THE SASSAFRAS SCIENCE ADVENTURES

VOLUME 6: ASTRONOMY

JOHNNY CONGO & PAIGE HUDSON

THE SASSAFRAS SCIENCE ADVENTURES
VOLUME 6: ASTRONOMY

First Printing 2020
Copyright @ Elemental Science, Inc.
Email: support@elementalscience.com

ISBN: 978-1-935614-93-7
Cover Design by Paige Hudson & Eunike Nugroho (be.net/inikeke)
Illustrations by Eunike Nugroho and Shubhangi Raheja

Printed In USA For World Wide Distribution

For more copies write to:
Elemental Science
PO Box 79
Niceville, FL 32588
support@elementalscience.com

DEDICATION

"If I have seen further than others,
it is by standing upon the shoulders of giants."

~ Isaac Newton

We dedicate this book to the giants—those authors and scientists—who have caused us to dream big. This series is the result of us standing on your shoulders.

MAKE THE MOST OF YOUR JOURNEY WITH THE SASSAFRAS TWINS!

Add our activity guide, logbook, or lapbooking guide to create a full science curriculum for your students!

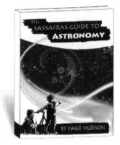

The Sassafras Guide to Astronomy includes chapter summaries and an array of options that coordinate with the individual chapters of this novel. This guide provides ideas for experiments, notebooking, vocabulary, memory work, and additional activities to enhance what your students are learning about space!

The Official Sassafras SCIDAT Logbook: Astronomy Edition partners with the activity guide to help your student document their journey throughout this novel. The logbook includes their own SCIDAT log pages as well as night sky journal sheets and an astronomy glossary.

Lapbooking through Astronomy with the Sassafras Twins provides a gentle option for enhancing what your students are learning about space through this novel. The guide contains a reading plan, templates and pictures to create a beautiful lapbook on astronomy, vocabulary, and coordinated scientific demonstrations!

VISIT SASSAFRASSCIENCE.COM TO LEARN MORE!

THE SASSAFRAS SCIENCE ADVENTURES

TABLE OF CONTENTS

THE SASSAFRAS SCIENCE ADVENTURES

THE SASSAFRAS SCIENCE ADVENTURES

THE SASSAFRAS GUIDE TO THE CHARACTERS

OLD FRIENDS THAT APPEAR THROUGHOUT THE BOOK*

★ **Blaine Sassafras** – A.K.A. Train and Rowboat, this boy is the male twin of the soon-to-be-famous Sassafras twins. He also has a wide range of acting abilities and a talent for finding things in space.

★ **Tracey Sassafras** – A.K.A. Blaisey and Fish Hook, this girl is the female twin of the soon-to-be-famous Sassafras twins. She also plays a mean game of Pass the Petri Dish and Copernicus Code.

★ **Uncle Cecil** – The Sassafras twins' talented, eccentric, and messy uncle who can never get their names right. He is an inventor with friends and colleagues that are out of this world.

★ **President Lincoln** – A.K.A. Linc Dog and The Prez, this prairie dog is Uncle Cecil's lab assistant. He doesn't say much, but without his talent for inventing, the twins' adventures wouldn't be the same.

★ **Summer Beach** – The sandwich-loving, excitable scientist who is a dear friend of Uncle Cecils. Her lab in Alaska is packed with out of this world tech!

★ **Ulysses S. Grant** – Summer's lab assistant, who happens to be an Arctic ground squirrel, and best friend of President Lincoln. He invents all kinds of technology, such as robot squirrels and zip-zop cuffs, when he isn't hibernating.

★ **The Man With No Eyebrows** – The memory-erasing, disappearing cape-wearing, eyebrow-less man who has tried just about everything he can think of to stop the twins. In the last volume we found out his name: Thaddeus.

★ **Adrianna Archer** – The former Triple S agent who the twins met during their Earth Science leg. She worked with the Man With No Eyebrows behind the scenes during their Geology leg.

★ **Evan DeBlose** – A.K.A. Agent Beans, this Triple S agent who serves as the twin's local expert on their Earth Science. He was friends and colleagues with Adrianna Archer until she went rogue.

ix

* **Q-Tip** – A Triple S's agent and resident expert in technologizing. The twins got a glimpse of his talents on their Earth Science leg.
* **Captain Marolf** – Head of the Triple S Agency. The twins met the captain during the Earth Science leg.
* **Yuroslav Bogdanovich** – The rogue scientist who bears an uncanny resemblance to Uncle Cecil. He tried to stop the twins during their Earth Science leg, but his memory was erased during the twin's Geology leg and now he works as a clerk at the Left-Handed Turtle Market.

CECIL'S NEIGHBORHOOD (CHAPTER 1)

* **The Guardian Beast (in name only)** – This miniature poodle is the stuff nightmares are made of, according to Cecil Sassafras.
* **Old Man Grusher** – Uncle Cecil's neighbor and owner of the Guardian Beast.

CHAPTERS 2 & 3 (SUMMER'S ALASKAN LAB)

* **REESE** – The robotic creation of President Lincoln and Ulysses S. Grant. His name stands for Robotic Exploration, Entertainment, and Scientific Enhancement. REESE joins the twins at several other locations throughout the book.

CHAPTERS 4 TO 7 (INTERNATIONAL SPACE STATION)

* **Yang Bo** – The twins' local expert in space. He is a Chinese astronaut living on the International Space Station, serving as the station's astrobiologist. He is also a former classmate of Uncle Cecil and Summer.
* **Captain Dianna Sturgess** – The decorated American astronaut who is currently in charge of the International Space Station.
* **Sander Petrov** – The Russian astronaut who serves as the International Space Station mechanic.
* **Bayard Clemence** – The French astronaut who serves as the International Space Station physician.

THE SASSAFRAS SCIENCE ADVENTURES

* **Anna Maria Bezerra** – The Brazilian astronaut who serves as the I.S.S. meteorologist.

* **Parth Banerjee** – The Indian astronaut who serves as the International Space Station mathematician.

* **SLIM** – The QA-700 robot aboard the International Space Station Its name stands for Super Literal Information Machine.

* **Brett Frye** – The billionaire space tourist who spent some time on the International Space Station.

* **Queenie Clemence (in name only)** – The sister of Bayard Clemence.

CHAPTERS 8 & 9 (HAWAII)

* **J.P. Jungos** – The twins' local expert for their time in Hawaii. He is a burn victim on the journey of his lifetime.

* **Peter Karko** – An employee at the Mauna Kea Observatories, who also turns out to be a very opportunistic and cranky tour guide.

* **Dr. Ellison Ocampo** – Lead scientist at the Mauna Kea Observatories.

CHAPTERS 10 & 11 (WASHINGTON, D.C.)

* **Paul Sims** – The twins' local expert as they explore the National Air and Space Museum. He is a very knowledgeable museum curator, but there is more to him than meets the eye.

* **Wiggles and Fidget** – The excitable museum security guards.

* **Sparks Sheen** – The leader of the family custodial crew, Shine-O-Mite.

* **Flash Sheen** – A member of the Shine-O-Mite crew.

* **Pat Sheen** – Short for Patina, she is the only sister on the Sheen Shine-O-Mite crew.

* **Lumin Sheen** – A member of the Shine-O-Mite crew.

* **Alexander Slote** – A member of the Rotary Club – not the one you are thinking, it's a club extoling the virtues of the rotary telephone.

* **Graham Slote** – Another member of the Rotary Club.

* **Belle Slote** – The final member of the Rotary Club. She is the only female in the three-member group.

CHAPTERS 12 & 13 (POLAND)

* **Minka Ziven** – The twins' local expert for their time in Poland and the clue guide for the Copernicus Code Escape Room.
* **Clive Stanek** – One of the players at the Copernicus Code Escape Room. He is Halley's brother.
* **Halley Stanek** – Another one of the players at the Copernicus Code Escape Room. She is Clive's sister.

CHAPTERS 14 & 15 (NEW ZEALAND)

* **Arty Stone** – He is the lead foreman for the Professional Gamer Championships and the twins' local expert for their time in New Zealand.
* **Mr. Sebastian** – The production manager and announcer for the Professional Gamer Championships.
* **Wayne Hammer** – The boisterous American gamer competing in the Professional Gamer Championships.
* **Ms. Pink Rocker** – The pink-clad Russian gamer competing in the Professional Gamer Championships.
* **Mohawk Wellington** – The preppy, Mohawk-wearing British gamer competing in the Professional Gamer Championships.
* **Agnes the Librarian** – The quiet, middle-aged Canadian gamer competing in the Professional Gamer Championships.
* **El Cohete Loco (The Crazy Rocket)** – The easy-going Mexican gamer competing in the Professional Gamer Championships.
* **Robbie Thistler** – The mysterious gamer who set an unbeatable record on Planet Prowess before disappearing from the gaming scene.
* **Kiwi Jones** – The young gamer who ends up shows up all of the top five gamers at the Professional Gamer Championships.

CHAPTERS 16 & 17 (MUMBAI, INDIA)

* **Ravi Chopraz** – The twins' local expert for their time in India and star of Bollywood's famous *Star Check* show. He plays the handsome Captain Cutta.

THE SASSAFRAS SCIENCE ADVENTURES

✮ **Varun Gowda** – The director of *Star Check.*

✮ **Preathi** – The digital effects specialist for *Star Check.*

✮ **Sana and Puji** – Two of the stylists for *Star Check.*

✮ **Jaya Amin** – She plays First Lieutenant Ursa, the captain's wiser and better-looking counterpart.

✮ **Rom Basu** – He plays the factual and stoic Second Lieutenant Denab.

✮ **Chiku Kapadia** – He plays a Worbflyster from the planet Worbflyse, who only speaks Worbflystian.

✮ **Dhruv Dalal** – The resident *Star Check* stunt man, who also plays the part of a Borbothian alien who is out to get the captain.

✮ **Aja and Ru Katri** – Executives from the company that is responsible for producing *Star Check.*

CHAPTER 18 (BACK AT UNCLE CECIL'S LAB)

✮ **Socrates and Aristotle** – The skeletons-turned-mannequins from the twins' Anatomy leg that Cecil frequently talks to as if they are friends.

VOLUME 6

ASTRONOMY

CHAPTER 1: TIME TO BOLDLY GO WHERE NO SASSAFRAS HAS EVER GONE

Pass the Petri Dish Gone Wrong

His voice was edged with anxious energy as he stood at the border of all that was familiar and the mysterious unknown.

"Everything in my life has led up to this moment."

He paused to take it all in.

"Fate now bids me to step up, over, and then out into the great unknown. What perils are out there? I know not. What terrible and fantastic discoveries await? I know not. Regardless, it is time. Time to slip the surly bonds of Earth and dance the skies on laughter-silvered wings. Time to step foot into the final frontier, to explore strange new worlds, to go boldly where no Sassafras has ever gone before!"

The redheaded man paused, took a deep breath, grabbed the border in front of him with both hands, hoisted himself up, and then said in his loudest and highest octave yet, "One small step for man! One giant leap for Sassafras-kind!"

The twelve-year-old twins who were standing with the man both rolled their eyes and shook their heads. Why did their uncle have to be so dramatic? All he was trying to do was hop over a fence to retrieve a Frisbee that had flown over into a backyard. It's not like he was traveling into space or anything. However, chuckles from both twins accompanied the eye-rolls and headshakes because they both loved their crazy uncle dearly, and neither would change one thing about him even if they had the power to do so.

"Oh, c'mon, Uncle Cecil! You can do it! It's just a backyard fence." Blaine, the older twin by five minutes and fourteen seconds, encouraged.

"Yeah, you can do it!" Tracey, the twin sister, echoed.

"Go over and get that Frisbee!"

Cecil Sassafras, with his wild, uncombed hair, white lab coat, and pink bunny houseslippers, was precariously perched on top of the six-foot wooden fence. He looked down at his niece and nephew with momentary confidence in his eyes, but the twins watched as that confidence melted back into fear. The redhead dropped back down to the grassy ground.

"B-b-b-but it's not just any fence. And that's no n-n-n-normal backyard," he stammered. "That is the d-d-d-domain of the Guardian Beast!"

Tracey rolled her eyes. Blaine shook his head. The "Guardian Beast" as their uncle called it, was actually a miniature poodle. The little dog was the pet of the neighborhood resident known as "Old Man Grusher." Grusher lived on North Pecan Street in a house just across from Uncle Cecil.

The three Sassafrases had been playing a game that Cecil liked to call "Pass the Petri Dish." Really though, they were just tossing the Frisbee around to get a little sunshine and exercise. Cecil's mind was so filled with science that it was hard for him to separate it from any activity he was doing. So, Uncle Cecil pretended the Frisbee was a petri dish, and he would shout out different scientific words as he threw the flying disk.

During the game of "Pass the Petri Dish," their uncle had gotten a little too animated and had launched the Frisbee over the backyard fence into Old Man Grusher's yard. Blaine had offered to hop over the fence to retrieve the Frisbee because he knew his uncle was, for some strange reason, deathly afraid of his neighbor's miniature poodle. But Uncle Cecil had rejected his nephew's offer. The scientist had said he was the one who threw the Frisbee over the fence, so he was the one who should go get it. He had also added that it was time to face his fear of the Guardian Beast.

Cecil's first attempt to hop the fence had consisted of him touching the fence and then backing away. His second attempt had included the amazing and spirited speech the twins had just heard, but those words hadn't gotten their uncle over the fence either. The twins now stood here wondering how far a third attempt would get him or if there even would be a third attempt.

"What about the zip lines?" Cecil suddenly asked and pointed at his niece and nephew.

"The zip lines?" The twins question-answered in unison.

"Yep, yes, yep, yessiree," Cecil quivered.

"I could use a harness and a specially designed three-ringed carabiner. I could set the coordinates for Old Man Grusher's backyard. Then I could zip through the fence on the invisible lines at the speed of light, retrieve the Frisbee, and zip back!"

Blaine and Tracey looked at each other skeptically. They loved the invisible zip lines, but in their opinion, this was much too short a distance for this fantastical mode of transportation.

About five weeks ago, Blaine and Tracey had rolled into to town on a hot and shaky bus with bad attitudes. They had both failed science, so their parents had sent them to their uncle's house for the summer to nip that problem in the bud. Uncle Cecil happened to be a pseudo-famous research scientist, and the twins' parents were sure that he could help the children improve their knowledge of science.

Over the past five weeks, that is exactly what had happened. They had morphed from kids who despised science into kids that absolutely loved it. The twelve-year-olds quickly found out that not only was their uncle not an ordinary person, but he was not an ordinary scientist either. On the contrary, he was extraordinary. And with the help of President Lincoln, his prairie dog lab assistant, he had invented invisible zip lines that could be used to travel at the speed of light to any destination on the planet.

Blaine and Tracey had been successfully using these zip lines for weeks now to study all kinds of scientific topics within the subjects of zoology, anatomy, botany, earth science, and geology. The zip lines were designed to drop the twins in precise, undetectable spots, where they would then meet local experts. These experts would help them learn about the scientific topics for the given locations. But now Uncle Cecil was proposing the idea of using the invisible zip lines to travel a distance of mere feet. Neither Blaine nor Tracey thought this was a good idea.

"Uncle Cecil, c'mon," Blaine hollered. "Just let me hop over the fence and get the Frisbee."

"No how, no who, no why, no way!" Cecil blurted. "This task is mine. This feat is something I must diggity diggity dig down and do!"

Even though he said this boldly, the twins could see that their uncle was still shaky and uncertain.

"Okay, Uncle Cecil, you do it," Tracey exhorted. "We know you can. You don't need to use the zip lines. You just need to hop over that fence and get that Frisbee!"

"But I've never been over that fence before. I have no idea what's back there!" Cecil answered, his courage retreating again.

"It's just a backyard," Blaine reminded. "It's probably like most other backyards with some grass, some bushes, maybe a shrub or two. It's just a backyard. It's probably pretty normal and…backyardy."

"But what about the Guardian Beast? What if he bursts out of the back door and comes after me?" their uncle whimpered.

"Maybe he's not even home," Tracey offered. "Or maybe he's taking a nap or something. Besides, doesn't he usually hang out on the front porch?"

"Okay, okay," the eldest Sassafras stammered. "But what about Old Man Grusher? He's the meanest old man in the whole neighborhood. You have to be mean to be the owner of such a foul creature as the Guardian Beast. What if he spots me in his backyard and then comes out to get me?"

At this point, all Blaine and Tracey could do was sigh. They were trying to be encouraging to their uncle, but their patience was wearing thin.

Cecil could sense what was happening in the younger Sassafrases. "Okie, okie, okay, so there is no need to use the zip lines, but what about your smartphones? Do you guys have any application on them that I can use to retrieve the petri dish; I mean flying saucer; I mean Frisbee?"

"Our smartphones?" the twins question-answered in unison. Cecil nodded vigorously.

Currently, neither of the twins had their smartphones with them. The devices were across the street in their uncle's basement. The smartphones and their applications were inherently tied to the invisible zip lines. For instance, the LINLOC application, which was short for Line Locations, gave the exact longitude and latitude coordinates in which the twins were supposed to land. They would set these coordinates on the rings of the carabiners. One ring was for longitude. One ring was for latitude. The third ring was to lock the carabiner securely shut. Then, the carabiner would automatically attach itself to the correct invisible zip line. The twins would hang in midair for approximately seven seconds before zipping off at the speed of light to the line location landing spot. Another thing the LINLOC app did for them was give them the name of the local expert along with the topics they would be studying at the location.

The SCIDAT app (short for scientific data) was another super important application on the twins' phones that they used to record all the scientific information they were learning. The twelve-year-olds would gather the data with the help of their local experts and then record that data in the SCIDAT app. Finally, they would text that data to their uncle's basement lab, where he could view it on his screen. This way Cecil was able to track and confirm the science his niece and nephew were learning. The basement data screen could also function as a tracking screen, enabling Cecil to keep tabs on the twins, represented by two green dots, as they zipped around the globe. Obviously, neither of these applications was going to help their crazy uncle retrieve the lost Frisbee, so why was he asking about phone apps right now?

Cecil was frantically running through the applications, grasping for hope. "L-l-l-let's see, there's the LINLOC and SCIDAT apps. Nope, nope, nopity, nope. Neither one of those can provide any help for this current situation we find ourselves in. How about the microscope application or the archive application, or the high-resolution cameras? Can I use any of those to get our Frisbee back?"

Blaine and Tracey answered with impatient, shaking heads. Those three applications were used for obtaining images of scientific topics—images that they sent in with their SCIDAT data.

"No-eee, no-eee, no-eee way. Taking a picture of the Frisbee will do us absolutely no good," Cecil screeched, "nor will picture taking protect us from Old Man Grusher or the Guardian Beast! Okay, okay, if those apps are a no-kay, what else is there on your phones? There is also a compass application. Will that help? No, no, I'm a frayed knot . . . What else? The phones are equipped with a waterproof casing . . . but that' not really . . . even applicable . . . Isn't there one more application that I'm forgetting? There's also . . . what else do we have? Oh, yes! Your phones each have tasers! Can I use the taser application to get the petri dish back? Can I tase the Guardian Beast?"

"No, Uncle Cecil, no," Tracey answered. "You can't taser Old Man Grusher's miniature poodle. You need to just hop this wooden fence and go get the Frisbee!"

"Oh, sweet sassy molassy. I just can't!"

"Yes, you can!" Blaine encouraged. "And you're going to do it right now, with our help!"

With that, the twelve-year-old boy stepped over to the fence and climbed to its top. He then waved for his uncle and sister to follow. Tracey hopped right to it and was up next to her brother almost instantly. Cecil wasn't quite as quick, but surprisingly he did make his way to the top of the fence. All three Sassafrases let their eyes wander across the backyard of Old Man Grusher.

Just like Blaine had guessed earlier, it was a pretty normal backyard with grass, some bushes, and a shrub or two. There was also a bird bath, a flower garden, and . . . a Frisbee. The flying disk had landed harmlessly right next to the bird bath. Now all they needed to do was hop down from the fence, walk over, and go get it.

Tracey was the first to jump down and plant her feet in the backyard. Blaine was a second and a half behind her but not Uncle Cecil. He remained frozen in fear on top of the fence. Blaine and Tracey looked at their uncle and then at each other. Uncle Cecil was ordinarily one of the bravest men they had ever known. It was just this one dog that scared him. However, today was the day their brave, visionary, and creative uncle was going to face his fear. They were sure of it.

The twins looked back toward their uncle, still on the fence. The scientist's face was wrinkled in fear as he looked out over this new and scary backyard—this domain of the Guardian Beast, as he called it. He might as well have been a first-time astronaut looking out into the dark unknown throws of space. The Sassafras twins kept looking hopefully at their uncle's face, silently cheering him on; and as they did, the wrinkles of fear slowly began to melt into a courageous face full of resolve. Cecil was a Sassafras after all, and Sassafrases never give up.

All at once, the scientist jumped down from the fence, his bunny slippers landing firmly on the surface of the Beast's domain. Upon Cecil's landing there were three Sassafras hearts soaring. However, zero Sassafrases noticed that at the exact same time Cecil's feet hit the ground, the backscreen door of Old Man Grusher's house began to slowly creak open.

A Look Back at Geology

"Where are those three silly-sassys, Prez?" A white-coat-clad female scientist with frizzy blonde hair exclaimed with no worry in her voice. Summer T. Beach was playfully curious as she questioned Cecil Sassafras's lab assistant, who also happened to be a prairie dog.

Summer was an old friend and classmate of Cecil's. Plus, she had served as a local expert for the twins on multiple occasions. She was beyond excited that she was in the lineup to serve in that capacity again during their upcoming astronomy study. The twins didn't know yet, and she was dying to share this information with them. However, before they zipped off to study astronomy, they were supposed to walk through a review of what they had learned about geology.

President Lincoln always put together a presentation using images the twins had captured during their studies and words Cecil would read aloud. The presentation could be viewed on the basement data screen that was affixed to the wall behind the computer desk. Even now, illuminated in bright lights on that very screen was a picture of President Lincoln with exciting text arched over his head saying, "President Lincoln's Ever-so-brief Presentation on Geology."

Summer Beach was ready for the presentation. President Lincoln was ready for the presentation. The only problem was that there were no Sassafrases present for the presentation.

Summer shot another question the prairie dog's way. "They were playing 'Pass the Petri Dish,' right? Oh my! What a fun game! But, wow, they have been playing for such a long time now. Prez, do you think something unpredictable happened?"

As the screen door opened wider, the hushed creaking turned into loud, rusty screeching. All three Sassafrases turned their heads toward the sound. As they did, their victorious smiles immediately turned to open mouths of shock and fear. There now, standing on the back porch, filling up the entire door frame, was Old Man Grusher himself. There was no Guardian Beast with him. It was just the lone man accompanied by an unasked question.

The man was big. He was wearing baggy, pleated khakis and a long-sleeved, button-up sweater. He had strands of gray hair swimming across his mostly bald head, and he was walking with the use of a gnarly wooden cane.

The aging man stepped out far enough onto the porch as

to let the screen door slam shut behind him. Cecil, Blaine, and Tracey all involuntarily jumped at the sound of the slamming door but otherwise remained frozen. There was a long, brief silence as Old Man Grusher stared the three down with slanted eyebrows.

The unasked question took its time, but it eventually made its way up through a scratchy throat to the man's lips. "What are the three of you doing in my backyard?"

Cecil remained silent. Blaine managed only a moan.

Tracey, however, was able to get an actual coherent response to come out of her mouth. "Our Frisbee flew over the fence into your backyard. We hopped over to get it."

Old Man Grusher glared at the three fence hoppers and then glanced at the Frisbee lying on the ground next to the birdbath. "Well, why didn't you three knock on the front door? I would've happily come back here and retrieved it for you." At the conclusion of this statement, Old Man Grusher's eyebrows moved up, all of his wrinkles disappeared, and the big man let out a bellowing, good-hearted, neighborly laugh that flooded the three Sassafrases with surprised relief.

A few minutes later, Tracey, Blaine, and Cecil came bounding down into the basement lab with bellowing, good-hearted, neighborly laughs of their own. They had retrieved the 'petri-dish.' They had not been attacked by any beast. They had made friends with Old Man Grusher. And now they were going to dive into some science!

Summer was there to greet the twins with one of her patented happy jumping dance hugs. Cecil, however, slid through the hug, somersaulted over a short file cabinet, sideswiped a plastic mannequin, bounced off a section of rock climbing wall, hurdled a potted plant, careened over a homemade rocket, and then finally slid to a stop in front of his muddled computer desk, where he immediately launched into his job as an orator. "'President Lincoln's Ever-so-brief Presentation on Geology,'" the redhead read.

The prairie dog stood on the desk with a proud smile that looked exactly like the one he was showcasing in the picture on the screen. The animal tapped at the computer keyboard, causing the presentation's next image to come up. Uncle Cecil read the new text.

"With the exception of a few islands here and there, all land on Earth can be divided into seven continents. These continents are: North America, South America, Europe, Africa, Asia, Australia, and Antarctica."

The picture being displayed was a very white picture. It was a picture of ice—or more specifically, "the Ice," otherwise known as the continent of Antarctica. The twins had taken the picture as they had trekked across the frozen continent with their brave local expert, Isaac Revvington. He was a blind adventurer who, with his Seeing Eye dog, Nyles, had been attempting to reach the South Pole in addition to the North Pole and the summit of Mount Everest. The twins were sure he was the bravest person they'd ever met.

"The Earth has three main layers: the crust, the mantle, and the core," Cecil read the next frame. The picture was now that of an erupting volcano. It was an image the twins had captured in Ecuador, where they had studied the topics of both "layers of the earth" and "volcanoes" with the help of a local expert who the twins were pretty sure was an actual superhero by the name of Brick Kid.

"Volcanoes can be active, dormant, or extinct," the twins' uncle narrated. "Active means they erupt periodically or continuously. Dormant means they have been known to erupt in modern times. And extinct means they have not erupted in modern times."

President Lincoln tapped the keyboard again. The picture changed to that of a rocky, shaking beach, and Uncle Cecil read on.

"An earthquake is a release of energy that happens when the Earth's plates rub together at places called fault lines, causing the ground to shake." It had sure been shaking on the beach of that island off the coast of Sri Lanka when the twins had taken this picture, and the poignant memory almost caused the ground to feel like it was shaking right now here in their uncle's basement.

The next picture to come up was of an igneous rock. It was a picture the two had taken in Norway while being chased all over the place by the Fjord Gerry Monster. "The three types of rock are igneous, metamorphic, and sedimentary," Cecil said in his own unique, upbeat way. "Igneous rock is formed by fire. Metamorphic rock is rock that has been changed by heat or pressure. Sedimentary rock is formed layer by layer from tiny bits of rocks, dead plants, and dead animals."

"And last, caves!" Cecil exclaimed as the last image appeared, "Caves, which are also known as caverns, are naturally occurring spaces or areas found under the surface of the ground."

The twins smiled as they saw the picture of the cave they had seen while in Australia. Their local expert, Jackie Ray Wagon, had successfully found a diamond in a cave full of dripstone pillars. He then used the diamond to successfully ask his love, Peggy Jo, to marry him.

"Stalagmites form on the floor of the cave, whereas stalactites form on the ceiling," Cecil said, wrapping up the ever-so-brief presentation. The redheaded scientist then clapped, gave a few fist pumps, wiggled all ten of his fingers above his head, and looked like he was about to make a big announcement.

But before he could, Summer stole his thunder. "It's time to study astronomy!" the female scientist exclaimed with wiggling fingers of her own.

"So sorry to interrupt you, Sizzle, er, I mean, Cecil," the excitable woman apologized. "I am just so pumped about these two brilliant little brainey-frasses starting their next scientific subject. They are going to get to learn all about the planets and the stars! They are going to study things like astronauts, telescopes, space travel, and more! It's all so fantastically exciting! So sorry I interrupted."

"No apology needed, Summer Thyme! I am super-sizzling-sassy-excited too! Why don't you go ahead and tell these two who their first local expert is going to be!"

Summer's eyes got excited and wide. She curled her upper body into a little ball with her head down and her arms and hands pulled in close to her chest. Blaine and Tracey could barely hear it at first, but Summer started a squeal of delight that crescendoed from a whisper into a shout. All at once she popped her head up with exploding frizzy hair and then threw her arms out as wide as they would go.

The loud, happy squeal then turned into actual words, "Your

first local expert is me!"

"Really?" The Sassafras Twins responded in a unified squeal of their own.

"Really!" Summer responded. "Go ahead and check it out on your smartphones!"

Blaine and Tracey both scrambled to find their backpacks and then both pulled out their phones. Tracey was the first to get the LINLOC application open, and she immediately read aloud the information it held. "Our first astronomy location is Alaska, longitude -163° 4' 12.24", latitude +67° 3' 58.91". We will be studying the topics of the solar system, asteroids, stars, and the International Space Station. And our first local expert is indeed the one, the only, Summer Beach!"

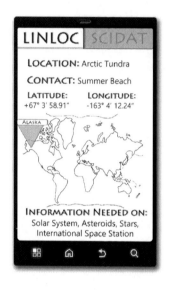

Summer squealed again. Tracey squealed. Cecil even squealed. Blaine attempted a manly grunt, but it came out as a . . . squeal. The one Beach and the three Sassafrases were more than a little excited to get started studying astronomy.

He had seen them. He had heard them. He knew all their plans. He smiled a wicked smile. The capabilities he had at his fingertips right now were light-years better and more advanced than anything he had tried in his old basement at 1108 North Pecan Street. One of his satellites had transmitted the video image of Cecil and those twins walking from Old Man Grusher's house back to their house at 1104. Then another new tech satellite had transmitted the audio about their plans to zip to Alaska, complete with LINLOC coordinates.

From this point on, nothing the Sassafrases did would be hidden from him. They would have no secrets.

Currently he was standing on his glossy, white pedestal, the one that stood right in the middle of his underground Siberian lab. He loved the feeling of standing higher than everyone else. He loved the view from here, looking out at the scores of submissive scientists that obeyed his every wish and command.

Even now, a group of them was working on building a new Forget-O-Nator machine. This one would be the size of a mobile home. Another group was working to duplicate the Dark Cape suit so that he could eventually have an army of invisible henchmen. Yet another group was putting the finishing touches on a personal spacecraft. This was a sleek vehicle that he was hoping might be useful as the twins attempted to learn astronomy.

And out among all the white coats was one black coat. It belonged to the gorgeous Adrianna Archer. The beautiful blonde used to be a Swiss Secret Service agent, but now she served as his loyal right-hand woman, helping direct and guide all the ant-like scientists.

His hope for vengeance against Cecil Sassafras was now stronger than ever. He had never felt more empowered to carry out revenge against the one that had taken his eyebrows.

THE SASSAFRAS SCIENCE ADVENTURES

Blaine did have a little question about the scientific subject at hand. "Hey, you know, I don't know all that much about astronomy yet, but isn't it kind of, well, you know, the study of outer space and stuff?"

Nods and shrugs came from both scientists that communicated a "pretty much" response.

"Well, then, how, you know . . ." Blaine stammered, trying to put his question into words. "How are we going to be able to study astronomy on Earth, you know, in places like Alaska? Shouldn't we, or couldn't we, I mean, can we zip to outer space?"

Now Uncle Cecil shook his head. "Sadly, the invisible zip lines are only built to connect with precise longitude and latitude coordinates on this planet, our planet, on planet Earth. They are not capable of breaking through the Earth's atmosphere to go into space."

Summer joined in, but she didn't look sad at all. "However, say we could get your specially designed three-ringed carabiners on the outside of the earth's atmosphere and have your zip origination point, or your Z.O.P., start from space. Then in theory the invisible lines would be able to connect to any point in our entire galaxy."

Cecil jumped in, "So what we need to enable you two to zip throughout space is some kind of craft that has the ability to break through the atmosphere."

"And guess what, you two Space-a-frasses," Summer exclaimed. "We happen to have access to such a craft!"

"We do?" the twins responded.

"Yes, we do," Summer shouted. "You know my underground lab in Alaska? Well, it just so happens that it is not only a lab. It also contains a . . . spaceship!"

CHAPTER 2: TO ALASKA AND BEYOND

Rocketing into the Solar System

All four of them had their harnesses on, and they were ready to zip. Blaine and Tracey smiled big smiles full of joyful anticipation. They were excited to start the study of astronomy. They were thrilled they were going to explore the solar system. Usually the Sassafras twins traveled on the invisible zip lines alone, but this time two friends would be starting with them. All four zippers turned the longitude ring and latitude ring to Summer's lab coordinates, and then they tightened the third rings to lock the carabiners closed.

As they did, all four zippers were pulled up a few feet into the air when the specially designed three-ringed carabiners attached themselves to the invisible lines that would take them to Alaska. They would remain dangling for approximately seven seconds before disappearing off into light-speed flight.

Blaine and Tracey looked over at their companions. Summer Beach and President Lincoln were both smiling as big as the twins. They had both traveled on the invisible zip lines before but never with the Sassafras twins.

"All-kay oh-right! You four have a far-out time!" Cecil cheered as he waved goodbye. "I'll be righty here in the basement tracking your progress and receiving your SCIDAT. Enjoy the smithereens out of this adventure!"

The twins waved goodbye to their uncle. President Lincoln waved goodbye to his boss. Summer waved goodbye to the man she loved . . . whoops . . . liked. And then . . . three, two, one . . . the four blasted off into swirls of rip-roaring light!

"Hurry up, you buffoon!" The Man With No Eyebrows commanded gruffly to the servile scientist who was trying to help him get buckled into the seat of his personal spacecraft. "They have already zipped off to Alaska! And if that lab of Summer's can break through the atmosphere and achieve flight, they'll soon be launching off into space as well. Hurry up! C'mon, get me buckled up! I want to be in space before them. I want to be there to greet them with fury! Hurry up!"

The poor scientist was trying his best to help his new boss. But with all the complaining and handslapping his superior was doing, it was making it next to impossible to truly be of assistance.

Click.

The last part of the harness-like seat belt finally connected. The sweating scientist now happily scurried away, hoping to never be asked to assist again.

Thaddaeus was dressed in the Dark Cape suit, which his scientists had deemed "space-worthy." Adrianna had the scientists also add a new zip-zop cuff to his gear, one that would allow him to move along Cecil's extraterrestrial zip lines. It was yet another scientific concept he had stolen from Cecil and his crew.

His personal spacecraft was a sleek black machine about the size of a car, and it was shaped somewhat like a more oblong , less-pointed version of his Dark Cape helmet. It was rounded and curved at the front with wings coming out of the back.

It was a craft that had originally been named *Yuro-1* after Yuroslav Bogdanovich, the craft's designer. But now that the Man With No Eyebrows had gotten rid of Bogdanovich and taken over his lab, Thaddaeus had decided to rename the machine after himself. The spacecraft, now called *Thad-1*, could travel at top speeds in space and was equipped with a powerful ray gun.

Any and all of the white lab coat-wearing helpers began backing away from the craft as its black-tinted windshield began to slowly close into place. The thick, see-through section served not only as a windshield but also as the only way in and out of the craft. It locked shut with a calculated thud and a small burst of steam. Then, through a recent audio upgrade to his helmet, Thaddaeus heard Adrianna Archer's strong, beautiful voice in his ears.

"Do you read me, our highly esteemed leader?"

"Loud and clear," Thaddaeus responded.

"Good. Everything is set. *Thad-1* is ready for launch."

"Roger that," the Man With No Eyebrows responded confidently.

He was confident right up until the countdown got to 3 . . . and then he began having dozens of doubts.

What am I doing?

I've never been to space!

But I have to do this if I want to stop the twins and crush the hopes of Cecil Sassafras, right?

Oh, well, it's too late now was his last thought as he heard Adrianna's voice cried out, "Blast off!"

"DeBlose, Evan!"

"Present, sir!"

"Archer, Adrianna!"

"Present, sir!"

"Sargent DeBlose, get your eyes off Sargent Archer. Wipe the smile off your face. Look straight ahead at only me, and stand at attention! Do you understand?"

"Sir, yes sir, Captain Marolf, sir!"

Triple S Agent, Evan DeBlose smiled again as he reminisced about the first time he'd met Adrianna. He had liked her since he met her on the first day in Sargent Training Academy for the Swiss Army. Even under the stern command of Captain Marolf and the demanding load of the academy, the two had become fast friends. Although he had often ribbed her, calling her "darling" or playing practical jokes on her, he truly did consider Adrianna to be one of his most trusted friends.

They'd been friends until just over a week ago when she had betrayed him. Freshly stung by this fact, the smile fell from DeBlose's face. Adrianna had not only betrayed him; she had betrayed the Triple S, the Sassafras twins, the country of Switzerland, and quite possibly all of Siberia as well.

Evan and Adrianna had risen together through the ranks of the Swiss Army. They had both been recruited into the Swiss Secret Service, a.k.a. Triple S, by the gruff Captain Marolf, who had transitioned from leadership in the Swiss Army to leadership in the Secret Service. For years, Evan and Adrianna and the other Triple

S agents had worked together to protect the interests of their home country of Switzerland and also the interests of freedom-loving people everywhere. But then, a few days ago, Adrianna had sided with a Siberian terrorist by the name of Yuroslav Bogdanovich.

She had helped him secure a vile of deadly chemicals as he escaped the custody of the Triple S. Not only that, but she had also damaged a Triple S satellite in the process. She had threatened the lives of many of her fellow agents plus a pair of twelve-year-old twins who had been in Switzerland studying earth science.

Evan shook his head and again asked himself the obvious question, "Why? Why had Adrianna done it? What had flipped her from good to evil?"

DeBlose walked down the long corridor and exited through the door at the end. He then began walking up several flights of metal stairs that would take him to his destination, his white boots making a loud sound on every step as he ascended.

He pulled at the sleeves of the silver suit he was wearing. This thing was so much less comfortable than the black suit he was used to wearing on his missions. This would be only the third time he had been thrust into space, and just like the first two times, he was not a fan of the apparel. He finished his climb up the metal stairs and entered the rocket. As he did, the tall metal staircase was moved by machines away from the vertical craft, and the name of the vessel, *Dauntless-12*, could now be clearly seen painted on the side in bright red.

The thick, heavy, reinforced door of the rocket closed behind the silver-clad Triple S agent as Evan shuffled over to one of the two chairs in the small cockpit area, took a seat, and immediately strapped himself in with the heavy-duty seat belt straps.

DeBlose let a short, almost silent laugh slip from his lips— sitting down in a chair like this never felt normal. He was lying down on his back, with his legs and feet pointed straight up in the air. He would be sitting like this until *Dauntless-12* broke through the Earth's atmosphere and made it into orbit, where it didn't matter which way was up or down because the lack of gravity made every direction virtually the same.

Evan looked over toward the other chair where his partner for the mission was already seated. It was this agent's first trip to space, and the poor guy looked as nervous as a balloon in a tack factory. In fact, if he thought about it, the little man's head was kind of balloon shaped. Evan had always thought it looked a tad too big for the man's skinny body. "You gonna be okay, Q-Tip?" Evan asked, using his partner's nickname. "Looks like you're sweating bullets over there."

"Oh, yeah, I'll be fine," the skinny agent responded, sounding about as confident as he looked.

Q-Tip laughed nervously, although it came out more as a squeak. The agent, whose main job for Triple S was serving as a technology expert, reached out toward DeBlose with an open palm to hand him something. Evan looked at Q-Tip's open hand with a smile and grabbed the item.

"Ah, yes, my pocketknife," DeBlose acknowledged. "I guess this can be useful even in space."

"It sure can!" Q-Tip responded with his normal enthusiasm now more apparent. "This Swiss Army knife still has all its normal utilities, such as a flat blade, a serrated blade, a corkscrew, a toothpick, etc. It also has some of its past upgrades such as the flashlight, the toothbrush, the glass cutter, the nun chucks, the small missile launcher, and the taser!"

Evan chuckled. It didn't seem possible for a pocketknife to hold all these utilities, but it did because Q-Tip had made it possible. That's why he was the expert technologizer. And really, that's why his nickname was Q-Tip in the first place. It wasn't only because his head was too big for his body—it was because his first invention for Triple-S had been a Q-tip with a taser in it.

"For this space assignment, I've added two new upgrades to the pocketknife: an oxygen supply and a propulsion system." Q-Tip paused and reached down beside him before adding, "Of course, I also brought along two thermoses that are full of Swiss hot chocolate and equipped with tasers!" He handed one to DeBlose and kept the other for himself.

Both men faced forward and focused their attention on making sure that everything in the cockpit was set and ready for launch. The two agents had been handpicked by Captain Marolf himself for this mission. Their task was to make it into orbit, find the damaged Triple-S satellite, and repair it. Evidently, when Adrianna Archer cut the feed to the satellite to help Bogdanovich, she didn't just temporarily block its communication abilities. She sabotaged the satellite by using her encrypted Triple S password to remotely shut down the satellite's defense shield, which made it vulnerable to flying space debris.

In the week since Archer's betrayal, none of the Triple S technicians had been able to remotely turn the shield back on. The conclusion of the agency was that the only way to get the shield back on was to make any needed repairs by hand. Captain Marolf had chosen Agent DeBlose for this mission not only because he had been to space before but also because he was leading the operation to find both Yuroslav Bogdanovich and former Agent Archer. Agent Q-Tip had been chosen because he was Triple-S's best technologizer. Captain Marolf expected him to not only fix the satellite but also to make a special top-secret upgrade to it.

Everything in the cockpit was set. The mission was clear. The two agents were as prepared and ready as they could be.

A voice echoed out over the launch site. "Operation Shield Recovery is a go. Launch time in T-minus ten seconds. Ten, nine, eight, seven, six, five, four, three, two, one . . . blast off!"

THE SASSAFRAS SCIENCE ADVENTURES

"What a blast!" Summer exclaimed. "Wow, just wow. The two of you get to travel through the solar system! And like I was saying, the solar system includes the sun and everything that orbits around it!"

Summer Beach was talking excitedly, sharing about the solar system as she led the Sassafras twins on a tour or rather what she was calling a "re-tour" of her underground lab. "This includes the planets, asteroids, moons, comets, and . . . all the space junk!" Summer waved her arms up high and grasped with her fingers as she said the end of this last sentence, almost like she was reaching for the stars herself, right here in the lab.

"In our solar system, the main objects are the eight planets that orbit the sun," the scientist continued. "Those planets are Mercury, Venus, Earth, Mars, Jupiter, Saturn, Uranus, and Neptune. There are also two large asteroid belts known as the Asteroid Belt and the Kuiper Belt. And, we have a few dwarf planets, including Pluto, which used to be considered the ninth planet, but now it is not."

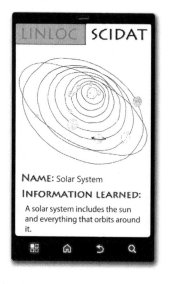

LINLOC   SCIDAT

NAME: Solar System
INFORMATION LEARNED:
A solar system includes the sun and everything that orbits around it.

Blaine and Tracey were following Summer down a long, egg-shaped hallway. This was the main corridor of her lab and served almost like a spine, connecting most of the lab's different sections. The twins had many questions rolling around in their minds—the biggest one being how Summer's lab could possibly be a spaceship. But the twelve-year-olds held their queries in for now.

"The gravitational pull of the sun keeps all the objects in our solar system orbiting around it. The sun is near one thousand times larger than all the other planets put together!" Summer was still waving her arms high above her head as she spoke. "Most of the planets in our solar system have an atmosphere, which is a thin layer of gas that surrounds the planet. However, Earth is the only planet in our system that has an atmosphere that can currently support life."

Summer paused briefly and then sighed happily. "Ahhh, that concludes your scientific data about solar systems. "I love the fact that you two little cuties are soaring so well through science. And I love the fact that you are starting your study of astronomy! What fun! You are going to have the amazingly unique opportunity to soar all around the solar system we just talked about. It's going to be such a blast!"

The twins nodded. It was going to be a blast, but first they needed to get some answers. "Are we going to be able to upload this SCIDAT data about solar systems to our phones later back in that part of the lab that has those big see-through, floor-to-ceiling data screens?" Blaine asked.

Summer giggled cheerfully as she turned from the long corridor to enter an adjacent one. "Nope! And here's why not. It's because Lincoln and Ulysses have a surprise for you!"

Blaine and Tracey generally liked surprises, but as Summer said the word, they both realized they might be on surprise overload.

"The two of them just finished up another one of their inventions. And it's something you two are absolutely going to love the bonkers out of!" Summer squealed. "Plus, it will be yet another way you can upload SCIDAT!"

"Hmmmm," Tracey mused. "I wonder if that's where President Lincoln ran off to."

Upon their landing in Summer's lab, President Lincoln had given a whoop and a holler when he had seen his old buddy, Ulysses S. Grant. Not only was Ulysses a furry animal named after a U.S. president like Linc Dawg, but Ulysses was an inventor and lab assistant, too. Ulysses S. Grant was an Arctic ground squirrel that worked in Summer's lab and helped the excitable scientist with everything from A to Z. President Lincoln and Ulysses S. Grant had been friends for a long time, according to Uncle Cecil. The two were both going to be pretty paws-on during the twins' study of astronomy. Upon landing here in Alaska, the two mammals had given each other a high five, a chest bump, and a long, complicated secret handshake. Then, they had scurried off like they were super excited about something. Tracey bet it was the surprise that Summer had mentioned.

Summer's Spaceship and Asteroid-sharing Robots

The young Sassafrases continued to follow their local expert through her large, underground lab. They had been here three times. The first time they had been impressed by the sleekness of the lab—especially the room with the floor-to-ceiling translucent data screens Blaine had mentioned. That room also had some cool specimen tubes and some cozy sleeping pods. During that first visit, they had also left the lab and taken a ride around Alaska on a super-fast helicopter that Summer called a "heliquickter." It was parked inside the lab, and it could come and go through a section of roof in the facility that opened and closed.

During their second visit to the lab, the twins had seen much more of the facility than the first time; however, that visit was kind of a hazy blur in their minds because robot squirrels had been chasing them, and they had been paying more attention to escaping the clutches of the metallic vermin than committing anything they were seeing in the lab to memory.

During their last visit to Alaska, they had briefly been down in the lab, but they'd spent most of their time in the field and forest above the lab playing paintball. In all of the visits to Summer Beach's lab, Blaine and Tracey hadn't seen anything they could recall that would've led them to ever believe this place could double as a craft worthy of space travel. Even so, the Sassafras twins continued to follow Summer, trusting that things would start to make more sense soon.

The three made their way down a couple more corridors. They climbed up a metal rung ladder through a hatch and slid down a well-lit tube slide. They approached a hallway that looked normal except for a large, circular opening in the ceiling.

"Run, lunge, and bounce!" Summer suddenly shouted as she ran, lunged, and bounced right off the floor and all the way up through the circle in the ceiling.

Blaine and Tracey looked at each other in surprise. Then Tracey recalled, "Blaine, remember? This is that trampoline floor! We came this way when the squirrels were chasing us!"

"Oh, yeah!" Blaine exclaimed with a smile as he followed Summer's instructions. He ran, lunged, and jumped, firmly planting both feet on the floor, which gave under his weight. The stretchy floor shot him back up, catapulting Blaine through the hole in the ceiling. Tracey giggled as she watched her brother, and then followed right behind him. The Sassafras girl landed safely up on the next level, and the trio proceeded to climb a spiral staircase.

The twins then saw they were inside a room that looked like a large cockpit. "Huh, this room looks like a cockpit," Blaine thought simply at first. Then the realization hit him. "Hey, this room looks like a cockpit! And cockpits are only found in vehicles that can . . . fly!"

Blaine's excited thought remained in his head, but Tracey spoke her thought. "Summer, this is the cockpit, right? The cockpit where you fly your lab, I mean, your ship, right?"

"Yes, it is!" Summer responded, exploding in smiles.

The female scientist reached up and wiggled her arms and fingers toward the stars once more, then she dance-walked over to the nearest wall where she began flipping switches.

Flick by flick, the cockpit became more and more alive with illuminated purpose as panels, boards, screens, buttons, knobs, and levers all clicked to "on."

The twins' eyes got wider with every flip. They felt themselves starting to believe that maybe this underground lab really could launch up out of this place to fly into space.

Summer Beach sat down in one of the sleek, almost triangular-shaped seats in the cockpit. Her seat was situated in front of a panel of controls. "One of the things that initially drew me to this job was the versatility of this lab," Summer explained. "Like your hunkle . . . I mean . . . uncle, I was really into research science. This Swiss-funded lab here in Alaska, in my mind, was the greatest place on the globe within which to conduct cutting-edge research using all the newest and fanciest scientific equipment known to man. And when they told me that the underground lab had the ability to fly into space, well, that was just the cherry on top!"

Summer reached out and patted the triangular seat to both the left and right of her, beckoning the twins to sit, which they both did happily. Summer swiped her hand across the panel that lay in front of them. As she did, a large section immediately began to slide away, revealing a window or maybe a windshield. Summer smiled and looked like she was about to reveal something interesting when all at once an electronic "Wooka, wooka, wooka" turntable sound rang out behind where they were seated.

Summer, smile intact, pulled a lever that turned all three seats around. The sight that met the four eyes of the twins immediately enthralled them. President Lincoln and Ulysses S. Grant were rolling into the cockpit with the coolest robot the twins had ever seen. If they were not mistaken, the robot was doing some kind of hip-hop dance as it entered the room.

"Wooka, wooka, wooka," the machine sounded out as it busted a move.

The robot was about four feet tall. It had a trapezoid-shaped head with two big, round eyes. It had a sleek, almost egg-shaped torso. The robot had tank-like, rubbery wheels instead of legs and feet. It had springy yet strong-looking metallic arms and neck. The robot had so many other bells and whistles that the twins couldn't even take it all in.

Summer Beach jumped up out of her chair with outstretched arms as she introduced the machine, "Blaine and Tracey, meet REESE!"

"REESE?" the twins asked through elated smiles.

"Yes, REESE," Summer answered. "R-E-E-S-E, which stands for Robotic Exploration, Entertainment, and Scientific Enhancement!"

"REESE," the twins repeated, now understanding a bit.

"REESE is Ulysses S. Grant's latest and greatest project," Summer proclaimed.

Upon this statement, the Arctic ground squirrel stood tall, looking proud of his handiwork.

"Ulysses and Linc Dawg put the finishing touches on him today!" Summer informed. "So, REESE is at your service and ready, ready, ready to join the two of you as you zip around the universe to study astronomy!"

"Wooka, wooka, wooka," REESE rang out again as he continued to hippity hop. Then a small, rectangular screen lit up at the bottom and center of his face. The lights within the small screen seemed to move, resembling a talking mouth. As this happened, the large screen on his torso also lit up, with the words of a hip-hop song as the robot began singing and dancing.

"Gravity! Wooka, wooka, wooka. Gravity!" Now a rhythmic beat was added into the song, reverberating from somewhere within the robot as he continued to sing the song's first verse:

Gravity, yep, is this song's subject, subject.

It's the force that does the pulling
Of an object to a larger object, object.
This is certainly a fact worth knowing.

The twins were already in sync with the cool robot's song, and both Blaine and Tracey began bobbing and bouncing in rhythm with the beat of the catchy song.

Gravity!
Wooka, wooka, wooka. Gravity!

REESE sang the chorus again and then moved to the second verse:

The gravitational pull of the sun, sun
Keeps the planets orbiting around it.
Instead of floating off into space, gone, gone.
You better believe it and resound it.
Gravity!
Wooka, wooka, wooka. Gravity!

The Sassafrases were already familiar with the song. They now sang the chorus with REESE. Linc Dawg and Ulysses were dancing and hopping along with the song, as was Summer Beach. But the female scientist was doing more of a disco dance than a hip-hop one.

REESE the robot sang one more verse:

Gravity also makes things go down, down.
When they slip, trip, detach, or release,
Go tumblin' fallin' to the ground, ground.
This force keeps us grounded, so be at peace.

The robot finished with a robot-style dance and then cranked out the chorus a couple more times.

Gravity!
Wooka, wooka, wooka. Gravity!
Wooka, wooka, wooka. Gravity!
Wooka, wooka, wooka. Gravity!

At the conclusion of his song, the screen on REESE's torso went from displaying the song's lyrics to an image that made it look like the robot was wearing a name tag that said, 'Hello, my name is REESE." The machine rolled toward the twins and then, not in a hip-hop voice but in a more stereotypical robotic voice, said, "Blaine and Tracey Sassafras. So nice to meet you. How may I be of assistance?"

Blaine and Tracey both stood with open mouths, awed at the fact that a robot had talked to them. Summer put a halt to her disco dancing and skipped over with a smile. "Hey, REESE, why don't you tell Blaine and Tracey about all your components?"

The lights that constituted REESE's mouth rose into a smile. Then the robot said, "Summer T. Beach, that is a wonderful idea. Blaine and Tracey, would you like to hear about all I am and all I can do?"

The Sassafras twins nodded eagerly, their faces still wearing open-mouthed smiles.

"All righty then," REESE said. "I provide robotic exploration, entertainment, and scientific enhancement, starting from the ground up. I am equipped with versatile, multi-speed, tank-like wheels and treads that are connected to the rest of my frame with a 360-degree spinning pelvic girdle joint. This allows me to move at a desired speed in any direction."

REESE demonstrated what he was talking about by rolling around in several different directions. "If I need to travel over uneven terrain, for instance, up a set of stairs, I can use my elasticized metal arms to assist in movement."

The robot then illustrated what he meant by stretching out his flexible arms all the way to the ground and lifting himself up off the floor and into the air a foot or two. Impressed, the twins clapped at REESE's display of strength and versatility.

"Next, on the largest section of my body, the torso, I have

two main components," REESE continued in his robotic voice. "First there is a touchscreen monitor, which can be controlled by hand or voice to view a large variety of videos, images, and text. For instance, I have a large library of movies, television shows, and even karaoke songs that can be viewed on the screen."

"You mean, kind of like the words to the song about gravity we just enjoyed together?" Tracey asked.

"That is exactly right, Tracey," REESE confirmed. "You can also view SCIDAT data on my screen, and then you can upload it onto your smartphones."

"Sweet," both twins thought.

"Second, on my torso, located beneath the monitor, I am equipped with a storage cell." As REESE said this, a storage compartment opened up, and the twins could see that it was already filled with all kinds of cool-looking things. "This storage cell can be used for an assortment of different objects. However, its main purpose is to store my many different hand attachments."

"Hand attachments?" Blaine asked.

"That is correct, Blaine. On the ends of my arms, I am able to attach suitor cups, vice grips, claws, grappling hooks, specially designed three-ringed carabiners, space-traveling cuffs, rocket launchers, karaoke microphones, and more."

Blaine's mouth opened in a smile again as he looked into the open storage cell and saw many of those attachments. REESE reached around with his current attachment, which was a metallic, humanlike hand. He pushed the storage cell closed before continuing.

"And finally, we have my head, which is connected to my torso with the same elasticized metallic material of which my arms are made." REESE moved and stretched his neck as he mentioned it. "Affixed to the top of my head, I have three small satellite power antennae that have the capability of picking up and transmitting radio frequencies from anywhere in the solar system. Second, my two eyes have telescope vision. You can tilt my head to gaze out in any direction in the cosmos, and then you can view what my eyes are seeing on my torso monitor. Third, the circular indentions on the sides of my head operate like ears, taking sound in. However, they can also pump sound out as they are high-watt sonic speakers as well. And fourth, the light box that makes up my mouth not only has the ability to appear as though it is a moving mouth, but it can also serve as a spotlight, movie projector, and disco ball."

The mention of the last component of REESE the robot was all Summer Beach needed to start dancing again. President Lincoln and Ulysses S. Grant, the inventor of this great machine, joined in and danced as well.

REESE, however, was not as eager to shake a leg. "Blaine and Tracey Sassafras, now that you have heard about all my components, would you like me to share some SCIDAT with you?"

"Sure!" The twins nodded in response to their new friend's question.

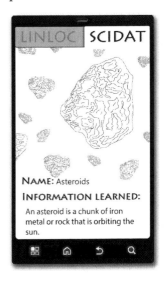

"All righty then. Your next topic is asteroids. An asteroid is a chunk of iron, metal, or rock that is orbiting the sun," REESE informed as his torso monitor lit up with the words he was saying.

"Asteroids have a jagged and irregular shape," he continued. "They don't always travel in an even, elliptical pattern around the sun. Most of the asteroids in our solar system orbit the sun in two places: the Asteroid Belt, which is between Mars and Jupiter; and the Kuiper belt, which is beyond Pluto. However, some asteroids orbit much closer to Earth. We call those NEAs for 'Near Earth Asteroid.' As these asteroids tumble through space, they can be pulled in by Earth's gravity. Once an asteroid enters Earth's atmosphere, it is called a meteor."

Blaine and Tracey wondered if any of the asteroids REESE was currently talking about would pose any kind of problem to them as they traveled around the solar system. Surely the different orbits of asteroids had been calculated by Uncle Cecil, right?

"Asteroids vary greatly in size," REESE spoke on as the SCIDAT on his monitor scrolled along with his words. "Some are only meters in length, whereas others are large enough to be named and considered planetoids. There are over ten thousand asteroids that are large enough to be named, such as Ceres, which is about six hundred miles wide and is also considered a dwarf planet. Another large asteroid, named Eros, actually had a robot spacecraft successfully land on it in 2001."

"Hmmm," thought Tracey, who was still dreaming about what it was going to be like to zip around the solar system. "If a robot spacecraft can successfully land on a moving asteroid, I bet we can too. I bet we can land and zip everywhere that's in the lineup for our study of astronomy."

As REESE finished giving scientific data, the twins both felt their phones vibrate.

"I have just uploaded the SCIDAT for both solar systems and asteroids to your phones," REESE notified with a smile showing on his voice box.

The twins smiled back—this robot was awesome! Summer, who was still disco dancing, slid over to a switch and dimmed the lights in the large cockpit. As she did, the speakers on the sides of REESE's trapezoid-shaped head began pumping out the rhythms of an upbeat song. At the same time, his screen mode switched from mouth mode to disco-ball-mode, and the robot began to dance. Ulysses was dancing. President Lincoln was dancing.

Summer Beach, of course, was still dancing.

Blaine and Tracey looked at each other. Several weeks ago, they had been bored to tears, hating science. Now when they looked at where they were, they had to laugh. They loved science now, and they loved all the crazy silliness that was happening in front of them. With no more hesitation, the Sassafras twins joined in the disco party.

CHAPTER 3: ZIPPING OUT OF THIS WORLD

Smashing Spray-Painted Stars

After the disco party ended, the twins, Summer, and the two lab assistants went outside to gaze up into the night sky. All five were now lying comfortably on their backs in the big, wide field of grass that lay above Summer's underground lab with their hands, or paws, behind their heads as they tried to take in the expansive mystery that was the cosmos. There were so many stars in the sky that it looked like some kind of celestial giant had spray-painted white speckles all across a huge, black canvas. It was so clear that the twins felt like they could see stars beyond the stars. It felt like they were looking out light years beyond into a universe that was still expanding. Space was such a big . . . space. There was so much that hadn't been explored and so much that hadn't been seen by human eyes or touched by human hands.

THE SASSAFRAS SCIENCE ADVENTURES

Blaine and Tracey both smiled and then let out long, dreamy sighs. They were on the cusp of such a wonderful opportunity. They were going to get to zip all across this wonderful universe of theirs. They still couldn't believe this was possible, even after Summer had explained it again. Her spaceship lab, which was buried just under a thin layer of this field, would thrust up and out of the ground by huge rockets. Then they'd fly into the sky and out of the atmosphere into space. Evidently, this whole lab, with its space-traveling capabilities, had been funded by some kind of private company in Switzerland. That company had originally named the craft-lab the *Triple-S 2*, which would have stood for either *Summer's Spaceship* or *Summer's Science Station*. However, Summer had vetoed that idea because she wanted to name the craft after her beloved lab assistant. She wanted to honor the Arctic ground squirrel and show him how much his hard work was appreciated, so the spaceship was named *Ulysses-1*.

But the name *Triple-S 2* reminded Blaine and Tracey of their time in Switzerland when they had been studying Earth science. They had been recruited by the Swiss Secret Service, also known as Triple S, to help stop Yuroslav Bogdanovich, the Siberian mad scientist. They hadn't succeeded in stopping Bogdanovich because one of the Triple-S agents, some lady named Adrianna Archer, had decided to be a turncoat and help the madman. Yuroslav had gotten away only to be caught a few days later, as strange as it was, by the Man With No Eyebrows.

However, to make things even stranger, Yuroslav Bogdanovich now worked as a clerk at a supermarket in Uncle Cecil's neighborhood. The Man With No Eyebrows had erased Yuroslav's memory, and Uncle Cecil had replaced the man's lost memory with those from a canister that he'd found in his basement. They were memories of a teenager named Preston who worked at the Left-Handed Turtle Market. So now Yuroslav though he was Preston, which was weird, but it was better than Yuroslav thinking he was Yuroslav.

"It's all moving! Wow! It's so amazing to think about how it's all really, really moving!" Summer suddenly exclaimed, cutting off the twins' reverie.

"What's moving?" Tracey asked.

"Everything that we can see up in the sky tonight," Summer answered. "Most of it looks stationary, but most of it is moving at tremendous speeds. Space is full of objects, some of which we can see from Earth with just our eyes, some we can see with the help of telescopes and some we can't see. But it' just so crazy to think about how so much of it is moving. We call everything in space the 'universe,' which includes all the matter, space, and energy that exists. Sometimes, we refer to this as the cosmos, but the cool thing is that the universe is constantly in motion! Even us, right now as we lay here in the field gazing up into the sky, we're moving! Isn't that amazing to think about?"

The twins agreed it was amazing. They smiled, sighed, and set their gazes back out into the remarkable universe.

"And the expanse of it! Wow! It's so incredible to think about the huge expanse of it all!" Summer continued, truly awed. "For instance, there are more stars than we could ever count, even using the most advanced technology. And some of them are so far away from Earth that our minds almost can't comprehend it."

Caught up in what Summer was saying, Tracey asked, "So what is a star exactly?"

"It's a huge ball of exploding gas," Summer answered with ever-present enthusiasm. "All stars go through a life cycle. They are born; they shine; and then one day they die out. These stages can take millions of years."

"Stars have a life cycle? What's that mean?" Blaine asked amazed.

"Stars are born in nebulas, which are large, swirling clouds of gas and dust," Summer answered. "Inside a nebula, clouds of gas clump together and then collapse inward, forming the core of a star. Once the core is formed, it grows hotter and hotter until eventually the gas starts to explode, and then the star begins to shine. As the gas in the star's core burns out, it begins to die. The star becomes a red giant, meaning it swells up and turns reddish. The gas on the outside burns up and dissipates into space, leaving a small ball known as a white dwarf. As the white dwarf cools, it fades away, and the star is gone. The larger the star, the quicker it burns out. The smaller the star, the longer it will shine."

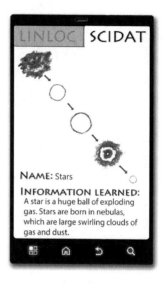

NAME: Stars

INFORMATION LEARNED: A star is a huge ball of exploding gas. Stars are born in nebulas, which are large swirling clouds of gas and dust.

As Summer spoke, the Sassafrases felt like their gazing out into the stars became even deeper, if that were possible. "I want to add one more thing before we go back down to the lab to upload all this SCIDAT about stars to your phones," Summer said. "A supernova is the explosion of a star that is larger than our sun when it's near the end of its life cycle."

Lying in the field looking into the sky had turned Blaine and Tracey into starry-eyed dreamers. It was almost as if their eyes were reflecting all they were seeing and hearing about stars, nebulas, and the ever-moving, limitless expanse of space. It was amazing, and they couldn't wait to be out in the middle of it all.

He couldn't believe it. *Thad-1*, his personal spacecraft, had made it out into orbit, and he was now soaring in space. A few days ago, he had been sitting in his basement at 1108 North Pecan Street thinking his revenge plot against Cecil Sassafras was over. But here he was, soaring through space, ready to blast Summer's spaceship to kingdom come as soon as it entered orbit.

Thad-1 was equipped with a ray gun that could, in theory, disable any other kind of spacecraft. The lasered spacecraft would then enter an endless orbit around the Earth with no working instruments. This would be the end of the Sassafras twins. Their science-learning would stop here in space. Their fate would be endless orbit in the great unknown.

This thought was so satisfying to him, so satisfying in fact that he was beginning to feel something inside. Was this courage rising from his stomach up to his throat? Was this resolve that . . . wait . . . no . . . this was not any of those things. This wasn't confidence. It was motion sickness, and that wasn't courage coming up his throat. That was . . . oh, no!

He was about to get sick!

"Hey, Q-Tip, toss me a cookie!" Evan DeBlose ordered. Q-Tip smiled and threw a cookie toward Evan. Both Swiss astronauts laughed as they watched the cookie then float slowly through the zero-gravity air. It was moving so slowly, in fact, that Evan was able to easily catch the cookie with his mouth. Evan crunched down the cookie and then chased it with a swig of floating hot cocoa.

Q-Tip had done so much better than he'd expected. Even though it was the agent's first trip into space, and he had been nervous, the little guy had done great.

Dauntless-12 had rocketed up out of Earth's atmosphere and into orbit with great power and velocity. It had been an intense experience, one that could have made the first-time astronaut freak out, but he hadn't. Q-Tip had remained composed, and Evan was proud of him.

The handsome, sandy-blonde agent gulped down the last of the hot cocoa with satisfaction. Now it was time for the task at hand: locate the broken satellite. They already had a tracker on it, and they could see its location on the screen in front of them. However, it was still quite a distance from where they were. It was going to take some time to get to it.

"Our trajectory is set at 0.37 degrees," Q-Tip announced as he processed through the data he was seeing. "Our path to the satellite is currently free and clear of any other spacecraft or space debris. By my estimation, we should reach our satellite by . . . wait . . . an unknown craft has just entered our vector."

"What?" Evan responded, leaning forward to see what Q-Tip was talking about. Sure enough his partner was right. The images and data on the screens in front of them confirmed it.

"Are we close enough to contact the craft?" DeBlose asked.

"Let's find out," Q-Tip offered as he reached for a headset.

Evan also grabbed a headset. He put it on, and he listened in as Q-Tip tried to connect with this surprise vessel in their vector. "This is *Dauntless-12* calling to unidentified craft. We want to avoid an unwanted collision. Our altitude is currently in low Earth orbit at 262.4 kilometers. Our trajectory is set at 0.37 degrees. And our speed is 28,665 kilometers an hour. Did you copy any of that?"

The Swiss Secret Service agents waited for a response, but none came.

"*Dauntless-12* to unidentified craft. Come in, please. Do you copy?" Q-Tip tried once more.

They were again met with silence.

Q-Tip rechecked the data on the screen in front of them. "By my estimation, the vessel should be well within range of contact," he informed, a little confused.

Evan's eyebrows scrunched down a little. Q-Tip never estimated wrong. Either the unidentified craft was unmanned, or its pilot was ignoring them.

"*Dauntless-12* to unidentified craft. Please come in. Do you copy?" Q-Tip repeated.

Still there was no answer.

They were traveling over twenty-eight thousand kilometers an hour, and according to their data, the other craft was traveling even faster, and it was headed in their direction. If they couldn't contact the craft, this could become a big problem.

"Should I change our velocity or deviate from our current trajectory?" Q-Tip asked, looking at Evan.

"Not yet," the three-time astronaut answered. "That will take us off our path to the satellite and could jeopardize our mission. Let's keep trying to contact that vessel."

Q-Tip nodded, but his nervousness was coming back. "*Dauntless-12* to unidentified craft. Please come in. Do you copy?"

Once more, there was no answer.

Again, "I said, *Dauntless-12* to unidentified craft. Please come in. Do you copy?" Radio silence was all they received.

"*Dauntless-12* to unidenti—"

"Listen here, buddy," Evan cut in on the transmission with a more authoritative voice than his partner was currently mustering. "This is *Dauntless-12*. We are coming fast, and we are coming right at you. If there is anyone in your craft, you need to answer right now or else!"

"Or else what," a third deep voice finally chimed in.

Evan and Q-Tip looked at each other. This person from the unidentified craft didn't sound nice.

"Our altitude is currently in low Earth orbit at 301.9 kilometers. Our trajectory is set at—"

Q-Tip started to give the specs again, but he was interrupted by the menacing voice. "I already heard all of that. Don't waste your breath."

"But you've got to change your current speed and trajectory, or else . . . or else . . ." Q-Tip stammered.

"Or else what?" the nameless voice scathed.

"Or else we'll all be Swiss cheese!" Evan blurted into the headset.

"How 'bout this," the voice answered, "I continue to do exactly what I'm doing. You, the *Dauntless-12*, change your speed and trajectory, and get out of my way. Or I will blow your ship out of space!"

"Blow our ship out of space? What are you talking about?" Evan exploded.

"Do as I say. Or else," the voice answered and then said, "*Thad-1*, over and out!"

"Whoa!" Blaine laughed with his sister. "We look like we're wearing marshmallows!" The two were giggling as they waddled around in their new space suits.

After last night's star gazing, the twins had rested deeply and well in a couple of the sleeping pods. They had woken up this morning to the sound of their pod doors opening and to the sight of two furry mammals presenting them with these cool suits. President Lincoln and Ulysses S. Grant, who had already been wearing custom space suits themselves, had handed the suits to the twins and helped them get the suits on.

Now the Sassafrases were laughing and bounding around the lab as they tried their new outfits out. They were in the main section of *Ulysses-1*, the one they had originally slid down into the first time they visited Alaska. It was a sleek and modern place with floor-to-ceiling, translucent data screens, brightly lit specimen tubes, and sleeping pods built into the walls, among other things.

As Tracey sat down in a chair to get a better look at her space boots, Blaine repeatedly pressed the button that opened and closed his dome-shaped space helmet. The twins were too busy playing with their space suits to notice the large, egg-shaped door beginning to open slowly. They did, however, notice when a figure ran into the room through the open door, wearing a fat white suit just like theirs.

"Summer!" The adolescent Sassafrases exclaimed.

Summer Beach skipped across the floor, swept up both the twelve-year-olds along with the other two mammals, and the group then experienced their first bulky-space-suit-clad, happy, jumping dance-hug.

"Today is the day!" Summer cried out. "Today is the day that we get to travel out into space! Today is the day *Ulysses-1* goes for launch!"

The group continued to hug until another figure entered through the doorway.

"Good morning," a robotic voice said as cheerfully as a robotic voice could sound. It was REESE, and he was the only one not wearing a space suit.

"REESE! Good morning," Summer's voice greeted as cheerfully as a human voice possibly could sound.

"Blaine! Tracey! REESE is here to tell us more about these cool, new space suits." Summer squealed as the lights resembling a mouth on REESE's light box lit up and made a bright smile.   "The ship may be named after Ulysses S. Grant, but the suits are named after his best friend, President Lincoln," REESE said in his robotic tone. "These are Linc 2.0 IEVA space suits, and they were designed by Linc Dawg and Ulysses to provide the durable versatility you will need to navigate the inside of any and all spacecraft as well as outside in space itself. IEVA stands for Intra-Extra Vehicular Activity."

The Sassafrases nodded, impressed, as REESE continued. "Your Linc 2.0 suits are equipped with internal pressurization, a seventy-six-hour supply of oxygen, carbon dioxide expulsion, temperature regulation, a shield against ultraviolet radiation, aluminized insulation layers to protect against micro meteoroids, as well as a communication system. On top of being life-sustaining, the Linc 2.0 suits are also agile. They will allow unrestrained mobility at every joint in your body. The boots are lightweight, sturdy, and puncture proof. The gloves are made of silicone, enabling a sense of touch, and are also equipped with fingertip flashlights."

"Wow!" Blaine marveled out loud as he immediately looked at the ends of his fingers.

"And two last things—the docking system and the propulsion system—both are located on the back of your suits," REESE informed, still smiling. "The docking system will securely connect you to any and all external setters, whereas the propulsion system shoots out bursts of air, allowing you to travel through space untethered."

"Wow!" Blaine blurted out again, and then he accidentally engaged the propulsion system REESE had spoken of. This caused a short burst of steamy air to shoot out of the back of his suit. The outburst made Blaine jump, while everyone else smiled and laughed.

Blast Off to the International Space Station

The outburst had made him jump, but evidently it had

worked. The two annoying astronauts had been contacting him and warning him over and over again. They had kept talking on and on, which was more than irksome, so he had blasted them. He had used the ray gun to shoot *Dauntless-12*, and it looked like he had made direct contact. The outburst of the gun had been surprisingly loud and jolting for him here in the cockpit of *Thad-1*, but he was no worse for the wear, and it looked and sounded like the ray gun had successfully shot the other craft.

He couldn't see their craft anymore, and they weren't nagging him over the radio, so it must have worked. He took a long, deep breath inside his Dark Cape helmet and even managed half a smile. Having an army of scientists at his disposal who could design and develop things like this sleek spacecraft wasn't half bad. This army of his was definitely going to help him get his revenge against Cecil Sassafras. He took another deep breath and smiled the other fifty percent of his smile.

Now it was time to focus on what he had flown out here into space to accomplish. He couldn't wait to use the laser to blast the Sassafrases. He flicked his big, black gloves around the tech in the cockpit and quickly gained access to the satellite that was keeping tabs on Summer Beach's lab. Immediately, he could hear the frizzy-haired female scientist yakking away, saying something about how the zip lines would work in space.

"What is taking these jokers so long?" He growled aloud. "Surely they are going to take off soon! Or is all they do talk, talk, talk? C'mon, Sassafras twins, blast off, so I can then blast away all your dreams of learning science!"

"So they won't zip through the Earth's atmosphere," Tracey

clarified. "But once we make it out into space, they will work like normal, right?"

"Right, Tracey!" Summer answered. "That's the theory! Linc Dawg and Ulysses are pretty sure they have worked out all the kinks, and once the two of you get out into orbit, the invisible zip lines should be right as rain!"

Both the prairie dog and the Arctic ground squirrel nodded that this was indeed true.

"So, once we get out there, where are we going first?" Blaine asked. "Maybe the moon, or Mars, or oh! Oh! My personal favorite: the planet of Irkazoid?"

Tracey looked down at the ground and shook her head. "Blaine, that's not even a real place."

"It's not?" Blaine questioned.

"No, that's just a made-up place in one of your video games." Tracey shook her head again.

"You're sure there's no planet called Irkazoid?" Blaine confirmed.

"Pretty sure," Tracey said with confidence.

"Your first location out in the great beyond is going to be the I.S.S!" Summer interjected with outstretched arms.

"The I.S.S?" Tracey asked. "What does that stand for?"

"I.S.S. stands for International Space Station!" Summer said excitedly. "It's the most expensive thing humankind has built to date."

"Whoa!" Both twins mouthed, responding in awe.

LINLOC   SCIDAT

NAME: International Space Station (I.S.S.)
INFORMATION LEARNED: The I.S.S. is made from several modules that clip together. It has a large array of solar panels to generate the power it needs.

"Simply put, a space station is a human-made structure that is launched into space and orbits around the sun, orbiting Earth," Summer expounded. "The I.S.S. is made from several modules that clip together, and it has a large array of solar panels to generate the power it needs. It is also covered with radio antennae and satellite dishes so that it can send signals back to Earth with the information it gathers from experiments and observations. Since the year 2000, the I.S.S has been continuously manned by a team of astronaut scientists. The researchers come from several different countries, and they perform experiments to learn how humans and plants are affected by space."

"Currently, there are six astronauts aboard the International Space Station," REESE interjected. "The astronaut in charge is Captain Dianna Sturgess from the United States. Also aboard are Yang Bo from China, Sander Petrov from Russia, Bayard Clemence from France, Anna Maria Bezerra from Brazil, and Parth Banerjee from India."

"It truly is a multinational crew and sort of serves as a blueprint for global cooperation," Summer mused, taking the reins back from her robot friend.

"Dianna, Yang Bo, Sander, Bayard, Anna Maria, and Parth live in a zero-gravity environment there on the I.S.S.," the female scientist continued as she herself pretended to float around the lab in zero gravity. "This means they must be strapped in when they sleep and exercise. Plus, any and all liquids float, so they have to use vacuums to go to the bathroom. And, wowie, washing their hair can turn into a water droplet-chasing adventure!"

Blaine and Tracey smiled. They could just imagine it, floating around in space, virtually flying, with anything and everything around them floating, too. This was going to be so fun!

Soon, what was now only in their imaginations would be a reality.

Soon, what was now only in his imagination would be their reality. He would blast *Ulysses-1* with his laser. The science learning of those twins would come to a wonderfully terrible end.

His vengeance against Cecil Sassafras would be complete. The loss of his eyebrows would have atonement.

"Okay, Thaddaeus. You are positioned exactly where you need to be," he now heard the voice of Adrianna Archer inside his Dark Cape helmet. She was transmitting clearly all the way from his underground lab in Siberia. "When *Ulysses-1* makes it into orbit, blast them at your leisure."

"Ten-four," he responded to his right-hand woman.

"C'mon, you silly science lovers," he growled impatiently to himself as he listened over satellite waves to Summer, who was still yakking away. "Quit talking SCIDAT, and get that spaceship off the ground!"

"So, it's traveling how fast?" Tracey asked with wide eyes.

"The International Space Station orbits the Earth every ninety minutes and is traveling at the speed of five miles per second!" Summer repeated what she had just said.

"Wow!" Blaine said. "That is . . . really fast!"

"Yes, it is!" Summer happily confirmed. "And now it is time for us to get up there and join them! Let's see what this research lab spaceship can do! Sassafrases, let's get back to the cockpit! It's time for blastoff!"

"Well, that was quite the whirly ride." Evan laughed in the direction of Q-Tip, who was not laughing but rather sweating and gasping for air.

"It looks like everything on board is still working," Evan said. "I guess that means you got the shield up in time?"

"Yes, we got our shield up in time but barely. However, the laser blast from that small ship still rocked us pretty good. We are now off our desired trajectory. And although it may not feel like it, we are still spinning uncontrollably."

"Can we recover and realign?" Evan asked.

Q-Tip didn't answer immediately as he looked over the information on the screen and quickly did the mathematical calculations.

"I think so," the skinny agent responded, now breathing normally. "But even if we can, it's going to add weeks to our mission."

Evan almost asked his next question quickly, but he caught himself and allowed a pause. Then he asked, "Could we use . . . what about . . . you know . . . the upgrade?"

Q-Tip looked at DeBlose perplexed. "But that was supposed to be for the satellite. Not this rocket."

"True, true," Evan responded. "But it's already functional and attached to this rocket, right?"

"Right," Q-Tip answered cautiously. "And the main purpose of our mission was to find the satellite, repair it, and turn its shield back on, right?

"Right, but the upgrade is top secret—it's a taser, right?

Everybody knows how much you love to add tasers to everything. Fixing the satellite's shield is of utmost importance, and the top-secret upgrade to the satellite is secondary. You know that. Why does a satellite need a taser, anyway?"

"Well, it doesn't . . . I just through that . . . but what will Captain Marolf say?"

"Q-Tip, forget about Captain Marolf right now. If the main purpose of our mission is to reach the satellite and repair its shield, and the taser can give us the boost we need to get back on track to do that, don't you think we should use it? It's operational and attached to this rocket and ready to go!"

"Well, yes, I guess it does make sense," Q-Tip answered, starting to see Evan's way. He shook away his nervousness and then said, "Not only could the taser give us the boost we need to get back on track, I could probably figure out how to attach it to the satellite even after use."

"That a boy, Q-Tip! Now you're thinking like a true field agent!"

Summer T. Beach, Tracey Sassafras, Blaine Sassafras, President Lincoln, Ulysses S. Grant, and REESE the robot were all now strapped securely in the cockpit of *Ulysses-1* and were ready for launch. They were about to shoot up from a field in Alaska out into the great beyond of space. REESE started an electronic-sounding countdown as numbers flashed across his torso monitor.

"Ten . . . nine . . ."

THE SASSAFRAS SCIENCE ADVENTURES

Oh! Oh! They were starting a countdown! It was finally time to blast them with the ray gun! Thaddaeus with no eyebrows grabbed the controls to *Thad-1*'s blaster and aimed straight for the point at which *Ulysses*-1 was calculated to exit Earth's atmosphere.

"Eight . . . seven . . ."

"Okay, I've checked and rechecked," Q-Tip squeaked out, a bit worried, excited, and nervous. He took a deep breath and continued. "The taser is indeed operational and should give us the boost we need. The only problem is that we're still spinning, so it's going to be virtually impossible to fire the taser at the exact right moment to put us back on the correct trajectory. If we get it right, then great. But if we get it wrong, then . . . not great. A misfire will put us even further off course and render this mission a failure."

"Then let me do it," Evan said. "Let me fire the taser."

Q-Tip looked at his partner with big, unsure eyes but then nodded.

"Six . . . five . . ."

Blaine and Tracey were unfathomably excited. They were about to rocket up into space.

They glanced over and saw that of course Summer had a

huge smile on her face, but so did Ulysses and President Lincoln. Even REESE's face held a huge smile as his countdown continued.

"Four . . . three . . ."

He held the controls of his ray gun with tight excitement, the leather of his black gloves creaking because of the intensity of his grip. "C'mon, Sassafrases. Come and get it!"

"Two . . ."

Q-Tip was about to give his partner a few more calculations and explanatory comments, but before he could, the intrepid Triple S agent, DeBlose, Evan, fired the taser unannounced.

As he did, a flume of electrified light as bright as a supernova shot from the spinning *Dauntless-12* out into space and thrust them into a defined trajectory.

"One."

With wicked excitement, Thaddaeus prepared to crush down the "fire" button for the ray gun, but a second before he did, a powerful flume of light came shooting directly toward him from some unseen place. Before the black-clad, eyebrow-less man could do anything to protect himself, *Thad-1* was hit by the shocking shot of electric light and sent spinning off violently into darkness.

"Blast off!"

The Sassafras twins were pushed to the backs of their seats because of the exhilarating force. Their smiles became bigger and wider with the of rushing velocity. Their minds and hearts expanded because of impending adventure *Ulysses-1* rocketed up from its Alaskan field. The spaceship launched forward with a power the twins had never experienced before. And with only a limited amount of atmosphere left before them, Blaine and Tracey knew they would soon be in . . . space!

CHAPTER 4: SPACE SANDWICHES AND PLANETARY POTATO CHIPS

Mechanical Mercury

"Yeppity yep. You thought that might happen," Cecil confirmed as he went from standing next to his desk to sitting at it.

The dots of light that represented his niece and nephew's location in the world had gone dark on the tracking screen. "It's like you said, Linc Dawg. Once Train and Blaisey break through the atmosphere and enter space, we will no longer be able to follow their progress here on the . . . Linc? President Lincoln, where are you?"

The redheaded scientist spun this way and that looking around somewhat frantically for his prairie dog lab assistant. "President Lincoln? Where did you go? Where . . . oh, yes, now I remember. You went with them."

Cecil chuckled at his own forgetfulness and then called out toward the other side of the basement.

"Can you believe that, Summer?" He chuckled. "I forgot President Lincoln zipped away with the twins for their astronomy adventure. Isn't that just the funniest thi— Summer?"

Cecil swiveled his head around again. Summer wasn't down here either. "Aha! Okity-okay. That's right! Summer, you're with the twins, too. In fact, it's your lab-ship that is being used to maneuver in space."

Cecil started to laugh again but then stopped because something was stuck in his throat . . . Was it . . . loneliness? If it was, he wasn't sure he'd ever experienced it before.

"Interesting. Scientifically interesting," the scientist said to himself. "It's no surprise that I miss President Lincoln; I have grown accustomed to his scurrying around this place working with me on project after project. But wow! I miss Summer Beach, too!"

Cecil scratched his head. "She was here for only a short time, and although we are old friends, her physical presence was an anomaly of sorts. So, it is more than a little surprising that I would feel this way because of her absence. Hmmm . . ."

The Sassafras man mused as he looked around this messy lab of his. "Pretty interesting, don't you think?" he asked the two men dressed in robes standing over by the closet.

"Well, don't you?" Cecil asked again. "Socrates, surely you've got an angle on this. Aristotle, I bet you've pondered the feeling of loneliness before. Surely between the two of you, you could muster some sort of thought on this matter. Well?"

Cecil waited for a response but then remembered the two plastic mannequins had never been much for words.

"Hmmm . . ." the scientist mused again.

"Sweet astronaut sandwiches on air compressed wheat!" Summer Beach exclaimed. "You two Space-a-frasses are about to zip all over the galaxy!"

The twins would have bounced with excitement upon this statement, but because they were now in space and experiencing zero gravity, they floated in excitement instead.

"You two, along with REESE, will be exploring the inner planets, the outer planets, the International Space Station, and more! Your Z.O.P.s, your zip origination points, out here in space will be on the I.S.S." Summer turned from the twins momentarily toward a screen. "As I said before, I can track your location in space on this cockpit monitor. And Ulysses and Linc Dawg have checked the equipment and confirmed that everything looks good to go."

The Sassafras twins nodded and then pulled out their smartphones.

"Okay, cutie squared!" Summer smile-shouted. "Open up those LINLOC applications and see what's on the horizon!"

Blaine and Tracey did just that and saw that their next local expert's name was Yang Bo; they would be studying about Mercury, Venus, Earth, and Mars; and instead of longitude and latitude, there was something LINLOC was calling a space coordinate. There was one listed for each planet, and they all ended in AU.

"Wow!" Tracey exclaimed. "Space coordinates? What does AU mean?"

"AU stands for astronomical unit, which is how we measure distances in space. It is equal to about 93 million miles, or 150 million kilometers. One AU is about the distance Earth is from the Sun. The space coordinates in LINLOC show you the average distance the planet is from the sun—isn't astronomy exciting!" Summer smiled. "And, oh! Oh! Just so you know, Yang Bo, your local expert, knows about the invisible zip lines."

"He does?" Blaine gaped.

"He sure does," Summer confirmed. "It so happens that Yang Bo is an old junior high classmate of your uncle and mine."

"He is?" Tracey asked.

"Yep!" Summer responded. "He came over as a foreign exchange student from China, and it became quickly apparent to all of us that he was uber smart. He was PhD brains walking around in a junior high body. It's no surprise that he went on to get a doctorate in astrobiology and then from there got commissioned to be an astronaut for the International Space Station."

"Wow, he does sound smart," the twins agreed.

"He's smart, and he's also super kind," Summer added. "Cecil and I have both kept up with him over the years. I was super-duper pumped when he agreed to help you two out with the study of astronomy! And you know, he's not the only one from that junior high class that will be involved in this leg of science learning. There's also . . . well, you know what . . . I'll let you two get your zip on so you can go and find out! Look at me. I'm so excited for you two that I've become quite the Chatty Kathy."

Summer laughed at herself and then raised her arms up high. "It's time to zip! The universe is out there waiting for you!"

"Wait . . . but . . . how do we put on our harnesses over these suits? And how do we spin the carabiners to the space coordinates?" Blaine asked, a bit confused.

Summer giggled before answering, "Oh my, REESE forgot to explain the zip-zop cuff, another one of your Uncle's brilliant inventions! President Lincoln and Ulysses have equipped the left cuff on your IEVA with this digital carabiner of sorts. All you need to do is enter the space coordinates into the screen on the zip-zop cuff, press the zip button, and you will connect to our invisible extraterrestrial zip lines. To get back, all you do is press the zop button, and it will automatically connect you to the line that returns you to your zip origination point, which Ulysses set as the International Space Station. If for any reason you need to unclip from the lines, simply tap the digital coordinate screen three times in rapid succession, and you will unclip. Otherwise, the cuffs will remain on the lines, floating in space until you enter a new coordinate or press the zop button."

"That sounds easy enough, but what about you, Summer?" Tracey asked. "And what about President Lincoln and Ulysses? What are the three of you going to do while Blaine and I explore the galaxy?"

"Oh, we've got some fun stuff planned," Summer giggled. "Linc Dawg and Ulysses are a couple of inventive, science-loving mammals, so even out here in space, they have a whole list of projects and experiments that they want me to help them work on. Don't worry about us; we'll be fine."

The twins nodded, inhaled, and then exhaled. It was time to see if the invisible zip lines worked in space, out here beyond the Earth's atmosphere. They weren't wearing their backpacks, harnesses, or helmets. They didn't need those for invisible zip line space travel. The twelve-year-olds looked good and ready, almost like real astronauts.

"Are you ready to ride the zip lines with us, buddy?" Blaine asked as he patted REESE on the back of his trapezoid-shaped head.

"Almost, Blaine!" REESE responded. "If you will be so kind as to reach in my storage compartment, grab the specially designed zip-zop-cuff-equipped hand attachment, and then secure that to the end of one of my arms, I would be more than grateful."

"Sure thing, pal," the Sassafras boy responded and then did exactly as the robot had asked.

"Okay!" Summer exclaimed. "To get to the I.S.S., you need to press the zop button and then for approximately seven seconds, you three will float here, or I should say 'continue to float here,' and then you will zip off for the International Space Station! Are you ready?"

"We're ready!" The two humans and one robot answered.

Summer, Ulysses S. Grant, and President Lincoln all smiled and waved as REESE, Blaine, and Tracey pressed the zop button on their cuffs. The Sassafras twins immediately felt their cuffs connect to the invisible lines. REESE, too, had his robotic arm immediately pulled up as his zip-zop-hand attachment connected to the line as well.

Then whoosh!

The three zipped off into mind-bending light. It was as if the stars around them were swirling around, beckoning them to come farther than they'd ever zipped before. The familiar rush made it seem like the invisible zip lines were working fine out in space.

Suddenly, an abrupt jerking motion interrupted the smooth ride, but this worried neither Blaine nor Tracey because this was the customary way an invisible zip-lining trip ended. The cuffs automatically unclipped from the lines, and the twins' bodies slumped down, blind and devoid of physical strength, which was also expected.

Their blindness slowly faded from bright, white light back into color. Their strength slowly returned as well. As it did, they found their bodies hadn't actually slumped down to the ground upon landing but instead were floating because of zero gravity. REESE had also landed safely, and he was floating with an electronic smile next to the Sassafrases.

"Welcome to the International Space Station," the robot greeted.

The Sassafras twins smiled and looked around at their first non-Earth location. The room they were in was small but not cramped. It was square with a window on one side. There was an adjoining tube-shaped hallway on the other side. The walls, ceiling, and floor of the room were all covered with an array of tubes, wires, levers, buttons, multi-language instructional stickers, and more.

All at once, a thick, circular door at the other end of the adjoining tube opened up. In floated a person dressed in bulky white. Blaine and Tracey gasped in awe—here was a real, live astronaut. He was a handsome Chinese man with kind eyes and a strong jawline that was turned up into a smile. The twelve-year-olds both opened up their space helmets and met the approaching astronaut with smiles to match.

"Blaine and Tracey Sassafras!" The Asian man greeted as he reached them. "Welcome to the I.S.S! I'm so glad the two of you are here!"

"Yang Bo?" the twins half asked, half stated.

"That's me!" Yang Bo confirmed happily. "Classmate and friend to both Summer and Cecil, local expert to both Blaine and Tracey, resident astrobiologist of the International Space Station, and the luckiest man in the solar system!"

The Chinese astronaut gave both the twelve-year-olds high fives before exclaiming, "It's so cool that the invisible zip lines work!"

"They definitely do," the twins nodded.

"When your uncle first told me the idea about zip lines that were going to be invisible, I thought he was joking. He then added that these invisible zip lines of his were going to be able to transport riders from location to location at the speed of light. That's when I thought my old buddy from junior high had truly lost it. But here the two of you are now! And although the zip lines don't actually travel quite as fast as light, they are fast and they do work!"

"Wait," Blaine paused, thinking about the swirls of light they had just zipped through. "The zip lines don't travel at the speed of light?"

"Not exactly," Yang Bo answered. "Light is super fast.

Beyond fast, actually. It travels about six hundred million miles an hour or more; precisely 5.88 trillion miles a year. And besides being fast, light also serves as our measuring stick out here. We measure distances in space by light-years."

Blaine's stunned face revealed how amazed he was at the information Yang Bo was telling him.

"When Cecil told me about the zip lines," Yang Bo continued, "he said they were going to travel at the speed of 'lound.'"

"The speed of 'lound?'" Tracey asked. "What's that?"

"That was my question when I first heard the word, Tracey," Yang Bo responded. "Your uncle explained to me that the speed of lound was somewhere in between the speed of light and the speed of sound.

"I don't remember the exact calculations," Yang Bo chuckled, "but I thought the word was silly even for Cecil, so I suggested that if he ever got the lines up and running, he should just say they traveled close to the speed of light."

The twins chuckled along with their local expert as they thought about how silly yet brilliant their uncle was. They might even say he was "silliant," or was it "brilly?" Maybe they were becoming more like him.

"Did your uncle invent this wonderful machine as well?" Yang Bo asked, referring to REESE.

"Nope, this guy was designed and invented in Summer Beach's lab," Tracey answered. The astronaut smiled at the mention of another one of his old friends.

"REESE, or R-E-E-S-E, stands for Robotic Exploration, Entertainment, and Scientific Enhancement," Tracey explained. "And as you can see, because of this specially designed zip-zop-cuff attachment, he can ride the invisible zip lines with us!"

Yang Bo nodded and smiled.

"Yeah, REESE is a real hoot," Blaine added, sounding a little more nerdy than he'd wanted to.

"Point of fact, REESE is not a real hoot," a new voice suddenly entered the conversation.

The twins looked and saw that some kind of skinny, little machine was floating through the tube-shaped hallway to join them. It was mostly white with some reflective orange stripes on it. It looked a bit like an upside-down tube of roller-ball deodorant or maybe a flashlight that was standing on end.

"A hoot is the natural throat noise of an owl," the thing said. "REESE is a robot."

"Meet QA-700," Yang Bo introduced. "He checks and confirms our mathematical calculations here on the I.S.S. He also gives factual answers for any questions we may have. He usually comes across as kind of a know-it-all."

"Point of fact, I am not a know-it-all," the robot droned. His digital face had minimal lines, but when he spoke some lights blinked in his face. "Knowing everything is not possible because 93% of—"

"Yeah, yeah, yeah," Yang Bo laughed, interrupting the machine. "QA-700 is not exactly a know-it-all, but as you can see, he takes things literally. So, most of the astronauts aboard the I.S.S. have stopped calling him QA-700. Instead, we call him SLIM."

"SLIM?" Blaine asked. "Is that because he's kind of skinny and looks like a knee-high flashlight?"

Yang Bo shook his head. "Nope, SLIM stands for Super Literal Information Machine."

"Oh," Blaine said. "That's cool."

"Point of fact, I am not cool," SLIM responded in his flat, robotic voice. "I operate anywhere from 30 degrees Celsius to—"

"Okay, okay," Yang Bo interrupted the robot again good-naturedly. "That's enough for now, SLIM. Blaine and Tracey are here to study astronomy, not receive comments about everything that's said."

The astronaut turned from the robot toward the twins. "The first topic on the docket is the planet of Mercury, right?"

The twins nodded.

"Point of fact, the planet of Mercury is the closest planet to the sun," SLIM interjected. "It is a small, hot pla—"

"Hold up," REESE suddenly interrupted his counterpart. "I'm the robot who is supposed to be giving these Twinkies their SCIDAT."

SLIM turned to look at REESE. "Point of fact, I cannot hold up any solid objects as I am not equipped wi—"

"Talk to the hand," REESE said, holding up his arm in front of SLIM.

"Point of fact, that is not a hand. That is a zip-zop-cuff attachment."

"Step off! Gear down. Chill out! Back awa—"

"Whoa, whoa, whoa," Yang Bo's human voice cut in. "Everyone take a moment, and let me explain how this is going to work."

The two robots stopped their conversation and looked toward the astronaut. Blaine and Tracey looked at Yang Bo, too, trying hard not to laugh out loud at the fact the two robots were fighting over the chance to share SCIDAT with them.

"I am the local expert here, so I will be the one to relay the scientific data to Blaine and Tracey," Yang Bo informed, looking like he was holding in laughter as well. "In some cases, I may pass along this responsibility to REESE, who has also been approved and commissioned to complete this task. Additionally, if applicable, REESE can show the SCIDAT on his torso data screen as well as upload it straight to the twins' smartphones. SLIM will serve as a backup in the case that neither REESE nor I are able to relay SCIDAT data. Does everyone understand?"

Blaine, Tracey, and REESE nodded. SLIM blinked.

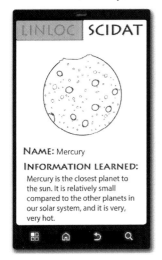

NAME: Mercury

INFORMATION LEARNED:
Mercury is the closest planet to the sun. It is relatively small compared to the other planets in our solar system, and it is very, very hot.

"Okay, good." Yang Bo sighed happily. "Then let me get back to Mercury. Like SLIM said, Mercury is the closest planet to the sun. It is relatively small compared to the other planets in our solar system, and it is very, very hot. During the day it gets up to over 800 degrees Fahrenheit. However, the temperature ranges on the surface of Mercury are the greatest of all the planets, so at night it can dip down to freezing temperatures that can nearly reach -300 degrees Fahrenheit."

"Wow!" The Sassafrases shivered. They had thought Antarctica was cold.

"Mercury, which is named after the Roman messenger god, is one-third the size of the Earth," Yang Bo continued. "However, it is almost as heavy as the Earth due to the fact that its core is made of dense metal. The first glimpse of the surface of Mercury was caught in 1973 from a space probe named *Mariner-10*, and it's a surface that is covered with numerous craters, the largest of which is called 'Caloris Basin,' and it is nearly 800 miles across."

"Wow," the twins thought again. "Studying the planets is going to be a lot different than anything we've studied so far on Earth."

Yang Bo floated over to REESE and touched the screen on the robot's torso, turning it on. "No need to text in this information about Mercury, Blaine and Tracey," he said. "This time around, we'll have REESE upload it straight to your phones."

The SCIDAT Yang Bo had cited could now be seen on the screen along with an upload tab, which Yang Bo promptly pushed.

"I would like to explain one more thing about how days and time work out here in space before the two of you zip out further from here to inspect these planets we'll be talking about," the astronaut said. "A year or a day for the different planets in our solar system doesn't necessarily work the same as they do for Earth."

"Really?" The twins responded as they felt their phones vibrate with the SCIDAT that was coming in.

"Really," Yang Bo responded. "A year on a planet is the time it takes for that planet to orbit the sun. And a day on a planet is the time it takes for that planet to completely rotate, resulting in both a sunrise and a sunset. For instance, a year on Mercury takes only about 88 Earth days. However, a day on Mercury lasts over 58 Earth days."

Even though Blaine and Tracey had both gotten A's in math during their last school year, this "space math" they were hearing about was boggling their minds. Their faces showed their bewilderment, which made the Chinese astronaut chuckle.

"Okay, that's enough data for now," he said. "Why don't you guys set those zip-zop cuffs of yours so you can actually go see the planet of Mercury!"

Venus Vapors

At this news, Blaine pumped his fist in elation, but he suddenly stopped. "Wait a second," the boy quipped. "Didn't you just say the surface of Mercury is either extremely cold or extremely hot? If we zip there . . . even with these space suits . . . won't we . . . you know . . . like . . . die?"

"That's an excellent point, Blaine," Yang Bo acknowledged. "I can see that you are well on your way to being as smart as your uncle."

Upon this comment, Blaine puffed his chest out a little.

"It is for this exact reason that you two will not be able to land on the actual surface of most of the planets," the astrobiologist explained. "The 'space coordinates' you will use for each planet, with the exception of Mars, will put you at the closest safe viewing distance to the planet."

"You mean we'll be kind of hanging out on the zip lines in space and looking down at each planet from sort of a bird's-eye view?" Tracey asked.

"Precisely," Yang Bo confirmed. "You will set the space coordinates on your cuffs. You will zip from here on the I.S.S. to those distances. When you reach the location, your zip lining will stop as normal, but you will not unclip from the lines. Stay clipped in. Take in the out-of-this-world breathtaking views. Get your pictures for SCIDAT. And then zip back to the I.S.S."

The Sassafras twins nodded in understanding.

"Okay," the astronaut said, clapping his hands once. "Let's get this show on the road! Let's call—"

"Case in point, Blaine and Tracey will not be traveling on an actual road. They will be—"

"Okay, thanks for your input, SLIM," Yang Bo said, patting the literal robot on its 'head.'

"That will be all for now. Blaine and Tracey, the space coordinate for Mercury is 0.387 AU. Go ahead, set your cuffs to that number, and get ready to zip!"

Everything was still spinning. What had happened?

"Adrianna?" He called out into the darkness in a weak voice.

"Adrianna, are you still there?"

There was no answer. The speakers in his helmet remained silent.

He blinked his eyes several times to make sure they were open. They were. But still all he could see was darkness. He could hear nothing. He could see nothing. But he could smell something. Uh oh, he may have tossed his cookies again.

He slowly exhaled and tried to remember what had happened. He knew he was in a one-man spacecraft out in orbit, but what exactly had he been doing? And why was he now spinning uncontrollably?

"Ouch." He winced. "It hurts to concentrate this hard."

He exhaled.

"Oh, yes," he painfully recalled. "I was about to blast Summer Beach and those twins, but I wasn't able to because . . ."

What was the reason? Why had he not fired his ray gun?

"That big flame of bright light!" He exclaimed. "I was blindsided out of nowhere by all that bright light!"

Where had that shot of light come from? Had he been hit by a shooting star? Had an alien spacecraft shot at him? No, aliens weren't real—were they?

"Wait, wait!" He shouted. "*Dauntless-12*! I was on a collision course with some ship called *Dauntless-12*. But didn't I . . . Yes, I blasted them into smithereens! Or did I miss them? Are they the ones that shot me with the light?"

He was on the verge of panic. His stomach threatened to toss his cookies again.

Suddenly the lights and controls in his cockpit clinked to life, and a crackling sound came through the small speakers in his helmet.

"Adrianna!" He called out again to his right-hand woman, who he desperately hoped was listening. "Adrianna, are you there?"

All at once, everything went dark again.

"No!" He shouted. This couldn't be happening. This couldn't be real. He was spinning out of control through space, entrenched in darkness with no one to help him and no one to communicate with.

"Adrianna!" He called out again. Clink. Clink. Thad-1's lights clicked on again. "Adrianna! Adrianna! Are you there? Help me! I'm scared!"

"Thaddaeus? Thaddaeus? Come in, Thaddaeus," the strong woman's voice suddenly transmitted clearly.

"Adrianna!" The Man With No Eyebrows yelped. "Can you hear me? Please, can you hear me? Can you help me?"

"Thaddaeus, I can hear you. Calm down. Just calm down. I can hear you. You are coming through fine. I'm with you, our highly esteemed leader."

"Adrianna! Help! I can't—I want—please—I'm—I can't—"

"Thaddaeus, slow down. Take a breath; you're going to hyperventilate if you don't calm down."

"Adrianna, help me. Bring me back! I don't want to do this anymore!"

"Thaddaeus, hold on." Adrianna Archer's voice went quiet for less than five seconds, although it felt like five hours to Thaddaeus.

"Thaddaeus, one of the technicians here says you need to locate the stabilization lever. Can you do that for me? Can you find the stabilization lever?"

The Man With No Eyebrows reached around the cockpit of *Thad-1* with his shaking black gloves until he found the stabilization lever. "Okay, Adrianna, I found it."

"Pull the lever up, Thaddaeus," Adrianna directed.

Thaddaeus obeyed the command. Immediately, his spaceship stopped spinning. "Okay! Okay, I'm not spinning anymore. I'm not spinning anymore!" The black-suited man exhaled, but his relief was short-lived and was immediately followed by more fear.

"But Adrianna! Where am I now? Can you see me? Are you tracking me? Or am I just floating out in space? Can you see me? What happened? Can you help me?"

"Calm down, Thaddaeus," Adrianna responded with a controlled voice. "We are tracking you, and you are still within reach of the Sassafras twins. You were hit with a ray gun or maybe some kind of taser from another spacecraft, but *Thad-1* is fine. The technicians here have given the green light to continue."

Thaddaeus gulped. "Continue? You mean I have to stay out here?"

"Well, yes, Thaddaeus. This mission was sanctioned under your direction."

"But . . . I . . . okay . . . okay . . . I will complete the mission. I will destroy the Sassafrases."

The eyes of Blaine and Tracey Sassafras were full of wonder as they floated in space, tethered to the invisible zip lines, overlooking the amazing planet of Mercury. They were thankful they had this privilege to be short-term astronauts and excited they were getting to take in views like the one they were seeing right now. These were views that almost no living person had ever seen before. It was almost too beautiful and wonderful to comprehend.

Tracey looked over at Blaine through the helmet of her

spacesuit. He looked back at her. Neither said anything. They just smiled.

This. Was. Awesome.

After several awe-filled minutes, both took pictures of Mercury from this vantage point. Then, they pressed the zop button on their cuffs to return to the International Space Station.

Their zip-zop cuffs zipped them back to the I.S.S. They landed with the usual jerk of the lines, and before their strength or sight even returned, they were already asking for more.

"Yang Bo! That was amazing!" Tracey exclaimed. "You've gotta zip out and see Mercury for yourself!"

"What's next?" Blaine asked excitedly but probably not patiently. "What's the next planet we get to study? We've gotta hear all about it! We've gotta zip out and see it!"

"Well, wow!" Yang Bo responded while laughing at the same time. "I guess you two thought that view of Mercury was something else."

The twelve-year-old twins nodded emphatically. "I was planning to introduce you to the rest of the I.S.S. crew right now," Yang Bo said thoughtfully. "But because you guys are loving it so much, I guess that can wait until after we study one more planet."

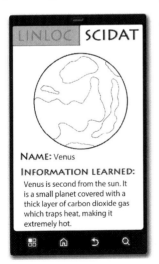

NAME: Venus

INFORMATION LEARNED:
Venus is second from the sun. It is a small planet covered with a thick layer of carbon dioxide gas which traps heat, making it extremely hot.

Blaine pumped his fist. Tracey clapped her hands. REESE did a happy twirl. SLIM looked like he was about to spew a fact or two but was cut off by the happy astronaut.

"Next up is the planet of Venus," Yang Bo said, obviously happy the twins were enjoying astronomy so much. "It is second from the sun, and it is a small, hot planet, even hotter than Mercury, in fact."

"It's hotter than Mercury, even though it's farther from the sun?" Tracey asked.

Yang Bo nodded. "Venus is covered with a thick layer of carbon dioxide gas that traps heat, making it extremely hot."

The twins nodded.

"After the moon, Venus is the brightest object in our night sky," the astronaut continued. "It appears like a bright star in both the early morning and early evening. The surface of Venus is not visible through its thick and hazy atmosphere. However, we do have pictures of the planet's surface, thanks to a series of satellites called Venera that were sent out by the Soviet Union. Additionally, the United States sent the orbiter Pioneer and the probe Magellan, to travel around Venus and use radar to map out the surface. So, we now know that the surface of Venus is rocky and covered with mountains, canyons, shallow craters, volcanoes, and hardened lava flows."

"Oh! Oh! Tell them about the planet's rotation!" REESE jumped in.

"Yes," Yang Bo smiled. "Can you believe that a year on Venus takes nearly 225 Earth days, but a day somehow takes even longer than a year?"

Dumbfounded, yet enthralled, looks covered the Sassafras twins' faces.

"A day on Venus takes more than 243 Earth days!" The astronauts gave the data with gusto.

"But that's not . . . How is that . . .?" Blaine tried to ask.

"Point of fact, a year on a planet is the time it takes for the planet to orbit the sun," SLIM interjected. "A day on a planet is the time it takes for a planet to completely rotate, resulting in both a sunrise and sunset."

"We know," the twins responded, half annoyed, half entertained by the robot's repeating what Yang Bo had told them earlier.

"But a day that's longer than a year," Blaine hesitated, still not able to comprehend fully. "That . . . that's . . . What is that?"

"That's awesome!" Tracey finished the thought for her brother.

"It is awesome," Yang Bo confirmed. "And right now, it's time to go see the planet!" Another fist pump came from Blaine and another clap from Tracey.

"Sassafras twins set your cuffs to the space coordinate 0.722 AU. Then ride those invisible zip lines out into space to view Venus!"

Adrianna Archer ended the transmission with her leader. She told all the technicians and scientists that were with her to leave. Then she sat for a silent second in her seat in the underground command station here in Siberia. She loved power. She was hopelessly attracted to it. That's why she had wanted to be in the Swiss Army. It's why she had pursued a position in the Swiss Secret Service. It's why she had betrayed her country to join the likes of Yuroslav Bogdanovich. The Russian mad scientist had oozed fearlessness and power until he was kidnapped and ousted by the Dark Cape.

Thaddaeus had taken command of this underground Siberian lab and had shown promise to be a man who had the power to take over the world. However, the way he'd just acted turned her stomach. She had been repulsed by his cowardice and fear. She realized now that she could no longer support or follow this man. She wanted to be near power, not timidity.

Adrianna sighed then scowled. "The Swiss Army is not powerful enough," she said to herself. "Triple S was close but no cigar. Yuroslav—toppled. Thaddaeus—puny. Where do I go next? Where or who has the real power that I seek?"

The blonde tapped her fingers on the counter in front of her. "What about this scientist Thaddaeus is trying to get revenge on?" She mused. "He must have a powerful mind if someone like the Dark Cape is trying to take him and his niece and nephew down."

Adrianna tapped at a couple buttons and quickly gained access to the satellite that was keeping tabs on Cecil Sassafras's house. She immediately gasped at what she saw. The redheaded scientist was carrying two full-grown men across his backyard— one in his right arm and one in his left. Adrianna quickly flicked the switch for audio so she could listen.

"Okity, Socrates; dokity, Aristotle," Cecil was saying. "Time to hit the tire swing for a little refresher on physics!"

Adrianna sighed, this time with no scowl, and leaned back in her chair.

"Wow," she proclaimed. "Cecil Sassafras. What a hunk. He has the physical power to carry two full-grown men at the same time and the mental power to master all things science. This man is the complete package. This is the man I need to be working for. This man possesses the power that I desire."

Adrianna clicked off the satellite image and stood from her chair. She was finished here—no more Siberia for her. 1104 North Pecan Street was her new destination.

CHAPTER 5: THE REST OF THE INNER PLANETARY SCOOP

Earth in Space

Venus was just as beautiful as Mercury had been. Floating in space with universal blackness all around them, and the huge, orange, perfectly round second planet from the sun right in front of them was surreal. The space coordinates Yang Bo had given them for Venus had put the twins above the planet on the opposite side from the sun, for which they were thankful because they assumed being out in space on the sunny side of any of these closer planets could be just a tad bit too bright and a tad bit too hot.

The two Sassafrases got their SCIDAT pictures, took in a last view, and then pressed the zop button to zip back to the International Space Station. As soon as they landed and regained their sight and strength, the kind and excited Yang Bo and the factual SLIM explained to the twins that they would now be leaving the docking port area and going to I.S.S.'s main laboratory, where they would meet the rest of the crew.

Blaine and Tracey followed their local expert and the flashlight-shaped robot with big smiles as they floated through a network of high-tech corridors. REESE floated along behind the twins, quietly singing the song about gravity, which he had taught them a day earlier in Summer's ship.

Even though they had already been on two spacecraft and had seen the planets up close, the Sassafrases were still not used to the zero-gravity reality. It was like they were flying in slow motion everywhere they went. For the most part, it was fun, but it was going to take a bit to get used to the sensations.

The corridors they were floating through eventually led to a fairly large, clean, well-lit laboratory, where four people were hard at work.

"Blaine, Tracey, and REESE, welcome to the main hub of the International Space Station!" Yang Bo declared happily. "Now, let me introduce you to the crew."

The Chinese astronaut began making his way toward his crew members, but before he could reach any of them, one of them came laughing, smiling, and spinning through the air toward him.

"Yang Bo! *Hola* and hello!" The short woman with a dark complexion shouted. "Who are these new members of the crew you have with you today?"

Yang Bo and the woman collided in the air, somewhat awkwardly. Then Yang Bo held out his arm toward the three newcomers.

"Anna Maria, this is Blaine and Tracey Sassafras and their robotic friend, REESE," the local expert introduced. "Blaine, Tracey, and REESE, this is Anna Maria Bezerra. She is from Brazil and serves as our resident meteorologist."

"Hello," the twins greeted.

"*Hola* and hello," Anna Maria responded with a big smile. "I love it when we get visitors!"

Now coming toward the group at a much more controlled pace was a tall astronaut with wavy brown hair and a large yet handsome nose. "Bonjour," the man greeted in French. "My name is Bayard Clemence, and I am the International Space Station's *médecin traitant.*"

"*Médecin traitant?*" the twins asked with confused faces.

"*Médecin traitant* is attending physician in French," Yang Bo explained. "Bayard is our resident physician who is doing groundbreaking research in the field of space medicine."

Bayard did a courtly midair bow and then backed away as the next astronaut came their way. Only he was not coming to meet them; he was chasing some kind of small, red disk through the air. The dark-skinned man, who was wearing glasses and had neatly combed hair with a perfect part, barely acknowledged them as he floated by, grasping for the red disk but continually missing it.

"That is Parth Banerjee," Yang Bo introduced. "He is our mathematician from the country of India, and he loves to play checkers."

"Actually, I despise checkers," Parth responded as he continued the chase. "I play checkers because I have lost my magnetized chess set."

Yang Bo chuckled at his apparently flustered teammate, as did Anna Maria and Bayard. Then he beckoned for the twins and REESE to follow him toward the last remaining astronaut in the room. She was floating next to a circular window on the other side of the laboratory and had remained stationary since the Sassafrases' arrival in the room.

Yang Bo seemed to be approaching this particular astronaut with great respect, so the twelve-year-olds followed suit. They reached the woman, and she turned to greet them. She was a strong yet pretty woman. With short, graying-blonde hair, her face held an expression that was confident and lay somewhere between a frown and a smile.

"Blaine, Tracey, and REESE, this is Captain Dianna Sturgess," Yang Bo introduced. "She is the one in charge here on the I.S.S., and she has more cumulative 'space time' than any other human being ever."

"Whoa, more space time than anyone ever—awesome!" The twins thought.

Tracey wondered what the protocol should be. "Should we salute the captain, or is a handshake okay? Do we need to bow?" the girl mused "Do we need to . . . Oh, no! He's not. Blaine isn't actually thinking about giving the captain a fist bump, is he?"

Tracey hung her head a little as her twin brother thrust a fist in Captain Sturgess's direction. The captain completed the fist bump with the boy, but she did not do the loud explosion fingers afterward as Blaine did.

"Are you young scientists or simply space tourists?" The captain asked.

"Well, we're . . . I mean . . . I think we're . . . ummmm . . ." Tracey stumbled through a response, a little intimidated by the captain.

"Both are okay," Captain Sturgess said. "It's just that I'll be a little more willing to spend time with you if you're scientists."

"Oh, well then . . . umm . . . I guess that makes us . . . you know . . . I think we're . . ."

"These two are definitely young scientists!" Yang Bo interjected, rescuing Tracey from her bumbling. "They are especially interested in studying astronomy with a focus on the eight planets of our solar system."

"Good," Dianna Sturgess affirmed. "Then welcome to the International Space Station. I specialize in life science myself, but I have a deep appreciation for astronomy, especially after being out in space so long."

Blaine bobbed his head up and down and offered the captain another fist bump, which she declined.

"Astronomers call the four closest planets to the sun the inner planets. There are Mercury, Venus, Earth, and Mars." The strong leader of the station continued. "The four planets that can be found beyond the Asteroid Belt are called the outer planets. They are Jupiter, Saturn, Uranus, and Neptune." Captain Sturgess paused and turned to look out of the large, circular window. "But that right there, third from the sun, is the planet I'm most interested in."

The Sassafras twins moved a little closer to the window and followed the I.S.S. captain's gaze out into space. There it was: Earth, their home planet. It looked so beautiful from here, from this vantage point on the orbiting International Space Station.

"I've spent all these days and years out here for one purpose," the captain continued. "That's to remain on the cutting edge of any kind of scientific research or advancement that can or will ensure the well-being of our planet."

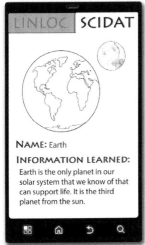

NAME: Earth

INFORMATION LEARNED:
Earth is the only planet in our solar system that we know of that can support life. It is the third planet from the sun.

The twins nodded. They appreciated the passion they heard from the legendary astronaut in front of them.

"Earth is the only planet in our solar system that we know of that can support life," she continued. "The atmosphere on Earth is a unique combination of oxygen, nitrogen, and other important elements. It's an atmosphere that extends out six hundred miles from the surface, protecting people from the harmful rays of the sun. Additionally, the presence of water in liquid form on Earth and Earth's dynamic weather patterns help provide the conditions needed for Earth's diverse plant and animal life, sustaining life as we know it."

"How many Earth days does it take Earth to orbit the sun?" Blaine asked.

"Blaine, they're just called 'days.' It is Earth," Tracey said like she was a little embarrassed.

"Huh?" Blaine again responded. "That's not right; is it?"

"It takes precisely 365.26 days to fully orbit around the sun," the captain responded without saying who was right and who was wrong. "And a full rotation of the Earth, or rather a day, takes 23 hours and 56 minutes."

The captain moved away from the window and made her way toward the center of the room. "Here on the I.S.S. we are traveling at a speed of five miles per second in LEO around our home planet."

"This means we orbit Earth every ninety minutes, and we experience sixteen sunrises and sunsets per Earth day," she explained to the surprised twins. "The station has been continuously occupied since November of the year 2000. In that time, nearly 250 people from eighteen different countries have visited. Some were scientists, and some were space tourists, but all were welcome because one of the main purposes of the I.S.S. is to serve as a blueprint for global cooperation, enabling multinational partnerships and shared advancements in science and space exploration."

"Wow, that's sick," Blaine blurted out, impressed. Then he began moving toward Captain Sturgess for another fist bump but stopped himself, remembering that she didn't seem to be a big fan of bumping fists.

Suddenly, a circular door swung open, and in floated a new

astronaut the twins hadn't met, and he looked angry.

"It vas sabotaged, Captain!" He shouted in a Russian accent. "The launch of the Mars Module vasn't accidental! It vas purposeful sabotage!"

"Sanders, calm down," Captain Sturgess commanded. "What are you talking about?"

"I'm talking about sabotage, Captain!" the angry astronaut repeated.

"Who is that?" Tracey cautiously asked Yang Bo.

"That is Sander Petrov," the local expert responded. "He is from Russia and serves as our engineer."

Tracey nodded, as did Blaine. Neither was sure yet if they liked the astronaut or not. "For some time now," Petrov continued aggressively, "ve have assumed ve lost Brett Frye because there had been some kind of malfunction or that somevun on board had accidentally sent that absurd space tourist off to Mars in the module, or that he himself accidentally launched the Module, but I vas just down in the bowels of the control pod, and I found that something had been jammed into the fuse board in the precise spot that controls the Mars Module!"

"*Au la Vache!*" Bayard exclaimed in French, seeming horrified.

"What is it?" Captain Sturgess asked. "What is jammed into the fuse board?"

"I don't know," the angry astronaut answered. "Vhatever it is, it is buried down deep in the board. It is going to take me avhile to dig it out."

"*Au la Vache,*" Clemence exclaimed again.

"But that's not all," the Russian astronaut continued shouting. "Not only am I sure that it vas sabotaged; it vas sabotaged by one of you!"

"*Au la Vache!*" Bayard cried out yet again.

"What do you mean?" Yang Bo spoke up.

"Vhat I mean is that the only people who have access to the control pod and the fuse board are long-term astronauts stationed on the I.S.S.! That means von of you did it!"

"*Au la Vache*! *Au la Vache*! *Au la Vache*!" The Frenchman yelped.

"No! *No es posible*!" Anna Maria shouted defensively in Spanish.

"I think you may be wrong about this," Yang Bo asserted. His voice was under control, but he was still clearly agitated at being accused.

Parth continued to float around in the background, frantically chasing his checker. Sander continued to shout, point, and accuse. Bayard, Anna Maria, and Yang Bo continued to defend and deny. Parth continued to chase. Finally, Captain Dianna Sturgess held up her hand, beckoning everyone to be quiet.

"Everyone stop!" She ordered. "The six of us have been stationed together for more than a year on this space station, and we have become more like family than colleagues. So, let's drop the he-said she-said and start acting like a family."

Sander quieted down and let his pointing finger fall. Yang Bo, Anna Maria, and even Parth visibly relaxed a little. Bayard calmed down too, but he did let one more "*Au la Vache*" squeak out.

"What in the world does '*au la vache*' mean?" Blaine asked it out loud, when he meant to think it only in his head.

"Point of fact, '*au la vache*' is French for 'oh my cow!' It is a common expression used when someone is surprised, flabbergasted, or scared," SLIM informed, unaware as a robot that the mood in the room was tense.

"Thank you, SLIM," Captain Sturgess said to the little robot.

Getting back to the subject at hand, the captain asked, "SLIM, can you remind us who Brett Frye is?"

"Point of fact," SLIM responded. "Brett Frye is a billionaire from the United States. He made most of his money as a real estate tycoon, but his real passion is commercial space travel."

"Okay, and can you tell us what happened to Mr. Frye precisely six months, two weeks, five days, and eleven hours ago?" Sturgess addressed the robot.

"Point of fact, Brett Frye boarded the I.S.S. as a business consultant and space tourist. Less than two weeks later he was launched toward the planet of Mars in the Mars Module."

"Thank you, SLIM," Sturgess acknowledged. The captain then turned from addressing the fact-giving robot to her astronauts. "Those are the only real facts we have. Even after Sander's findings at the fuse board, anything more than these facts, at this point, is simply speculation. Let's stay calm; let's be honest; and let's talk through this."

Everyone nodded except for Petrov, who grunted instead. Dianna Sturgess then looked from her astronauts toward the Sassafras twins.

"Blaine and Tracey," she said. "You two are the only non-partial non-robotic scientists on board."

Both twelve-year-olds suddenly had "who me?" looks on their faces.

"Would you be willing to conduct individual interviews with each astronaut to see if any one of us had the motive or the means to send Brett Frye off to Mars in a sabotaged module?"

Tracey was too stunned by the sudden proposal to answer. Blaine was stunned, too, but he did manage to answer by holding up his hand up to give the captain another fist bump. This one was reluctantly returned by Captain Sturgess.

Everything in *Thad-1* was running properly again. He had calmed down and regained his composure and his focus on the main goal: to destroy Cecil Sassafras by thwarting the science learning of Cecil's niece and nephew.

According to the information he had gathered via satellite, he now knew those twins had zipped successfully from Summer's spaceship, *Ulysses-1*, to the International Space Station, where they were now in contact with the six astronauts currently manning the orbiting laboratory. He had missed his chance to blast the twins with his ray gun while they were onboard *Ulysses-1*, but now he could blast them while they were on board the International Space Station.

With his confidence back in place, he smiled a wicked smile, adjusted his trajectory a bit, and then rocketed in the direction of the I.S.S.

Mars Module

Blaine and Tracey both sighed and leaned back in their floating space suits. They were down in the control pod next to the fuse board, where they had conducted the first of six interviews. Captain Dianna Sturgess had volunteered to be interviewed first. Still intimidated by the great woman, the twins had been a little awkward in their questioning. Regardless, if any of the fault rested on the I.S.S. captain, the Sassafrases sure didn't see it.

"When I grow up, I want to be just like her," Tracey whispered to Blaine as Captain Sturgess left the pod.

Then, as Bayard Clemence came into the pod for the next interview, Blaine muttered back, "Aloe vera . . . Avalanche . . . I love bocchie? How do you say 'oh my cow' in French again?"

"*Avoir le Cafard!*" Clemence announced with a disheveled face.

"That's, 'oh my cow,' right?" Blaine asked as if Bayard had answered his whim of a question.

"No," the French physician replied. "It means 'have the cockroach.'"

"Have the cockroach?" Tracey asked.

"Yes, 'have the cockroach,'" Clemence confirmed. "I think the English equivalent would be 'down in the dumps.'"

"*Avoir le cafard*: down in the dumps," Tracey repeated, before asking, "Why would you say that?"

"Because that's how I feel about Brett Frye and the sabotage of the Mars Module," the Frenchman said. "I'll admit that I didn't like the guy very much, but I have the cockroach because of his displacement."

Blaine had to hold in a laugh because of how the cockroach phrase sounded when it was translated into an English sentence. But his sister remained on task.

"Why didn't you like Brett Frye?" Tracey asked.

"Well, besides the fact that he was a smug billionaire while he was in space," Bayard answered, "he was also arrogant when on Earth. He was always hitting on my little sister, Queenie."

"You have a sister named Queenie?" Blaine asked.

"Yes, Queenie Clemence, my only sibling. And Brett was always flirting with her and wanted to marry her so that she would become a French Frye."

"Why would marrying her make her a French fry," Tracey asked.

"She is French . . . his last name is Frye . . . French Frye,"

Clemence explained.

"Oh . . . French Frye." Tracey nodded, now understanding. Blaine was mostly successful in holding in another laugh as he nodded—adults could be so weird!

"However, my disdain for Brett did not lead me to sabotage the Mars Module," Bayard informed sincerely. "At the moment of the untimely launch, I was in the lab working on a medical experiment."

The twins nodded again, asked the space physician a few more questions, and then sent him out. Tracey looked at her brother. "This is going to be tough. We just got here. We don't know these astronauts. We're not detectives or trial lawyers. How are we going to find out who sabotaged the module?"

Blaine shrugged as Anna Maria Bezerra came into the pod. Completely opposite of Clemence, the Brazilian astronaut came in cheerful and bouncy. "*Hola* and hello!" She greeted. "How are the interviews going?"

"Pretty good," the Sassafrases answered in unison.

"Anna Maria, you seem so nice," Tracey smiled. "You didn't have any reason to ship Brett Frye off into space several months ago; did you?"

"Well, of course I did," the meteorologist answered to the shock of the twelve-year-olds.

"You . . . did?" Blaine gulped.

"*Si* and yes!" Bezarra confirmed. "I was a hot, jealous mess. That handsome, space-traversing billionaire was in love with Bayard's little sister, Queenie, instead of me!"

"So . . . you were jealous enough to sabotage the Mars Module?" Tracey asked cautiously, suspecting that they may have found the saboteur.

"Yes, at the time I might have been jealous enough to do it.

But . . . I didn't. I didn't sabotage the module."

"You didn't?" The twins asked.

"No, I didn't," Anna Maria answered and then chuckled.

"I get crushes pretty easily, but I get over them easily, too," the astronaut explained. "I liked Brett and was jealous that he pursued Queenie and not me, but I got over it. And truly, I love the I.S.S. and being an astronaut more than I love anything else at this point in my life. I would never do anything to jeopardize the integrity of this space station."

The Sassafras twins believed her. Although the whole picture hadn't been painted yet, they believed that Anna Maria Bezerra didn't sabotage the Mars Module. They believed that Bayard Clemence didn't either, and of course it wasn't Captain Dianna Sturgess. That wiped out three possibilities but left three more.

Next in the pod was the Indian mathematician, Parth Banerjee. By this point he had caught the red checker he had been chasing, yet he still seemed flustered.

"Are you okay, Mr. Banerjee?" Blaine asked. "You look a little nervous."

"That's Dr. Banerjee," the mathematician corrected, not gruffly but matter-of-factly. "And no, I'm not nervous. I am a little impatient. Ready to get back to my important pile of calculations."

"Well, we don't want to keep you, doctor," Tracey quipped. "We need to ask you if you had any reason to harm or sabotage Brett Frye."

"By my calculations, 'harm' and 'sabotage' are words that are too strong," Parth answered. "But I did not like the man. Actually, I despised him."

"You despised him?" Blaine asked.

"Yes," Banerjee confirmed. "He was constantly second-guessing my computations, even though he was no mathematician himself. Rather he was simply a glorified realtor. Also, he got so mad he couldn't beat me at chess that he stole my magnetized chess set. Now, I am consigned to months of playing checkers, which I very well may despise more than Brett Frye. Even so, I did not harm or sabotage that man or the Mars Module that he was launched away in."

"Hmmm," Blaine and Tracey both responded, thinking not only about what Banerjee had said but also about everyone else's denials.

After Parth left the pod, the twins' local expert, Yang Bo, came in. The twins both took long, deep breaths. Now they could rest easy for at least a few moments because they knew there was no way this astrobiologist and former friend and classmate of their uncle was the culprit in this case.

"Are you two getting any answers?" The Chinese astronaut asked. "No, not really," Blaine sighed.

"Everybody seems to have motive for sabotaging the Mars Module," Tracey said. "But nobody seems to have had the malice strong enough to take action."

Yang Bo nodded. "But really, more than being worried about what happened back then with Brett and the module, I am worried about him now."

"What do you mean?" Tracey asked.

"Well, it would have taken Brett at least six months to reach the Red Planet," Yang Bo explained. "And even if everything went perfect with the flight, the module was only stocked with a seven months' supply of food for one astronaut, but we hadn't finished preparing the module yet. Brett may have already run out of food, especially if he didn't ration what was there properly. But even if he did, it's been more than six months since the incident, and we haven't heard a thing from him. His food could be gone, or dangerously low, or he could be hurt. Brett is a space tourist.

He's not an astronaut or a scientist or even a young scientist like you two. He has been all alone for a long time now and may have no idea what to do or how to survive. He wasn't trained for a mission like this."

The twins' mouths dropped open. The gravity of the incident was now hitting them, and they were understanding more and more why the prospect of sabotage was such a big deal to the crew.

"This year, there were three attempts to rescue Brett using other rocket-powered modules," Yang Bo continued. "But all three attempts failed for one reason or another."

The twins' shoulders slumped. Could anything be done to rescue Brett Frye?

"But I've got an idea," the astrobiologist offered optimistically.

"You do?" the Sassafrases asked.

Yang Bo nodded and then pointed directly at Blaine and Tracey. "The two of you can go to Mars to rescue him!"

Again, the twins' mouths dropped open.

"But . . . you know . . . we're kind of new to this whole astronaut thing," Tracey reminded.

"True, but you're not new to the whole invisible zip line thing," Yang Bo countered. "The two of you can zip to Mars and find Brett so much faster than any kind of craft or module can, and truly at this point, you may be his only hope."

Tracey took a deep breath and looked at Blaine. The Sassafras twins knew what the right thing to do was. Both looked at their local expert, nodded, and replied in unison, "We'll do it."

Now Yang Bo took a deep breath and nodded in the same fashion. "Thank you," he said. "You two are as brave as your uncle and Summer said you were."

Yang Bo patted both kids on the shoulders. "And you know," he added thoughtfully. "If you find Brett alive and well, you can ask him what happened instead of only having to rely on these interviews you're doing."

The twins hoped they would indeed find Brett Frye alive and well.

The Chinese man continued. "I don't think the atmosphere or terrain of Mars will pose any threat to you as long as you remain in your Linc 2.0 IEVA space suits."

"Additionally, REESE and SLIM can zip to Mars with you," Yang Bo suggested, resulting in smiles from the twins. "REESE has extra zip-zop cuffs in his storage cell, so you can use one of those to zip Brett back if and when you find him."

Yang Bo paused and pulled out a smartphone of his own. "Let me give you all the coordinates to the outer planets, just in case you want to zip from Mars to visit them instead of coming back here first."

Looking at his phone, Yang Bo read off the numbers. "The coordinates for Neptune are 30.1 AU; Uranus is 19.2 AU; Saturn is 9.58 AU; and Jupiter's coordinates are 5.20 AU. But let me start out by giving you space coordinates that will land you precisely where Brett's Mars Module was supposed to land on Mars: 1.589AU."

"What's it like?" Blaine asked. "Have you been to Mars?"

Yang Bo shook his head. "I haven't yet been afforded the privilege," he replied. "But I hope to be able to visit in the future. As an astrobiologist, I am confident that scientists traveling to Mars will be the next great leap for both scientific advancement and space exploration. The planet was first visited in 1976 by the space probe Viking 1. But most of the photos that we have

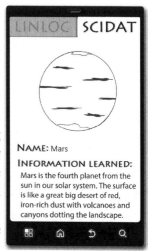

LINLOC **SCIDAT**

NAME: Mars

INFORMATION LEARNED:
Mars is the fourth planet from the sun in our solar system. The surface is like a great big desert of red, iron-rich dust with volcanoes and canyons dotting the landscape.

today of the surface of Mars were taken by Pathfinder, a probe that was sent to the planet in the 1990s."

"So, to answer your question," Yang Bo said, looking at Blaine, "Mars is the fourth planet from the sun in our solar system. The surface looks like a great big desert of red, iron-rich dust with volcanoes and canyons dotting the landscape. The biggest volcano on Mars is called Mount Olympus, and it is the largest known volcano in the entire solar system. The largest canyon on Mars, Valles Marineris, could spread across the whole United States."

"Wow," the twins mouthed.

"Mars does have storms, clouds, and fog, similar to what we have on Earth, but it's much colder than our home planet. There is a thin atmosphere of poison gas covering the planet, and each of its poles is covered with frozen ice made from a mix of carbon dioxide and water. It is half the size of the Earth and is the closest planet to Earth. In fact, from Earth, you can see Mars, along with several other planets, with only a simple telescope or even binoculars."

Upon hearing this, Blaine made fake binoculars with his hands and began pretending like he was looking around for Mars. Tracey looked down and shook her head, embarrassed at the antics of her twin brother. Yang Bo laughed and finished giving the SCIDAT about Mars.

"A day on Mars is similar to a day on Earth. It takes right around 24 hours and 37 minutes for the Red Planet to complete a full rotation. And a year on Mars takes 687 Earth days."

Blaine smiled and was about to switch from looking through his "hand binoculars" to looking through a "hand telescope." But before he could get reconfigured, the door to the control pod burst open, and in came Sander Petrov.

"Oh, hello Sander," Tracey said. "Are you here for your interview?"

"Nyet!" Petrov huffed in Russian. "I'm not going to be

interviewed by a couple of punk kids who just got to the I.S.S!"

The angry astronaut then shoved his way past the Sassafrases and Yang Bo toward a large panel on the other side of the pod.

"I'm not here to talk," he growled as he yanked open the panel and pulled out a pair of needle-nose pliers from a pocket in his suit. "I'm here to actually find out vhat happened to that space tourist!"

The open panel revealed a large fuse board. Wasting no time, Petrov jammed the pliers into a particular spot and began trying to dig out whatever he thought was stuck inside.

"Sander," Yang Bo declared sternly. "You need to give these kids a chance to help us find the truth."

"Nyet," Petrov barked again. "They are space tourists, and I don't have time for space tourists! Brett Frye vas a space tourist, too, and look vhat happened to him!"

"With an attitude like that, who's to say you didn't sabotage the Mars Module?"

"I didn't."

"How will we know if that's true if you refuse to do an interview?"

"I'm not doing an interview!"

"Sander, you need to rethink your attitude on thi—"

"*Hola* and hello!" The astronauts' argument was interrupted by the cheerful Brazilian voice of Anna Maria Bezerra. "Are the interviews finished?" She asked as she floated into the control pod, followed by both Bayard Clemence and Parth Banerjee.

"No, they're not," Yang Bo answered.

"Oh, but they are!" Petrov countered defiantly.

Yang Bo shook his head. "Sander doesn't want to do an interview with Blaine and Tracey," he said. "Instead, he wants to dig through the fuse board to find whatever it is that he thinks got jammed into the fuse slot that sent Brett off in the module."

"*Devenir chèvre!*" Bayard exclaimed in French, and then translated for himself. "He's become a goat."

"Become a goat?" The twins asked, looking at each other.

"Sander has become a goat," Bayard repeated, before he explained. "How do you say it . . . it means . . . he's been driven mad."

The twins looked at the Russian astronaut as he tore through the board with the pliers, trying to find something that didn't seem to be there. Maybe he had gone mad. Maybe Sander Petrov had been in space too long, and he had actually lost his mind.

Sander's four fellow astronauts watched their crazed teammate as he continued to dig. They all seemed to have more sorrow in their eyes than anger.

All at once, Petrov stopped and exclaimed, "Queenie!"

"Queenie?" Everyone asked.

"That's right," Sander confirmed. "Queenie did it!"

"*Devenir Chèvre*," Bayard said again, aghast. "You think my younger sister is the one who sabotaged Brett and the Mars Module? You are crazy! That's not possible! My sister has never left France, much less been aboard the I.S.S!"

"Not that Queenie," Petrov said as he yanked the pliers out of the fuse board, revealing that he had indeed found something that had been jammed into the slot. "This queenie!"

Everyone gasped.

Now everyone could see what was held in the grasp of the pliers: the white queen from a chess set. Parth's face reddened with guilt.

Everyone remained shocked and silent except Blaine, who slowly announced, "Oh . . . my . . . cow."

CHAPTER 6: THE RED PLANET RESCUE MISSION

Jumping Jupiter

"There has to be some other explanation," Yang Bo mused as Blaine, Tracey, and REESE all entered 1.52 AU, the space coordinates for Mars, into their zip-zop cuffs. "Even though the evidence seems to be there, I don't think Parth sabotaged the Mars Module. There must be another explanation. That's why it's all the more important for you two to find Brett, not only to save his life but also so we can get Brett's side of the story."

The twins nodded. They had felt so bad for Parth Banerjee as the angry Sander Petrov took him from the control pod up to the main laboratory, where Petrov declared him guilty before Captain Dianna Sturgess. The captain had remained calm and even, but she did say that if Banerjee was truly guilty of sabotaging Brett Frye, then he would be sent back to Earth, where he would more than likely spend a major portion of the rest of his life behind bars. Parth hadn't said one word to defend himself, and to the twins he had looked a lot more scared than guilty.

"So, do you think it might have been an accident?" Tracey asked.

The astrobiologist nodded. "I do."

The International Space Station was now finally in his sights. He grinned and placed his finger on the "fire" button for *Thad-1*'s powerful ray gun. He was going to blast those twins, and they weren't even going to know what hit them.

Wait.

He was listening to them and that local expert of theirs over satellite, and they were talking about zipping from the space station out to Mars. Could he blast them in time?

Could he hit them with the ray gun before they took off?

The two humans and the one robot pressed the zip button on their cuffs—all three devices immediately found and connected to the correct invisible line. They now had approximately seven seconds until they zipped away for the Red Planet. Blaine and Tracey were nervous but excited. They had seen Mercury and Venus from afar, but they were actually going to get to land on Mars.

REESE's mouth box was lit up, giving the robot an excited look as well. Even though he was a machine and couldn't actually experience emotion, he sure acted like he could. SLIM, on the other hand, was as emotionless as usual and was packed away and quiet for the moment inside of REESE's storage cell.

"You four be safe and complete your mission," Yang Bo warned with a serious face that quickly gave way to a smile. "But don't forget to have some fun, too! After all, you're traveling to Mars!"

NO! He wasn't going to be able to blast them in time!

Those twins were going to zip away before the laser from his ray gun reached them. But he had to try anyway. Maybe if he aimed out from the I.S.S. a little he could hit them as they began invisible zip line travel. He didn't know if that was even possible, but he was going to try it anyway.

"Ahhh," he shouted in vengeful anger as he pressed down hard on the fire button.

"Ahhh! Ha, ha, ha!" the twins and REESE shouted in elation as they zipped off from the International Space Station into swirls of light. The twins loved this! Riding these lines with enamoring light spinning all around them like . . .

Smash!

Slam!

THE SASSAFRAS SCIENCE ADVENTURES

Crash!!

Something was wrong! Usually the ride was fairly smooth with the light spinning and swirling around them, but this time it had been jolting and the light around them wasn't spinning. It was . . . wobbling. What was wrong? Was a calculation slightly off? Was there a new glitch in the zip line system?

Their cuffs remained attached to the invisible line. It felt like they were still moving, but the wobbling light continued, and it definitely felt like something was off. Blaine and Tracey's minds involuntarily jumped back to the time when they had tried to ride the invisible zip lines in the middle of a typhoon while studying Earth science. The lines hadn't worked then because of a storm. Were they traveling though some kind of space storm right now? Were their zip-zop cuffs going to hold and stay clipped in, or were they going to detach, sending them twirling off helplessly into the blackness of space?

"Poi- of fa—, someth- is wrong wi- flight to Ma—," the muffled voice of SLIM now cut off the twins' fearful thoughts.

The Sassafrases could hardly hear the robot because he was inside of REESE's storage cell, and the rushing and wobbling of light around them were loud. But what they had heard was definitely SLIM's emotionless voice, and at this juncture they were interested in what he might have to say.

"Speak up, SLIM!" Blaine shouted out. "What did you say?"

To be helpful, REESE opened his storage cell. SLIM then repeated what he had said. "Point of fact, something is wrong with our flight to Mars."

"What is it? What's wrong?" asked Tracey.

"Our coordinates were initially correct," SLIM responded. "We started out directly for Mars, but an instant after we took off, something affected our flight. According to my calculations, which take into account speed and trajectory, we are now zipping around in the solar system with no destination."

"What?" Blaine shouted, on the edge of panic, but he stopped himself and asked, "What about those other coordinates Yang Bo gave you, SLIM? Can we switch to one of those? Is it even possible to recalibrate our cuffs mid-flight?"

"Point of fact . . . I don't know."

"What?" This time it was Tracey shouting. She, too, was on the edge of panic. "Well, that's our best option. We can't keep zipping around in space with no destination. Let's try to recalibrate our cuffs. Let's put in new coordinates."

"Which coordinates would you like?" REESE asked.

"Let's try Jupiter," Tracey answered, remembering it was the planet that was up next for study.

"Point of fact, the space coordinates for Jupiter are 5.20 AU." SLIM responded. Blaine and Tracey looked at each other. There was fear in their eyes, but they knew they had to try this. They both reached up and began entering the new numbers into their cuffs. REESE followed their lead. Blaine and Tracey's fingers worked nervously and slowly, but they eventually managed to get the desired coordinates set. As the last number was set into place, the unthinkable happened. The zip-zop cuffs unclipped from the invisible lines.

Had he gotten them? Had the blast from his ray gun worked? The Man With No Eyebrows looked at the screens in front of him. He listened intently to the satellite feeds. He didn't see anything. He didn't hear anything. There was no trace of the twins anywhere. What had happened to them?

For a second that felt like eternity, the three remained unclipped. Then all at once, Blaine, Tracey, and REESE's cuffs found the new invisible lines set for Jupiter and securely connected to them. The wobbling light continued, but off to the side a new tunnel of light instantly opened up, and the four travelers were sucked into it, riding the new lines.

The normal swirls of light now rushed around them, and then in a matter of seconds, the zip line traveling came to the customary, jerky stop. When their sight and strength returned, the only thing that the twins could see was a circle. It was a big circle, a circle that looked like it was made up of swirly, delicious ice cream.

"Point of fact, that is Jupiter," SLIM informed.

Blaine and Tracey let themselves take big sighs of relief. They had made it through whatever the problem had been with the invisible zip lines, and now here they were, floating a safe distance from the planet of Jupiter, in the same fashion as they had with Mercury and Venus.

"Outer planets! Wooka, wooka, wooka, outer planets!" REESE suddenly exclaimed with an explosion of happy lights.

The twins looked over and allowed themselves to smile. Their favorite robot was singing another science song.

"Outer planets! Wooka, wooka, wooka, outer planets!" REESE sang again, and then he launched into a verse:

> Outer planets can be found out beyond the belt
> Not a belt for pants, not a belt for Orion,
> But a belt made of rocks that are spinning flyin'.
> That's the place in space called the Asteroid Belt.

Happy light continued to flash as REESE sang the "wooka" part again. "Outer planets! Wooka, wooka, wooka, outer planets!" Then he went directly into a second verse:

> *Jupiter, Saturn, Uranus, and Neptune—*
> *These are the outer planets. Count them: four.*
> *We don't count their moons; if we did there'd be more*
> *That's it, that's a wrap, that's my Outer planet tune.*

Blaine and Tracey pumped their fists, clapping and singing along with REESE as he finished the song, grateful for the joy he had just infused them with.

"Outer planets!" They sang. "Wooka, wooka, wooka, outer planets!"

"Point of fact, Jupiter is known as King of the Planets," SLIM said, starting to give SCIDAT data on the planet they were currently floating over.

"Whoa, whoa, whoa. Step off, Lil' SLIM," REESE interjected somewhat defensively. "When Yang Bo isn't present, it's my job to give Blaine and Tracey their SCIDAT, not yours."

The emotionless SLIM didn't object, so REESE proceeded. "Jupiter is the largest planet in our solar system and can easily be spotted with the naked eye from Earth. It is the fourth-brightest object in the night sky and is sometimes referred to as King of Planets."

NAME: Jupiter

INFORMATION LEARNED:
Jupiter is the largest planet in our solar system. Jupiter is made mainly of gas, which is why we call it one of the gas giants.

Blaine and Tracey chuckled a little as REESE repeated what SLIM had said, thinking it funny that the two robots were still arguing a little over giving them their SCIDAT data.

"Jupiter is made mainly of gas, which is why we call it one of the gas giants," REESE continued. "Jupiter mainly has hydrogen gas, but there is some helium as well. Below its thick layer of gas, there is a layer of liquid hydrogen surrounding an iron core. The atmosphere covering Jupiter has both dark and light clouds. Scientists have divided these strips of clouds into different bands and zones. The wind flows in one direction in the zones and in the opposite direction in the bands. With all of these interesting wind patterns, Jupiter has an atmosphere that is not only extremely cloudy but also extremely stormy. One of the largest of these storms is known as the Great Red Spot." REESE pointed to the spot to which he was referring as he said this.

"This spot has been visible for more than 400 years, and it generally looks like a large, red oval. It changes in size and shape from year to year. Overall the Great Red Spot is three times the size of Earth."

"Wait, wait, hold up," Blaine interrupted in amazement. "You're telling me that huge red spot is a storm? A storm that never stops. A storm that never stops that's three times bigger than Earth?"

REESE nodded.

"That's crazy," Blaine said in awe.

From this vantage point not only could they clearly see the red spot REESE was talking about. They were close enough to see the spot moving and swirling.

"A year on Jupiter takes about twelve Earth years, and a day takes about ten Earth hours," REESE continued. "A lot of what we know about Jupiter came from data that we received from Galileo, a probe that began studying the planet. For instance, we know that Jupiter has more than fifty moons. These moons vary in size from about six miles across to quite a bit larger. The four largest of Jupiter's moons—Ganymede, Callisto, Io, and Europa—can be seen from Earth with a telescope. In 1995, after two years of orbiting, the probe entered Jupiter's atmosphere."

Tracey was overcome by the beauty of Jupiter and was thinking about all the mixtures of different gases flowing around it that were creating these colors, affording them this breathtaking view. Blaine was suddenly overcome with hunger, thinking that the Great Red Spot looked like a hurricane-sized cherry on top of a giant scoop of ice cream.

REESE blinked his robotic eyes. Then in a sign of goodwill toward his counterpart, he asked, "SLIM, can you tell Blaine and Tracey what exactly a moon is?"

SLIM, who was peeking out from inside REESE's storage cell, immediately answered. "Point of fact, a moon is a celestial body in orbit around a planet. Most moons are solid, and a few even have atmospheres. Earth has one moon. All the outer planets have multiple moons."

"That's right, brother from another mother board," REESE replied. "Thank you for that data. And just so you know, Blaine and Tracey, the planet we are zipping to next, Mars, has two moons."

The Sassafras twins nodded and took that as a cue to take a picture of Jupiter and then to reenter the AU numbers into their cuffs for the surface of Mars. REESE shut SLIM safely back inside his storage cell and then followed suit with his zip-zop cuff. Blaine and Tracey both gulped as the numbers were set. They knew they had to get to Mars to try to rescue Brett Frye. They hoped that whatever had affected them or thrown their lines into a wobble the first time they had tried to zip there didn't do it again.

Seven seconds after the three set the new coordinates, off they zipped. The twins breathed sighs of relief—whatever had happened to them before must have been an anomaly because they were now zipping through normal light in a normal fashion. In no time, the zip-lining motion came to a jerking stop. They all tapped their cuffs, causing them to unclip from the invisible lines and drop to the surface of Mars with a thud.

As their senses returned, Blaine and Tracey blinked their eyes open and closed repeatedly like something might be wrong. They had gone from swirls of color to the customary blinding white to red. All they could see now . . . was red.

Red! All he could see now was red.

Red, red, red! He was red with anger!

A screen in front of him revealed that those twins were alive and well! They had popped back up, and now they were on Mars! They had made it to Mars! The ray gun blast had not worked.

His hairless brow sank into a deep scowl. His black-gloved hands clinched into tight fists. His whole body seethed. These twins were intolerable. They were unstoppable. No matter what he tried, they kept moving forward in their science learning. Over air, land, water, and now even through space—they kept moving forward! Not even a powerful blast from his fancy spaceship had been able to stop them.

In frustration, he unclipped his seat belt and grabbed his own zip-zop cuff, one he had stolen from Summer's lab. If *Thad-1* was going to fail, then he was going to try the invisible zip lines again.

"Adrianna? Adrianna? Come in, Adrianna?" He spoke into his headset, trying to connect with his right-hand woman back at his base. "Adrianna, I don't know if you can hear me or not, but I wanted to let you know I'm going to use the invisible zip lines to go after those twins on Mars. Over."

No response came to him over the radio waves.

"According to what the twins just learned, it would take *Thad-1* months on end to reach Mars from where I am now, so I have to use the lines if I want to get to them on Mars. I heard the coordinates over the satellite. Come in, Adrianna, come in."

There was still no response from his base and his blondeheaded lady.

"Okay, then! I'm zipping to Mars, and I'm zipping now!" He shouted as he pressed the zip button on his cuff.

He was a little frustrated that he wasn't hearing from anyone in the Siberia lab, but he was a lot more frustrated that the twins were still on the move. Seven seconds after the numbers were set, off he zipped from the cockpit of *Thad-1* to the planet of Mars. He was going to stop those twins if it killed him.

Searching Saturn

"Point of fact, it is called the Red Planet because of the color of the iron-rich dust that covers the planet's surface," informed SLIM, who had jumped out of REESE's storage cell and was now traveling on his own via his underside roller ball.

The Sassafras twins nodded in thanks toward the little robot, even though they had already figured out why everything looked so red, remembering the SCIDAT data Yang Bo had already shared with them.

Blaine and Tracey scanned their eyes across the barren, rocky, red landscape as they traversed Mars with their robot companions. They were here to find the lost Mars Module and the space tourist who had ridden it, but at the moment, they could see nothing but iron-rich, red wilderness.

They were having a little trouble concentrating on the task at hand. Maybe it was because of all the red. Maybe it was because they still weren't used to the spacesuits they were wearing. Maybe it was the lower level of gravity, or maybe it was because they were . . . on Mars!

They were actually taking steps on a completely separate planet. They had blasted out of the Earth's atmosphere. They had visited the International Space Station, and they had floated over the surfaces of three other planets. All those experiences had been beyond amazing, but here they were now, walking (or rather bounding) across the planet of Mars. Their minds were having some trouble processing how amazing this fact actually was.

They were on Mars!

The group continued to walk, roll, and bound, scanning their eyes out across the landscape and looking for the module. Yang Bo had given them the coordinates of where it was supposed to land, but evidently its trajectory had been a bit off because they had been walking five minutes now and hadn't seen anything.

Wait, what was that? The twins saw the spot at the exact same time. Off to the right, in the distance, it looked like an object vehicular in nature.

"Look, REESE!" Tracey exclaimed. "Off to the right. Do you see that? Do you think that could be the module?"

The robot turned his trapezoid-shaped head and looked in the direction Tracey was pointing.

"Well, I'll be a monkey's uncle," REESE responded. "You're right, Tracey. That is it. That is the lost Mars Module."

"Point of fact," SLIM interrupted. "REESE, you are not a monkey's uncle. That is an impossibility due to the fact that you are—"

"Yeah, yeah, yeah," Blaine laughed, bringing a stop to the super literal information machine's statement. "Monkey's uncle or not, let's get over there and check it out!"

With a quickened pace, the group of hopeful rescuers made their way toward the objects. As they got closer, they saw the object was indeed the Mars Module. The two humans and two robots cautiously approached the module.

Blaine's first thought was that the flying vehicle looked like a big candy corn lying on its side. Tracey was wondering why the door to the vehicle was ajar.

REESE reached the module first, and as he did, he slowly extended his flexible neck to peek inside the open door. The Sassafras twins followed and took slow, cautious looks inside themselves. Even SLIM leaned in for a peek.

The inside of the Mars Module wasn't a big space. Even for one person, it would have felt fairly cramped, especially if one were in it for months on end. There were instruments, screens, buttons, and levers affixed to the module's walls. There were crumpled food wrappers, empty drink containers, and tattered pieces of paper with calculations on them lying about. What there was not was a person. The module was empty, and Brett Frye was nowhere to be seen.

"Point of fact," SLIM stated, "the provisions of this module have been exhausted, and the passenger is currently absent."

Neither Blaine nor Tracey listened to this obvious statement from SLIM because something else had captured their attention. There were footprints in the red dust leading away from the module.

Without saying a word, Blaine turned away and began following the trail of footsteps. There was no doubt about it; these were the footsteps of Brett Frye. That was the only possibility because, other than the twelve-year-olds, he was the only human to have ever set foot on this planet. Blaine bounded cautiously in front. Tracey followed closely behind him. Then came REESE and finally SLIM. As the Sassafras twins led the way, the question on their minds was not where the footprints led but what the footprints led to. What would they find at the end of this trail?

THE SASSAFRAS SCIENCE ADVENTURES

Footprints. Look at all these footprints.

What had they done—had a dance party when they arrived? By the looks of all the prints on the red ground, those twins had had a great time upon their landing on Mars, jumping, bounding, and moving around. Why couldn't they stay in one place or walk in a straight line. Not only that, but the two robots had made marks all over the place as they rolled around, too.

He stood up and growled, now fully recovered from his zip-lining arrival. He had landed on this planet after them, and he couldn't currently see them, so the only thing he could do now was to try and follow their trail. But that was going to be easier said than done.

He scanned the area until he finally found a straight trail of footprints and robot roll prints leading away from the zip line landing area.

Oh, what was that?

Something else—was that what he thought it was? Had they dropped an extra zip-zop cuff? He walked over and picked up the item he had spotted. How had they forgotten or misplaced such an important thing?

He growled again, but this time he was a bit more optimistic as he set his black boots in the direction all the prints were leading. He looked ahead through his black-tinted visor. He couldn't see anything yet except barren landscape, but he was certain he would eventually find those twins. They couldn't have gone that far on this miserable planet.

"And when I do find them," he said to himself, "I want it to be a surprise. A big, scary surprise."

He clinched the cuff he had found, snickered, and then pulled the vanish string that was located on the inside of his Dark Cape suit. As he did, he immediately became invisible.

As soon as they saw him, they stopped. Even the two robots halted, joining the twins in a sort of shocked stupor. They had found him. They had found the lost space tourist, Brett Frye. But was he okay?

The trail of footprints had led the twins and the robots across a long stretch of flat landscape and then down into a craggy canyon. It had been a much longer traverse than the twins were first expecting, and they had begun to wonder if they would ever find the missing man. And because of the anxiety the search had caused, their minds had begun to play tricks on them. Tracey had wondered if maybe this was all a dream. Blaine had imagined he'd seen a Martian or two lurking behind rocks, spying on them. Being as smart as they were, they knew these things were not true, but they were feeling weirded out, nonetheless.

So now, here they were, staring at a motionless man in a white space suit, wondering if they were seeing him or if he might be a figment of their imaginations. Had they truly found the missing billionaire, or were they seeing things?

SLIM broke their trance as he was the first to go over and assess the man. "Point of fact, this man is still alive," the skinny robot stated as he stood leaning over Brett.

The twins let out huge sighs of relief and then rushed over to join SLIM. The factual robot was right—Brett Frye was alive. His chest was rising and falling as he took slow breaths. The glass on his see-through helmet would slightly fog with each breath the man took. But he didn't look healthy. His face was gaunt, and his skin almost looked like it was a yellowish-green color.

"We've got to get this man back to the I.S.S." Tracey said

urgently. "Let's hurry up and get that extra cuff on him so we can zip out of here."

Fully aligned with his sister, Blaine hopped over to REESE, opened his storage cell, intending to grab the extra zip-zop cuff, but to the boy's shock and dismay, it was not there. Blaine was about to shout out this fact in panic, but before he could, he was interrupted by SLIM.

"Point of fact, I may have knocked the extra zip-zop cuff out of the storage cell when I alighted back at the zip line landing spot."

"What?" Blaine exclaimed, slightly agitated. "You mean, we've got to walk all the way back there before we can harness him up and zip him out of here?"

"It's okay," Tracey interjected, attempting to calm her twin a bit. "We can make that trek, and we can get Brett out of here."

"How are we going to drag an unconscious, full-grown man all the way back there?" Blaine asked.

"Allow me!" REESE was now the one interjecting as he pulled what looked a little like a skateboard hooked to a metal cord out of his storage cell.

"What is that?" Blaine asked.

"It's a roller board hand attachment," REESE answered as he connected it to his strong, flexible arm.

"What does he not have in there?" Blaine thought. "I mean; besides the cuff we need."

Wasting no more time, they all worked together to get Brett loaded onto the roller board, which was virtually serving the purpose of a stretcher. When the unconscious space tourist was loaded up and safely strapped onto the board, REESE began pulling him up out of the canyon. The versatile robot made it look effortless, as his tank-like treads powerfully churned over the rocky

Mars terrain. SLIM followed on his single roller ball that was set mostly inside the bottom part of his slender frame, and then the Sassafrases brought up the rear in their Linc 2.0 space suits.

The trip back from the canyon seemed shorter and quicker to the twins than the trip out had been. Look! They could already see the Mars Module!

Look! He could already see those twins and those robots coming back! He had to come up with a plan and fast! He had tried so many times and failed to squelch their science learning. He had virtually thought of everything, and yet they always overcame and then continued on. He couldn't seem to stop them . . . them . . . them . . . Wait!

Maybe that was the problem. Maybe instead of trying to stop them directly, he should try to stop them indirectly. Maybe instead of attacking them, he should try to attack whatever task was right in front of them or what they were currently trying to accomplish.

He gazed across the terrain toward them now. What were they currently doing? It looked like they were carrying something. If they were, that would become his target. Whatever they were hauling was what he was going to attack.

He looked down to make sure he was still invisible.

He was.

He checked to make sure he still had their lost zip-zop cuff.

He did.

"Okay, Sassafras twins," he silently growled. "Come to papa."

Blaine and Tracey were feeling optimistic. They were making great time. They had already passed the Mars Module. And they were certain they were going to find the lost cuff once they reached their landing spot.

Suddenly REESE violently fell over to his side, as if he had been hit by some unseen force. Then, before the twins could process what was happening, the unconscious body of Brett Frye was somehow pulled off the roller board, and a zip-zop cuff, floating all on its own, attached itself to the space tourist's wrist.

REESE quickly picked himself up. SLIM rolled over toward Brett for a closer look. But the Sassafrases stood like frozen shocksicles. Their shock deepened when all at once, Frye's body began dragging across the ground all on its own!

Oh, snap! What was he supposed to do now?

He had the person the twins had been trying to rescue. He even had the extra zip-zop cuff successfully attached to the guy's wrist. But what was he supposed to do now?

His mind was spinning.

Numbers! Numbers!

What were the last coordinates he had heard? Hadn't that Chinese astronaut given these twins some coordinates?

Blaine snapped out of his trance a second before his sister, and he began chasing Frye's body. It was now clear to him what was happening. Brett's unconscious body was not being moved by a see-through Martian or by some scientifically unknown force of Mars. Brett Frye was being pulled across the ground by the Man With No Eyebrows!

Blaine didn't know how or why, but the Man With No Eyebrows was still stalking them. He had somehow made it to Mars, and he was currently wearing the invisible Dark Cape suit. And for some unknown and twisted reason, he was trying to pull poor Brett Frye away from them.

Blaine was determined not to let that happen. With every low-gravity step, he was gaining on the invisible Dark Cape and his abductee.

He was now filled with fear because that boy twin was showing no fear. That boy was chasing him now, he was quickly gaining, and he looked beyond determined to catch up.

"What am I going to do?" He screamed silently to himself. "What were those numbers? I need coordinates! Any coordinates!"

All at once, a sequence of numbers rushed to his brain: 9.58 AU. He didn't know where these numbers would take him and this unconscious astronaut to, but he was certain they were actual coordinates he'd heard somewhere before. And anywhere was better than here.

He calibrated his cuff while on the run, and then he stopped. He had to. He had to stop and crouch over this unconscious man to get the coordinates entered into the other cuff.

Oh, no! Here came that boy twin like a rocket!

Only a few paces ahead of him, Blaine saw that the body of Brett Frye had suddenly stopped. Had the invisible Man With No Eyebrows dropped him and fled? Blaine surged forward and made one last jump toward Brett's body. And as he did, two things happened.

First, he saw the coordinates on Brett's cuff as clear as day: 9:58 AM. And second, he slammed into an invisible frame. When he did, the man in the Dark Cape suddenly became visible.

Ouch and oh no! Oh no and ouch! That boy had slammed right into him, and it had hurt, but even worse than that, the boy had hit him so hard that it had yanked the vanish string and made him visible again.

Here he was now, crouched in the Dark Cape suit, right in front of the boy. And not only that, the girl and those robots were fast approaching! It was a good thing he had gotten the coordinates set into the zip-zop cuffs.

Blaine's mouth dropped open, surprised but still determined. Here he was, on Mars—the Man With No Eyebrows, the Dark Cape—one in the same. Blaine wanted to ask a million questions he knew the man wouldn't answer, so instead of talking, the Sassafras boy lunged. Just as he did, the Man With No Eyebrows was gone. And not only that, Brett Frye disappeared, too.

Blaine slumped to the ground.

"Was that . . . was that who I think it was?" Tracey asked as she finally caught up with her brother.

Blaine nodded.

"And he took Brett? Why would he do that? Why would he take Brett?" Tracey stammered, confused. "Now we can't rescue him. Now we can't get him back to the I.S.S."

"Oh, we're going to rescue him," Blaine announced with resolve. "I saw the coordinates on Brett's cuff. We're going after him."

Seconds later, with the same space coordinates that Blaine had seen on Brett's zip-zop cuff entered into their own cuffs, the two humans and the two robots found themselves floating in space a safe distance above another beautiful planet. This time, however, instead of gazing at the planet, they were gazing around to find two individuals.

"Point of fact, this is Saturn," SLIM peeked out from inside REESE's storage cell, evidently unaware of the urgency reverberating through his companions. "Saturn is one of the outer planets. It is the sixth planet from the sun. The outer planets are all known as 'gas giants' because they are large planets made up mainly of gas. All of the gas giants have rings of rock and dust that orbit them, but Saturn's are the most visible."

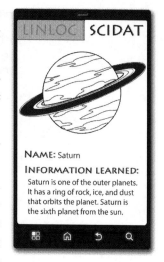

NAME: Saturn

INFORMATION LEARNED:
Saturn is one of the outer planets. It has a ring of rock, ice, and dust that orbits the planet. Saturn is the sixth planet from the sun.

"SLIM, shut your trap," REESE interjected. "It is my job to share SCIDAT with the twins."

"Point of fact, I do not have a trap, I—"

"Anyway," REESE interrupted and continued. "It is not the time to share SCIDAT. A villain in a Dark Cape has abducted Brett Frye and brought him to this place. We must help Blaine and Tracey find him."

"Point of fact, Saturn is the second-largest planet in our solar system," SLIM continued on with the fact giving, totally disregarding his robot counterpart. "It is light for its size because it is composed mainly of gas. Point of fact, Saturn is so light, it could float on the ocean if there were one big enough to hold it."

Blaine and Tracey were hearing what SLIM was saying, and they were amazingly somehow committing it to memory, but like REESE had just said, their focus was finding Brett Frye and getting him back from the Man With No Eyebrows.

"Point of fact, Saturn's rings are made up of ice, rocks, and dust that orbit the planet," SLIM continued. "The ice rings reflect light, which is why Saturn's rings are so visible, and because of these rings, Saturn is largely considered to be the most beautiful planet in our solar system."

Blaine had thought he had seen the coordinates on Brett's cuff correctly, but now he was second-guessing himself. Where were those two? Had the Man With No Eyebrows pulled the vanish string in his Dark Cape again?

"Look, Blaine!" Tracey shouted out. "There! I see them!"

Blaine looked in the direction his sister was pointing. Tracey was right. There they were: the Dark Cape and the limp body of Brett Frye, floating out over the planet of Saturn, a distance away from them.

"Okay," Blaine exclaimed. "Let's fire up the propulsion systems on these Linc 2.0 suits and get over there quick!"

"Point of fact, the atmosphere of Saturn is made up of ammonia, water, and methane that is colored by phosphorus and other elements," SLIM droned on, as though he was still completely unaware of the current priority. "This gives Saturn its colorful shades of cream, yellow, and brown. The rest of Saturn is composed of liquid hydrogen with a solid iron core, like Jupiter. Also, like Jupiter, Saturn has frequent, violent storms."

The propulsion jets were working well. They were closing distance on the Dark Cape and his abductee. Both Sassafras twins were feeling not only confident they would catch up but also that when they did, they would be able to retrieve Brett from the eyebrow-less man.

They had spotted him. They had pursued him. And now they were going to catch him.

He had no kind of propulsion system on this Dark Cape of his like they had on those white suits of theirs, so they were quickly gaining, and they were going to catch him. He had to do something!

Should he pull the vanish string and try to elude them that way? No, they would still be able to see the body of the astronaut.

He had to put new coordinates in the zip-zop cuffs.

"Ahhh!" He screamed as he nervously fidgeted with the numbers on the screen.

"Point of fact, Saturn has more than fifty confirmed moons that are mostly made of ice, except for Titan, which is Saturn's largest moon," SLIM recited calmly as the chase raged on and the four got closer and closer to the two. "Titan has a thick atmosphere and is a bit larger than our Earth. Scientists gathered much of their information from Cassini, the probe that was launched with the purpose of studying Saturn. Point of fact, it took seven years for Cassini to get from Earth to Saturn. A year on Saturn takes nearly 30 Earth years, but a day takes only about 11 Earth hours."

As SLIM finished the SCIDAT data, the Sassafras twins found themselves within pouncing distance of the Man With No Eyebrows and the unconscious billionaire, Brett Frye. They both took big, excited breaths inside the translucent domed helmets of their Linc 2.0 suits.

They reached out to push away their enemy and save their friend, but as they did, the two forms disappeared again—into thin air. And this time, neither Blaine nor Tracey had seen the coordinates on the zip-zop cuffs. Those two could now be anywhere in the entire solar system.

CHAPTER 7: WHERE IN THE SOLAR SYSTEM IS MR. FRYE?

Unique Uranus

"We made it," his voice squeaked in excitement. "I almost can't believe it. We actually made it!"

"Of course, we made it, partner," a much calmer and more confident voice said. "You never doubted that we would make it; did you? That boost from the taser worked brilliantly and got us right back on track. Of course, we made it. We are Triple S agents after all."

Swiss Secret Service agents Evan DeBlose and Q-Tip were sitting in the cockpit of *Dauntless-12,* and they were staring out at a satellite that floated directly in front of them. It was the satellite that belonged to the Triple S. It had been damaged by the turncoat, Adrianna Archer. Its shield was down, and it had been hit by space debris, causing the Swiss Secret Service to lose all its surveillance capabilities, meaning they couldn't track the whereabouts of Archer the fugitive or her evil counterpart, Yuroslav Bogdanovich. Q-Tip and Evan were here to fix it.

Evan looked at Q-Tip and smiled. "Now all we have to do is climb out into space, away from the safety of our rocket, float over to the satellite without getting hit by any space debris, and fix the shield by hand as it orbits twelve thousand miles above the surface of the Earth. Then, if we are still alive and functioning at that point, we'll add the taser upgrade. No sweat."

Q-Tip responded with a chuckle and a smile of his own, but both were nervous. "Yeah, no sweat," the skinny agent repeated as he actually started sweating.

There he was, the man of her dreams. Adrianna Archer was crouched down and cautiously peeking into the basement window of the house at 1104 North Pecan Street. Inside, Cecil Sassafras sprinted back and forth across the room from one project to the next with ferocious, untamable energy.

"What power," Adrianna thought. "Power of the body and power of the mind. He has more power than Yuroslav and Thaddaeus put together."

The beautiful blonde pulled herself back from the window, sat on the grass with her back against the house, and sighed. How was she going to convince this redheaded man that he needed her to join him? Yuroslav, whom she thought looked similar to Cecil, had been fairly easy to convince. Thaddaeus had been even easier. All she had had to do with him was grab his hand and say some flattering words.

But Cecil Sassafras, she assumed, was going to be much

harder to join forces with. A man of his brilliance, power, and moxie would surely be a tough nut to crack. She would need to study the man a little more, do her research, and watch his every move. Once she had gathered enough information, then she would approach him and try to become his companion in power.

Adrianna sighed again, stood up, and left the house. She would be back, and she couldn't wait to be by Cecil Sassafras's side.

"Point of fact, a year on Uranus takes about 84 Earth years, and a day takes a little over 17 Earth hours. Uranus is also a gas gia—"

"Stop, just stop, stop, stop," REESE's robotic voice interrupted SLIM's. "Step off, back away, gear down, big shifter."

"Point of fact, I am not equipped with any kind of gea—"

"That is not my meaning," REESE interrupted SLIM again. "You must stop giving SCIDAT data. First off, it's my primary directive to give Blaine and Tracey the SCIDAT. Second, the priority now is finding Brett Frye, not covering any kind of data."

Even though they were feeling bucket loads of angst because of Brett's abduction by the Man With No Eyebrows, Blaine and Tracey had to chuckle at REESE and SLIM. It was more than a little funny to hear two robots continue to argue about who was going to give them their scientific data.

What was not funny was the fact they hadn't found Brett. They figured the Man With No Eyebrows still had spying capabilities and that he had heard their local expert, Yang Bo, give the space coordinates for all of the planets they were visiting. The Man With No Eyebrows had snagged the zip-zop cuff SLIM had dropped and had calibrated it to the coordinates for Saturn. The only way the eyebrow-less man could've known those coordinates was if he had overheard Yang Bo give the twins those numbers back on the I.S.S.

So now here the Sassafrases were, floating over the planet of Uranus in search of Brett, thinking that if the Man With No Eyebrows had the coordinates for Saturn, maybe he had the coordinates for Uranus, too. But as they looked out across the expanse in front of them, they did not see the black-clad man or the white-clad man he had kidnapped. To make this search even more complicated, the Man With No Eyebrows had a suit that enabled him to become invisible. So not only could he zip anywhere in the solar system that he had coordinates for, but he could operate invisibly while doing so. Plus, the twins were pretty sure that if the Man With No Eyebrows threw the large cape of his suit over the body of Brett Frye, he could make their unconscious friend invisible too. This search wasn't like looking for a needle in a haystack. It was like looking for a needle in a haystack the size of the entire galaxy.

"Point of fact," SLIM started again. "The correct way to say Uranus is 'you-rah-nus' not 'your-a—'"

"Oh, no, you don't," REESE interrupted the skinny robot before he got going again. "Don't you dare start giving SCIDAT. That's my job."

"Oh, it's all right, REESE," Tracey said. "Let the little guy give us the SCIDAT on Uranus. Blaine and I could use something good and fun right now. And then, maybe after SLIM does that, you could sing us another song?"

REESE looked from SLIM to Tracy. His light box mouth changed

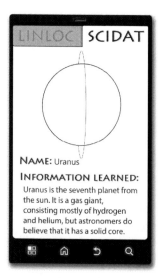

SCIDAT

LINLOC

NAME: Uranus

INFORMATION LEARNED:
Uranus is the seventh planet from the sun. It is a gas giant, consisting mostly of hydrogen and helium, but astronomers do believe that it has a solid core.

from a frown to a smile. That was all SLIM needed to start right back up again. "As I was saying before, point of fact, Uranus is a gas giant. This seventh planet from the sun consists mostly of hydrogen and helium, but astronomers do believe that it has a solid core. The planet's blue color is due to the presence of methane gas. Point of fact, Uranus has a system of eleven rings that are all quite thin. It also has more that twenty confirmed moons, the largest of which is half the size of Earth's moon. Uranus is unique in our solar system because it orbits the sun on its side. We received most of our information about Uranus from the space probe Voyager 2. It visited the planet in 1986, and it took more than twelve years to get to Uranus from Earth."

Now, with a more cooperative spirit, REESE illuminated his torso screen with text for everything SLIM had said. The bigger robot then immediately jumped into a song about dwarf planets. This time, though, instead of being a hip-hop song, it was a rock ballad. He even kind of bobbed his head and did some air guitar moves with his arms as he sang.

Ohhhh, Ohhh, dwarf planet!
Ohhhh, Ohhhh, dwarf planet!

REESE sang in a loud, raspy voice out into the Uranus night. He then broke into the first verse.

You are a celestial body with a spherical shape that orbits the sun,
But you're not large enough to disturb other objects
From your orbit—nobody, no one!
Ohhhh, ohhhh, dwarf planet!
Ohhhh, ohhhh, dwarf planet.

Blaine and Tracey liked this song as much as all the other songs this robot who was designed for exploration, entertainment, and scientific enhancement had sung before. They even found themselves almost involuntarily bobbing their own heads and strumming their own air guitars as REESE belted out the second verse.

Out of all of the dwarf planets by far the most famous—Pluto
But what used to be thought of as the ninth and final planet
Is now no longer, no, no!
Ohhhh, ohhhh, dwarf planet!
Ohhhh, ohhhh, dwarf planet!

REESE finished his song with a soundless jam session that even had the emotionless SLIM's lights blinking. The Sassafras twins clapped and laughed, and then they took big, long, deep breaths. It was time to focus on finding Brett.

Yang Bo nervously tapped his fingers on the armrest of his seat. He was looking at Parth Banerjee, his friend, who sat across the room in a pair of handcuffs, strapped down in a seat of his own. The Indian mathematician was accused and seemingly convicted of a crime that Yang Bo didn't think he had committed.

A white queen from Parth's chess set had been found jammed into a slot in the main circuit board. This had caused the Mars Module to deploy with Brett Frye inside it. Banerjee was blamed and was now going to be sent back to Earth to go to jail. Brett was lost on Mars and was probably now on the brink of survival if not already dead.

The Chinese astrobiologist stopped tapping his fingers and let out a long sigh through nervously clinched teeth. The only hope left for both Parth and Brett rested in the hands of two twelve-year-olds. Blaine and Tracey Sassafras were the only ones who could save both of these men. He hadn't heard from them in more than an Earth day's time, but Yang Bo was still daring to believe that the twins were alive and were up to this seemingly insurmountable challenge.

Sander Petrov, the Russian engineer, burst into the room

and with him Captain Dianna Sturgess. "The vessel that vill serve as this scumbag's transport back to Earth is fast approaching," he said gruffly, pointing at Parth. "Let's get him down to the docking port."

Yang Bo unfastened himself from his seat and floated up to get in Sander's way. "Sander, settle down. What's the rush?"

"Vhat's the rush? Are you kidding me right now, Yang Bo? Parth is a sabotaging piece of trash, and it's time to get rid of him."

"But Sander, Parth is, er, was our friend. Stop being so cruel to him. And stop referring to him as trash."

Disregarding the astrobiologist, Sander pushed past Yang Bo and made his way over to where Banerjee was secured. "No friend of mine breaks the trust of his peers or sends people off to their deaths," Petrov barked as he roughly unfastened Parth from his seat.

Captain Sturgess also made her way past Yang Bo with a sorrowful look on her face. She reached the spot where the engineer was yanking the mathematician out of the chair, and she put a gentle yet firm hand on Sander Petrov's shoulder.

"Yang Bo is right, Sander," she declared clearly. "We all need to settle down. We can wait until the transport vessel arrives to move Banerjee to the docking port. Parth very well may have sabotaged the Mars Module to get back at Brett for constantly mocking him. But instead of treating our fellow astronaut roughly for his moment of weakness, let's treat him with respect for his many years of strength and brilliance."

Sander paused from manhandling the terrified Banerjee and looked at his captain.

Yang Bo held his breath as he waited to see how Petrov would respond to what the captain had said. The engineer made a huffing noise, and the angry look on his face didn't change, but he did let go of the mathematician. The Chinese astronaut let out a silent sigh of relief. Petrov had settled down, but there was no telling how long that would last.

"C'mon, Blaine and Tracey," Yang Bo's mind pleaded. "Find Brett and get back here quick!"

Nearing Neptune

"Neptune is the farthest planet from the sun and is about four times bigger than Earth. However, even being that large, it appears only as a tiny blue star when we look at it through a telescope from Earth." REESE was sharing SCIDAT data with the twins in his normal robot voice. SLIM was quiet for the moment and packed away in REESE's storage cell.

Blaine and Tracey were quiet right now too, partly in awe, but mostly in discouragement.

Floating above the surface of Neptune, the planet looked much larger than a tiny blue dot. Its size, beauty, and depth were awe inspiring. It looked like a huge spherical ocean of swirling dreams or a giant wishing well they could toss a dime or a nickel into and make a cosmic wish. But they were discouraged because they had hoped to find Brett Frye here above Neptune, and they hadn't. Maybe Neptune, this dreamy planet, could grant them a wish.

Just one wish. Their only current wish—their wish to find Brett Frye alive.

"Neptune is another gas giant with a small, rocky core," REESE continued. "It is composed mainly of hydrogen and helium, but it also has methane gas, which gives the planet its blue color, and ammonia gas, which

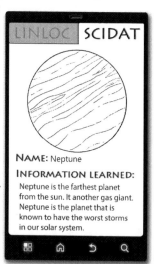

UNLOC **SCIDAT**

NAME: Neptune

INFORMATION LEARNED:

Neptune is the farthest planet from the sun. It another gas giant.
Neptune is the planet that is known to have the worst storms in our solar system.

forms the pure white clouds on the surface. Neptune is the planet that is known to have the worst storms in our solar system. In 1989, the probe Voyager 2 sent back images of Neptune that depicted a raging storm that was named the Great Dark Spot. But then in 1994, the spot mysteriously disappeared."

There it was again, that word, 'disappeared.' It was a word that seemed to stalk them now. The Man With No Eyebrows, who had been stalking them from the beginning of the summer, was always disappearing and then showing back up and then disappearing again. Now, he had made Brett Frye disappear with him. The twins were not fans of this word.

However, as they stared down at the big, swirling blue planet and thought about the Great Dark Spot that had disappeared, they could imagine it coming back. With all of the movement of the gases on Neptune, the twins could easily envision a big, dark storm reappearing. And this is how they needed to think about the Man With No Eyebrows and Brett Frye with him. They had to hope with all of their hearts that their big storm—the Dark Cape— would reappear. And when he did, they would not only rescue Brett Frye from his clutches, but they would also get an answer to the question of why the Man With No Eyebrows wanted to sabotage their summer of learning.

"Neptune has more than ten confirmed moons, the largest of which is Triton," REESE's voice broke back in through the Sassafrases' thoughts. "And a year on Neptune takes 165 Earth years, where a day takes only a little over 16 Earth hours."

How many Earth days or Earth hours would it take the twins to find Brett? Brett hadn't looked good when they had found him on Mars. He had looked like he was on the brink of death, so they really needed to find him before he went all the way over. Didn't the Man With No Eyebrows know how serious the situation was? He was horrible, but he didn't want anyone to die; did he?

The Sassafras twins snapped pictures of the swirling blue

planet in front of them with their smartphones. They had visited all the inner planets. They had visited all the outer planets. They had had experiences and seen things that were out of this world, and for that they were thankful. But their wish right now, as they floated over Neptune, was to find Brett Frye. He wasn't here. Where was he?

Here he was now. He was a step away, always just a step away from having the perfect plan to stop those Sassafras twins. He had made it all the way to space to stop them, and yet he couldn't do it. He was still a step away, and his plan to thwart them was still a little bit off.

Yes, he had abducted this unconscious astronaut whom those twins were trying to rescue, but what did that do? It didn't accomplish what he wanted to accomplish—revenge against his nemesis, Cecil Sassafras.

And besides that, this astronaut looked like he was in pretty bad shape. And although he knew he himself was full of vengeance, he was not so vile that he wanted anyone to die. He simply wanted revenge for the loss of his eyebrows.

He thought to himself as he hung there, "It was a bad plan to abduct this man. I cannot let this man die, but where should I take him?"

Thaddaeus looked through his dark visor one more time at the man. Should he take him back to Mars, where the twins had found him? Or should he take him to someplace that the poor man could actually get some help?

They had failed.

They had not found the needle they were looking for in the galaxy-sized haystack. They had let the Man With No Eyebrows escape with Brett Frye. They could keep zipping all over the solar system and search until their own faces turned green, but the likelihood of finding Brett alive was slim to none.

Blaine and Tracey Sassafras hung their heads low, pressed the zop button on their cuffs, and zipped through swirls of light from the planet of Neptune back to the I.S.S. They'd had Brett Frye in their grasp, but they had lost him. And now they had to return and face Yang Bo, their local expert, empty-handed.

The twelve-year-olds and their robot friends, REESE and SLIM, landed with a jerk. Their cuffs unclipped from the invisible zip lines, leaving the twins in the same square room they had originally landed in on the I.S.S. This time, however, when the twins' sight and strength returned, they saw that their local expert was not here to greet them. Tracey looked at her brother with a sorrowful and dissatisfied look on her face.

"We're going to have to go find Yang Bo, Blaine," she stated. "And we're going to have to tell him that we weren't . . . we couldn't . . . we didn't bring Brett back with us."

Blaine nodded his low-hanging head. Tracey was right about their next step, and like her, he was sad and didn't want to reunite with Yang Bo without having Brett. But they had to. Blaine led the way from the room into the adjoining circular tube that served as a connecting hallway to the rest of the station. Tracey slowly followed her brother, floating through the zero-gravity air, as did

REESE, and also SLIM, who was now out of REESE's storage cell.

Before the four could exit the circular tube, another figure entered from the other end. It was Yang Bo, and he seemed uncharacteristically rattled. The Chinese astrobiologist looked like he was about to say something, but Blaine beat him to speaking first. "Yang Bo, we tried, we really tried, but we didn't . . . well, actually we did find Brett Frye on Mars. It's just that . . ."

"Blaine," Yang Bo tried to cut in, but the Sassafras boy either didn't notice or didn't let him.

"It's just that, well, see, the Mars Module wasn't where our space coordinates for Mars landed us, and then . . ."

"Blaine," Yang Bo tried again to no avail.

"And then," Blaine continued to fumble, "when we found the Mars Module, Brett wasn't even there, so we ended up having to hike down into a ravine, and then he was there, and he looked green and was barely breathing. But we didn't have an extra cuff, so we had to . . ."

"Blaine." This time it was Tracey who was trying to interrupt her brother who was almost absent-mindedly apologizing and talking a million miles an hour.

"So, we had to hike back to our landing spot, but then all of a sudden, The Man With No Eyebrows was there in his invisible Dark Cape Suit, and he took him. He took Brett Frye. He took him away from us, and there was nothing we could do. We tried. We tried our hardest, we really did, but we couldn't get him back. We just couldn't. We zipped to Saturn and Uranus and Neptune, but we couldn't get him back. We couldn't find him. We failed. We didn't complete our mission. And now Brett is probably going to die, and Parth's probably going to get arrested and, and, and I am sorry. We are sorry, we failed, and we—"

"Blaine!" This time Yang Bo and Tracey said the name together, finally causing the boy to cease his bumbling monologue.

'Blaine, look!" Tracey said emphatically and pointed, along with Yang Bo, out a circular window.

The Sassafras boy looked out into space in the direction in which the two fingers were pointing and saw something that rendered him awestruck. A lone astronaut, in a white spacesuit, floated limp and lifeless out about a hundred yards or so from the space station.

"Is that . . . is that Brett?" Blaine asked, astonished.

Yang Bo nodded his head. "I don't know how, especially after your summarization, Blaine, but you guys did it. You brought Brett Frye back from Mars!"

"We did?" Blaine asked, dumbfounded.

"You did," Yang Bo answered. "But now we need to go out and get him before he floats off by himself into space."

A few minutes later, Blaine and Tracey Sassafras found themselves soaring out from the International Space Station, aiming to retrieve the body and hopefully the life of the free-floating billionaire. They were tethered to the space station with strong cords of interwoven steel that were securely attached to an external platform of the ship and to the backs of each of their suits. These lines they were currently attached to weren't invisible, and they didn't allow the twins to travel at the speed of light, but they were the best way to get Brett Frye back.

Yang Bo had quickly hooked the twins to the external tethers and had given them some instructions on what to do and what not to do. So far, the Sassafrases were doing a good job of following those instructions. They were being careful not to get their two lines crossed, and they were using the propulsion systems on their suits to point them in the most direct, and therefore fastest, trajectory toward the space tourist.

Brett was still floating about a hundred yards out from the I.S.S., seemingly on the same orbit as the ship. Their tethers were approximately 200 yards long, meaning the twins should have plenty of length to reach Frye, securely connect to him, and then bring him back in.

The female Sassafras ended up a little in front of her brother, although neither of the twins were viewing this as a competition. Both wanted to rescue Brett, and both wanted him to be all right, so both were now reaching out in their Linc 2.0 spacesuits to get to Frye.

It was strange to the twins that although they were traveling at thousands of miles an hour in orbit, it only felt like they were floating in slow motion. Also, the Sassafrases thought it might have been extremely loud, flying in their spacesuits outside of the I.S.S, but all each of them could hear was the sound of their own breathing inside their illuminated helmets.

They were now more than halfway out to where Brett Frye was free-floating. Blaine glanced back toward the I.S.S. and saw that Yang Bo, REESE, and SLIM were all looking out one of the small circular windows, nervously monitoring their progress. Blaine turned his attention in front of him and prayed a silent prayer that he and Tracey could pull this off without incident.

They floated forward in as straight a line as they could manage, and after what seemed like a much longer time than it actually was, the twelve-year-olds finally reached Brett Frye.

Tracey securely clipped the unconscious man to her line. Blaine double-checked to make sure everything was fastened correctly and then gave a thumbs-up. The twins then turned and began propelling themselves, with Brett in tow, back toward the I.S.S.

What was this feeling he was feeling inside his dark heart right now? Was this joy? Was light creeping into his darkness? Was he actually happy? Floating here invisibly in his Dark Cape suit, an actual smile made its way to his eyebrow-less face. He had watched those twins float out from the space station and safely retrieve that unconscious astronaut.

At this moment, they were successfully getting him through the open cargo bay door, back into the craft. Thaddaeus was not only feeling happiness and joy right now; he was also feeling pride. He was proud of those twins for having the courage and capacity to save this lost astronaut.

Was this how Cecil felt all the time? After the twins successfully learned a scientific subject or persevered through a trial, did Cecil feel this kind of abounding pride for the twins? It was a good feeling, but it was scaring him a little.

On top of being proud of the twins, Thaddaeus was also proud of himself. He had actually chosen to do the right thing. Instead of letting that astronaut die or letting him float off somewhere in space, he had returned him here to the orbit of the International Space Station, where he knew he would be seen and then rescued. Yes, he had done the right thing, and he was feeling good about it.

But, wait! Did all these positive feelings mean he was changing? Did this mean he no longer desired revenge on Cecil Sassafras? Were these good feelings potentially as fulfilling as any kind of vengeance could be? For the first time since junior high school, Thaddaeus was thinking maybe so.

Sure, Cecil Sassafras had caused the accident that had taken his eyebrows, but was it that big of a deal? Was life without eyebrows so bad?

Maybe not—maybe instead of spending all his time and energy pursuing revenge on Cecil, he should instead be committing acts of kindness. The smile on his face got even bigger. Yes, he was having a change of heart.

It felt sudden, but maybe this process of heart change had been marinating for a while! Saving this astronaut seemed to be setting him on a different course. Right now, he was going to zip back to *Thad-1*, and then he was going to return to Earth to his underground Siberian science lab. There he would inform Adrianna Archer, his strong and trusted companion, that there was now a new trajectory. They were now going to stop stalking the Sassafrases, and they were going to start serving humanity. All the scores of scientists he had at his beck and call would now become an army for goodwill. All this sudden positivity almost made Thaddaeus feel like actual light was shooting out of his heart.

"Look out world," the Man With No Eyebrows declared as he looked down at the actual globe. "Here I come! And I am bringing a lot of light with me! Thaddaeus Wazeezy now exists to serve the good of humankind!"

Tracey's eyes moved occasionally behind her eyelids. Blaine mumbled unintelligible sentences. Even so, both Sassafrases slept soundly after hours on end of intense space travel. After Blaine and Tracey had gotten Brett Frye safely on board the International Space Station, he had been rushed by Yang Bo straight to the infirmary, where Captain Dianna Sturgess and space medicine expert, Bayard Clemence, attended to him.

Yang Bo had then shown the Sassafras twins to the crew quarters and instructed them to get some rest because there was no telling what was going to happen with Brett or how long it would take. The twins had strapped themselves into their beds so they wouldn't float away and had fallen asleep within seconds.

Blaine was dreaming that he had hopped the fence into Old

Man Grusher's yard, except that it wasn't a yard—it was Mars. And Old Man Grusher's dog, the Guardian Beast, wasn't just a dog, it was a Martian. It was chasing him to try and steal the Frisbee out of his hand.

Tracey was dreaming that she was standing on a starlit stage, holding one of REESE's karaoke microphones, and she was singing a beautiful, moving song. She was about to get to the climax of the song, but suddenly she was interrupted by an annoying robotic voice.

"Time to wake up."

"Stop," Tracey mumbled. "I need to finish this song."

"Point of fact, it is time to wake up," the robotic voice informed again.

"SLIM? Please let me finish . . . wait, what?" Tracey opened her eyes and saw that the skinny little robot was there, hovering by her bed.

"It is time to wake up," he said again. "Point of fact, Brett Frye is conscious. He is weak, but all signs point to the probability that he will live."

"Brett is okay? He's awake?" Tracey questioned in exclamation.

"Affirmative," SLIM answered.

"Blaine! Blaine, wake up!" Tracey shouted as she reached over to shake her brother out of his slumber. "Blaine, wake up. Brett's okay! He's alive!"

"Give me back my Frisbee, you . . . alien . . . dog . . . Martian . . . what?" Blaine mumbled as he sat up groggily in his bed.

"Blaine! Brett's okay! Let's go see him!"

Blaine nodded, unstrapped himself from the bed, and then followed SLIM and his sister out of the room.

A few minutes later, the Sassafras twins burst into the main laboratory of the I.S.S, expecting to find a scene of excitement and joy, but instead it was a packed room of thick intensity. Everyone was there: Captain Dianna Sturgess, their local expert Yang Bo, Bayard Clemence, meteorologist Anna Maria Bezerra, Russian engineer Sander Petrov, REESE, SLIM, the accused Parth Benerjee. Then, sitting in the middle of everyone, was billionaire and space tourist, Brett Frye. He was conscious. He was coherent. He still looked a little weak, but he was no longer green.

"Welcome, Blaine and Tracey," Captain Sturgess greeted. "Brett, these are the two who saved your life."

Frye looked at the twins. He said nothing, but, in his eyes, there was a heartfelt look of gratitude. Captain Sturgess looked like she was about to say something else, but before she could, she was interrupted by the factual and socially unaware SLIM.

"Point of fact, Brett Frye was about to tell us who sabotaged the fuse board and sent him off alone in the Mars Module."

"Eh, hmmm, yes, thank you, SLIM. That is what is happening," the captain said. She looked at Brett Frye. "Brett, as you just found out, Sander discovered a queen from Parth's chess set lodged deep into the fuse board down in the control pod. This queen caused the short circuit that sent you off alone in the Mars Module. Our question to you now is, if you remember and have the strength to answer, did Parth Banerjee or any other member of this crew intentionally commit this crime?"

Brett remained silent, looking like he couldn't or didn't want to answer.

Parth sat fidgeting and sweating.

Everyone else remained completely silent, waiting to see if an answer would come from the one that Blaine and Tracey had traveled across virtually the entire solar system to rescue.

CHAPTER 8: BACK TO EARTH
Gawking at Galaxies

Pretty much everyone seemed to have motive, but who on the I.S.S. would've had the audacity to sabotage the fuse board and send Brett Frye off alone to Mars?

Parth Banerjee was sick and tired of Brett belittling him for being a "rookie." It was his white chess queen that had been found in the fuse board. Sander Petrov, the one who had found the queen and then blamed Parth had already admitted that he wasn't a fan of the space tourist billionaire. The Frenchman, Bayard Clemence had motive as well. He was not happy with Frye because Brett was always flirting with his younger sister, Queenie, saying that he would marry her and call her his little "French Frye." And then there was Anna Maria Bezerra; although happy and kind, she admitted that she was jealous that Brett had directed his affections toward Bayard's younger sister.

Blaine and Tracey sat silently, as did everyone else, looking intently at Brett Frye and waiting for an answer. If he was ever arrogant before, you couldn't tell now. The man sat, humble, broken, and grateful to be alive. He had crawled into a canyon, thinking he would die alone on Mars. And yet, now here he was alive, desperately needing to give the answer everyone was waiting for with bated breath.

The billionaire lifted his head as high as he could. He made eye contact with everyone in the room. Then he opened his mouth to speak. "I did it," he confessed. "I short-circuited the fuse board that led to the launch. It was my fault."

A collective gasp filled with an unvoiced "why" pulsing from the group.

Brett mustered his strength and offered an explanation. "I

was smart. I was rich. I was always the best at everything. But no matter how hard I tried; I could not beat this brilliant man right here at chess." He pointed toward Parth. "I belittled him relentlessly because I was jealous of his chess skills. Eventually, I got so frustrated about it that I stole his chess set and took it down to the control pod. In a moment of pure foolishness and extreme frustration, I took that white queen and slammed it deep into the fuse board. Sparks started flying everywhere. I got scared, and I dove into the Mars Module where I thought I would be safe. Then like a bombshell, the realization that the module was taking off hit me. I was immediately filled with dread as I flew off for Mars. And for the last six and a half months, I have thought over and over that a single momentary decision was probably going to be the last mistake I ever made."

Brett paused and looked like he was going to say more, but either he didn't have the strength, or he was too choked up to continue. Really, though, he didn't need to continue. He was now safe. Parth was exonerated. And the mystery was solved.

Sometime later, the twins found themselves back in the square room they had originally landed in. REESE, SLIM, and Yang Bo were floating with them. The Sassafrases were ready to use their zip-zop cuffs to head back to *Ulysses-1*, but they were not ready to leave their three friends behind.

"Blaine and Tracey," Yang Bo said, looking at the twins proudly. "You are the bravest and most amazing young scientists I have ever met."

The Sassafrases dipped their heads bashfully.

"Not only did the two of you travel to all the inner planets and all the outer planets," the Chinese astrobiologist continued, "but you also saved a man's life. I am so grateful that you came and visited the International Space Station."

THE SASSAFRAS SCIENCE ADVENTURES

Yang Bo looked down and patted the fact-giving robot that was next to him. "SLIM and I are going to miss you guys, and REESE as well, but I hope we'll bump into you three somewhere sometime."

"Point of fact, the probability of actually bumping into these three—"

"Never mind your explanation right now, SLIM," Yang Bo interrupted the little robot with a laugh. "Just say goodbye to REESE and the Sassafrases."

"Point of fact, goodbye," SLIM voiced.

"Bye!" Blaine and Tracey chuckled together.

"Now, go ahead and zip out of here, you three!" Yang Bo encouraged. "There is so much more astronomy to be discovered and explored!"

The twins nodded and pressed both the "zip" and the "zop" buttons. REESE did the same on his cuff-hand attachment.

This sequence would send them soaring back to Summer Beach and her ship. The cuffs immediately connected to the invisible zip lines.

"Tell Summer and your uncle I said hello," Yang Bo said as he waved goodbye.

The twins gave an affirmative thumbs-up. Then, along with their trusty robot sidekick, they disappeared from the I.S.S, zipping off at the speed of light back toward *Ulysses-1*. When they arrived, they were greeted with squeals of delight. Before their sight and strength fully recovered, they were being pulled up into a happy, jumping dance-hug by the exuberant Summer T. Beach herself.

"Blaine and Tracey Cutie-Super-frasses! You're back! You did it! You zipped to the International Space Station and back! You met my old buddy Yang Bo, and you zipped to all the planets! Oh, you two are the cutest and the best! And REESE—you made it back too! Great job, you three!"

When the twins could finally stand on their own legs and see again, they saw that it wasn't just Summer here in the cockpit room with them. Both President Lincoln and Ulysses S. Grant were here too. The two animals were, of course, not as vocal as Summer, but they looked happy to see the twins. They were holding up some pretty fancy-looking rocks in their paws for Blaine and Tracey to see.

The twins tried to ask about the rocks, but before they could get the question out of their mouths, Summer was giving an answer. "Oh, Blaine and Tracey, you've gotta see this! Ulysses and the Prez are so excited and have been waiting to show you what they found on their own space adventures!"

Blaine took one of the rocks from President Lincoln, and Tracey took one from Ulysses, and they looked them over. They were rough and grainy rocks with all different kinds of sparkles shimmering through them as though full of jewels.

"It had always been President Lincoln's dream to travel to Pluto," Summer explained. "So that was going to be the project that Ulysses was going to help him tackle while the two of you were studying the planets. However, on their way to Pluto, something went haywire with the zip lines, and these two little furry dudes landed on an asteroid instead."

"They landed on an asteroid?" Blaine asked.

"Yessirree, they sure did," Summer confirmed. "And not only that, they landed on an asteroid that was made up of this beautiful rock that you are looking at now!"

"Wow!" Tracey exclaimed. "It looks like it's full of jewels. Do you think it really is?"

"We don't know for sure, but priceless jewels or not, we are excited to get back to Earth, show it to Cecil, and see what he thinks."

President Lincoln nodded proudly as Blaine and Tracey handed the cool asteroid rocks back to him and Ulysses.

"And, speaking of getting back to Earth . . ." Summer smiled as she excitedly pointed to the actual planet Earth, which was directly in front of them out of the cockpit windshield. "Are the two of you ready to reenter the atmosphere and continue your study of astronomy back on our home planet?"

The twins nodded resolutely.

"Okie-awesome-dokie then!" The female scientist giggled. "As you obviously remember, the invisible zip lines cannot zip through the Earth's atmosphere, so you will have to wait until we get back to our home planet to zip to your next location, but even so, go ahead and open up the LINLOC apps on your phones to see what you will be studying next and where that location is!"

Still wearing their Linc 2.0 suits, the twins felt around until they found their individual smartphones. Tracey got to the information on her LINLOC first and excitedly read aloud what she found.

"We are going to Hawaii! Longitude -156°01'41.8", latitude +19°47'27.7". Our local expert's name is J.P. Jungos, and we will be studying the topics of galaxies, telescopes, satellites, and space probes!"

LINLOC SCIDAT

LOCATION: Hawaii

CONTACT: J.P. Jungos

LATITUDE: LONGITUDE:
+19°47'27.7"   -156°01'41.8"

HAWAII

INFORMATION NEEDED ON:
Galaxies, Telescopes,
Satellites, Space probes

"Wow, Hawaii!" Blaine repeated excitedly.

Feeding off the twins' excitement, Summer Beach got even more excited herself, if that were even possible. She stood in place and clapped her hands close to her body, seemingly as fast as a machine gun. She then quickly transitioned into another happy, jumping dance-hug, which included herself, the twins, the two furry mammals, and REESE the robot.

Then, after the hug went long enough for her but too long for everyone else, she announced, "Hey, everybody, before we go back to Earth, let's have one last space disco party!"

As if he had been waiting for the command, REESE immediately changed the light box on his face to disco mode and began cranking out the outdated yet fun music of the 1970s. Then the one robot, two animals, and three humans . . . danced.

He was so happy he could dance. For the first time in a long time, or maybe even for the first time ever, he was choosing good over evil, and it was making him feel so fine that he thought he might actually want to . . . dance.

Yes, he wanted to dance. Maybe he could even ask Adrianna to dance with him once he got back to the lab. Maybe all of the white lab coat-clad scientists would dance with them too. He smiled as he thought about it.

Safely back in the pilot seat of his black spacecraft, *Thad-1*, he was headed back to Earth. And once he got there, everything was going to change. First, he was going to tell Adrianna that the plans for revenge against Cecil Sassafras were off, and now they were going to seek out missions of goodwill only. Next, he would ask the beautiful, blonde headed Adrianna Archer to dance with him. Then, just maybe . . .

Nope, he couldn't go and start thinking too far in the future. He knew he shouldn't go and count his chickens before they were hatched.

A laugh now joined the smile on his face as he pointed his spacecraft in the direction of Siberia. The absence of eyebrows was the last thing on his mind. He was going home, and he knew that everything was going to change.

They had their helmets back on. They had their backpacks back on. And they had left their space suits behind, back on *Ulysses-1*, which was now parked safely underground in that familiar field in Alaska. They had enjoyed their time zipping around in space, but it was nice to now be back on Earth. The twins smiled as the swirling light caressed their faces. They had just said goodbye to Summer, Linc-Dawg, Ulysses, and REESE, and they were ready to say "hello" to J.P. Jungos, their new local expert.

Eventually, the two Sassafrases landed with a jerk, and their tingling bodies slumped down, sightless and without strength. Quickly, Blaine and Tracey realized they were going to desperately need both sight and strength because the coordinates for Hawaii had landed them directly on top of two surfboards! Tracey was tempted to be scared by this fact, but instead she took a deep breath and began to remember all she and Blaine had learned from professional surfer Emeraldine Hendrix, their local expert in Sri Lanka.

As a good wave broke in the perfect spot behind her, the Sassafras girl hopped to her feet, assumed a good stance on the board, held her arms out, bent her knees, and lowered her center of gravity. Tracey caught the wave! She maintained her balance and began surfing toward the shore.

Tracey glanced over her shoulder to see if Blaine had panicked or if he'd managed to stand up on his board and surf. Sure enough, her brother was not only surfing, but he also had a big goofy smile on his face. He was flashing some surf's-up symbols with both of his hands.

Tracey turned her head forward and smiled as she rode the wave all the way to the beach. Blaine hit the sand a couple seconds after his sister. Both twins expected everyone on the beach to be somewhat surprised at seeing a couple of twelve- year-olds surf a wave into the shore fully clothed and with backpacks and helmets on. But none of the twenty or so people who were there were paying any attention to them at all.

Instead, everyone was staring intently at an older man bent over something in the sand. As the twins got closer, they heard the murmuring crowd, "Sandcastle . . . must have taken hours . . . what happened to him . . . how can he . . . can you read the words?"

Blaine and Tracey laid their surfboards down and looked at each other. What was going on?

Somebody in the small crowd bravely shouted out toward

the old man, "Why are you doing that?"

"I just want to write a poem and make some sandcastles in peace. Please leave me be," the older man pleaded. He then turned in the direction of the twins and looked up. The Sassafras twins saw why everyone was staring, and it wasn't the amazing work he was creating. The man's face appeared . . . melted from the top of his head all the way down around his eyes, nose, mouth, and all the way to his neck. The man's skin was obviously scarred. It looked as though he had been burned badly. Additionally, his right ear was no longer there, and his entire right arm was burned from his shoulder all the way down to the fingertips on his right hand.

He was wearing a tank top and board shorts, so his scars were easy to see. He wasn't trying to hide them from anybody. There were tears streaming down his face as he looked back down and began writing in the sand once more.

Eventually, the waves began to lap away at the old man's work. The small crowd began to dissipate. People went back to their spots on the beach, resuming whatever activities they had presumably been doing before the Sassafras twins had arrived. However, Blaine and Tracy stayed close by. Moved with compassion, they moved closer to the burned man to see if there was anything they could do for him.

"Sir, my name is Tracey, and this is my brother Blaine. We were wondering if you need any help—can we do anything for you?" Tracey offered gently.

The man looked at the twins and began to tremble, either out of sorrow or anger. It was hard to tell. Then, instead of answering Tracey, he pulled off a backpack he was wearing, held it up with two hands in front of himself, and began speaking to it, "My darling. My cherished. I am so sorry."

The twins glanced at each other with an amount of alarm on their faces. Did he love his backpack enough to speak to it? Was he in his right mind?

THE SASSAFRAS SCIENCE ADVENTURES

"My darling, I tried," the man continued speaking to the backpack. "We did get to go surfing together . . . I built the sandcastle . . . I wrote a poem for you on the beach . . . but now the waves have washed most of it away . . . It's gone . . . just like you."

It was apparent to the twins now that the man's trembling was coming from sorrow. The man was not only a burn victim, but he seemed also to be rather old. Where the skin on his body wasn't burned, it was weathered and wrinkled. His movements were rather slow, and there were a couple of wisps of white hair clinging to the back of his head.

The twins looked down into the sand where the man had been building a sandcastle and writing something down. His work was being washed away by the waves. Nothing was recognizable as a sandcastle, but the twelve-year-olds could still read some of the words the man had written down.

"My darling, my . . . stars from their . . . compare not . . . brighter . . . to the end of the galaxy and beyond. Our love . . ." And that was all the twins could make out. The rest of the words were gone.

Tracey looked up at the man who was still clutching his backpack in front of himself, now mumbling to it. The compassion inside her was still stronger than any awkwardness she might be feeling.

"To the end of the galaxy and beyond. Our love . . ." Tracey quoted. "That's beautiful. What else did you want to write down?"

The man looked from his bag to Tracey. He stared at her for a moment and then clamored. "What else? What else? Do you two want me to write it down so you can watch it be washed away once more?"

The Sassafrases were taken aback. "No, no sir. We just . . ." Tracey stammered. "We thought maybe we could, I don't know, maybe you might want . . . we came over to . . . It looked to us like maybe . . . I liked the galaxy part."

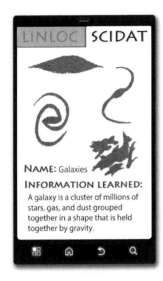

NAME: Galaxies

INFORMATION LEARNED:
A galaxy is a cluster of millions of stars, gas, and dust grouped together in a shape that is held together by gravity.

"Galaxy?" The man questioned Tracey. "A galaxy is a cluster of millions of stars, gas, and dust grouped together in a shape that is held together by gravity," his voice strengthened as he continued. "There are four main shapes of galaxies: spiral, elliptical, barred spiral, and irregular. You want me to write that down? You want me to write it down here in the sand so you can sweep it away with your feet?"

Both twins shook their heads "no" with emphasis, but the man dropped to his knees and started writing in the sand anyway.

"Spiral galaxies have a pinwheel shape with a bulge and thin disk in the center. They have lots of gas and dust with both young and old stars," the man wrote with his finger as fast as he could. "Elliptical galaxies have a round or oval shape with a bulge in the center but no disk. They have a little cool dust with both young and old stars."

The man spoke as he wrote, quoting word for word what the twins were watching him write in the sand.

"Barred spiral galaxies have a pinwheel shape with a bar of gas, dust, and stars running through the center. They usually have lots of gas and dust with both young and old stars." As the man continued to write, Blaine and Tracey were realizing that this was, in fact, their local expert: J.P. Jungos.

"Irregular galaxies contain a hodgepodge of shapes, basically anything that is not spiral or elliptical, meaning they have no regular shape. They normally have lots of gas and dust with both young and old stars." J.P. paused here and looked up at the twins.

"Do you want more? Do you want me to write down more that will be washed away?"

The twins shook their heads "no" again, but Jungos continued. "The galaxy within which the Earth is found is called the Milky Way. It is part of the Local Group cluster, which contains about thirty galaxies. Astronomers believe the Milky Way is spiral shaped."

"On clear nights, you can see bands and trails of light and dark up in the sky. These are actually clusters of stars and trails of dust within the bands of the spiral galaxy." Jungos paused and looked down at the water that had begun to swirl around his feet.

The twins watched as the ocean ate away at the last of the words J.P. had written. The burn victim began trembling again as he picked his backpack up out of the sand, clutched it tightly, and began speaking to it once more. "We always dreamed of coming to this beautiful place together, my cherished one," he said with tears. "This was supposed to be a poignant experience, but it's just . . ." He stopped and couldn't finish.

Blaine and Tracey did think their new local expert, J.P. Jungos, was a little strange, but clearly he was quite intelligent. He had moments of lucidity and moments where he seemed pulled back to the past. The old man was obviously a burn victim, but what had happened? And why were the backpack, sandcastle, and poem so important?

Towering Telescopes

The twins followed the poor old man at a distance as he slowly hobbled up the beach. They were at a loss for words and weren't sure how best to approach him again. They were certain he was their local expert for this location. If they were going to get any more SCIDAT, then he was going to be the one that would give it to them. Even more than that, the Sassafrases truly wanted to help him if they could. They didn't know what he really even needed, but they did know their hearts were full of empathy for him.

The sun began to set over the Pacific Ocean as the twelve-year-olds slowly walked up the beach behind their local expert. The fading light of day cast some of the most amazing colors across the sky the twins had ever seen. Deep oranges and pinks and purples stretched out over the gently moving, watery horizon like a masterpiece of a painting that only a prodigy could have rendered. Hawaii was such a beautiful place. Blaine and Tracey wished they could be enjoying it instead of feeling the lump in the pits of their stomachs on behalf of the poor man they were following.

They typed into their phones as they walked, putting in all the information about galaxies they'd learned. The twins found pictures in the archive app to add to the information. They would send this data to Uncle Cecil down in his basement, along with all the other data they were supposed to gather here, that is, if they could figure out a way to enter into conversation with their local expert again. They didn't know where he was going or if he would get frustrated with them again if they approached him or asked him another question.

Eventually, they reached what looked like a resort that had a restaurant on the beach. There were beautiful strands of lights strung over the sand. There were tables set up with crisp, white linen tablecloths that were topped neatly with flickering candles. There was gentle island music floating through the air, coming from the strings of some unseen instrument. The smell of savory meat being roasted over an open flame combined with the other sensory experiences to create an overall wonderful impression.

J.P. walked straight up to the hostess of the restaurant and asked for a table for two. The shock of seeing his burned face and arm formed her initial expression, but she recovered quickly. She grabbed a couple menus and then led him to an open table. The restaurant was already fairly full of patrons, mostly with what looked like couples who were having candlelit conversations, gazing into each other's eyes, enjoying each other's company.

As soon as J.P. was seated, most of the conversations ceased, and the eyes began gawking. They stared at Jungos's burns, and many began whispering rudely, like he couldn't hear them. The old man, however, seemed used to this reaction to his appearance. He ignored the stares and the whispers, took off his backpack, put it in the chair across from him, and began conversing with it again. Blaine and Tracey saw this and shook their heads slowly. They were concerned about the old man's state of mind, and they were also a little embarrassed for him.

Instead of following Jungos into the restaurant, the twins stayed outside its perimeter and took seats in the sand. They weren't sure what to do. They wanted to help their local expert, but they didn't know him. The first and only time they had approached him, it had seemed to make him frantic and frustrated. They didn't want that to happen again. So, the twins watched and listened as J.P. sat in the breezy restaurant, enjoying dinner and conversation with his backpack.

Eventually the strangeness and novelty of seeing a burn victim talk to an inanimate object wore off. The restaurant patrons went back to their conversations. For the Sassafras twins, the fatigue and exhaustion of days adventuring in space finally set in. They fell asleep right there on the beach next to the rhythmic swelling and sinking of the Pacific and under the stars and planets twinkling up in the solar system they had just explored.

After dreams of billionaires, galaxies, and asteroid-wielding rodents, the brother and sister woke up groggily. "Good morning, my cherished," they heard someone say. "How did you sleep with only the stars as your blanket?"

Once the twins got their eyes all the way open and sat up, they saw the voice they had heard was not speaking to them. It was the voice of J.P. Jungos, and he was still talking to his backpack. He was up the beach about thirty or forty yards from them, sitting up on a roll-out mat. It looked to the twins like he had slept overnight on the beach like they had.

"Now, my darling," J.P. crooned as he unzipped the backpack and reached for something inside. "It's time to start our hike up through the Hawaiian rainforest."

The local expert pulled out an item from his bag that was about a foot long and tubular in shape. He squinted his right eye and then put his left eye on one end of the tube. He then tilted his head back and pointed the tube away from the ocean and looked up like he was looking through it.

Tracey looked at Blaine. "We've got to try again," she said. "Even though he sorta got mad at us last time, we have to try to talk with him again, not only to get our SCIDAT data but also to see if we can help him in any way."

Blaine agreed.

The twelve-year-olds stood, dusted the sand off themselves, and then began walking gingerly over toward the old man.

"It's hard to see from this vantage point, my darling," he was saying. "But it's up there: the summit of Mauna Kea. And we're gonna make it all the way there together."

"Good morning . . . Mr. Jungos, right? . . . Mr. Jungos?" Tracey greeted him bashfully.

J.P. took his eye off of the gizmo he was gazing through and turned to look at the twins. "Oh, it's you two again. Blaine and Tracey, right?" He said through what the twins thought was probably a scowl.

Blaine and Tracey braced themselves for some shouting or maybe some crazed writing in the sand. Instead J.P. bent down and looked at both twins directly in their eyes. Facial expressions were a virtual impossibility for him because of the burn scars, but as the twelve- year-olds looked into the old man's eyes, they saw it clearly: kindness.

J.P. Jungos's eyes were shining with kindness.

"Did you two young'uns sleep the entire night out on the beach?" He sounded concerned.

The Sassafrases nodded, pleasantly shocked at how seemingly different J.P. was acting this morning.

"Yesterday . . . we're sorry . . . we didn't mean to . . ." Blaine started to try to explain, but he was cut off by the old man.

"Don't you worry about yesterday. And don't apologize. It is I who needs to apologize. I am on a journey that is important to me. That crowd and the oncoming tide about ruined the experience back there on the beach yesterday. I was upset, and I was definitely too harsh with you two. For that I am sorry."

The twins nodded with immediate forgiveness.

"Thankfully, mercies are new on this beautiful Hawaiian morning, and attitudes can change after a good night's sleep. My journey will continue." J.P. held the black tubular object out toward the Sassafrases. "Here, take a peek through this telescope, and see where my journey is going to take me."

"This is a telescope?" Blaine asked, taking the tube from the local expert and putting his eye up to it.

"It sure is," Jungos confirmed. "Telescopes are designed to make far away objects look closer."

The old man helped Blaine direct the telescope up into the mountains of the island. "This little one you are looking through now is pretty nice, but it's not even close to as powerful as the telescopes that I'm going to see up there on the summit of Mauna Kea."

"What's Mauna Kea?" Blaine asked, craning his head and squinting his eyes, still trying to get a good view through the telescope.

"Mauna Kea?" J.P. asked like he was surprised the twins didn't already know. "Why, Mauna Kea is this huge mountain you see right in front of you. Mauna Kea, also known as White Mountain, or more simply Mount Kea. It is home to the Mauna Kea Observatories."

"What kind of observatories?" Tracey asked, patiently waiting her turn to look through the telescope.

"The world's largest astronomical observatories," J.P. Jungos answered. "There are currently thirteen working telescopes, being operated by astronomers from eleven different countries. Nine of the telescopes are for optical and infrared astronomy. Three are for sub millimeter wavelength astronomy, and one is for radio astronomy."

"Ooooh, oooh! I think I see something," Blaine said excitedly, still gazing through the black, handheld telescope. "Whoa, it's way up there."

The local expert nodded in response to the enthusiastic boy. Then, he continued talking about telescopes. "In an optical telescope the more light that hits the eyepiece, the brighter and clearer the image will be. There are two main types of optical or light-collecting telescopes. Refractor telescopes use a curved mirror to collect light and send it to another mirror, which focuses it in front of the eyepiece that magnifies it. Reflector telescopes use a lens to collect light toward the eyepiece which magnifies the image."

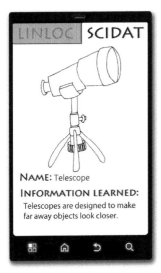

NAME: Telescope
INFORMATION LEARNED:
Telescopes are designed to make far away objects look closer.

Blaine now handed the handheld telescope to his sister. Tracey eagerly grabbed it and began her turn in trying to catch a glimpse of the summit of Mauna Kea.

"In addition to light, telescopes can also collect radio and energy waves," J.P. continued. "Radio telescopes collect radio waves in a dish and reflect them to a receiver where they are processed by a computer and turned into images."

"Hey, I think I can see it!" Tracey exclaimed. Then she asked, "That's an observatory? Way up there?"

Jungos nodded. "We have telescopes you can hold in your hand like the one you're looking through now. We have telescopes at observatories like the ones up at Mauna Kea. And we even have telescopes in space, for instance, the Hubble Telescope. The great thing about telescopes that are out in space is they don't have to deal with all the haze and pollution of our atmosphere so the images they send back are much clearer. And really, that's the same reason an observatory was built on the summit of Mauna Kea."

Tracey finished her turn looking through the telescope and handed it back to J.P. "So, the summit of Mauna Kea is kind of like space?" She asked.

"Mauna Kea is the highest island mountain in the world," Jungos explained. "It's a dormant volcano that rises almost fourteen thousand feet above sea level, which places its summit over forty percent of the world's atmosphere. The broad, rocky, barren summit might not feel exactly like every place in space, but I bet it's kind of like being on the moon or maybe Mars."

The twins shot each other smiling glances at the mention of Mars. "The exceptionally stable atmosphere above Mauna Kea is extremely dry. It's cloud free, and it's far away from city lights so that is what makes it kind of like space when it comes to using telescopes up there," the old man explained. "So like the Hubble Telescope can send us back pristine pictures from space, the telescopes up on Mauna Kea can capture amazing pictures as well because it's so clear up there on the summit."

Blaine and Tracey nodded.

"Did you know that the Hubble Telescope actually didn't work properly when it was first launched," the local expert continued. "Three years after it was sent into space, astronauts had to go out and repair it by hand. It now sends back clear pictures of our universe from the surface of the sun to the faintest galaxies, to the craters on many moons, and to the rings of Saturn. Yes, we have come a long way since Galileo. He was the first astronomer to make a telescope, which he used to discover those rings around Saturn. Pretty amazing to think about; isn't it?"

The twins nodded again, and then Blaine asked, "And now you're going to hike all the way up there to the summit of Mauna Kea on this important journey you're on?"

"Yes, I am, Blaine," J.P. Jungos affirmed, happily and resolutely. "And it's not just an important journey that I want to take. It's also a romantic journey."

"A romantic journey?" Tracey asked excitedly.

The old man nodded with bright eyes. To this, Tracey swooned and Blaine scrunched up his nose skeptically.

"Fifty years ago, I married the prettiest girl I'd ever seen." J.P. said this like it had happened yesterday, not a long time ago. "I was working on a ranch in Idaho, and she was working for the summer down at the hardware store. The first time I walked in and saw her, my heart did such a somersault that it nearly flipped right out of my chest. Eventually, after a few failed attempts, I finally worked up enough courage to speak to her. She was kind enough to speak back to me, and we fell in love almost immediately. We were married within weeks, which many thought was crazy, but I knew I'd found the treasure of all treasures in her. We were young. We were poor. But we were in love."

"But what about the journey you're talking about?" Blaine asked, getting a little impatient with all the mushy stuff.

"Hold your horses, little tyke. I'm getting to that," J.P. said with a chuckle. "We had so little money at the beginning that we weren't even able to go on a honeymoon," the man continued. "Our dream was always to go to Hawaii together where we could surf, enjoy the beach, and even hike all the way to the summit of Mauna Kea, where we heard they were going to build the world's biggest and best observatory, but . . . but . . ."

The joy in J.P.'s voice ebbed away and was replaced by sorrow. He looked like he was going to explain, but then suddenly his eyes drifted toward the ocean, and his voice was silenced.

CHAPTER 9: HAWAIIAN DREAMS AND SIGHTINGS

Satellites Switchbacks

It had taken him awhile, but Thaddaeus Wazeezy had finally managed to get his spacecraft, *Thad-1*, back into the Earth's atmosphere. For some reason, he hadn't been able to gain a connection with Adrianna Archer on his headset. So, when he had gotten back into the atmosphere, it had taken a long time to find his laboratory. There must still be some kind of malfunction or glitch in the communications system. Even so, at this moment he was bringing his sleek, black spaceship to a sliding stop inside his lab.

He smiled as he unclicked his safety harness and opened the door of the craft to get out. His heart was still full of joy, light and goodwill, and he was ready to share that goodwill along with his new purpose and vision with Adrianna and all of these white lab coat-clad scientists that were scurrying his way even now. After choosing to do the right thing in helping save that lost astronaut, his trajectory in life had changed. He was sure of it.

No longer would he seek revenge on Cecil Sassafras. Instead, he would seek to shower humankind with acts of kindness. He stepped out of *Thad-1* and took his Dark Cape helmet off, showcasing the smile he was sporting.

Some of his scientists saw the uncustomary smile and became confused because of it. Most seemed to be avoiding any and all eye contact with him and continued to scamper around, trying to look busy.

The Man With No Eyebrows chuckled and was happy to see all these little guys running around, but they weren't who he wanted to see. Where was Adrianna?

Where was the mind of their local expert? Blaine and Tracey wondered as they waited for J.P. to continue his story. Instead, he was staring out at the waves with a faraway look in his eyes. The early morning sun glistened on the tears that were streaming down his face. The memory he was reliving must have been painful.

Tracey broke the silence by gently asking, "Mr. Jungos, can we get you anything?"

J.P. startled, waking up from the memory he was reliving. He wiped the tears from his face, stared down at his backpack, and cleared his throat. "I need to go there. I need to finish what we started together."

Tracey and Blaine looked at each other—what did he mean?

Where did their local expert want to go, and what did he mean by "started together?" Was he talking to them? They didn't think so because it seemed as if he was talking to his backpack

"Where do you need to go, Mr. Jungos?" Blaine asked.

Jungos turned towards their direction and blinked a few times as if he were seeing them for the first time in a long time. "To the summit of Mauna Kea to look through the telescopes at the observatory there. Would you two like to join us on the journey?"

Blaine and Tracy nodded as they both replied, "Yes."

"Wonderful!" J.P. exclaimed to the twins before he turned back to the backpack and said, "Did you hear that, my darling? These lovely children are going to join us on our hike."

The Sassafras twins stood up, brushed the sand off, and gathered their things. At the same time, J.P. carefully slung his beloved backpack over his shoulders and then turned to face the mountain. His sorrow seemingly evaporated. "It's time to start the journey up to the Mauna Kea Observatories. Are you two ready?"

The twins nodded with smiles of their own. They followed their local expert as he left the sand of the beach and headed up into the green of the forest.

The terrain the old man chose was immediately steep, but it was also immediately beautiful. Just as last night's Hawaiian sunset had been full of color, this Hawaiian forest was also bursting with an amazing array of colors. From the flowers that were showcasing their petals to the birds that were flying to and from different perches, this forest was blooming and moving and alive with color. And the green it offered was not simply green but green that came to the senses through different shades and shapes, all deep and wonderful.

As they continued to hike up through the beauty, the story about J.P. and his wife was in the forefront of Tracey's mind. The old man's story had been cut off by the pain of the memory, but

Tracey was hoping their local expert would be willing to finish it as they hiked the trail. "Mr. Jungos? What happened with your wife? Were you two ever able to make it to Hawaii together?" Tracey asked respectfully.

Upon hearing Tracey's question, J.P. slowly stopped his movement. He turned, looked at the twins, and although his entire face was deformed because of the burn scars, Blaine and Tracey could see sorrow all over it.

"No," he answered. "I lost her."

Upon this response, the twins became silent and still. Empathy flooded their hearts. Blaine wanted to ask questions of "how" and "why." Tracey wanted to let her tear ducts open up, but instead the two twelve-year-olds kept silent and waited for their local expert to say the next word.

J.P. stood still for several long moments, and then as his trembling returned, he said it again. "I lost her."

The old man gulped painfully with closed eyes. The trembling turned to shaking, and through his shut eyes, the tears began to come. He tried to explain. "There was a fire . . . in our home . . . I knew that she was upstairs sleeping so I rushed up and tried to . . . but it was too late . . . The support of the first floor had already burned away so the second floor was collapsing, and . . . I was able to reach out my right hand and grab her hand, but . . . I held on for as long as I could . . . She was falling . . . She was slipping . . . I held on for as long as I could . . . Even as the flames consumed my face and my right arm, I held on, but . . . the entire second floor gave way . . . Our hands were jerked apart. I was thrown in one direction . . . and she in another . . . I lost her." J.P.'s shaking brought him down to his knees.

Upon hearing this dear man tell his story, Tracey could hold her emotion in no longer. She began sobbing. Blaine even began crying. The Sassafras twins rushed over and wrapped J.P. Jungos up in a big hug. J.P. hugged them back, appreciative for the twelve-year-olds' kindness.

After a good, long cry, the three continued their trek up Mauna Kea. J.P. Jungos led the way, climbing steps with labored consistency. He was followed by Blaine, and then came Tracey.

"So that's what makes this journey so important, right?" Blaine broke the silence. "You were going to do this hike with your wife, weren't you?"

J.P. nodded in confirmation.

"And romantic," Tracey added, smiling. "Important and romantic."

Blaine scrunched up his nose a little bit again at the thought of romance, but it wasn't that bad. Love, real, true, sacrificial love, like J.P. Jungos had for his wife was definitely a good thing. Actually, that kind of love was a great thing.

Blaine did wonder, though, if maybe the traumatic experience of the fire had done more than physical damage to J.P. Maybe the reason he was always talking to his backpack was because the loss of his beloved wife was too much for him to bear. Maybe conversing with the backpack had become some kind of coping mechanism. Whatever the reason, it wasn't bothering Blaine anymore.

The trail remained steep as the group of three gained altitude quickly. The twins could feel it more in their legs than in their lungs at this point, but even with all the rigorous climbing, they felt good. Not only did the blooming forest around them have an ever-present beauty that was enthralling, but they were also still pretty overwhelmed with joy to be on Earth again. Sure, floating around in space had been fun, and they were grateful for the opportunity, but they liked having their feet firmly planted on their home planet.

Jungos kept moving forward ahead of them, his mood now joyful and light, despite a gradual growing difficulty with his breathing and movement. "Blaine! Tracey! Look!" He shouted and pointed up ahead. "A rainbow!"

The Sassafras twins raised their eyes from the trail to the sky and saw the sparkling arch of refractive color.

"Whoa," Blaine exclaimed.

"Beautiful!" Tracey said.

It was no small, ordinary, barely visible rainbow. It was a huge, brilliant ribbon of color that was seemingly shooting out of the ground before them. It arched way up into the sky and then disappeared somewhere higher up the mountain.

"Let's see if we can find the other end of it!" J.P. shouted as giddy as a child. Then, with a shot of energy to his steps, he glided up through the green of the forest, looking for the end of the rainbow.

Blaine and Tracey looked at each other, shrugged, smiled, and then took off up the trail after their local expert. Yes, he talked to his backpack. Yes, he chased the ends of rainbows. Yes, he was a burn victim with terrible scars. The twins liked him anyway, and they were perfectly happy following this old man to the rainbow's end if that's where he wanted to go.

The three pushed upward, dancing around trees, swatting through bushes, and maneuvering every large rise and short fall the mountain had to offer. The rainbow remained visible, yet elusive for quite a long time. Then it eventually faded away into the beauty and color of Mauna Kea. When it became apparent that the rainbow was truly gone, J.P. Jungos stopped and sat down. At first, the twins thought maybe he was discouraged. However, when they reached his spot, they found him laughing and happy.

"We are doing it, my darling," he spoke to the backpack. "We are living the dream! Did you see that rainbow? Did you see the brilliance of its colors and the height of its arch? Ha, ha, we didn't find the end, but it sure was fun trying; was it not?"

J.P. gave the backpack a big hug, then set it down, and opened it up. From it, he pulled out a pen and a piece of paper. He made one simple mark on the paper, then quickly put it back in the bag, and zipped it back up. The old man looked at the twins and then stood back to his feet.

"Keep going?" He asked happily.

The resilient twins nodded yes. The group hiked and after hours of gaining altitude, the three mountain climbers and rainbowhunters finally stopped for a good, long rest. J.P. shared some snacks he had with the twins. The old man also pulled out a couple hammocks from his backpack.

"I have an extra," he offered, tossing the tightly packed hammock in Blaine's direction. "You'll have to share it with your sister so it may not be the most comfortable night of your lives. But it's better than sleeping on the ground."

The Sassafrases found that the hammock was actually long enough for them to sleep in end to end with their heads on opposite sides and their feet touching in the middle. The two set their hanging bed up a few yards away from J.P.'s spot. He was already gently snoring before they even climbed in. The twelve-year-olds laid their weary heads to rest and within minutes were fast asleep as they slightly swayed back and forth under a starry sky.

"The word 'satellite' comes from the Latin word for attendant," J.P. Jungos was saying as he continued to lead the way up the mountain the next morning. "A satellite is technically an object that orbits something bigger than itself. For instance, the moon is a natural satellite of the Earth. But when talking about satellites, typically man-made machines are being referred to."

The Sassafras twins nodded as they huffed and puffed, hiking up behind their local expert. They had woken up early this morning and continued their climb of Mauna Kea before the sun had even come up. It was well up into the sky now, casting bright light on everything around them. And although the twins' legs were sore, and their lungs were burning, there was an excitement in the air because they were learning science. In addition to that, they were also about to reach the Mauna Kea Observatory's Visitor Center. It was situated below the tree line at 9300 feet. And according to Jungos, it had all kinds of high-quality pictures and interactive information about astronomy, including satellites, which he was talking about right now.

"There are thousands of man-made satellites out there," J.P. informed, huffing and puffing. "Some look down on our planet, and some look out into space as they orbit the Earth. Some are working and operational, and some are not. Those that are not working are called 'space litter' or 'space debris.'"

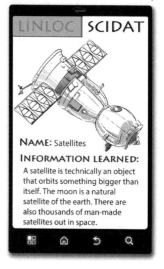

NAME: Satellites
INFORMATION LEARNED:
A satellite is technically an object that orbits something bigger than itself. The moon is a natural satellite of the earth. There are also thousands of man-made satellites out in space.

"How many different kinds of man-made satellites are there?" Blaine, who was in the back of the line today, asked.

"Hmmm, let me think," J.P. mused as he stopped for a break and tried to catch his breath. "I guess there are about five main types. You've got communication satellites, which are satellites that help capture and transfer radio waves. There are navigation satellites that allow us to establish our position on Earth, that is, Global Positioning System, or G.P.S. There are resource satellites that take pictures of the Earth's natural resources for scientists to turn into maps. And there are weather satellites that help us learn about and forecast the weather. Then there are military satellites that are used for communication, navigation, and other tasks by the different militaries of the world."

The twins nodded, made mental notes of the SCIDAT, and

then when their elderly local expert was ready, they started hiking uphill again, toward the visitor center.

Evan DeBlose chuckled and nodded his head proudly as he watched his secret service partner furiously tapping around on the computer and other instruments here in the cockpit of *Dauntless-12*. Sure, the little man was kind of nervous, fast paced, and a bit squeaky, but he was also talented, capable, and brave. This was Q-Tip's first mission into space. It had not been an easy mission and had lasted days longer than expected. But even through all of this, Evan had watched Q-Tip come through with flying colors.

"Oh! Oh! Oh! Aha! Aha!" Q-Tip squeak-shouted as he took a short break from punching on the computer. "It looks like . . . I think it's . . . it is! It's operational! Our satellite is up and running! We did it! We fixed it!"

The two Swiss Secret Service agents flashed huge, teeth-baring smiles, then reached out, and gave each other an elated, low-gravity high five. They had spent days attempting to fix the satellite that Adrianna Archer had sabotaged, and they had finally done it! In the process, they had nearly been blown to smithereens by the mysterious *Thad-1* vessel. They'd made countless space walks. They had dropped and lost several of their tools out in space. But in the end, it looked like they had accomplished the task they had launched into space to do.

They had fixed the broken satellite by hand, and it was again operational. They could now use it to pinpoint Archer's location along with Yuroslav Bogdanovich's location. Maybe they could even use it to figure out who that despicable fellow in *Thad-1* had been.

Startling Space Probes

"She what?" Thaddaeus screamed.

"She . . . she . . . she . . . quit and she left," the shaking little scientist repeated, barely audibly.

Thaddaeus, who was still in his Dark Cape suit, used both of his gloved hands to grab the sniveling man by the collar of his white lab coat and pick him up off the ground. He glared at the man from behind his dark-tinted visor as the man's feet dangled helplessly in midair. All the goodwill and kindness that was in his heart had immediately left with the news one of the little minion scientists had confirmed.

"What do you mean she quit and left?" The eyebrow-less man asked, still screaming.

"She . . . she just quit . . . and then she left," the little scientist restated.

Thaddaeus let go of the man and then stomped off in no particular direction. He had been looking for Adrianna Archer ever since he had gotten back to the lab from space, but she was nowhere to be found. He had waited overnight for her to turn up and had approached a countless number of his scientists asking about Archer's whereabouts, but she had not shown up.

Nobody seemed to know anything. His frustration had grown and grown, overtaking and replacing the positivity he had been feeling after he had saved the astronaut. But now he had his answer.

Adrianna had quit and left! How was that possible? Adrianna was loyal and true. She would never quit and leave; would she? He had so many future plans that included her. She made him feel important, capable, and strong. She just couldn't be gone—he needed her.

He walked around a corner and literally bumped into a small cluster of his scientists. He grabbed one of them before he could scurry off and get away.

"Satellites!" He shouted at the one he had caught. "Come help me access our satellites! I want to find Adrianna Archer, and I want to find her now!"

There had indeed been some cool pictures and information regarding satellites at the Mauna Kea Observatories Visitor's Center. The Sassafras twins were enjoying themselves, that was, until a small crowd being led by a tour guide entered and joined them in the center. It was immediately apparent the group leader was in a cranky mood, and the hot and sweaty group looked more than ready to be done with their tour.

"Okay people, this is the last stop of the tour. Thank goodness—after this, we will get loaded back up in the van, and I will finally get to take you back to the base of the mountain," the guide paused, took a deep breath, and continued to address the group. "The place we are in now is the visitor's center, and it is—"

The man suddenly stopped when he spotted J.P. and the twins. "Excuse me? What are the three of you doing here? This building is supposed to be closed for my private tour. I am the leading resident astronomer. How did you three even get up here? And what's wrong you, sir?" The scientist directed his last question at J.P.

He stared at Jungos as he continued. "I'm sorry to say it, but you look too . . . umm . . . handi . . . gro . . . old . . . You look too old to be up here."

The widower was used to people gawking and using thoughtless words in his presence. He didn't say a thing in response. Instead, he dipped his head and clutched his backpack tighter to his body.

The Sassafras twins, however, couldn't stand by and say nothing. "You shouldn't talk to him like that," Tracey declared to the astronomer. "Mr. Jungos is trying to complete a journey that he and his deceased wife dreamed about taking together."

"Yeah!" Blaine added for emphasis.

"Plus," Tracey continued boldly. "The sign on the door said, 'Welcome, we're open!'"

"I know what that sign says," the cranky scientist growled. "But I say, not everyone is welcome. We can't just let anybody walk in here. What if this man has malicious intentions? What if he wants to vandalize or steal? What if he is really a monster?"

"A monster?" Blaine repeated in disbelief.

"Yes, a monster—just look at him!" the astronomer spat out as he pointed toward J.P.

The Sassafras twins were finding it hard to believe that this tour-guide-astronomer felt it was okay to behave so rudely. And by the looks on their faces, the tour group the man was leading agreed with the twins.

"He's not a monster," Tracey said calmly. "He is a brilliant and kind man who happens to have scars from burns on his face and arms."

"That may be the case, but he needs to leave," the rude astronomer replied.

Blaine sighed in exasperation at the man's insolence but then folded his hands in front of him and tried a more refined approach,

"Sir, like me, you are a man of science, right?"

The man looked at the twelve-year-old boy in front of him in bewilderment. Tracey also looked at her brother with bewilderment mixed with amusement. What was Blaine doing?

"As a man of science," Blaine continued, "let us look at this matter scientifically. Factually, we know that burn scars usually only affect the external appearance of a victim and have no bearing on the—"

"Stop talking," the now angry scientist interrupted Blaine. "Save your sentiments for the base of this mountain because that's where you are going. All three of you! Right now!"

"But . . . but . . ."

"No buts! Step outside the visitor's center right now. Get in my vehicle. I am going to drive you down!"

At this point, J.P. Jungos started to mutter. "My . . . my . . . darling . . . I'm so . . . sorry . . . We didn't quite . . . make it." He was trying to talk to his backpack in between labored breaths.

The Sassafras twins wondered if maybe the elderly man's body was not dealing so well with the altitude. The tour guide, however, was not concerned about anyone's physical or emotional state. He was only concerned with their locational state. He was lumbering toward them right now as if he were going to move all three of them by force.

Tracey glared at the mean scientist in disbelief. Blaine jumped into a defensive karate stance, although he, in fact, had never actually studied the art of karate. Before any kind of physical altercation went down, the door to the visitor's center burst open, and another scientist walked in. The man was taller, fitter, and thankfully, kinder looking than the cranky astronomer.

"Peter Karko!" He declared with authority. "What in the world are you doing?"

Peter Karko, evidently this was the name of the tour-guide-astronomer, stopped his advancement toward the three and turned to look at the other scientist. "I'm, I'm getting this old man and these two kids out of my . . . this center."

"Your center?" The new scientist asked, aghast. "Peter, you . . ."

The man looked like he was about to blast Peter with his words, but instead, he took a breath, gathered himself, and then said in a controlled voice, "Peter, you left the observatories without telling anyone, and no one knew where you were. I needed you to run a test on Keck II, and you were nowhere to be found."

"But my cousin Jimmy called me and told me . . . these people were coming and . . . that they would pay good money for a tour . . . and then this strange-looking man and these kids were . . ."

"Peter, this man is obviously a burn victim, and he and his friends have every right to be on this island, this mountain, and here at this visitor's center. Frankly, Peter, I believe it's you who no longer has the right to be here."

"What?" the misguided astronomer now asked, aghast.

"Peter," the man said, "you're fired."

"What?"

"You're fired."

"You can't fire me."

"I certainly can. And as your supervisor, that's exactly what I'm doing. Peter, you're fired. You can go back up to the observatories, gather your things, and then you need to go down, call that cousin of yours, and leave this area. I'm sorry, Peter, but your services are no longer needed here on Mauna Kea."

Surprisingly, without any more argument, Peter Karko dropped his head, slumped his shoulders, and shuffled slowly out of the building. When he was gone, the supervisory scientist made his way over to the Sassafrases and their local expert, who was still breathing heavily.

"Hello. My name is Dr. Ellison Ocampo. I'm so sorry that my former employee treated you with such contempt. Let me now give you a proper welcome to the Mauna Kea Visitor's Center."

"Thank you," the twins responded in unison.

"I would also be happy to take the three of you up to the observatories and give you a tour if that's something you'd be interested in doing."

The twins nodded and then looked at J.P. Jungos, who was still trembling and clutching his backpack. The old man looked like he might now be smiling. Also tears were forming in the corners of his eyes.

"Thank you so much, Dr. Ocampo," he said gratefully. "We would love to go up to the observatories with you."

Ellison then turned and extended the same offer to the group Peter had been guiding. They looked grateful and relieved as they nodded to accept Dr. Ocampo's offer of a proper tour.

Later in the evening after the tour, J.P. had perked up a bit. He started to share about space probes with Blaine and Tracey, "Space probes are similar to man-made satellites . . . except they travel throughout space . . . and don't just orbit the Earth," J.P. breathing seemed to be a bit labored, and the twins were glad they were taking a break, resting on the cool grass.

There no longer seemed to be any sorrow in the old man's voice—only joy, fulfillment, and peace. He had reached the summit at Mauna Kea. Here he was at the observatories, a place he had been waiting fifty years to visit. He had finished all that he and his wife had planned to do so many years ago.

Dr. Ellison Ocampo had driven the three from the visitor's center up to the observatories in his Jeep, and then he'd given them an interesting and informative tour of the world class facilities. Dr. Ocampo answered every question J.P. had and shown him everything he wanted to see. The kind astronomer has also offered to assist the elderly man anytime he looked to be physically struggling. After their tour was over, he generously allowed the widower to freely roam the observatory grounds, along with the twins, to his heart's content. Dr. Ocampo had promised to return in an hour or so to take them down off the mountain in his vehicle.

The three had visited most of the twelve facilities that housed the thirteen telescopes on Mauna Kea, and during their gazing through the last telescope, J.P. was sure they had spotted a space probe, which was an exciting sighting indeed. This had led him to give the information he knew about probes, which the twins were eager to hear.

"Space probes are unmanned spacecraft . . . These probes typically carry cameras and send back pictures of the . . . distant places they visit," Jungos continued as he and the twins gazed over terrain that looked like a moonscape in between the large, white buildings that housed the telescopes up higher on Mauna Kea's summit. "Space probes have helped scientists . . . learn about the sun, planets in our solar system, asteroids, comets . . . black holes, and more," the Sassafrases' local expert informed.

"Space probes have visited . . . all the planets in our solar system," the widower continued. "Some have even landed . . . on those planets. Voyager I and Voyager II . . . are space probes that have gone further . . . than any manned spacecraft have gone before.

NAME: Space Probes

INFORMATION LEARNED: Space probes are unmanned spacecraft These probes typically carry cameras and send back pictures of the distant places they visit.

The first space probe, Sputnik I . . . was launched out into space by the Soviet Union . . . in 1957. The United States . . . launched its first space probe, Explorer I . . . a year later."

"That is fascinating, Mr. Jungos. But are you okay? Do you need anything?" Tracey asked gently.

"I am fine. I have finished all that I set out to do as best as I could. And now, I want to sit here and rest a bit. Will you both sit with me as we enjoy the amazing sky?" J.P. Jungos replied.

Blaine and Tracey nodded their affirmations.

J.P. leaned his head back against the wall and gazed out into the clear, night sky that was brilliantly ablaze with millions of stars. An evening breeze swept up and across the flat, rocky landscape of the summit and caressed the three with a calming pace as it gently whipped at the children's light brown hair and the old man's whisps of white hair. It was so calm, and the stars were so bright that it almost made Blaine and Tracey feel like they were floating out in space again with the cosmos swirling all around them.

J.P. Jungos let out a long, satisfied sigh, and then with slow, trembling hands, he reached over, opened his backpack, and pulled out a piece of paper. The twins were pretty sure they'd seen this paper earlier in the day. J.P. made another mark on it, then the local expert reached in his backpack again and now carefully and almost reverently pulled out an ornamented jar of some kind. He set it down on the ground, looked at it fondly, rested a gentle hand on top of it, and then let his gaze drift back out into the night sky.

"My darling, my cherished . . . our love shines brighter than the constellations," the old man's breathing was still a bit labored. The Sassafras twins were worried, but they were glad to hear how peacefully he spoke, as though he were walking in a dream.

"The stars as a throng; they sing, they shine, from their locations far and wide, out in the expanse of space," Jungos said dreamily.

Tracey excitedly, yet quietly nudged her brother. "Blaine, I think he may be quoting that poem he had written on the beach when we first met him!"

Blaine nodded, thinking his sister was right.

"But their beauty and grandeur compare not to the love we possess. Our love shines brighter than a million exploding supernovas. To the end of the galaxy and beyond our love shines. My darling, ny cherished, how our love shines!" J.P. Jungos, the burn victim, the victor, the romantic, the brilliant man of science finished his poem with a burst of energy and joyful exclamation. He then leaned his head back against the wall of the building once more, breathed deeply one more time, and closed his eyes.

Blaine and Tracey looked through star-cast light toward the man, and even though his face was deformed because of the scars, the twins thought they could actually see a smile on it. The Sassafrases smiled and leaned their heads back against the wall of the big, white building as well. They were thankful for J.P. Jungos, their local expert at this beautiful location. They were thankful for his eccentricity, heroism, and romanticism. They were also thankful for all the scientific information he had imparted on them, and they were ready and listening if he wanted to impart more.

The twelve-year-olds kept smiling and kept waiting, but evidently Mr. J.P. Jungos was content to be done. His eyes remained closed. His smile stayed on his face, and he said no more. Blaine and Tracey looked back out toward the sky thinking about everything from J.P.'s poem to space probes to telescopes.

After a few minutes, the twins heard the sound of shoes crunching over rocks and looked over to see Dr. Ellison Ocampo walking up to join them. The doctor of astronomy smiled kindly as he approached and joined the three seated on the ground, leaning his back up against the wall.

"It sure is beautiful, isn't it?" he offered.

The twins nodded.

"Did the three of you get to see everything you wanted to see?"

Blaine and Tracey both paused and waited for J.P. to answer, but when they looked over, his eyes were closed, and it looked like their local expert had gone to sleep. Blaine gave a response. "I think so. We got to see most of the telescopes."

Dr. Ocampo nodded, then reached over, and put a hand on J.P.'s shoulder. "I am so glad that you realized your dream of coming up here, my friend," Ellison said. "I hope it was everything you hoped it would be."

Instead of responding in any way, J.P. Jungos remained silent.

"Mr. Jungos?" Dr. Ocampo asked. "Mr. Jungos, are you okay?"

The twins looked at their silent local expert with a sudden tinge of fear.

"J.P., can you hear me? Are you okay?" Ellison leaned in closer to examine the old man. Then came words that Blaine and Tracey were not prepared to hear. "Oh, no, he's not breathing."

CHAPTER 10: THE NATIONAL AIR AND SPACE MUSEUM

Solar Gumballs

Completely content and full of years, J.P. Jungos died peacefully on the summit of Mauna Kea. The brave man had accomplished everything he had set out to do

The Sassafras twins sorrowfully began gathering their local expert's things, and when they did, they found two items that filled them with awe and helped everything make sense. The piece of paper Blaine and Tracey had seen J.P. marking on was a list—a list of things to do that were now all checked off.

Things to do in Hawaii

✓ Surf
✓ Build sand castles
✓ Write a poem in the sand
✓ Have a candle-lit dinner on the beach
✓ Sleep under the stars
✓ Hike up through the rainforest
✓ Find the end of a rainbow
✓ Make it to the summit of Mauna Kea to stare at the galaxies through the observatory's telescopes

The second item in the pack was the ornamented jar. The twins found that it was actually an urn filled with the ashes of J.P.'s beloved wife. J.P. had not been talking to his backpack. He was talking to his wife. He was hugging the urn that held his darling's ashes. The widower had not been making the journey to the summit of Mauna Kea alone. As young newlyweds, they had dreamed of doing everything on the list together. J.P. Jungos had spent all the strength and energy left in his frail body to ensure that the list was completed, that the journey was finished, and that he and his darling had done it together. To the end of the galaxies and beyond, their love had shined. The Sassafras twins were grief-stricken that their local expert had passed away, but in the end, it was a fitting conclusion to a beautiful love story.

Several hours later, Blaine and Tracey found themselves traveling through a swirling tunnel of light. As they zipped along the familiar invisible lines, they couldn't help but wonder if J.P. Jungos's passing from life had gone something like this. They hoped so, and they smiled as they pictured J.P. without his burn scars being reunited with his lovely wife.

The twins landed with a jerk. Their sightless, strengthless, tingling bodies slumped down, automatically unclipped from the lines. After they had entered all their pictures and SCIDAT about galaxies, telescopes, satellites, and space probes, they found on the LINLOC app that they would next be zipping to longitude -77° 1' 12.23", latitude +38° 53' 14.95", which would land them in Washington D.C. Here they would be studying the topics of the sun, the day/night cycle, the moon, and eclipses with a local

LINLOC SCIDAT

LOCATION: Washington, D.C.
CONTACT: Paul Sims
LATITUDE: +38° 53' 14.95"   **LONGITUDE:** -77° 1' 12.23"

INFORMATION NEEDED ON:
The Sun, The Day/Night Cycle, The Moon, Eclipses

expert named Paul Sims.

The Sassafrases' senses normalized, but their emotional senses did not. Something was wrong. They had not landed in Washington D.C. They had somehow landed back in space!

By the looks of it, they were back inside the International Space Station! Fear shook them because they knew they could not survive up here without their space suits on.

Tracey reached out and began grabbing at the instrumentation on the walls of the space pod they had landed in. Blaine began desperately gulping for fresh air.

"Tracey!" He shouted in between breaths. "How is this possible? The zip lines aren't supposed to be able to zip us outside the Earth's atmosphere! How did we get ba—"

"Blaine," Tracey interrupted, but her brother didn't stop.

"Ba . . . back out . . . you know . . . back out . . . here in space! We're . . . not going to . . . make it out . . . here!

"Blaine," Tracey tried again, but still her brother didn't stop.

"We're . . . we're . . . at any second . . . we're going to . . ."

"Blaine!" Tracey shouted emphatically.

"What?" The male Sassafras asked incredulously. "Blaine, we're not floating."

"Yeah, but we're . . . wait, we're not floating . . . so that means we're . . ."

"Not actually in space," Tracey finished for her brother, and then she pointed out of the space pod's window. "Look."

Blaine looked, and he did not see stars or planets or astronauts out on spacewalks. He saw . . . schoolchildren?

"Blaine, we didn't land in space. I think we landed in . . . a museum."

Blaine and Tracey both stood to their feet and made their way toward a circular-shaped open doorway they were just now seeing. The twelve-year-olds stepped out of the space pod and into a large and wide room that was filled with people, young and old. There were classes of schoolchildren. There were families and individuals all slowly walking around, quietly chattering and observing one of the coolest-looking museums the Sassafras twins had ever seen.

There were all kinds of different aircraft hanging from the ceiling. There were huge missiles protruding up in the center of the room. There were multiple exhibits with comparatively smaller items such as engines, instrumentation, flight equipment, and more. Blaine and Tracey looked back and saw that it was not the International Space Station they had stepped out of, but instead it was something titled Spacelab Module.

Blaine was about to make another comment, but he was interrupted by a voice that stood out, shouting louder than all others in the crowd. "But it looks like a giant, yellow gumball!" A little girl's voice exclaimed.

"Yes, yes, I guess it does," a man's voice responded. "But it's actually a giant ball of exploding gas, also known as the fiery star at the center of our solar system."

THE SASSAFRAS SCIENCE ADVENTURES

The Sassafras twins moved over to where the voices were coming from and saw a little girl holding hands with a woman, presumably her mother, talking to a man who looked like he worked for the museum. He was pointing up to a giant solar system mobile that was hanging from the ceiling.

The girl, who looked to be six or seven, was wearing a baggy T-shirt, a polka-dot skirt and untied sneakers. She continued, talking loudly, "You're sure it's not a gumball? 'Cause, mister, it looks like a gumball to me—a ginormous gumball with a bunch of other gumballs floating all around it."

The mother squeezed her daughter's hand gently and laughed nervously. "Honey, quiet down a bit and let the nice man tell us all about that giant yellow . . . gumball . . . solar . . . thing."

The little girl looked at her mother and smiled and nodded.

"That giant yellow gumball solar thing in the center of all those other floating gumball solar things is called the sun," the man informed with the girl listening eagerly. "It is so big that a million of our Earths could fit inside of it."

"Wowie!" the girl exclaimed.

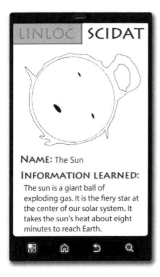

NAME: The Sun
INFORMATION LEARNED:
The sun is a giant ball of exploding gas. It is the fiery star at the center of our solar system. It takes the sun's heat about eight minutes to reach Earth.

"And the sun is really hot," the man continued. "It is over ten thousand degrees Fahrenheit. It takes the sun's heat about eight minutes to reach Earth. Life has the ability to exist on Earth because we are just the right distance from the sun. In addition to light and heat, the sun sends out a stream of particles known as solar winds. When these particles pass by the North and South poles, they can make the surrounding air in the atmosphere glow red, blue, green, and purple. This phenomenon is known as the Aurora Borealis at the North Pole and the Aurora Australis at the South Pole."

As the man explained this, he pointed above the solar system mobile, where projected lights were recreating an aurora-like sky on the ceiling.

"Wowie, Mister!" The girl exclaimed. "That's beautimus! It looks like a magical, upside-down, cotton candy pond!"

The twins chuckled at the girl's imaginative descriptions.

The man from the museum also laughed before continuing, "We have sent out space probes, Ulysses, SoHo, and TRACE, to study the sun, so we know the surface of the sun is constantly in motion. Because of this, there are often darker or cooler spots that we call sunspots. There are also whiter or hotter spots called faculae."

The girl jumped up and down in excited understanding.

"Another feature on the surface of the sun is called a prominence. This is a place where a mass of burning gas sweeps up, almost like a leaping flame of fire. Solar flares are similar to prominences except for the fact they travel much farther from the surface of the sun."

Now more projected light shined on the yellow ball representing the sun, making it look like the model had moving dark spots, light spots, prominences, and sun flares. This received another spirited "wowie" from the girl.

The man pulled out a museum-branded pair of kid-size sunglasses from his back pocket and handed them to her. Her mother nodded that it was okay to take them, so she energetically grabbed them and put them on.

"It is dangerous to look directly at the sun," he said. "Not even sunglasses can protect our eyes from the damage the sun could do if we were to look directly at it. But I thought you might like a pair of these to view the rest of the museum through."

The girl gave a couple big, happy nods to the man, then looked at her mother, and pulled at her hand. "C'mon, Mom! Let's go see what's next!"

The mother mouthed a silent "thank-you" to the museum worker as she was pulled off to another exhibit by her joyous, skipping, sunglasses-wearing daughter. The Sassafras twins smiled as they stepped forward to introduce themselves to the museum representative to see if maybe he was their local expert.

However, before they could get their names out of their mouths, someone else shouted them out. "Blaine! Tracey! Cutiefrasses! You're here!"

The twins looked to their right where the excited voice had come from none other than Summer Beach who was running toward them with outstretched arms ready to engulf them in a laughing, jumping dance-hug. The twelve-year-olds received the hug and even hugged back a little themselves, but they were confused—what was Summer doing here?

The man from the museum witnessed the dance-hug and then stepped forward with acknowledgment on his face. "Summer T. Beach," he said with a big smile. "So nice to see you again, old friend."

Summer dropped the twins out of the hug they were in, turned, and then wrapped the man up in a hug of his own. "Paul Sims!" She smiled. "Golly, great, goodness, it's nice to see you again, too!"

The twins were about to ask how the two knew each other, but before they could get any words out, they were again interrupted by the sound of their names. "Blaine and Tracey," a robotic voice rang out. "What's up, my friends?"

Now the Sassafrases turned to see more familiar faces. REESE the robot was rolling toward them, along with President Lincoln and Ulysses S. Grant, who were trailing up behind him. The twins leaned forward to give the three high fives, but before they could, they were interrupted once more—this time by their faces being . . . feather dusted? Yes, Blaine and Tracey were pretty sure they had both just been fluffed in the face by rainbow-colored feather dusters.

As the Sassafrases both did a kind of awkward half-sneeze and swatted the feathers away, they saw that it was not them but REESE that was actually the one who was being bombarded by feather dusters. A group of haphazard janitors had stumbled in between the twins and their friends and had begun to vigorously dust the pieces and parts of the robot. The group of four was also poking and prodding REESE with brooms and mops.

This didn't seem right to the twins, and they were about to say something to the janitors, but they were interrupted yet again.

"Hey, Shine-O-Mite! What in the world are you doing?" It was Paul Sims addressing the group of janitors. "Leave that poor robot alone and go over to the Milestones of Flight Hall. I heard earlier there was quite a mess over there. Go see if any more cleanup needs to happen."

"Yessir, sorry sir, Mr. Sims, sir," one of the janitors responded apologetically.

The four sheathed their mops, brooms, and feather dusters, grabbed their rolling janitor's cart, and moved along. However, as they left, they gave Blaine and Tracey some pretty strange sideways looks, which further confused the twins as to what in the world was happening around here.

"Blaine and Tracey! Meet Paul Sims!" Summer introduced, sweeping in with her ever-present joy. "Paul is an old junior high classmate of your uncle's, Yang Bo's, and mine. And now he serves as the head curator here at the National Air and Space Museum in Washington, D.C."

The female scientist then turned to her old classmate and

said, "Paul, meet Blaine and Tracey Sassafras. This is Cecil's niece and nephew! They are the ones who are traveling all over the place this summer, learning science."

Paul Sims smiled, reached out, and shook the twins' hands.

"And behind the twins there," Summer continued excitedly, "are Ulysses S. Grant the Arctic ground squirrel, President Lincoln the prairie dog, and REESE the robot. Ulysses is my lab assistant. Lincoln is Cecil's lab assistant. And REESE is helping us all!"

The smile remained on Paul Sims's face, but there was an understandable undertone of confusion as he reached out and shook the "hands" of the robot and the two animals. The museum curator quickly turned his attention back toward the humans.

"Summer, I was so glad when you messaged me to let me know Cecil's niece and nephew were going to pay a visit to the museum. And then you added a little mystery when you said you were coming and that you had something to show me?"

Daytime Here, Nighttime There

Summer nodded with excitement. "Yes, Paul! Oh, yes! You're gonna love this!"

Summer skipped over to REESE and opened up his storage cell. She reached in and pulled out a rock—a rock the twins had seen before. "This, my friend," Summer announced as she proudly presented the rock to her old classmate, "is an asteroid rock!"

Paul Sims's face still held a hint of surprise, but more than that, he looked excited. "An asteroid rock?" He asked.

Summer nodded.

"Meaning a rock from an actual asteroid?"

Summer nodded again.

"Ulysses and Lincoln procured this piece during our recent travels in space," Summer smiled.

Paul Sims looked at Summer, then at Ulysses and Lincoln, and then back at the piece of asteroid he was holding in his hands. The museum curator was speechless.

Summer clasped her hands expectantly together under her chin and began doing little, quick jumps up and down. "Paul, we were hoping this rock is something you might want to display here at the museum!"

Still speechless, Sims smiled and nodded.

"I was also hoping you could walk Blaine and Tracey around your museum and help them learn about the topics they are here to study?"

Paul smiled and nodded again. "Of course," he replied, no longer speechless, but still staring at the asteroid rock. "Where do you want to start?" He asked the Sassafras twins. "What's the first thing you want to learn?"

The twins took another wide look around. There were so many cool things to see and experience, and they wanted to learn about it all, but they figured they should probably start with the topics listed in LINLOC.

"Well, we heard you tell that little girl and her mom all about the sun," Tracey answered. "Maybe next we could learn about day and night?"

"That's a great idea," Sims agreed, finally pulling his gaze away from the precious stone in his hands. "Follow me right this way, all six of you!"

The Sassafras twins jumped in step behind the museum curator as he started off in a particular direction. Summer squealed and continued bouncing up and down like it was Christmas morning. She jumped in line behind Blaine and Tracey to go see some more of the museum, followed by Ulysses, Linc Dawg, and REESE the robot.

The eclectic group of seven made their way through the

National Air and Space Museum, weaving in and out of the crowded halls. The curator, Paul Sims, led the way, even though he was looking at the asteroid rock in his hand the whole time. It was apparent he knew this place like the back of his hand. Blaine and Tracey were excited and kept their focus on where they might be going, not noticing that the four strange janitors were following them.

The four custodial workers were sweeping, mopping, and dusting, but they were doing those things at a rapid pace in the exact same direction that the Sassafrases and their companions were walking. Additionally, there were two security guards who seemed to have the same trajectory and tempo as the rest.

After walking past all kinds of cool artifacts and exhibits, the twins with their group arrived in a small, oval-shaped theater. Paul Sims pressed a couple buttons on an almost hidden keypad in the wall. All at once the little theater's oval-shaped screen was illuminated all around them with images of the Earth and the sun.

NAME: The Day/Night Cycle

INFORMATION LEARNED:
As the Earth turns and rotates, day changes to night on one side of the globe. At the exact same time, on the other side of the globe, night changes to day.

"As the Earth turns and rotates, day changes to night on one side of the globe," Sims informed with his gaze on the screen's images. "At the exact same time, on the other side of the globe, night changes to day. We call this the day/night cycle."

The twins nodded in wonder as they looked at the moving images of the sun and the Earth rotating all around them on the oval screen. Although they had seen the Earth and the sun from the vantage point of space, this was still pretty awesome.

"The day/night cycle occurs because as the Earth turns, different parts of its surface face the sun." Sims continued. "For instance, during the morning, our side of the Earth is turning to face the sun. This is when we see the sunrise ushering in a new day. During the evening, our side of the Earth is rotating away from the sun. This is when we see the sunset marking the beginning of a new night. This day/night cycle takes about twenty-four hours to complete."

Blaine and Tracey, along with the others, did slow, wide-eyed circles as Paul Sims talked, keeping their attention on the screens around them. They did not notice when eight feet and four feather dusters entered the oval theater.

"Even on cloudy days, the sun is shining, but you may not be able to see it or feel it due to the clouds. The only time it is dark during the day is the rare occasion when the moon moves in front of the sun, blocking out its light. This is what we call an 'eclipse.' In a way, we create a sort of mini-eclipse when we stand in front of the sun to create our shadows."

Just as Sims said the word "shadows," several big shadows could be seen on different parts of the oval screen. Tracey wanted to gasp. Blaine wanted to jump. But before either did, they saw what was casting the shadows. Those janitors were back, and they were dusting the projector that was displaying the screen's images.

"Hey, Shine-O-Mite!" Paul Sims greeted, perturbed. "I thought I told you to go clean up that mess in the Milestones of Flight Hall?"

The same janitor who had responded to the museum boss earlier responded again. "Yessir, you did, sir, but we're already finished with that, sir. So we thought we would come clean the theater, sir."

Sims shook his head. "No, not right now. I don't know how you even had enough time to . . . You know what . . . Why don't the four of you go . . . why don't you go take a break down in the janitors' closet?"

The museum curator didn't seem mad at the crew, but he was definitely annoyed. The custodial crew of four reluctantly stopped their dusting and slowly made their way out of the oval-shaped theater. Before they were gone, however, they shot some more sideways glances at the twelve-year-old twins and then also some inspective looks at REESE. The twins wondered who these curious janitors that Paul Sims kept calling Shine-O-Mite were.

Just as the janitors made their way out of the theater, those two short, round security guards stumbled in. One was male; one was female. Both were decked out in tight-fitting navy-blue security uniforms. The male spoke first in an energetic, high-pitched voice. "Mr. Sims, how are you? Were those four bothering you again? Do you want us to go have a 'talking to' with them?"

"Oh, hey, Wiggles," Paul answered. "No, no, it's fine. They are acting a bit jumpy, but they are on their way to the janitors' closet for a break."

"Are you sure, Mr. Sims?" The female security guard chimed in, a little hyper herself. "A little 'talking to' by us would probably set them straight for at least a little while."

"No, Fidget, it's fine. Really," Sims responded. "Thank you for offering, but I think it'll be fine."

"Okay, Mr. Sims," the male security guard evidently named "Wiggles" answered. "If you change your mind, hit us up on the walkies and let us know!"

"Until then," Fidget, the female security guard added, "the two of us will go back out into the museum to serve the general public and protect against all kinds of mayhem, misconduct, and malfeasance!"

"Okay, thank you, and if I do need anything, I will contact you two." Paul Sims nodded and smiled as he touched the walkie talkie on his belt.

At that, Wiggles and Fidget quickly rolled out of the small

theater back into the wide museum. Paul turned back to the those he was hosting with a smiling sigh and held the piece of asteroid up in his hand.

‘Okay, you five, let's go present this rock to a few more of the ‘higher-ups’ back in the office and see what they think.” He then singled out Summer with a look and a wink, adding, “And just so you know, I think they are all definitely going to want to display this thing right here in our museum.”

A couple hours later, the Sassafras twins found themselves bored. Bored is not a feeling they had experienced in a long time. Spending their summer break zip lining around the globe at the speed of light, studying science, didn't lend to many boring moments. But right now, they were finding themselves bored.

They were grateful for the opportunity to meet all the important, suit-wearing people who ran the National Air and Space Museum. They truly were, but goodness sakes, there were so many “higher-ups” to meet, and so many of those “higher-ups” were extremely long-winded. Thankfully, Blaine and Tracey were able to check out because it was the grownups who were doing most of the talking. They were kind of trailing behind, watching Paul and Summer talk with other people.

Evidently, to get something like an asteroid rock displayed at a museum, this is the gauntlet one had to go through. To lighten things up a bit, Blaine was about to tap Tracey on the shoulder and ask if she thought he might look dashing in a suit, when suddenly he was swatted in the face . . . by a feather duster!

“Not those janitors again,” Blaine thought as he turned in the direction of the swat with an incredulous look. Sure enough, it was a custodial feather duster that had made contact with his face. But this time it was one of the janitors, not all four of them.

“You need to come with me,” the janitor whispered urgently.

"Come with you? Are you kidding me? Why do I need to come with you?"

"Because your life is in jeopardy!"

This chilling statement brought Blaine to a stop. "My life is in jeopardy?" The boy asked, not believing it. "What are you talking about?"

Tracey noticed her brother had stopped, causing her to pause as well.

The janitor looked at both of them with desperation. "Both of you need to come with me now!"

The expression on Tracey's face matched her words perfectly. "Are you crazy? There is no way we are going with you!"

"We were afraid the two of you would respond like this," the janitor sighed.

And as he said this, the other three janitors emerged from around the corner, pushing the custodial cart. Then, in a tidy flash, before the Sassafrases even knew what was happening, the four janitors grabbed the twelve-year-olds, stuffed them inside the large, underside compartment of their cart, and rolled away. It happened so quickly and so quietly that none of the adults noticed that Blaine and Tracey were gone.

The big lab room of the Triple S headquarters inside the Zytglogge clock tower in Bern, Switzerland, was bustling with nervous excitement. Agents DeBlose and Q-Tip had returned from space after having successfully repaired the damaged satellite. The Swiss Secret Service was now back online at full capacity. They were about to use the repaired satellite to pinpoint the location of the traitor, Adrianna Archer.

THE SASSAFRAS SCIENCE ADVENTURES

"Okay, everyone, settle down. Settle down now," came the deep authoritative voice of Captain Marolf.

The barrel-chested leader of all the secret agents of Switzerland, with his flat-top haircut and permanent mustache, motioned for everyone present to stop talking. He then gestured toward a computer keyboard-covered table situated directly in front of a huge screen where the two returned space-trekking agents were sitting. "Agent Q-Tip? Agent DeBlose? Are we ready?"

"Affirmative!" Q-Tip squeaked.

"More than ready, sir!" Evan added with a confident smile.

"Okay, then," Marolf barked. "Work your magic on that keyboard, access our repaired satellite, and show all of us exactly where in the world that slimy turncoat is!"

"Yes, sir!" The two responded.

The large, white room of the underground science lab in the middle of Siberia was bustling with nervous dread. Thaddaeus, the Man With No Eyebrows, the Dark Cape himself, had finally managed to get one of his minion-like scientists to not only access the correct satellite but also to successfully bring the images from that satellite up on a stadium-sized screen here in the biggest room of his underground lab. He, along with his many servile sidekicks, were now about to find out the location of Adrianna Archer, the blonde bombshell who had quit on them.

Thaddaeus stared at the screen with seething eyes. The image of Adrianna was now coming into focus. Their vantage point, via satellite, had gone from space view down to street view, and they could all clearly see Archer about to walk into some sort of building. She wasn't outfitted in her normal black color. Instead, she was wearing what looked like a dirty, white lab coat and a pair of what had to be fake coke-bottle eyeglasses.

Thaddaeus's expression suddenly went from seething to acknowledgment and then back to seething as he saw the name of the building his former ally was entering.

"No, she isn't," he said through gritted teeth.

"What does that sign say?" Captain Marolf questioned. "What is the name of that building Archer is about to enter?"

"I believe it says . . ." Q-Tip started to say before pausing, thinking there could be no such actual place. But then the agent continued nonetheless and read the title of the building Adrianna was walking into, "The Left-Handed Turtle . . ."

CHAPTER 11: A BALLISTIC HEIST

The Lunar Rap

Light spilled into the cramped space as the compartment door was opened, and the twins were pulled out of the bottom of the janitors' cart. They were immediately greeted by four familiar feather dusters.

"Hey, stop!" Blaine shouted as he swatted at the rainbow-colored dusters. "What's the big idea? Why did you stuff us in the cart? Why do you keep dusting us?"

"We're sorry, Blaine, we are," the janitor's spokesperson apologized. "We are trying to clean you up. The underside compartment of our cart can't be all that clean."

Both twins continued to swat at the feather dusters.

"Stop, just stop!" Tracey screeched.

"Okay, Pat, Lumin, Flash, that's enough."

All the feathers dropped away from the faces of the twelve-year-olds. Blaine and Tracey found themselves standing in a large janitors' closet staring face-to-face with the four threatening custodians. Blaine was suspiciously annoyed. He was suspicious because these four had stuffed Tracey and him in a tiny cart, and he was annoyed because they kept sticking their feather dusters in his face.

"Who are you guys, and what do you want with us?" The Sassafras boy asked.

"Who are we?" The only janitor who had talked so far responded. "Why, we are Shine-O-Mite! The quickest and cleanest custodial crew in the capital area!"

All four smiled with sparkling, pearly white teeth.

"And what do we want with you?" The leader of the crew continued. "We want you to help us with a heist!"

Blaine and Tracey stared at the four in disbelief. Surely, they hadn't heard what they thought they'd heard.

"You want us to help you with a what?" Tracey asked.

"A heist," the man repeated.

Now the twins turned and looked at each other. What was going on here?

"We have to steal the guidance component before it's stolen by the Rotary Club!" One of the other janitors finally spoke up.

"That's right, Flash," the leader confirmed. "But let's back up a bit and start from the beginning. I can tell by looking at Blaine and Tracey's faces that they aren't buying, believing, or even understanding any of this."

The Sassafras twins' frozen faces indeed confirmed what the man had just said.

"Blaine and Tracey, we truly are the most stellar custodial

crew in the area," the lead janitor began. "But more than that, we are a family. We are the Sheen family. I am the oldest. My name is Sparks. Next is Flash. Then our only sister, Pat, which is short for Patina. And last but not least is the youngest brother, Lumin. From poverty we started our business, Shine-O-Mite, with only the clothes on our backs. We have worked our way up to being the best janitors around—the custodians of clout, if you will. We are the exclusive cleaning crew of the National Air and Space Museum!"

"If all this is true," Tracey interrupted, breaking her pose. "Then why ruin everything by trying to pull off a heist?"

"Because of the Rotary Club," Flash answered.

"The Rotary Club?" Blaine questioned. "I thought a rotary club was a bunch of old ladies who do humanitarian kind of stuff together. Why would a rotary club ever want to steal anything?"

"Not that kind of rotary club," Flash explained. "It's a rotary telephone club that is dedicated to the destruction of all the cell phones and smartphones in the whole world."

This sentence made both of the Sassafras twins turn back into statues of disbelief.

"It's true," Sparks confirmed what his younger brother had said. "The nefarious Rotary Club is made up of only three people: three siblings to be exact—two brothers and a sister. They are the Slote family: Alexander, Graham, and Belle. Their plan is to create a rocket that will travel into space and destroy all communication satellites, therefore, rendering all cell phones obsolete. This, in their minds, will usher in a new era of rotary telephone use, which they just so happen to have a racket on."

"And the only thing they need to complete this rocket of theirs is the guidance component from the SS-22 ballistic missile that we display here at our museum," Flash interjected.

"How do you know all of this?" Tracey asked, breaking from her statue-like stance again.

"Because we have repeatedly seen them here at the museum," Pat spoke up for the first time. "We have overheard their hushed conversations. They seemed suspicious to me from the first time I saw them. I told my brothers I thought those three Slotes were fishy, so we started getting close to them under the guise of cleaning and dusting. And, sure enough, we found out they were casing the museum, preparing to take the guidance component from that old Soviet missile."

"If all this is true," Tracey questioned, "then why didn't you report it to museum management or tell those two security guards that work here?"

"We did," Pat continued. "We told Wiggles and Fidget first, but instead of reporting the threat or helping us in any way, they ratcheted up their security in regard to us."

"They've never trusted us," Sparks added. "Not from the start. We don't know why. Maybe it's because we're so quick and efficient that it's hard to believe we're actually doing our job. But for whatever reason, they don't trust us, and reporting the potential Rotary Club heist just made them more suspicious and untrusting."

Pat nodded like everything her brother had said was true. Then she continued. "After Wiggles and Fidget didn't take us seriously, we reported the heist threat to Paul Sims, the museum curator you've been hanging out with, but he didn't take us seriously either. He said there was no way such a Rotary Club existed, and that even if they did, they would never be able to pull off a heist like that here at the National Air and Space Museum."

Pat sighed in exasperation and let her shoulders slump a bit. And as she did, Flash exploded with another seemingly outlandish comment. "They're gonna blow it all up!"

"What?" Tracey asked, confused.

"They're gonna blow it up," Flash repeated. "The Rotary Club! They're . . . ahhh . . . they're gonna . . . oh, man!"

Sparks patted his brother on the back and then explained, "The Rotary Club is not only known for their love of rotary telephones; they're also known for their love of using dynamite."

"Dynamite?" Blaine asked, rejoining the conversation.

"Dynamite," Sparks confirmed, "meaning that if they come here and follow through with their plan to pull off this heist, they will more than likely destroy many of the priceless pieces of flight history that we display here at our beloved museum with the dynamite they typically use."

Sparks paused and then said almost sorrowfully, "So you see, Blaine and Tracey, if we want to protect that old Soviet missile, its guidance component, and everything else inside this museum that we love, our only option is to pull off this heist ourselves before the Rotary Club does."

Blaine and Tracey looked at each other. Everything was beginning to make sense, but they were still skeptical.

"Why do you need us?" Blaine asked, turning back toward the Shine-O-Mite crew.

"Because you know the robot," Flash blurted out. "And to pull off this heist, we need that robot."

"Robot?" Blaine questioned. "You mean REESE? You need REESE to pull off the heist?"

All four Sheens nodded.

"When your crew arrived at the museum today and we saw that robot, we all got excited," Sparks explained. "And after a brief inspection with our feather dusters, we confirmed that REESE has all the tools needed to complete our plan. The SS-20 is an old, intermediate-range ballistic missile being displayed near the entrance of the museum. It stands upright at fifty-four feet tall and weighs over thirty-seven tons. The guidance component is located near the top of the missile beneath three layers of titanium plating. We feel that REESE's hand attachments have the strength and precision to safely remove the guidance component from the SS-20. And he also seems to be equipped with a storage cell big and secure enough to hold and carry the component without damaging it."

"Please," Pat cut in, adding emotion to her brother's facts. "Please help us, Blaine and Tracey. Please bring REESE to us and allow us to use him to pull off this heist. Please help us save the museum!"

The Sassafras twins glanced at each other, both still unsure about this cleaning crew and this whole heist business, especially if it meant using REESE. What if this was a big lie? It seemed like it could be.

"You know," Blaine fumbled. "REESE isn't designed for . . . you know . . . heisting. He's a robot made more for exploring, entertaining, and scientifically enhancing."

Sparks nodded and then said," Yes, yes, but we don't just need REESE. We need the two of you as well. With a good strategy, a team of six, and a nifty robot, we are fairly confident we can pull this heist off."

"I don't know," Tracey stalled, shrugging and shaking her head. "We . . . we're not sure if . . ."

"You know what," Sparks said, reaching out and gently touching both twins on the shoulders. "I know this is a lot to process all at once. Why don't the two of you take some time on your own to talk it over and decide whether or not you want to help us."

"But Sparks, we ne—" Flash started before he was interrupted by an authoritative, raised hand by his older brother.

"It's okay, Flash. We aren't going to force Blaine and Tracey to join us. They are free to decide."

Flash nodded in agreement. Pat and Lumin also nodded their confirmation. The twins sighed simultaneously, relieved and burdened at the same time.

"When is all this supposed to go down?" Blaine asked.

"Tonight," Flash declared.

"Tonight?" The twins responded in alarm.

All four Sheens nodded in unison.

The twelve-year-olds sighed again. "Well, thank you for giving us some time to think about it," Tracey said. "We'll talk it over and try to make a quick decision. Now, um, how do we get out of this janitors' closet?"

Pat pointed toward a door in the corner. "That will lead you out into the Lunar Exploration Vehicles exhibit," the Sheen woman told them. Then as the twins turned to leave, she added, "Blaine and Tracey, thank you. Thank you for even considering helping us."

The twins nodded and then exited through the door, which did indeed take them out into an exhibit on the first floor of the museum. As the door shut behind them, the brother and sister exhaled again. The information they had just received had become an immediate burden to them—a burden they wanted to share with someone they trusted. First though, they turned toward each other to talk about all they had heard. However, before they could say anything, they heard their names.

"Blaine! Tracey!" It was Summer Beach, and she was running straight toward them with outstretched arms.

"Guess what! Guess what! You're never gonna believe it!" She exclaimed as she reached them and started shaking them happily. "They're gonna display it!" She burst into a huge smile. "The museum wants the asteroid rock, and they're going to display it starting next week!"

The twins smiled. They were happy for Summer, Ulysses, and President Lincoln, but more than anything, they were feeling weighed down by the urgency of their impending decision.

"It was all Paul!" Summer continued. "You should've heard him sweet-talk those higher-ups! Manny, oh man, he sure knew what to say! But I guess, that rock is so cool that it probably sells itself, right?"

The Sassafrases smiled and nodded.

"Speak of the angel!" Summer exclaimed as she stopped shaking her favorite twins and gestured toward the now approaching museum curator, who was being trailed by Ulysses, Lincoln, and REESE. "Paul, I told Blaine and Tracey the great news!"

Sims smiled as he reached the spot where the three were standing, and then he said, "Blaine, Tracey, good to see you again. I noticed you disappeared back in the offices. I don't blame you. It's pretty boring back there compared to all we have out here."

The twins chuckled, somewhat nervously, knowing there was much more to their disappearance than boredom.

"And now I see that you two have found the Lunar Exploration Vehicles exhibit," Paul continued. "I'm excited about the asteroid rock, too, but I don't want to forget that the two of you are here to learn. Because you are standing here at this exhibit, do you want to learn about the moon and some of these cool vehicles that have landed on it?"

"Yes, for sure, of course," Tracey answered, fumbling a bit.

Paul Sims smiled and proceeded. "The moon is Earth's closest neighbor. It orbits the Earth in the same way the Earth orbits the sun."

The museum curator then pointed at one of the vehicles in front of them. "You see that one right there?

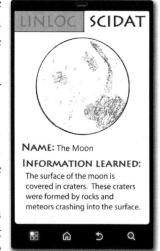

LINLOC **SCIDAT**

NAME: The Moon

INFORMATION LEARNED:
The surface of the moon is covered in craters. These craters were formed by rocks and meteors crashing into the surface.

That is the Apollo Lunar Module 2. It is the vehicle that first landed man on the moon."

The Sassafrases stared forward with wide eyes.

"Also on display here," Sims informed as he continued to point around. "Are a Ranger Spacecraft, a Survey Lunar Lander, a Lunar Orbiter, and an engineering model we call Clementine. Because of vehicles like these, we have had the ability to explore the moon more than any other celestial body outside of Earth. We know the surface of the moon is covered in craters. These craters were formed by rocks and meteors crashing into the surface. We also know that you won't find any clouds or weather on the moon. The moon does have an atmosphere, but it is composed of different gases than Earth's atmosphere. It has gases like sodium and potassium, so there is no air that humans are able to breathe on the moon."

This information caused both twins to take big, deep breaths just for the fun of it.

"The moon takes about twenty-seven days to go around the Earth, and it takes about a month to spin," Paul continued. "Because of this, we only see one side of the moon here on Earth."

"Really?" Blaine asked.

"Really," the local expert confirmed. "As the moon moves, parts of it are 'lit' by the sun, which makes it look like the moon is changing shape. We call these different shapes 'phases,' and we call the pattern they follow the 'lunar cycle.'"

"Lunar cycle! Wooka wooka wooka, lunar cycle!"

The room suddenly exploded with sound and lights. Blaine and Tracey spun on their heels to see that their robot friend, REESE, had launched into another one of his creative, hip-hop science songs.

"Lunar cycle! Wooka wooka wooka, lunar cycle!"

REESE belted out again. Then he went into the first verse.

First let me rap about the phase that makes us swoon.
When it's lit all the way up, it's called full moon.
Say it with me, "Full moon! Full moon!"

Summer, who was still standing there, suddenly shouted out, "Full moon! Full moon!" in perfect sync with REESE.

The Sassafrases stood still and silent for now, having almost forgotten about the musical side of their robotic companion, but they were smiling as he rapped:

Next phase: we can't see it all, but please don't grimace.
When three-fourths of the moon is lit, we call it gibbous.
Say it with me, "Gibbous moon! Gibbous Moon!"

The twins were tempted to be embarrassed because of how loud and flashy REESE was being, but all the museum visitors in the area seemed to be enjoying the performance more than being bothered by it. President Lincoln and Ulysses S. Grant seemed to be especially enjoying it as they actually began break dancing to the song.

Now REESE's third verse came:

Is it half lit, or half shaded? I'm on the border.
When we see half our moon, it's called a last quarter.
Say it with me, "Last quarter moon! Last quarter moon!"

At this point, Blaine and Tracey were all in as they shouted out, "Last quarter moon!" with REESE and Summer. Paul Sims, however, did not look interested.

The hip hop song continued:

Now this phase always seems to bring dreams that are pleasant.
When a fourth of our moon is lit, we call it crescent.
Say it with me, "Crescent moon! Crescent moon!"

Lights continued to flash, and dancing continued to happen as one last verse resounded from REESE the robot:

And now for the moon's final phase, please don't say boo.
When it's dark and none of it's lit; we call it new.
Say it with me, "New moon! New moon!"

Now even those passing by were shouting out along with the robot's rap about the cycle and phases of the moon.

"Lunar cycle! Wooka wooka wooka, lunar cycle!"

REESE finished in style with a last flash of sound and color. He then quieted down with a smile with his light box.

Lincoln and Ulysses stopped their break dancing. Summer stopped her sounds and movements too. Still quietly smiling, the twins turned back toward Paul Sims, whose current expression was hard to read. The museum curator looked from the twins to the rodents to his old classmate to the robot and then finally back to the twins. The Sassafrases silently wondered if he was annoyed, the smiles slipping from their faces.

"Regarding lunar cycles," Sims started flatly and slowly and then pointed toward REESE. "What he said." The museum coordinator then suddenly broke into a smile.

Blaine and Tracey laughed with chuckles of relief.

"And one last thing about the moon," Paul added, still smiling. "It is said to be waxing if it is appearing to grow larger, for example, as it moves from a gibbous moon to a full moon. And it is said to be waning if it is appearing to grow smaller, that is as it moves from a last quarter moon to a crescent moon."

The twelve-year-old science absorbers nodded in understanding and then turned their eyes one more time toward the vehicles on exhibit. Although they had been in space themselves and had even set foot on Mars, seeing these vehicles on display, especially the one that had first landed men on the moon, truly was inspiring.

"Yee haw and woo hoo!" Summer shouted out. "That was a blast, everybody! REESE, great song. Linc Dawg and Ulysses, nice moves. Paul, wonderful information. Twinkie-frasses, I can actually see your brains expanding! Come on in, everybody! I think this calls for a hug!" Blaine and Tracey immediately found themselves in a happy-robotic, jumping-animal, dancing-scientist hug.

Eclipse Escapade

Several minutes later, at the conclusion of the hug, Summer opened up REESE's storage cell and pulled out the asteroid rock. "Now let's go and look around at all the places this little beauty could be displayed!"

She skipped away, closely followed by the animal assistants and the rapping robot. Paul Sims looked like he was about to follow as well, but before he did, the Sassafrases grabbed his attention. They had to tell him about the heist. Even if he already knew about it, like the Sheens said he did, they couldn't keep it a secret.

"Mr. Sims, we have to tell you something," Tracey started but was then interrupted by her not-so-eloquent brother.

"Shine-O-Mite gonna heist! Gonna use REESE! Gonna steal the component! Before Rotary Club blow it all up!"

"I'm sorry, what?" Paul inquired with an expression of confusion.

Tracey laughed nervously, patted her twin brother on the back, and then explained. "The four members of Shine-O-Mite told us they are going to try and pull off a heist tonight. They want to take the guidance component from the Soviet missile you guys have here. They say they are only doing this to protect the component from a group called the Rotary Club, a group that is apparently known for using dynamite to accomplish their purposes. We had to tell you, Mr. Sims. Shine-O-Mite said they already told you and security, but in case they were lying, we had to let you know."

The museum curator remained silent for a few moments and looked at the twins as though he were studying them. He then began, "Blaine and Tracey, thank you for telling me about this. And just so you know, Shine-O-Mite is not lying. Earlier this week, they did indeed divulge this information about the Rotary Club and the heist threat to the guidance component."

The Sassafras twins both exhaled deeply. Nobody was lying, and they didn't have to carry the secret anymore.

"However," Paul continued, "it's ludicrous."

The twins inhaled quickly. They had been expecting this response from Paul, but they were still a bit shocked.

"First off, that Sheen family is known to have vivid and fanciful imaginations. Second, there is no way there is a group of people called the Rotary Club that are committed to the annihilation of cell phones. And third, even if there is, our security here at the National Air and Space Museum is too tight for anyone to be able to pull off a heist of something like a guidance component from one of our missiles."

The museum curator paused, and shook his head with a scoff. Then he gazed at the Sassafrases with an almost angry look before saying, "So please don't bring this up again. Frankly, between you two and those ridiculous janitors, I'm a little tired of hearing about it."

Blaine and Tracey stood there, blinking. They were so shocked by this response from their local expert that they could hardly breathe.

"Let's get back to science," Paul barked. "That's the reason the two of you are here; is it not?"

The Sassafrases nodded shyly.

The museum curator beckoned for the twins to follow him as he moved on from the Lunar Exploration Vehicles exhibit back over to the big, hanging sun and planets mobile, where the twins had first seen him earlier in the day talking to that spunky little girl and her mother.

"The last topic you guys needed to learn about was eclipses, right?" Paul asked but didn't wait for an answer before he launched into the data. "An eclipse is when one celestial body obscures the light from another celestial body. There are two main types we can see on Earth: solar eclipses and lunar eclipses," Sims shared, talking quickly, like maybe he didn't even want to be taking the time to give this information.

NAME: Eclipses
INFORMATION LEARNED:
Solar eclipses occur when the moon passes between the sun and the Earth, temporarily blocking out some of the light from the sun.

"Solar eclipses occur when the moon passes between the sun and the Earth, temporarily blocking out some of the light from the sun. This makes it seem like night in the middle of the day. A total solar eclipse is when the sun is completely blocked out by the moon's shadow. A partial solar eclipse is when it looks like a bit has been taken out of the sun because the moon's shadow is only covering a portion. Solar eclipses occur about every fifteen months."

The museum curator paused, reached in his back pocket, and pulled out a couple pairs of National Air and Space Museum-branded sunglasses. They were like the ones he had given the little girl earlier. "You must take special precaution when observing a solar eclipse because it can damage your eyes if you look directly at the sun."

Paul tossed the sunglasses to the twins, who were now barely breathing. "These glasses are not safe to view a solar eclipse through. I'm not even sure why the museum ordered them. I'm trying to get rid of them by giving them to every kid who comes through here. You don't need them to view a lunar eclipse, which is perfectly safe to watch without any special precautions."

Sims sighed as he looked at the unresponsive twins. Then he turned back toward the large mobile. "Lunar eclipses occur when the Earth is between the sun and the moon, causing the moon to move into the Earth's shadow. The moon appears dark and takes on a reddish glow. Lunar eclipses happen during a full moon about two times a year."

An awkward silence encircled the three as the curator finished giving SCIDAT data.

Paul stared at the hanging mobile for several long, silent seconds. Then he slowly turned back toward the twins. "Blaine and Tracey," he started, "I am sorry that I barked at you like I did. I know you two were trying to help. It's just that I am so sick and tired of those cockamamie janitors."

"It's okay," Tracey responded quietly.

"It's not okay," Paul returned. "And I'm sorry."

Both twins nodded their forgiveness.

"I'm gonna go see if I can't track down Summer," Sims declared, now in his normal temperament. "You two feel free to explore the rest of the museum. There is a lot of cool stuff here to see."

The twelve-year-olds smiled weakly as the curator said goodbye, turned, and walked away, eventually disappearing around a corner. Blaine and Tracey didn't say anything as they turned in the opposite direction and began wandering the halls of the national museum.

They passed Amelia Earhart's red plane and the first plane of the Wright brothers. They saw aircraft used in World War II and even the fastest jet created: the X-15. But the twins couldn't enjoy it because they were so stuck about what to do with the whole heist thing. Other people were moving around excitedly and worryfree, pointing toward this or that, but not the Sassafrases. They shuffled forward in silence, their minds on the decision they needed to make.

Around them there was chatter about all kinds of things like time and navigation, early jet engines, trying out flight simulators, blowing things up with dynamite, taking a stewardess test with a . . . wait! What was that group of three talking about?

Tracey grabbed her brother's arm as both twins abruptly halted. They were pretty sure the two men and one woman they had passed said something about dynamite.

The Sassafrases nonchalantly shuffled back a few steps and hovered in the area of the dark-haired, dark-clothed group of three. They were trying to hear a little more of what they were saying.

"Alexander, really?" The woman was saying in a hushed voice. "Why did we have to come one more time?"

"Easy, Belle. We are making sure everything is still in the same place," the man named Alexander responded.

"Who cares what place everything is in?" The second man asked. "It doesn't matter if we're going to blow it all up anyway."

"It does matter, Graham," Alexander responded calmly and authoritatively. "The less time we take, the better. If they moved the missile to another exhibit area, we would've needed to know that. Now we see it's still in the same location, so we proceed exactly as planned."

"Right," Graham responded. "Blow the front doors with dynamite, blow the bottom half of the missile to shreds so we can easily reach the top where the guidance component is located, rip the component out with crowbars and pliers, and then we get out of here."

"Right," Alexander confirmed.

"And if we run into those two security guards?" Belle asked.

"Then let's say we will have to use . . ." Alexander started with a wicked smile. "Excessive force."

The three shared a quiet but sinister laugh.

"And once we have the component in our grasp, we will have everything we need to destroy all the cell phones in the whole world." Belle cackled.

Another hushed but ominous chuckle came from the three grown Slote siblings, who hadn't noticed the twins were listening to them. The trio of darkly dressed, rotary telephone-using villains turned and left the spot they had been plotting in. They walked around the exhibit where the SS-20 missile was being displayed, found the front doors of the museum, and then disappeared outside.

Blaine and Tracey stared up at the impressively big and tall missile. They pondered the history, knowledge, and grandeur that it brought to the museum. They imagined the guidance component way up at its tip, hidden under layers of titanium. They then imagined it all being blown to bits. The two siblings brought their gazes down from the missile to each other. Without saying a word, they both knew what the other was thinking. They had to help Shine-O-Mite. They didn't know exactly how they were going to do it, but they needed to help protect the museum's property from the three rotary telephone-using villains.

Suddenly, each of the twins felt a hand on one of their shoulders. Blaine and Tracey turned to see that Paul Sims was now standing there with them. He had a contemplative look on his face.

"I can't believe it, but now, I see that it's true. I couldn't have been more wrong. I should have believed Shine-O-Mite. I should've trusted you both," he disclosed thoughtfully. The twins realized that he must have been standing there the whole time as the museum curator paused to let out a sigh.

"Tonight, we are going to protect that missile and this museum together!" Paul resolutely declared.

A few hours later, after night had fallen and the museum had long been closed, the Sassafras twins again found themselves in the janitors' closet. Paul Sims was with them, along with the four Shine-O-Mite team members and REESE the robot. When Paul had told them earlier that they were going to protect the museum, his plan had included local police involvement. But when he placed the call to tell the police about the Rotary Club threat, they reacted in the same way as he originally had. He couldn't blame the dispatcher; the whole thing did sound a bit ludicrous. The end result was that the protection duty fell on the shoulders of Paul, the twins, and the four janitors.

Sims had gone down to the janitors' closet and apologized profusely to Sparks, Pat, Lumin, and Flash. He had listened to their heist plan in detail, but he didn't like it one bit. However, he did agree to consider their idea if a few changes could be made. The Shine-O-Mite team was overjoyed to know that the museum curator believed them and were more than ready to have his input.

The first change to the heist plan Paul wanted to make was to call it their defense plan. Shine-O-Mite agreed that the heart of their plan was not to steal but to defend. The five put their heads together and came up with a new plan, one that all involved were proud to be a part of.

So, now here they all were, in the janitors' closet, going over the plan one more time. In mere moments, they were going to rush out into the museum corridors to defend its contents from the evil telephone swirlers.

"Okay, so one team will be stationed as lookouts near the front doors. Keep your eyes peeled for those Slote siblings. And if you do see them, your job is to engage the first line of defense—the water sprinklers." Sparks was reminding Paul, Blaine, and Lumin. The three members of the first team nodded.

"If the shock of the sprinklers turning on, soaking them

and their dynamite, doesn't stop the Rotary Club, then team two you need to be ready to go next." Sparks turned to address Tracey, REESE, Pat, and Flash. "Pat and Flash will be holding the ropes for Tracey and REESE, who will be hoisted up in harnesses hanging near the top of SS-20's tip. You two will be ready to retrieve the guidance component if, and only if, the Rotary Club makes it into the museum with their dynamite." The members of the second team nodded.

"Meanwhile, I will serve as the point man for the entire operation," Sparks informed, his voice humble yet resolute. "I will help you teams keep on task. And as we previously discussed, when, or rather if, the Rotary Club does show up, I will look for alternative ways to thwart their plans and apprehend them without any of us having to touch the SS-20 missile."

The eight members of the defense team nodded as they looked at each other in determination. They were ready to defend the National Air and Space Museum . . . together. Sparks looked them all in the eyes before placing his hand on the doorknob of the janitors' closet.

Before he opened the door, Blaine blurted out, "Hey, hey wait! What about Wiggles and Fidget?"

Sparks's hand dropped from the door. "Ahh, yes . . . Wiggles and Fidget," he said as he looked at Paul Sims. "Mr. Sims, sir, you know the museum security guards do not trust us one bit. If they are still making their nightly rounds and see us in the museum after hours, this whole plan will be in jeopardy.

Paul nodded as he took a moment to think. He then reached into his pocket to take out a small item. "Sparks, maybe we need a third team—a diversion team of one."

Sparks eyed Paul curiously but waved his hand for Sims to continue.

"This is a laser pointer." Paul held the small object up for all to see before handing it to Blaine. "If I know Wiggles and Fidget like I think I do, Blaine could easily use this to divert the attention of those quirky security guards.

Sparks nodded as if he liked the plan before saying, "That settles it. We now have three teams and all of our bases are covered. Is everyone ready to do this?"

The response was resolute nods all around.

"Then, here we go!" Sparks announced as he pushed open the door.

CHAPTER 12: LINLOC FAILURE TO LAUNCH
Abort the Astronaut Adventure

The blast sent Tracey into a temporary paralysis as she hung near the top of the SS-20 soviet missile. The front doors of the National Air and Space Museum had just been blown off by the dynamite of the Rotary Club. Evidently the sprinklers had not deterred Alexander, Graham, and Belle.

The Sassafras girl remained wooden-like for only a few seconds. Snapping quickly out of that state, Tracey swung back into action. REESE, hanging by his own rope next to her, immediately began working on loosening the titanium panel with his screwdriver hand attachement.

"Alright, REESE, finish unscrewing the last screw right here, and then I think we can safely pull off the panel and get to the guidance component," Tracey directed as she watched the three black-clad members of the Rotary Club rush through the smoke into the museum.

The blast sent Blaine into a temporary paralysis as he hid like a silent shadow in a dark corner. "The Rotary Club is here," Blaine thought to himself. He snapped out of his frozen stance quickly and scanned the area for Wiggles and Fidget. Where'd they go?

To the surprise of the twelve-year-old, the laser pointer had been working like a charm in diverting the attention of the two security guards away from the missile exhibit. He had been shining it all around, and they had been chasing its green dot like a couple of rambunctious kittens. Blaine guessed that was over now because the sound of the dynamite blast must've drawn the security guards toward the missile exhibit.

Blaine raced that way himself, and when he got there, he saw six things that made him stop in his tracks. Tracey and REESE were hanging high in the air, with the guidance component in their hands. The three members of the Rotary Club had blown the front doors of the museum clean off, and now they were all pointing angrily at the dangling two. Pat and Flash, who were standing on the ground holding Tracy and REESE up in the air, looked to be close to losing their grip on the ropes. Paul Sims and Lumin were standing with their hands on their heads. The expressions on their faces said that the defense plan wasn't going as they expected.

Wiggles and Fidget had indeed followed the sound of the dynamite blast and were here, but they looked overwhelmed with fear as their short, round bodies shook in fidgeting wiggles. And the sixth and final thing the Sassafras boy saw was Sparks Sheen standing with the custodial cart directly in front of Alexander, Graham, and Belle, glaring at them in confident indignation.

"Look, Alexander! They've already got the thing! What are we going to do now? Should we use more dynamite?" Graham Slot asked his brother.

Alexander shook his head. "No more dynamite. There's no need. They've already done our job and gotten the guidance component out for us. Now, we need to go take it from them!"

All at once, the brave Sheen janitor shouted out with a voice like that of a mighty and bold warrior "Shine-O-Mite vs. dynamite!" He then grabbed two rainbow-colored feather dusters from the custodial cart and started spinning them around like nunchucks with the speed and skill of a ninja.

Sparks Sheen advanced so quickly upon the three members of the Rotary Club that they had no time to react or defend themselves. They were swatted, thwacked, and biffed seemingly a thousand times in a matter of only seconds by spinning feathery rainbows. They were then immediately subdued and detained by Sparks Sheen alone. Their hands were tied behind their backs with lengths of black plastic trash bags.

There was another moment of temporary paralysis for both Sassafrases. It was a shocked but happy paralysis. They snapped out of it quickly, laughing triumphantly along with the other defenders. Pat and Flash lowered Tracey and REESE safely to the ground as Paul Sims went over to look at the item Tracey was holding in her hand. The museum curator reverently took the guidance component to the SS-20 missile from the Sassafras girl and then walked it over to where Alexander, Graham, and Belle were sitting on the floor.

"I'm not sorry to say it, my friends, but now it is impossible for you to carry out your plans to destroy all the world's cell phones."

The Rotary Club reacted by somberly hanging their heads in defeat. Sims then moved to where the two National Air and Space Museum security guards were standing with looks of amazed disbelief on their faces.

"Wiggles and Fidget, we were wrong about Shine-O-Mite. If it wasn't for them, this guidance component and quite possibly many more of the items in this room would have been lost. Can the two of you take this and put it in a safe place in my office? But before you do that, I'm sure you have something to say to the Sheens," he said as he held out the guidance component toward them.

Both Wiggles and Fidget nodded. Then Wiggles held out his plump, little hands, took the guidance component with firm resolve, and said, "I'm sorry for doubting you, Shine-O-Mite."

Fidget added, "Yeah, I'm so sorry we ever doubted you and your family."

The Sassafras twins looked at each other and smiled. The defense plan had been a success. They had been a part of protecting a national treasure. And as a result of it all, the museum curator, the janitors, and the security guards were now all on the same page. This location was a wrap.

She had made a move on him yesterday at the Left-Handed-Turtle, but it hadn't worked. She had decked herself out in mad scientist apparel, which she thought would've been difficult for Cecil Sassafras to turn away from, but he hadn't been the least bit interested.

She had sidled up next to the redhead on aisle six of the grocery story with her messy, white lab coat and her coke-bottle glasses. She had asked him a question about a fake physics experiment she wasn't working on. She had expected him to make some sort of comment back with great interest and maybe even some googly eyes, but Cecil had remained completely silent. He hadn't responded to her. In fact, he didn't even make eye contact. He continued to stare intently at a can of orange juice concentrate that he had been holding in his hand.

Adrianna asked the physics question again and even tried to pour on a little more charm. Nothing. Cecil had acted as though she wasn't even there. She had felt rejected and impressed all at the same time. This Sassafras science man truly was the most powerful person she had ever tried to align with—it looked like he was going to be next to impossible to join.

However, that did not mean she was going to give up—quite the opposite. She was now even more determined to combine efforts with this great man. She had left the Left-Handed-Turtle in a huff, somewhat frustrated, but after hitting the drawing board again last night, she felt optimistic about today's plan.

Here she stood now, on Cecil's front porch at 1104 North Pecan Street. She was wearing her normal stylish and feminine black power suit. Her long, blonde hair was perfectly styled and flowed down over her shoulders in vibrant waves. She had the right amount of makeup on, accenting her natural beauty in a complimentary way. And what did she have in her hand? A vacuum. That's right; she had a vacuum.

Today, Adrianna Archer was a door-to-door vacuum saleswoman. One thing she had seen as she had spied on Cecil's house over the last few days was that the scientist's dwelling was messy. Very messy. Very, very messy. How could he say no to a beautiful vacuum saleswoman? Right now, Adrianna was feeling confident that he couldn't.

Archer took one last deep breath, straightened her suit, and then knocked on the door. She waited, expecting the door to open any second, but that is not what happened. Instead, the wooden porch suddenly opened up underneath her, and she found herself falling into darkness with her vacuum in hand. In a split second, she hit a wide, metal slide. She careened smoothly down the slide toward a growing light and then shot out onto a pile of old, musty pillows.

Upon landing, she lost control of her vacuum. It swung up,

flew out of her hand and across the room over piles of scientific junk, straight toward a computer desk. Adrianna watched in embarrassed horror as the cleaning device crashed directly into the computer's keyboard, smashing it before knocking it off to the floor between the desk and the back wall.

With her power suit now wrinkled, her makeup smeared, and her hair in disarray, Adrianna looked toward the chair behind the computer desk where the redheaded scientist was presently sitting. The former Swiss Secret Service agent smiled bashfully and asked, "Hello sir, would you be interested in purchasing a vacuum?"

Cecil Sassafras responded only with silence and a raised eyebrow.

After a good night's sleep in the museum's guest quarters, near the Spacelab Module where they had originally landed here in Washington D.C., the Sassafras twins were ready for more face-to-face science learning. Yesterday had been exhausting, but in the end they had also been successful. The guidance component to the SS-20 Soviet missile was safe and sound. The museum's front doors were already being repaired. And they had finished one delicious breakfast consisting of freeze-dried space food, the same kind that they sold in the museum gift shop.

Blaine and Tracey each opened up the LINLOC apps on their phones to see where they would be going next. The familiar application opened up successfully, at least at first, but then it began cutting in and out.

"Hey, what's up with LINLOC?" Blaine blurted, shaking his phone as though that would fix the problem.

Tracey held her smartphone still, staring at its flickering screen. "You don't think it's another glitch; do you?" She asked her brother, who continued to shake his phone like it was a can of spray paint.

"I don't know, maybe," was his reply.

Tracey tried to glimpse the needed information as LINLOC continued to quickly flash on and off. "I think I saw the . . . nope . . . oh wait . . . there's the . . . yes! It was astronauts . . . and, wait . . . was that space shuttles . . . Yeah, I think it was space shuttles . . . And there is . . . oh no." LINLOC had blinked off to a black screen, apparently for good.

"Oh, great," Blaine huffed, finally letting his phone rest. "What are we going to do now?"

Just then the Sassafras twins heard someone singing their names, and the song was getting louder and closer:

Blaine and Tracey Sassafras,
Learning science really fast.

It was Summer Beach, and she was dance-skipping toward them.

Learning science that will last.
Blaine and Tracey, what a blast!

Summer stopped and giggled as she reached the two. "That's a little song I made up, just now, on the spot."

The twins nodded and smiled, even though they weren't sure if they were fans of the song or not.

"So, where are you two zipping off to next?" The female scientist asked with excitement.

"Maybe nowhere," Blaine answered.

"What? Why?" Summer responded with a puzzled look.

"Because it looks like there might be a new glitch on our phones," Tracey explained. "The LINLOC app started flickering when we were trying to look at it; then it switched off completely."

Tracey handed her phone to Summer, who began looking it over. After a few seconds of examination, Summer nodded. "You're right. LINLOC doesn't seem to be functioning at all."

She handed the phone back to Tracey. "Did you get any info from it before it clicked off?"

"I didn't see a location or a local expert's name, but I think I saw something about astronauts and space shuttles?" Tracey answered.

"Astronauts and space shuttles?" Summer questioned before exclaiming, "Oh! Oh! I bet those are two of the next four topics you are supposed to study!"

The Sassafrases agreed that the she was probably right.

"Okay, Tootie-Cutie Twinkie-frasses, here's what I think we should do," Summer said, smiling and moving her fingers when she talked. "Because we are already here at the National Air and Space Museum, why don't you two go see if you can't find Paul and get him to give you the data you need about astronauts and space shuttles. In the meantime, I will give your Tootie-cutie super handsome, really wonderful and brilliant—oh, he's brilliant and super spectacular—I'm sorry, excuse me. While you're talking to Paul, I will give Cecil a call and see if we can't figure out what is going on with LINLOC and whether or not we can fix it."

Blaine and Tracey chuckled and nodded, thinking this sounded like a good plan. They didn't know why Summer Beach had a hopeless crush on their uncle, but they did know they wanted to learn about astronauts and space shuttles. So, go look for Paul Sims they would.

"Sir, I am so sorry. Can I help you with that?" Adrianna Archer blubbered as she approached Cecil Sassafras sitting at his desk and then tried to pick up the smashed computer keyboard.

"No, no, nope-ity, noper-sons," Cecil answered fairly gently but as mad as he was capable of getting. "I think I can manage fine myself. I probably need you to leave, so I can fix this keyboard."

"I insist, sir," Adrianna pleaded. "Please let me help you."

She reached down to pick up the crumpled keyboard at the precise moment that Cecil did, and the two bumped heads.

"Oops, I am so sorry, sir."

"Yes, well, okay, you see, let me just get my keyboard, and maybe you should grab your vacuum," Cecil said, rubbing his head and then pointing toward the cleaning machine.

Adrianna obliged, as Cecil got the keyboard back up to the top of his deck. He looked it over for a few seconds, plugged it back in, and then looked at his desktop monitor. "Welp, welp, welpity, it looks like it might still work, but I think the blow to the keyboard may have affected the operational capabilities of LINLOC."

"LINLOC? What's LINLOC?" Adrianna asked as she grabbed the handle of the vacuum cleaner and pulled it back upright.

"Well, you see, LINLOC is a smartphone application that enables my niece and nephew to . . ." Cecil started with a short-lived smile but then abruptly stopped. "Wait, wait, wookie. Stop, stop, lookie. Why are you still here?"

"Oh, I'm sorry. Did you want me to leave?"

"Yes, I do. I really do. I need to get this keyboard fixed and this program back up and running. I think I can accomplish all this a little quicker all by my lonesome."

"Are you sure, sir, that you don't want to purchase a vacuum? I mean, by the looks of it, your house could use a little TLC."

"TLC?"

"Yes, TLC. Tender love and care," Adrianna said, batting her eyes, which Cecil didn't see because he was still looking at his monitor, thinking only of fixing LINLOC for Blaine and Tracey

"I'm pretty good at TLC myself," Adrianna continued.

"Uh huh, whatever you said. Please find your way to the exit as quickly as possible so I can workity work on fixty-fixing this."

Adrianna was stung a little by Cecil's rejection, but she was not out of the game. Cecil Sassafras didn't know it yet, but she would be joining his side. She was sure of it. The determined blonde-headed woman wasn't about to start looking for the exit to this place.

"The first man to walk on the moon was Neil Armstrong, but the first man to travel to space was a Soviet astronaut named Yuri Gagarin," Paul Sims shared, smiling as he and the Sassafras twins stood in front of the same Lunar Exploration Vehicles exhibit where they had stood yesterday to receive SCIDAT about the moon.

The museum curator was behaving extra nicely toward the twelve-year-olds today after they had been correct about the Rotary Club and the threat to the museum. Sims had apologized profusely about not believing them, and he had thanked them over and over again for saving the missile guidance component from the clutches of the would-be robbers. He had been more than happy to give

NAME: Astronauts

INFORMATION LEARNED:
Most astronauts train for several years on how to work and live in space. They have to learn how to function in zero gravity.

them a private tour when they asked him about the topics of astronauts and space shuttles.

"Most astronauts train for several years on how to work and live in space," Paul continued. "They have to learn how to function in zero gravity, how to escape a space shuttle quickly, and how to move and work in a spaceship."

The twins nodded, remembering how hard it had been to get used to zero gravity and what it had been like to float around in a space suit. Luckily, their Linc 2.0 space suits had been cutting edge, but yet they knew they could've used years of training instead of hours.

"Because space has no air, it is deadly to humans," Sims informed. "So astronauts' space suits are to them almost like personalized spacecraft. They must wear one to work and function out in space. The spacesuits are outfitted with tubes throughout the entire suit. These tubes are filled with water that can quickly cool or heat the astronaut. The outer layer of the suit helps protect the astronaut from the extreme temperatures of space and from meteoroids and small pieces of space debris. The astronaut also wears a helmet fitted with a radio, a drinking tube, and a visor to protect the eyes and face from the sun. The astronauts put on a backpack-looking appliance called the Primary Life Support System, which contains the air needed to breathe and helps monitor and regulate the astronaut's temperature. Altogether, the suit can weigh upward of 310 pounds."

"Three hundred ten pounds!" Blaine meant to only think but instead accidentally blurted out loud. He was sure their Linc 2.0 suits hadn't been that heavy. "That's . . . that's like . . . like wearing a sumo wrestler!"

Tracey made a grossed-out face.

Paul laughed and continued. "Of course, out in space, 310 pounds doesn't matter because everything is weightless due to zero gravity. So, everything floats, even liquids. Astronauts must use vacuums and specialized containers for everyday tasks like eating and drinking to be made possible."

Blaine heard what Paul said, but he whispered the words, "like wearing a sumo wrestler" again, partially because he was still thinking about the space suits and partially because he wanted to gross out his sister one more time.

"An astronaut's training is second to none," Paul continued, still smiling. "They must train to do their tasks while in their suits, immersed in water, because floating in water is somewhat similar to floating in space. Astronauts also have padded gloves with rubber tips so they can easily feel things."

The Sassafrases both nodded, thinking that floating in space was indeed similar to floating in water.

"One of the most extreme training tools for astronauts is called the Vomit Comet," Paul forced out with his own version of a grossed-out face. "To learn and feel what it's like to be weightless, the astronauts are put in a plane that climbs steeply for thirty seconds and then suddenly takes a dive for thirty seconds. During the dive, a feeling of weightlessness overtakes everyone. The opposite effect occurs during the climb, and people often get sick. That's why they call it the Vomit Comet."

Now there were grossed-out faces all around.

"All in all, astronauts are some of the most hearty, brave, and brilliant scientists there are," Paul summated, finishing the SCIDAT about astronauts. "Now let's go over to the Space Race exhibit, and I can tell you what I know about space shuttles."

"Alright," the Sassafrases said excitedly.

Space Shuttle Stalemate

"Hello, Cecil Sassafras residence. This is Adrianna. How can I help you?" An unfamiliar female voice answered.

"What?" Summer asked in confusion as she pulled the phone away from her ear and looked at the screen to make sure she had dialed the right number. It said, "Cecil Sassafras," and it was the correct number.

Summer put her phone back up to her ear. "Yes, hello . . . is . . . Cecil there?"

"Yes, he is, but he's busy right now. May I ask who's calling?"

"Ummm, yes. This is Summer. Summer Beach. Can you . . . wait, who are you again?"

"My name is Adrianna, and I am Cecil's new assistant. Would you like to leave a message for him?"

"Would I like to leave a message for him?" Summer repeated

"Yes, Susan, that's kind of how this works. You call. I answer. You leave a message. I give it to him." Adrianna responded sarcastically

"It's not Susan. It's Summer. Well, I guess . . . l could leave a message . . . Can you tell Cecil that LINLOC seems to have a glitch, and—"

"Okay, thank you so much for your call, Sierra. I will pass that message along to Cecil. Have a terrific day. Goodbye."

The call abruptly clicked off on the other end. Summer pulled the phone away from her ear and looked at it again, now with an even deeper level of confusion. What had just happened?

"The early trips into space were done via rockets that were not reusable, but then the reusable space shuttle was designed," Paul told Blaine and Tracey as the three now stood in the middle of the Space Race exhibit. "We have been sending rockets into space since 1957, and as I said earlier, Yuri Gagarin was the first person to travel into space in April 1961. He circled the Earth one time on his trip. The first American astronaut to enter space was Alan Shepard, and that happened a month after Gagarin in May 1961."

As Sims spoke, the twins looked around at all the Russian and American spacecraft being displayed in this exhibit. They imagined what it might have been like to compete for so many amazing "firsts."

"Space shuttles have taken space travel to steps beyond what rockets did," Paul Sims continued. "The space shuttle's main three components include two boosters, a large fuel tank, and the main reusable shuttle. When the space shuttle is launched, it is blasted off of a launch pad. The booster rockets use up their fuel first, fall away, and parachute back to Earth. Then the large fuel tank powers the main engine and falls away when it runs out of fuel, which happens once the shuttle has been delivered into space. The space shuttle has compartments to hold the crew, including the cockpit in the front where they fly the shuttle. In the middle is a large cargo bay that can carry telescopes, satellites, and/or other parts for a space station. The wings on the shuttle help guide the aircraft back to the Earth."

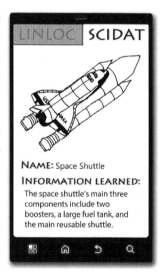

LINLOC SCIDAT

NAME: Space Shuttle

INFORMATION LEARNED:
The space shuttle's main three components include two boosters, a large fuel tank, and the main reusable shuttle.

"Wow, it is amazing what science has accomplished," Tracey wondered out loud.

"Wow, I wonder if a sumo wrestler has ever traveled to space," Blaine muttered under his breath.

"Today, there are many scientists and engineers who are working on new designs for aircraft to see if we can send people into space at much cheaper costs," Paul finished. The museum curator then sighed contentedly and smiled as he looked at the two twelve-year-old learners. "Thank you, Blaine and Tracey," he acknowledged. "Thank you for helping to save the guidance component, yes, but even more than that, thank you for visiting this museum. And thank you for caring about the science of it all—you two have reminded me of my own love for science. Thank you!"

"We thank you!" Tracey responded for herself and her brother. "Thank you for letting us help you and Shine-O-Mite and for taking the time to walk around this wonderful museum with us, giving us so much incredible information!"

Paul Sims nodded and smiled. "It's been my pleasure."

Just then, the three heard a familiar voice, but it was unfamiliarly forlorn. "Hey, guys, Cecil knows about the glitch in LINLOC. At least I think he does." It was Summer Beach, and she was approaching with slow steps and a downcast face.

"What?" The twins thought. "No smile or hug or jumping up and down?" They had never seen Summer like this before, ever. Something must be very wrong.

Paul sensed the obvious difference as well. "What do you mean, 'at least you think he does?'" He asked.

"Well, I called his number, but he's not the one who answered," Summer started. "It was some lady named Adrianna. She said she was his new assistant."

"New assistant?" the twins asked, flabbergasted.

"That's what she said," Summer continued. "I told her about the LINLOC glitch, and she said she would pass the information along to Cecil. But to be honest, she didn't sound trustworthy to me. Or nice. Or kind. Or happy. But she did sound pretty. I hope she's not pretty."

"New assistant?" The twins asked again, this time more inspective then flabbergasted.

"But what about President Lincoln?" Blaine asked. "This doesn't mean he's been replaced; does it?"

Nobody had an answer.

"Now, I think that's unnecessary," Cecil said, aggravated. "I don't need anyone to answer my phone for me."

"Oh, but I could be such a big help to you," Adrianna disagreed with a non-disagreeable voice. "I could be—"

"Also, I still don't need a vacuum cleaner," Cecil interrupted. "Lookie here, lady, I asked you to leave, and I thinkity think that is persactly what you should do right now. It's my fault you fell through the trapdoor on the front porch. That was an accident, and it's on me. I thought I had pushed the ejector floor button, not the trap door button. But since you've been down here, you've been quite the nosy-posy nuisance. And I would love it if you would leave. Righty right now. There is the staircase that leads to the exit. I don't want to be rude, but you can show yourself out."

Freshly stung by the powerful redheaded scientist's rejection, Adrianna Archer hung her head, grabbed the handle of her vacuum cleaner, and dragged it up the stairs. She would leave for now, but she would be back. Right now she was feeling defeated, but she was too much of a determined person to let a couple instances of rejection stop her from achieving her aim—a resolute aim that was still to stand by the side of this amazing man as his partner.

As soon as she disappeared through the basement door, Cecil let out a huge, relieved exhale. The weird vacuum salesman lady was gone. Now he could get back to fixing LINLOC.

He grabbed the smashed keyboard with both hands. "A couple more adjustments and this thing should be up and running like a Sassafras to sizzling bacon," Cecil whispered to himself with a smile.

"Well, there's only one way to find out whether or not Cecil's new assistant gave him the message about the LINLOC application," Paul Sims suggested. "And that is to open your phones and try again."

The Sassafras twins nodded. Paul was right. A few minutes had passed since Summer had made the call to their uncle's residence, so maybe that had been enough time for Uncle Cecil to receive the message and fix the app. Both twelve-year-olds opened their phones and then tapped on the LINLOC icon.

In a matter of seconds, they had their answer—LINLOC worked! It was back up and running!

"Well, where are you zipping off to next?" The female scientist asked with returning excitement.

"Poland!" Tracey shouted out. "Frombork, Poland, to be exact. Longitude +19° 40' 49.04", and latitude +54° 21' 27.58". We will be studying the topics of astronauts, space shuttles, comets, and ancient astronomers with the help of Minka Ziven, our local expert."

"Well, we've kind of already studied astronauts and space shuttles, thanks to Paul," Blaine summated. "I wonder what that means about those two subjects in the SCIDAT world?"

LINLOC SCIDAT

LOCATION: Frombork, Poland

CONTACT: Minka Ziven

LATITUDE: **LONGITUDE:**
+54° 21' 27.58"   +19° 40' 49.04"

INFORMATION NEEDED ON:
Astronauts, Space shuttles,
Comets, Ancient astronomers

Nobody had an answer, but everyone was excited that the adventure was continuing for the two young science learners.

A few minutes later, Blaine and Tracey were harnessed up and ready to zip. Their helmets were on, and their three-ringed carabiners were calibrated to the coordinates that would land them in Poland. Paul Sims and Summer Beach waved goodbye along with President Lincoln, Ulysses S. Grant, and REESE the robot, who had joined the group as the twins had been putting on their harnesses. Blaine and Tracey waved back and then, with a zip, disappeared and were gone.

Goodbye, Washington, D.C. Hello, Frombork, Poland. After traveling through swirls of light, they landed with a jerk. Their bodies were tingling and devoid of sight and strength. Where had LINLOC landed them this time?

When their senses came to, the Sassafras twins saw quite possibly the strangest place they had ever landed. As a matter of fact, it looked more like a dream than a scientific landing spot. They were in an open space, or it could've been a room. They couldn't tell because there was darkness all around them except for one source of light directly in front of them. Under that dim source of light swung a giant pendulum.

The pendulum, which looked to be made of copper, made no sound. It swung back and forth, back and forth, from one side to the other. Back and forth, back and forth, back and forth like the only time that mattered in all existence was the time this pendulum was keeping with its swinging.

Back and forth, back and forth, back and forth the tip of the large, copper pendulum was centimeters from touching the ground when at the center of its swing and then arched up slightly at the edges.

Back and forth, back and forth, back and forth. It swung from its hidden fixed spot over the circle made from dim light and what looked to be small, rectangular-shaped, wooden blocks standing on end at the circle's edges.

What was this place they had landed in? Was any of this even real? Had Uncle Cecil truly fixed LINLOC, or had a glitch sent them somewhere otherworldly?

Blaine and Tracey looked toward each other. They couldn't see each other's faces all that well because of the lack of light, but each twin knew the other twin had a look that was perplexed on their face.

The two slowly looked back; as they did the silence of the place was abruptly broken as the tip of the pendulum swung out and knocked one of the wooden blocks over with a slap and thud. Then back across to the other side of the circle it swung and knocked over an opposite block. The loud sound in the quiet blackness was eerie.

Suddenly the darkness was pierced by a rectangular shape of light off to the twins' right. It was almost as if a floating doorway had opened up, providing an exit to this strange place. Or maybe it was an entrance because all at once two children about the twins' size stumbled in through it. Then, as soon as they had entered, the doorway of light closed behind them. Blaine and Tracey remained silent, partially out of fear but mostly out of confusion.

The two newcomers stayed silent, but the Sassafrases knew they were there because they could hear the two rustling around a bit. The doorway had cast enough light to lead the Sassafrases to believe they were in a large room, a large, circular room with maybe a domed ceiling. Testing this theory, Blaine reached back behind him in the darkness and felt a slightly curved wall. He was certain now they were in a big, round room.

All at once, a circular light appeared, situated near the spot where the Sassafrases were sitting, but it was above them about fifteen to twenty feet, near the top of the wall. The new light looked to be about three feet or so in diameter, and it was not stationary. The moment it appeared, it began moving in a large horizontal oval above them like it was skimming the top of the circular room's wall. It moved at a seemingly consistent pace, but it was never able to make a complete circle before it would disappear only to eventually reappear again.

Then, as if things couldn't have gotten any stranger, another light appeared. This one was on the far side of the room on the other side of the pendulum from where the twins were sitting, and it was rising up out of the floor. It wasn't rectangular or circular. It was . . . person shaped? It wasn't just light rising up out of the floor; it was light that was shining on a person who was rising up out of the floor. Blaine and Tracey looked at each other again in the dim light.

What in the world was this place?

Eventually, the person rose all the way up and was fully visible. It was a young woman with pale-looking skin, dark hair that was cut perfectly straight across her forehead, and stoic features. All was quiet for a moment, and then she spoke slowly, deliberately, and with a Polish accent.

"A dark room. A swinging pendulum. Only one way out. Good afternoon. My name is Minka Ziven, and I will be your 'clue guide' today here at Copernicus Code Escape Room."

CHAPTER 13: THE COPERNICUS CODE

Comet Circumvention

Tracey's mind was racing as questions and answers were clicking into place. So, our local expert is a clue guide. Well, all of our local experts have kind of been clue guides, I guess, but what's the Copernicus Code?

As if sensing Tracey's question, Minka Ziven continued her melancholy introduction. "Nicolas Copernicus was a famous astronomer and scientist who is from right here in Poland. We will do a brief dialogue on his life and work, as we will with several other ancient astronomers. This escape room is named in his honor."

"Ummm, yes, Miss Minka, I have a question," the Sassafrases heard a girl's voice call out from the darkness, presumably one of the two children they had seen earlier. "You said there is only one way out. That out is not the door we came in through; is it?

Because if it is, that would be kind of boring."

Instead of answering directly, the stoic hostess answered by repeating and then expounding. "A dark room. A swinging pendulum. Only one way out. The emergency exit is not that way."

As Minka said this a green exit light dinged on above the doorway where the two other children had entered.

"Your goal is to capture the circular light that seems to be moving overhead. You capture the light; you find the way out."

"But that's impossible," the same girl's voice exclaimed. "It's too high up, and it keeps disappearing!"

Not responding to the child's comments, Ziven continued. "A series of clues, if solved correctly, will lead you to the circular light, which will lead to your escape from this room. You must escape before the pendulum knocks down all the blocks."

As if in response to Ziven's last sentence, the large, copper pendulum hit another block and struck it over. Although they weren't scared anymore because they knew they were in the correct location with the right local expert, the Sassafras twins still shuddered when the block fell over. They wanted to capture that moving light and get out of this room before this eerie pendulum finished its job.

"Is everyone willing and ready to proceed?" Minka Ziven asked the four children.

"Yes," the other two kids answered.

"Yes," the Sassafrases responded, speaking for the first time at this location.

Without moving from her spot or changing her expression, Minka began, "Then here is your first clue."

Suddenly, the floor, the wall, and the domed ceiling all lit up with stars. They weren't real stars, of course. They were small lights embedded in the surfaces of the room, but they looked real. It gave Blaine and Tracey the sensation they were floating in space again. The wall curving all the way around and the domed ceiling also lent to this feeling. The only thing that didn't look like space was the pendulum. It knocked another set of wooden blocks over before Minka guided the four children into their first clue.

"Space, the universe, the cosmos. It has been a mysterious marvel for all humankind for all time and has been contemplated and studied by some of the most brilliant minds."

As Minka said this, the Sassafrases noticed that many of the lights representing stars around them were blinking or fading in seemingly random intervals, making it look like the whole space was twinkling. Also, there were small, quick streaks of light that looked like shooting stars. And then the twins saw even bigger and slower streaks of light they thought might have been . . .

NAME: Comets

INFORMATION LEARNED:
Comets are made from dust and ice, meaning they are somewhat like giant space snowballs.

"Comets," Minka Ziven stated, pulling the Sassafrases' thought into a word. "Comets are your first clue. They are named after their description in Greek: Aster Kometes, which means 'hairy star.' Comets are made from dust and ice, meaning they are somewhat like giant space snowballs. They come from the outer edge of the solar system and orbit the sun traveling between planets. As a comet passes Jupiter and gets closer to the sun, the ice starts to melt, causing clouds of dust and gas. This cloud, called a 'comas,' forms around the comet, making a visible tail that seems to glow. A comet's tail always points away from the sun because the gases and dust particles are being pushed by solar wind."

Because of their local expert's description, Blaine and Tracey were now finding it even easier to differentiate between shooting stars and comets. They were both taking big 360-degree looks all around the room, watching as all kinds of comets zipped above, below, and around them.

"Every year a few comets do come close enough for us to view them from Earth with a telescope, but they usually look like fuzzy stars. In 1997 a comet named Hale-Bopp came close enough to Earth for telescope viewing. It's tail and all could be seen clearly. It won't return near to Earth for another 2,300 years."

"Twenty-three hundred years! Whoa, that's a long time!" The twins heard the girl exclaim.

The Sassafrases turned their attention toward the voice and could see there was now enough starlight to recognize that the other two children were a boy and girl who looked to be about the same age as they were. They were gazing around with as much wonder in their eyes as Blaine and Tracey.

"The most famous returning comet that is visible from Earth is Halley's comet," Minka continued, only to receive another exclamation from the talkative girl.

"Halley's comet? That's just like me! That's my name! There's a famous comet with my name!"

Not nearly as excited as the girl, Minka Ziven continued pensively. "This comet returns about every seventy-five years and is set to be seen in our sky again in 2061. It's named after scientist Edmond Halley, who predicted its return in 1705. He noticed there were similar descriptions of a comet being seen in the sky recorded at regular intervals. He used Isaac Newton's recent discoveries of gravity and motion to predict when the comet would be seen again. He didn't live to see it, but sure enough, his comet appeared in the sky once again in 1758."

"Wow! Halley's comet! That's awesome. A comet with my

name. That's pretty awesome, isn't it, Clive. Hey, Clive, I wonder if there's a comet with the same name as you?" The girl blurted out as she slapped the boy on the shoulder.

"Probably not," the boy said flatly. "But more important than what's named after who, I'm pretty sure that was the end of the first clue."

All four children looked toward Minka Ziven, who confirmed what the boy had said with a slight nod of her head as she stood stationary at her post with the eerie lights shining up on her, casting foreboding shadows on her pale face.

"How was that a clue?" the twins thought. That sounded more like SCIDAT information than any kind of clue.

They continued to look around the amazing room as they thought about all Minka Ziven had said. Were her words cryptic? Or had she stated what they needed to hear as plain as day?

"I've got it," the boy named Clive said faster than the twins though possible to figure out any kind of clue and with too small an amount of excitement, if indeed he had solved it. Clive walked over to a spot on the floor, followed by the girl, and pointed down.

"Watch this spot right here." He pointed. "It's the only point in the room at which all the comets intersect."

The Sassafrases walked over and joined the two at the spot Clive had pointed out and watched. The lights representing comets were flying all around the room in their rotations—on the walls, on the domed ceilings, and across the floor. It didn't seem like all these comets would ever get to the same spot, but as they waited, they saw that Clive was right. At just the right moment, and only for a second, all the comets intersected at this precise spot.

"How did you see that?" Blaine asked the boy.

"He's got a gift for things like this," the girl answered for the boy. "Hi, we're the Staneks, Halley and Clive Stanek. We're twins!"

"We're the Sassafrases, Blaine and Tracey Sassafras, and we're twins too. Nice to meet you guys," Blaine responded, holding out his hand for shaking. All four shook hands.

"We're from America, but we are here in Poland visiting the land of our parents' birth. How about you guys?"

"We're also from the good ol' U.S. of A.," Blaine answered. "We are here to study astronomy."

"So cool," Halley responded with a smile.

Suddenly, the pendulum knocked another block over, bringing everyone back to the reason they were standing where they were.

"Okay, so all the comets intersect at this spot. Now what?" Tracey asked.

Everyone shrugged except for Clive, who bent down and examined the intersection point. He studied the spot for only a few seconds, and then he used his hand to push down. This immediately caused a Frisbee-sized circular section to pop up out of the floor. Everyone gasped except for Clive, who reached into the cavity under the revealed circle and pulled out a . . .

"Quadrant," Minka declared, putting the children's thoughts into a word again. "This quadrant is your second clue. Quadrants are used to measure the angles and heights of heavenly bodies above the atmosphere. They can also be used to calculate longitude, latitude, and the time of day. This instrument was originally proposed by an ancient Egyptian astronomer named Ptolemy as a better kind of astrolabe. Several different variations were later produced by Middle Eastern astronomers."

Blaine and Tracey smiled. Although they had failed science in school last semester back before they had learned to love science, they remembered making a version of a quadrant in class. Their handmade quadrants had been pretty rudimentary, but they looked similar to this nice, copper-looking one they had just found. This one looked a bit like a protractor with a point on one side and then a curved edge on the other. There was a lightweight chain hanging from the point with an ornamented copper piece on its end. If the Sassafrases were remembering correctly, you were supposed to look down one of the straight edges toward the sun or moon or whatever you were trying to find the angle of. The chain, held down by the weight on its end, would stop at a precise degree point along the quadrant, giving the number of the angle you were looking for.

"Find the quadrant's proposer, and then use the instrument to find your next clue," Ziven instructed.

As she did, half a dozen portraits were suddenly projected around the room at different heights.

The Sassafrases immediately concluded these were all portraits of ancient astronomers, but they had no idea which one was Ptolemy, the proposer of the quadrant.

Clive, however, did. "It's that one right there," he said pointing. "That's Ptolemy."

"Are you sure?" Tracey asked.

"Oh, he's sure," Halley answered for her brother. "I got the brawn and he got the brains. Mom and Dad say that he's got a photographic memory."

"Huh," was all the Sassafrases could muster for a response, although they were intrigued and impressed.

"Either one of you guys know how to use this thing?" The gregarious girl asked as she yanked the quadrant out of her brother's hand and gave it to the Sassafrases. Clive didn't seem to mind at all.

Blaine took the instrument in his right hand and held it up in the direction of the portrait that Clive had said was Ptolemy. He closed his left eye then placed his right eye near the point of the quadrant. Blaine looked up the straight edge of the copper tool toward the Egyptian astronomer. As he did, the chain hung down and rested on a certain number of the quadrant's edge.

"Seventy-nine!" Halley Stanek shouted out. "Seventy-nine degrees is our next clue!"

All four children instinctively looked toward their hostess, Minka Ziven, who confirmed their correct guess with a slight, nonemotional nod of the head. Upon her nod, another set of previously darkened lights turned on all around the top of the wall. These lights were numbers zero to ninety, like the numbers on the quadrant. The Sassafrases liked how every time they got a new clue, more lights turned on. But still, the light they were going after, the ever-moving circular light, eluded them. The two sets of twins quickly looked for the number seventy-nine.

"Before you continue, a brief discourse on Ptolemy," the clue guide interrupted the children's hunt. "Claudius Ptolemy was an Egyptian with Greek heritage who studied math, the Earth, and the stars. He is believed to have been alive during the second century, but we don't know for sure because not much is known about his life. We do know, however, that he wrote several scientific books, including one that detailed his work in cataloging the stars and the position of the planets. He believed that all these

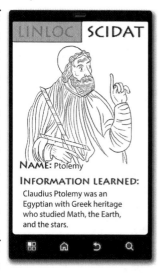

things orbited around the earth. His work was the astronomical authority for thousands of years. Even today, forty-eight of our constellations bear the name Ptolemy gave them."

As soon as Minka was finished talking about Ptolemy, all four kids rushed over to the number seventy-nine. Now as they stood beneath it, they found themselves facing the wall, staring directly into the face of another portrait.

"Who's this?" Halley whispered a little too loudly to her brother.

NAME: Copernicus
INFORMATION LEARNED:
Nicholas Copernicus changed astronomy when he proposed that the sun, not the earth, was at the center of our universe.

"Copernicus," Minka Ziven answered. "Nicolas Copernicus. Not only is he the one who pushed us to name this escape room after him, but he is the one who pushed astronomy forward into the modern age. He lived during the fifteenth and sixteenth centuries in Royal Prussia, which pushed on to eventually become Poland. Copernicus pushed science forward, and he changed everything the world knew about astronomy when he pushed the theory of our universe. He said the planets moved in a uniform path around the sun instead of an irregular path around the Earth, which was also the theory Ptolemy had pushed. Copernicus was pushed away by many of his contemporaries because of his new theory, and his ideas were not officially adopted until about a hundred years after his death. He truly pushed the envelope of astronomy, and his mark is still felt today."

"Was there a clue somewhere in all of that?" Halley asked, looking up at the number "seventy-nine."

Blaine put the copper quadrant in his back pocket and started looking around for any clue he could see. Surprisingly, Clive Stanek didn't have an immediate answer. This time around, the wonder boy actually looked stumped. Tracey, however, was not stumped. She wasn't looking around. She had heard the next clue clearly, and she knew exactly what they needed to do.

"Isn't it obvious, guys?" the Sassafras girl asked, now totally into this whole escape room thing. "Minka said 'pushed' like a hundred times when we were talking about Copernicus. I'm pretty sure we are supposed to push on this picture of him."

"Eight," Clive blurted out.

"What?" His sister asked.

"She said 'pushed' eight times, not a hundred."

"Whatever, Clive, help us push."

All four children put their palms on the portrait of Nicolas Copernicus. They all knew beforehand, and could now feel, that it wasn't an actual portrait but only projected light depicting his portrait. They were all fairly certain that pushing this picture was the next step toward their escape.

AWOL Ancients

The eight hands pushed and heaved, and upon their first effort, the section of the wall they were pushing moved backward. A rectangular shape about the same size as the projected portrait depressed inward, revealing a now window-type opening in the curved wall.

"Well, I guess you were right, sis," Blaine affirmed, proud of his sister.

"Yeah, great job, Tracey," Halley agreed. "Wait, does this mean we've solved the Copernicus Code? Is this window the way out of this escape room?"

"No, I think we still somehow have to get our hands on that light," Blaine reminded, pointing toward the three-foot light that had been rotating overhead almost from the beginning.

"Oh yeah, that's right," Halley remembered.

"Just as Copernicus opened up a whole new view of astronomy, the four of you have opened up a hole to another section of this escape room," Minka Ziven informed in her now familiar melancholic tone. "Proceed if you dare."

"Oh, we dare," Halley exclaimed, jumping through the window in the wall first.

She was followed closely by Tracey and Blaine. Clive, the slowest of the group, brought up the rear. The pendulum behind them knocked over a couple more blocks, bringing the number of standing blocks to a dangerously low number. The group of clueseekers needed to hurry.

Once through the opening in the wall, the twins found themselves in a small, square room about the size of a standard walk-in closet. The only thing in the room was a door. Halley stepped forward and pulled on the door handle.

"Locked," she declared. They'd all suspected as much.

The Sassafrases were tempted to lean their heads back out of the window and ask their clue guide for the next clue, but before they did, her monotone voice came through some speakers located somewhere in the new room.

"Johannes Kepler lived during the fifteenth and sixteenth centuries and built on Copernicus's work." As she spoke a projected portrait became illuminated on the lone door. It was one they had seen out in the first room, and they were now assuming it was a portrait of Johannes Kepler.

"Kepler agreed that the planets orbited the sun, but he said they do so in an elliptical path rather than the perfect circle that Copernicus had suggested. He accomplished much significant work in astronomy, mathematics and optics, but he is best known for his three laws that explain the relationship between a planet's distance from the sun and the length of its orbit. One of his most famous quotes is 'I demonstrated by means of philosophy that the Earth is round and is inhabited on all sides; that it is insignificantly small and is borne through the stars.'"

As soon as Ziven said the word stars, the small room lit up with stars in similar fashion to the first room. Feeling brash and confident, Blaine went up, put both his hands on the face of the door where the portrait was, and pushed. He pushed and he grunted.

Nothing. The door did not budge.

"No two clues are the same," Minka clarified over the speaker.

"Yeah, I know, I just," Blaine stammered. He was laughing, but he was also slightly embarrassed. "I thought, maybe you know . . ."

"No matter, Blaine," Halley encouraged. "Let's think this through a little more. The next clue has to be hidden in something we are seeing or something Minka Ziven said, right?"

The sound of more pendulum blocks falling echoed into their current room. Clive, who had been the star early on, looked perplexed and didn't seem to have anything to help them. Halley was full of spirit but was not full of answers. Tracey had come through for the group on the Copernicus clue, but she had nothing now as she stared at Kepler.

Blaine, still a little embarrassed about pushing on the door, didn't have anything either. He sighed and put his hands in his back pockets. "Ouch," he huffed. His right hand had hit . . . what was that? Oh, yeah, the quadrant.

He had slid the copper quadrant into his back pocket earlier. The Sassafras boy pulled the instrument back out and started fidgeting with it as he stared at the door and kept contemplating possible clues.

"Are there any obvious formations or intersections of the stars, shooting stars, and comets that are shining in this room?"

Blaine asked himself. It didn't seem like it.

Are there any visible numbers in this smaller room, or is there any way we can use the quadrant here? Blaine mused. If there was, it wasn't obvious.

Did Minka repeat anything over and over again in her last monologue? The mind of the scrambling boy asked. If she had, Blaine hadn't heard it.

The male Sassafras swung the chain of the quadrant around as he rehashed in his mind what Ziven had said about Johannes Kepler. "He did this, studied that, he accomplished lots of great things, and what was that quote she had recited? 'I demonstrated by means of philosophy that the Earth is round and is inhabited on all sides; that it is insignificantly small and is borne through the stars' or something like that? What a thing to say."

Blaine continued to muse. It seemed kind of true and kind of not true at the same time. "Is the Earth insignificantly small? Based on the scope of the universe, yes, Earth is minuscule. But insignificant? On the other hand, it doesn't seem small at all. Tracey and I have spent most of this summer zipping all around this wonderful planet, and we haven't even seen half of it yet."

"Insignificantly small and borne through the stars," Blaine replayed again, but this time he said it out loud.

"What did you just say?" Tracey asked.

"Oh, nothing," Blaine shrugged. "It's just part of that quote by ole' J. K. He said the Earth was insignificantly small and borne through the stars."

"Insignificantly small and borne through the stars?" Tracey repeated in question form.

Blaine nodded.

"Insignificantly small and borne through the stars!" The female Sassafras said again, this time excited.

"That's it!" She clapped. "That's the clue! Blaine, give me the quadrant."

Tracey yanked the instrument out of her brother's hand and held it up for examination. Blaine didn't seem to mind. After a couple seconds, Tracey grabbed the small, ornamented copper piece that was hanging at the end of the chain and held it up for her three companions to see.

"See? This is pretty insignificantly small; isn't it? But look closer. Do you know what it is? It's a key!"

Tracey excitedly took the newfound, tiny key and went over to the door. She bent over and looked all around the locked doorknob. "Borne through the stars," she repeated next as she examined every embedded starlight in the general area.

"Aha!" Tracey exclaimed rather quickly. She then slid the miniature key into the small keyhole she had found and carefully yet confidently twisted it. As she did, they all heard the lock mechanism inside the door click, and immediately the door opened.

The two sets of twins gasped in delight at first but then saw there was only darkness beyond the open doorway. Then, as before, some new lights turned on. These lights were altogether different from anything they had seen up until now. It looked to be a long, slightly curved hallway full of doorway-sized panes of glass that were reflecting light off each other and every which way. But it was not the ricocheting light that had captured their attention and given them pause.

When they looked into the space beyond the doorway, what the four saw was dozens of . . . themselves!

"It's a . . . it's a . . ." Halley started to say, but she was interrupted by the speaker with Minka Ziven's voice on it.

"Mirror maze," the dark clue giver provided. "The four of you are getting closer to your goal of capturing the elusive circular light, but before you reach it, you must make your way successfully through the mirror maze before you. Use haste, for at the current moment, there are only six blocks left unstruck by the ever-swinging pendulum."

Even as Ziven finished her statement, the twins heard another block fall back in the other room. However, any dread they may have felt was washed away by the positivity of Halley Stanek as she got her full statement out with excitement.

"It's a mirror maze!" The female exclaimed and then rushed forward into the labyrinth. She immediately smacked right into a mirror, but that didn't dampen her spirits, and it didn't stop her from recalibrating to look for the correct passage through the mirrors. Blaine and Tracey smiled and then followed their new friend into the life-size puzzle. Clive didn't smile, but he did follow with determination.

"Sir Isaac Newton was the first to use mirrors to make a telescope," the Polish local expert said over the speakers as the four children spread out into the mirror maze. "But it was Hans Lippershey who is actually credited with inventing the first telescope as he is the one who first applied for a patent on an instrument that used two lenses to magnify an object."

Blaine had laughed when he had seen Halley walk into a mirror, but now, seconds later, he found himself doing the same thing. Smack went Blaine as he bumped into an image of himself. He was still laughing but now at himself.

"I could've sworn that was an opening and not a mirror," Blaine chuckled.

"Galileo Galilei, who lived during the sixteenth and seventeenth centuries, came along and improved on Hans Lippershey's invention," Ziven continued. "He made telescopes that could magnify an object by twenty times. He made telescopes capable of viewing objects in space. He's the one who discovered Jupiter's moons, but probably most important of all, he used the telescope to prove that Copernicus's theory about the sun being the center of our solar system and not the Earth was correct."

NAME: Galileo

INFORMATION LEARNED:
Galileo Galilei made telescopes that could magnify an object by twenty times and were even capable of viewing objects in space.

Tracey was listening to every word Minka Ziven was saying so she could enter it correctly into SCIDAT later. At the same time, she was holding her arms and hands out in front of her so she could make her way through this maze without running face first into a mirror like she had seen a couple others do.

"Galileo had some ideas about falling objects that Isaac Newton later built upon as he wrote his theory of gravity and the Three Laws of Motion," Minka's voice continued over the speaker. "And as was alluded to earlier, Sir Isaac Newton began several experiments with light. In so doing, he came up with the idea to use mirrors to make the first reflecting telescope. What this accomplished was to reduce the haloes of colored light that would appear around objects when viewed through Galileo's telescope."

The Sassafrases had figured out that all the light in this room was actually coming from one source and, like Newton's telescope, was reflecting from mirror to mirror, making it look like there was more light than there was. However, figuring this out hadn't yet helped either of them figure out this maze.

Smack!

Another twin went face first into a mirror. It was Blaine again. It was a weird thing to see countless reflections of yourself seemingly walking around in different directions, then spotting an opening and taking it, only to run into a mirror and a version of yourself who came directly at you at the last second. Each child would also occasionally see images of one of the other three children.

It was eerie not knowing if an image was real or an illusion.

Tracey took a step to her left, walked three steps forward, and then found an open passage to her right. There she saw Halley, or at least an image of her. Halley smiled and reached out her hand toward Tracey. Actual contact was made as Halley's hand touched Tracey,s arm.

"Oh, good, it is you," Halley greeted happily. Then the Stanek girl pointed. "Look."

Tracey looked, and for the first time since entering the maze, she saw something other than mirrors. Tracey saw stairs. The two girls rushed forward, finally free of the labyrinth, only to run smack-dab into a reflective wall. The two fell backward and laughed about having been tricked one last time because now they looked to their right and saw their brothers had made it together to the real-life staircase.

The girls stood up and cautiously joined their twins on the bottom step. Behind them now lay the tricky mirror maze. Before them lay a staircase leading up to more darkness.

"Your successful passage through the mirror maze means that the four of you have solved all the Copernicus Code clues correctly up to this point," Minka the stoic clue guide said over the speaker. "Now all that's left to do is walk up the stairway before you and capture the light. If you can accomplish this last task, you will escape from this room. But be warned: the pendulum still swings, and there are only two blocks still standing."

At that, all four children looked at each other with urgency, then rushed up the staircase together. At the top of the stairs, they saw two things that rocked them. To their left, they were looking down on the room they had started in. The stairway had brought them to a small ledge or overlooking platform they hadn't been able to see from the big room earlier. From this vantage point, they could see all the stars twinkling everywhere. Minka Ziven was still standing over the eerie light and the ever-swinging pendulum. This meant the Kepler room and the mirror maze had been situated in a hallway that ran adjacent to the main room.

To their right, though, the two sets of twins saw something even more mind-blowing. There was a long, horizontal opening about five feet high and dozens of feet long. This opening looked to lead out of the escape room and toward the circular light they had been seeking. The mind-blowing part was that the circular light wasn't moving. It was perfectly still, situated on an exterior platform. The thing that was moving was them. Not just them, but the entire escape room they were in was moving.

"Oh, now I get it!" Clive shouted with his first smile of the day. "I feel silly for not getting it right off the bat. It's so simple!"

"Get what, Clive?" His sister responded. "Because there is nothing simple about this. The whole room is moving!"

"Exactly," confirmed Clive with delight. "That's the Copernicus Code."

"What?" Halley asked, still not getting it.

"Just as Copernicus came up with the universe-altering theory that the Earth revolved around the sun, this Copernicus Code Escape Room is revolving around that circular light, even though at first it looked like the light was the object that was moving."

"But at the beginning, that Minka lady told us to go capture the light that was moving," Halley said, pointing down at Minka.

"Actually, what she said was, 'Capture the circular light that seems to be moving,'" Clive corrected.

Halley paused and then nodded her head. "You know what, bro? You're right. You're absolutely right."

"I don't mean to butt in," Blaine interrupted. "But regardless of who's right, there's about to be only one block still standing. Look!"

Everyone looked down toward the pendulum and saw that Blaine was right.

"It's time to jump out of this moving room and onto that platform to capture the light!" Blaine charged.

"Yes!" Tracey, Halley, and Clive responded.

The two sets of twins then waited at the edge of the long opening to their right for the circular light and its platform to show back up, and when it did, they all jumped!

CHAPTER 14: THE NEW ZEALAND SPACE GAMES

Sporty Space Walk

With the help of their new friends, Halley and Clive Stanek, the Sassafras twins had cracked the Copernicus Code and gotten out of the escape room. They had captured the light just in time. Upon their successful exit, they were greeted by a cheerful, spunky young Polish woman who had her dark hair cut in a perfectly straight line across her forehead. It was Minka Ziven, and outside the confines of the dark escape room, she was a true delight. She had shown the two sets of twins around the Nicolas Copernicus Museum, where the escape room was located, on the beautiful grounds of the Frombark Cathedral.

Minka continued to serve as a kind of clue guide as she gave them more information about Copernicus and a few other astronomers. She also offered to share information about astronauts and space shuttles, but as she did, the Stanek twins' parents showed up and said it was time for them to go. Everyone had said goodbye and parted ways, and evidently, Minka thought Blaine and Tracey were a part of the Stanek family because when the Staneks left, so did Minka Ziven.

Blaine and Tracey had taken the time to put all the gathered data into SCIDAT. First, they uploaded all the needed pictures from the archive app, which had been the case for most of this astronomy leg of learning. Then they texted in the data about astronauts and space shuttles, which they had received from Paul Sims, and then the data about comets and ancient astronomers, which they had received from Minka Ziven.

The twelve-year-olds had crossed their fingers as they hit the upload button, hoping that having data from two different local experts wouldn't mess anything up . . . It hadn't! Not only did the SCIDAT data go through, but the LINLOC app also opened up this time without a hitch. Their next location was New Zealand, longitude +174° 3' 54", latitude -39° 4' 13'. Their local expert's name was Arty Stone, and they would be studying the topics of spacewalks, rockets, dwarf planets, and black holes.

Here the Sassafras twins were again, harnessed up and ready to zip through swirls of light. Their three-ringed carabiners snapped shut, calibrated to the correct coordinates, and off they zipped—two science explorers through transcendent light to their next scientific adventure.

The invisible zip lining came to a jerking stop, and the twins slumped down with no sight and no strength. After a few moments, both returned, and the twins saw they had landed in front of one of the most beautiful mountain-scapes they had ever seen. Even after all the amazing places they had been privileged to visit this summer, the twelve-years-olds were still enthralled with the beauty of the world they lived in, both outside the atmosphere and here under the atmosphere. The sun was beginning to set, and it was casting an amazing mix of colors onto the grandiose mountains as well as spreading color on the sky canopy above them.

The Sassafrases were truly filled with thanks. Tracey was about to voice her admiration but was interrupted by a voice that didn't sound thankful.

"Hey, you two, what are you doing?"

The twins turned to see a skinny, bald man with a headset glaring at them.

"Hey, I know it's pretty out here," he continued. "But you two are space walkers, and as space walkers you're not here to look at the scenery. You're here to work. So get back to work. Do you understand? We've got a show to put on here, and it's not going to put itself on!"

The man looked like he was about to say something else, but he was interrupted on his headset.

"What?" He questioned whoever it was that was speaking in his ear. "Mixer number three is down? Oh, for the love of peanuts, we are never going to get this thing up and running by tomorrow."

The man then scurried off, disappearing behind the small ridge he had been standing on.

The twins looked at each other, confused. Show to put on? Space walkers? What in the world had that guy been talking about? And where in the world did he come from? All the twins could see, even now that they were looking all around, was mountains. Maybe there was something on the other side of the small ridge the man had disappeared behind.

The twins got up and went to investigate. They were floored when they got to the top of the little ridge. It had been hiding a large, wide valley from their view. The valley was beautiful, like the mountains that surrounded it, but that's not what had floored the twins. The astounding thing was that the valley was full of people and equipment, and it looked like they were setting up for a huge, outdoor concert. There was already a large stage in place, but there also looked to be scaffolding, trusses, lights, speakers, and more that needed to be set up or was in the process of being set up. Now the twins knew what the man was talking about when he said there was a show to put on, but why had he called them "space walkers?"

"Hey! You two space walkers!" Suddenly, they heard the man's excited voice again. "I told you to get back to work, and I mean now! So, stop your gawking and get to it!" They saw him walking down the hill a little to their right.

"What should we get to work doing?" Blaine asked, trying hard not to sound sarcastic.

"You don't know what to do?" The man asked incredulously.

"Nope," Tracey answered.

"You're not joking; are you? You two really don't know what to do. Oh, for the love of pistachios, what kind of space walkers are they sending me these days?" The man let out an exasperated sigh and then turned and looked down into the valley where all the hustle and bustle was happening.

"Tell you what," he said. "Why don't you two go talk to Arty. He's one of our lead foremen, and he's always got a lot on his plate. Surely, he can put you to work."

The busy little man then pointed in a certain direction before he continued to scamper down the hill to join the anthill-like scene in the sprawling valley.

"Did you see who he was pointing at?" Blaine asked his sister.

"Not really," Tracey answered as she started down the hill.

"But he said 'Arty,' and the name of our local expert is Arty Stone. So, let's go find him."

Blaine followed Tracey down into the valley, and after asking only a couple of people if they knew where Arty was, they found him. He was a fairly tall, middle-aged man with a salt-and-pepper shortly trimmed beard. He was wearing a ball cap, long-sleeve T-shirt, and blue jeans. He was a lot calmer and nicer than the skinny, bald man wearing the headset had been, and when the twins asked him if there was anything they could do to help, he waved his hand with a smiled. "Sure! Follow me right this way."

He led them through bunches of workers, some of whom were doing heavy lifting-type work and others who were doing fine technical-type work, all for the successful setup of this outdoor concert or whatever it was, assumed the Sassafrases. Arty Stone eventually reached the big stage, and when he did, he climbed the steps and led the twins right up onto it.

"Okay, little space walkers," he said with a twinkle in his eye. "I need you to help me power up the old school Planet Prowess machines."

Sensing the man's kindness, Tracey thought she would go ahead and ask their question. "What's a space walker?"

"And what's Planet Prowess?" Blaine added.

Arty Stone looked at them at first like they were joking, but when he realized they weren't, he asked good-naturedly, "Where have the two of you been? Middle Earth? Planet Prowess is only the most successful and exciting arcade game ever invented. Besides, the two of you are here in New Zealand to work as space walkers, right?"

The blank look on the twins' faces spoke more clearly than any verbal response would have.

"Okay, none of us are real space walkers," Arty explained. "A real space walk is a period of time spent outside a real spacecraft in actual outer space by an astronaut. And really, it's usually more like space floating then space walking because of the whole zero gravity thing. Astronauts will do space walks to repair man-made satellites, to check the exterior of their spacecraft, or to help construct parts of the International Space Station."

The twins nodded in understanding—not because they understood why they were being called space walkers but because they had firsthand experience on the I.S.S.

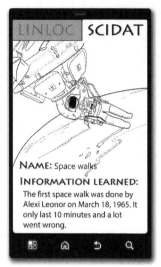

UNLOC   SCIDAT

NAME: Space walks
INFORMATION LEARNED:
The first space walk was done by Alexi Leonor on March 18, 1965. It only last 10 minutes and a lot went wrong.

"Astronauts have to use special space suits to survive space walks," Arty Stone continued.

"Oh, I know about those!" Blaine interrupted. "The space suits are equipped with water-filled tubes that can quickly cool or heat the astronaut. Because when a space walk is in the sun, it's boiling hot, and when it's in the shade, it's way below freezing."

"You're right, Blaine." Arty acknowledged. "Their space suits can be heavy and cumbersome, making even small tasks difficult, but it's totally worth it to help keep the astronauts safe."

The Sassafrases nodded, glad their Linc 2.0 space suits had kept them safe while they were in space.

"The first space walk was done by Alexi Leonor on March 18, 1965," Arty shared, clearly enjoying the scientific information more than the production setup they should be doing. "Leonov's space walk only lasted about ten minutes, and lots went wrong. Alexi almost died before making it back into the spacecraft, but the Soviets accomplished their goal, which was to complete the first space walk before the United States did. Shortly after that, on June 3, 1965, Ed White became the first American to complete a space walk. His space walk lasted about twenty-three minutes."

Arty looked up into the sky like he was envisioning those first space walks as he continued. "Probably the most famous space walk of all time happened on July 12, 1969. That's when American astronauts, Neil Armstrong and Buzz Aldrin, were the first humans to walk on the surface of the moon. All in all, less than six hundred people have been in space, and only twelve of those people have walked on the moon."

Blaine and Tracey took that part of the data to heart. They had joined this small, but mighty group earlier on their astronomy leg.

"But seeing that probably none of us have ever been to space, that's not why they call us space walkers," Arty Stone's words brought the twins back down to Earth. "We're roadies, for all intents and purposes, but they call us space walkers because Planet Prowess is a game about space. And although the professional gamers are the ones who get all the glory, we're the ones who do all the actual work, much like an unnamed astronaut doing the grunt work out on a space walk."

Now the twins understood, and they nodded. Stone pointed to the front center of the stage where even now, a dozen or so roadie-space walkers were working on situating two large arcade game machines. One looked old to the twins, and the other was a little newer looking, with a seat and steering wheel section attached to it.

"These are the first two editions of Planet Prowess," Arty said as he and the twins walked in that direction. "The original edition came out in the summer of 1981. It is a classic arcade machine with an upright chassis, inlaid and angled display, two simple speakers, a joystick, and one firing button."

As the three reached the machine Arty was talking about, he patted it like a proud papa. He then turned and put his hand on the other machine. "This baby here came out in 2001 for the special twentieth anniversary of the original Planet Prowess. It has all the same key components as the original. They added a player cockpit with an adjustable seat, a steering wheel, a rocket thruster pedal, and two buttons—a firing button and a view mode button. As you can see, it was a little bit of an upgrade from the '81 version."

The twins chuckled at the obvious statement from the foreman as did the roadies in the area. They finished placing the two arcade games in their spots and then scurried off to complete other tasks.

"Why are they being set up on this big concert stage?" Tracey asked.

"Concert stage?" Arty responded. "Why, this is no concert stage. This is a competition stage."

The blank looks returned to the Sassafrases' faces, so Arty continued his explanation. "This year, Planet Prowess is the marquee game for the PGC, the Professional Gamer Championships. So tomorrow, the best gamers from all over the world, plus a few local favorites, will be here to compete against one another at Planet Prowess for $500,000 in cash and the title of World's Best Gamer."

"Wow, World's Best Gamer. That would be a pretty epic title to have," Blaine thought out loud as he walked over and stood in front of the original machine. "So, what's the goal of Planet Prowess?" He asked the space walker foreman.

"The goal," Arty answered, "is to race your rocket past the planets to the end of the galaxy in the fastest possible time while avoiding asteroids, black holes, and shots fired from alien spacecraft."

Blaine nodded his head excitedly. "So, it's a space race!"

"You could say that," Stone responded. "But the real-life Space Race happened from 1957 to 1975 between the United States and the Soviet Union. Both countries wanted to be the first to send people to space, the first to walk in space, the first to land and walk on the moon, and so on. The world had never seen anything like it. The race between the two countries, combined with humankind's general awe and wonder about space, inspired all kinds of space-themed pop culture in the decades that followed, including the wonderful arcade game you are standing in front of now."

Blaine now looked at the game in front of him with a little more esteem. Tracey, feeling a little appreciation herself, took a seat in the 2001 version and put both her hands on its steering wheel.

"The Space Race actually began as a military plan to send secret satellites into space to spy on the other nation," Arty continued. "But thankfully, in the end, the two nations agreed to cooperate in their space ventures. And nowadays, Russia and the United States. work together on the International Space Station."

The Sassafrases knew this to be a fact. They had interacted firsthand with several astronauts on the I.S.S., including Captain Diana Sturgess from the United States and Engineer Sander Petrov from Russia.

Arty Stone paused on the history he was giving and knelt down to look at each twin with a smile. "You guys wanna try these babies out?" He asked.

The brother and sister looked at each other, then back to their local expert, then nodded emphatically.

"Okay," said Arty, jumping back upright to his feet. "Then help me get these two machines powered up, and let's do it!"

The twins happily obliged and followed the foreman's instructions as the three worked together to remove some floor panels from the stage and access the correct power cords running underneath. Then they connected the two game machines safely to the appropriate power sources. When this task was complete, both versions of Planet Prowess blinked to life.

"Ha ha! There you have it!" Arty laughed happily. "We've got them up and running. Now you two little space walkers get over there and try them ou—"

Suddenly Stone's sentence was interrupted by a shout from the edge of the stage.

"It's time to bring the hammer down!" A loud, obnoxious voice yelled.

Rocket Recreations

The three looked in the direction of the shout and saw not one person but a whole group of people walking up the stage's stairs. The group was being led by the skinny, bald, headset-wearing man the twins had met earlier. But he was not the one who'd shouted. The shouter had been the boisterous young man just behind the bald man

"Who's gonna Wayne? I'm gonna Wayne!" The big kid now shouted as he ran up onto the stage. He was the first on the stage. He was wearing black clothes with golden hammers printed all over them and was holding a smartphone in his extended right hand like he was having some kind of video conversation with somebody.

"Okay, Mr. Hammer . . . and everyone else," headset guy said. "This is obviously the main competition stage, and over there are the two old-school editions of the game."

"Whoa," the hammer-draped character exclaimed as he ran over to where the two Planet Prowess machines were situated. The two Sassafrases were still standing next to the machines along with Arty Stone.

"Get a load of this, Hammer Fans!" He shouted into his phone. "Look how old and dated these two machines are! They are ancient relics compared to the current VR version of Planet

Prowess! But no matter. I will soon destroy Thistler's records on both of these editions. And I'll maintain my status as champion on the current and relevant VR edition! It's time to bring the hammer down!"

"Vhatever, Hammer," a girl with pink hair and dressed totally in pink said with a Russian accent. "Nobody is going to take down the Thistler records. They vill stand forever."

"That sounds like something a number two would say, Pink Rocker," the hammer kid shot back.

"Vhatever, Hammer," the Pink Rocker snapped, rolling her eyes.

Hammer turned his attention back to his smartphone. "Okay, live-cast Hammer Fans. This is your gaming hero, Wayne Hammer, live from this year's PGC in New Zealand, signing off. I will be back online tomorrow when I will dominate all my fellow gamers as well as any local gamers that have the guts to step up and challenge me at Planet Prowess. Who gonna Wayne? I'm gonna Wayne!"

With that, the cocky video gamer finally pocketed his phone.

"Are these two games up and running, Arty?" The bald, skinny man asked the space walker foreman.

"Yessir, Mr. Sebastian. They sure are." Stone responded.

"Well, good, it's about time," the cranky man named Mr. Sebastian snipped before turning to the people with him. "Everyone, this is Arty Stone. He is one of our lead space walkers, and he is responsible for these two retro versions of Planet Prowess, among several other responsibilities."

Sebastian turned back to Stone and the twins. "I'm sure you probably already recognize them, but these are the current top five-ranked gamers in the world. We are so thankful they have all graced the PGC with their presence."

The twins weren't sure if Mr. Sebastian was being sarcastic or authentic.

"First we have the American Wayne Hammer," Sebastian continued.

"Who's gonna Wayne? I'm gonna Wayne!" The hammer-clad gamer shouted with a raised fist, actually audacious enough to repeat the silly slogan again.

"This is number two in the world, hailing from Russia, Ms. Pink Rocker."

The pink-clad girl gave a half-hearted wave, folded her arms, and then rolled her eyes again.

"Number three is standing right behind her, and his name is Mohawk Wellington. He is from Great Britain."

The twins saw why this gamer's name was Mohawk. He had the biggest and tallest Mohawk they had ever seen. But strangely, his hairdo didn't fit the rest of him. He literally wore what looked like a prep-school uniform.

"From Canada and currently ranked number four in the world, is Agnes the Librarian."

At first the twins didn't see the fourth-ranked gamer because they were looking for another young person. But then they realized Mr. Sebastian was referring to a middle-aged lady, probably in her fifties, wearing a long, brown skirt and a sweater vest. She looked very much like an actual librarian.

"She's a gamer?" The twins whispered as the bald man introduced the last gamer present.

"And, last but not least, from the country of Mexico, we have the number five ranked gamer in the world: *El Cohete Loco*." This one looked more like a Mexican luchador than anything else.

"It means The Crazy Rocket." The Mexican gamer's smile showed through his brightly colored mask. It was a carefree smile the twins immediately liked, and it made them smile too.

They smiled until Wayne Hammer stepped over and basically shoved them out of the way so he could get a better look at the 1981 and 2001 versions of Planet Prowess.

"Oh, yeah," he trumpeted as he started grabbing at all the controllers. "This is going to be even easier than I thought. Thistler's records are definitely going down."

He then looked over to the lower-ranked gamers. And none of you stand a chance against me. Tomorrow, I'm gonna Wayne as I bring the hammer down!"

"Vhatever, Hammer," the Pink Rocker responded again, probably voicing the thoughts of everyone present.

"Ok, gamers," Mr. Sebastian announced, raising his hand. "The caterers have contacted me on the headset, and dinner is ready. So please, follow me this way."

The cranky bald man and the world's best gamers filed off the stage. The Sassafrases weren't super sad to see them go.

"Oh, the sweet, sweet professional gamers," Arty chuckled. "They tend to be a little full of themselves."

Blaine and Tracey snickered back in agreement.

"And I do also apologize for my cranky, crusty old production manager," Stone remarked. "Mr. Sebastian can be a little snarky, but he's actually a good manager. He has a high standard for the PGC and for everyone involved in putting it on. The poor guy is overworked. Plus, he has to deal with those pro gamers all the time."

"Wayne Hammer and the Pink Rocker were maybe a little self-absorbed, but the rest of them seemed pretty nice," Tracey tried to be positive.

"Yeah, I especially thought *El Cohete Loco* was cool," Blaine added.

"Yes, *El Cohete Loco*," Arty smiled. "He wasn't even ranked in the top 100 last year, so he kind of came out of nowhere. He does seem like a cool guy, and I like his gamer name, especially for someone who will be playing Planet Prowess."

"How so?" Tracey asked.

"Well, you know, because his name is The Crazy Rocket, and Planet Prowess is a game about racing rockets."

"Oh yeah," Tracey responded, remembering the basic premise of the game.

"The rockets you race in the game are based off real rockets, which are responsible for carrying things and people into space," the local expert explained. "There are many types of rockets, including reusable space shuttles, military rockets, firework rockets, and experimental rockets. The first rocket to ever be launched was launched by Robert Goddard in 1926. It reached a height of forty-three feet, and the flight only lasted 2.5 seconds. Since then, rockets have gotten more complex and more powerful. The largest and most powerful rockets ever built were the Saturn V rockets. They were used between 1968 and 1972, thirteen times, including being used for the first moon landing."

NAME: Rockets

INFORMATION LEARNED: There are many types of rockets, including reusable space shuttles, military rockets, firework rockets, and experimental rockets.

"What a versatile expert," Blaine thought as Arty Stone spoke. "He's deep enough to know all about real rockets and cool enough to know all about video games."

"A rocket's payload, or the cargo it's carrying, is what determines what size the rocket needs to be," Stone continued. "Liquid fuel is burned to produce a stream of hot gas to propel the rocket up. Correct propulsion calculations are important as well. For example, to escape the Earth's gravity, a rocket has to travel greater than seven miles per second. This speed is known as escape velocity."

"Seven miles per second?" Tracey couldn't help but wonder out loud. "Wow, that's fast!"

"It sure is," Arty agreed.

Blaine was amazed by the rocket data and was taking mental notes for SCIDAT. He was also still wondering about a couple things Wayne Hammer had said. "What was that Hammer guy talking about when he said something about Thistler's records and VR or whatever?" He asked the foreman.

Stone acknowledged the question by chuckling again and shaking his head. "Yeah, Wayne Hammer was talking about Robbie Thistler. You guys ever heard of him?"

The twins shook their heads no.

"When Planet Prowess was originally released in the summer of 1981, there was a nationwide competition to help promote the game," Arty said. "Well, a nine-year-old boy nobody had ever heard of before, named Robbie Thistler, came along. He not only won but he also set a Planet Prowess record during that competition— one that still stands today as nobody has ever been able to top his score."

"Whoa," Blaine responded. "He was a video game prodigy! Is Robbie still a top-ranked gamer today?"

"Well, that's just it," the space walker said, shrugging his shoulders. "After his victory in '81, Robbie disappeared, and nobody ever heard from him again.

"Really?" Both twins asked, shocked.

Stone nodded, but then he paused with a smile on his face. "That is, until he emerged twenty years later for the release of the

Planet Prowess anniversary edition. And would you believe it?" Arty continued, still smiling. "Robbie sat down at that new 2001 edition, played one game, and set a record on that machine that also still stands today. Two editions. Two records. Both by Robbie Thistler."

As Arty Stone said this, he stepped to each machine and brought up the high scores. Immediately, Blaine and Tracey could see, plain as day, at the top of each leaderboard were four letters: T-H-I-S, the first four letters of Robbie Thistler's last name.

"Thistler disappeared into obscurity again after that 2001 record. And again, nobody has seen him or heard from him since."

"Do you think he'll ever resurface?" Tracey asked. "I mean, if he's so good at it, how can he not want to play again?"

"Nobody knows," Arty answered. "He was kind of a shy and reserved kid, so his appearance in 2001 surprised everyone. Some thought since he was older at that point, maybe he would stick around. But he didn't. When the VR version of Planet Prowess came out in 2016, many thought Robbie would show up again to set a record on it, but he never did. Gamers around the world speculated the reason for his absence. They figured he was an old man by now and an old school player, meaning the VR version was probably too fast and high tech for him. In the end, no one knows, and Robbie Thistler remains absent, almost like a ghost of the game."

"What does VR stand for?" Blaine asked.

"Oh yeah. VR stands for virtual reality. It's a mode of game play that makes you feel as though you are inside the game experiencing it as opposed to outside the game watching it."

"Oh, okay, now I get it," Blaine said, understanding.

"As you've seen, the 1981 version of Planet Prowess had a joystick and one button. In it your rocket basically races straight up the screen." Arty pointed at the original arcade machine.

Then pointing to the one with the seat, he continued, "The 2001 version makes you feel a little more like you're in the rocket, with the seat and the steering wheel and the different view modes. However, the virtual reality version of Planet Prowess is a whole new ball game! Not only do you feel like you are piloting your rocket, but you also feel as though you are truly in space. You can see the asteroids zipping right by you. You can feel the power of the black holes as they try to suck you in. You can use your hands to grab your blasters to fire at the alien spacecraft before their blasts take you and your rocket out. VR really does bring a whole new level of exhilaration to Planet Prowess."

"That sounds cool!" Tracey exclaimed. "Is the VR version going to be part of this PGC?"

"Oh, yes, definitely," the foreman answered. "Really, the VR version of Planet Prowess is the main event. First, all the professional gamers, plus one local gamer who will be chosen tomorrow morning, will compete against each other on the 1981 machine. The four highest scores will move on to see how they stack up against each other on the 2001 machine. Then, in the grand finale the two winners from the 2001 version will compete against each other at Planet Prowess, VR style. It's gonna be awesome!"

The Sassafras twins agreed. This whole thing was very exciting to them.

"Well," Blaine offered. "What else needs to be done? How can we help finish with the setup?"

Arty Stone was still smiling, but he sighed as he looked around at all the production set up that was still happening. "All these space walkers are working hard like ants," he said, proud of his coworkers. "But there is still so much that needs to be done. Why don't you two go over and help that group that is hanging the backdrop, and I will go check with the lighting guys."

The twins nodded and immediately obeyed. They were excited and honored to be a part of this grand competition, especially because they were working under the leadership of Arty Stone.

He was back in his old neighborhood—back in front of his old house, actually. When he had left here the last time, he didn't think he would ever come back, but here he was, standing invisibly in front of the house at 1108 North Pecan Street. Why? Because this is where Adrianna Archer had led him.

She had deserted him in Siberia, and out of all the places in the world she could have gone to, this is where she had come. Rescuing the lost astronaut had spawned dreams and ideas in his heart of how he and Adrianna could have ruled the world together in virtue, but when he returned from space to see she had abandoned him, all the malice in his heart had come rushing back. He had pursued her here, and over the past couple days, he had watched as she had tried to woo Cecil Sassafras. He had to give his nemesis some credit because Cecil had rejected her affections.

Adrianna, seeing that the house had been vacant, had decided to use 1108 as a sort of base—probably to work on another plan to snag the heart of the redheaded scientist and join his side.

Standing here now, invisible in the Dark Cape suit, he furrowed his completely hairless brow in determination. He was back on track to stop the twins from learning science, but he was now as equally bent on revenge against Adrianna Archer.

Blaine exhaled and wiped the sweat from his brow. Tracey yawned, tired but also fulfilled. They had both worked extremely hard all evening as space walkers, helping get everything set up for the PGC. The work was complete now, and everything looked great. The stage was set for an epic gaming competition that would happen here in beautiful New Zealand tomorrow. The twins had left their backpacks on the main stage next to the Planet Prowess arcade machines, and they were headed that way now to retrieve them.

All the space walkers slept in RV's parked at the edge of the venue, and Arty Stone had shown the Sassafrases which one they could use to get some rest that night. They needed to get their packs, and then they could get some much-needed sleep.

The stage lights were off, and it was pretty dark as Blaine set foot on the stage first, but it was Tracey who was the first to see the strange individual, a lone figure with raised arms standing in front of the 1981 version of Planet Prowess. She pulled on her brother's shirt and pointed, causing him to see the person as well. Upon the sighting, Blaine let out a surprised squeak, which in turn surprised the figure, who immediately turned and sprinted off the stage and out into the darkness.

The Sassafrases remained frozen for a second, not sure what to do. Then, more than a little shaken, the twelve-year-olds carefully made their way over to the arcade game where the figure had been standing. What the twins saw on the screen nearly made their hearts stop beating. It was the high scores for the '81 edition, and at the top of the leaderboard it no longer said T-H-I-S. Now there were four new letters at the top of the game: K-I-W-I.

Somebody had just broken Robbie Thistler's record.

CHAPTER 15: THE PLANET PROWESS LEADERBOARD

Dwarf Planet Diversions

Tracey giggled as she watched her twin brother Blaine clamber around the stage with the wireless virtual reality headset on. He was taking awkward steps, reaching his arms and hands out in front of him like he was attempting actual tasks. She knew he felt like he was in a real rocket racing his way through space, dodging asteroids and black holes and trying to elude alien spacecraft, but he looked more like a newborn colt learning how to walk.

His movements were awkward and jerky, and it was tickling her funny bone. She couldn't stop laughing. The funniest part was that she knew Blaine thought he looked awesome. She had tried this VR version of Planet Prowess herself. Tracey hoped she hadn't looked like her brother did now.

Arty Stone was standing next to Tracey, and he was laughing too. The Sassafrases had woken up early, as had their local expert. Because they hadn't gotten the chance to play Planet Prowess yesterday, Arty was giving them that chance this morning. The PGC didn't officially start for a couple more hours, and no fans had been allowed into the venue yet, so the old space walker thought it would be good fun for the twelve-year-olds to try their hand at the legendary game.

They had started at the 1981 arcade machine, then moved on to the 2001 version, and now they were getting to play Planet Prowess in virtual reality. Right now, only Blaine could see what was happening in virtual reality. Later during the actual competition, Arty said all the games would be up on the big screens where everyone could see what the professional gamers were doing. Blaine had topped Tracey's score on the first machine. She had beaten him on the second. And right now, their scores were close in virtual reality. Of course, neither of their points came even close to any of the top scores, but they were having fun nonetheless.

Last night the mysterious figure the twins had seen standing in front of the 1981 arcade machine unsettled them quite a bit, especially because whoever it was had topped the Thistler record. They told Arty about the incident, and he had immediately gone to check the machine. He looked to see if the machine had been tampered with. It hadn't. He ran diagnostics to make sure the new K-I-W-I record was real. It was. Whoever that shadowy figure had been, he or she had truly set a new record on the original Planet Prowess.

Arty Stone hadn't seemed overly concerned about the new record, but he had seemed surprised. "The Thistler records were thought to be unbeatable," Stone said. "Wait until the general public hears about this. They're gonna go crazy."

The three space walkers had spent some time speculating as to who the mystery gamer could've been. Was it Hammer? Probably not—he would have been shouting the whole time about how great he was. Was it Robbie Thistler himself coming back out of the woodwork? If so, why did he enter K-I-W-I instead of T-H-I-S? Was it one of the other top-ranked gamers? There was no real way to tell. Eventually they had put the questions behind them and enjoyed playing the games.

"Ahh!" Blaine shouted as he leaned left like he was dodging something Tracey couldn't see.

"Oh man," he then said, sounding disappointed.

"Your rocket got shot down; didn't it?" Tracey said smiling. "You're out; aren't you?"

"Yes," Blaine said. "Don't rub it in."

"Oh, I'm gonna rub it in, bro, because I'm looking at the scores up on the screen, and I can see who won, and it's not you it's . . . Oh who is it . . . It's me!"

Tracey did a little victory dance as Blaine took the VR headset off and looked at the scores. When he saw that Tracey was right and that she had indeed won, a good-natured smile of defeat formed on his face. Arty Stone chuckled at the twins as he took the headset from Blaine.

"So, in the first one," the boy started. "You kind of race your rocket straight up the screen as the asteroids and stuff slowly but surely grow in number and speed."

Arty and Tracey nodded.

"Then in the second one, there were actually checkpoints you had to make it to in a certain amount of time, right?"

"Right." Their local expert confirmed.

"But, man oh man, in this virtual reality version, the asteroids and alien spacecraft seem to come at you from all directions faster and faster, the black holes seemed real, and there were checkpoints, but they were a little different than in the 2001 version of the game, right?"

"That's correct." Arty confirmed and then explained. "In the 2001 edition the checkpoints are only the traditional planets of our solar system, but in virtual reality the checkpoints also include all the dwarf planets."

"Dwarf planets?" The Sassafrases asked out loud, thinking that they had heard a song about those somewhere.

Stone nodded. "A dwarf planet is a celestial body that orbits the sun, has a nearly round shape, and is not a satellite, meaning, it does not orbit around another planet. However, they do not meet all the criteria it takes to be considered a planet," the space walker said.

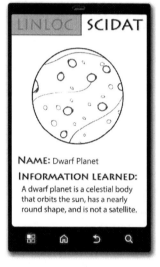

NAME: Dwarf Planet

INFORMATION LEARNED:
A dwarf planet is a celestial body that orbits the sun, has a nearly round shape, and is not a satellite.

"Right now, we have five planets in our solar system that are considered dwarf planets: Pluto, Eris, Haumea, Ceres, and Makemake."

"Pluto?" Tracey questioned. "Wasn't Pluto once considered to be a traditional planet?"

Stone nodded. "It sure enough was, but in 2006 the International Astronomical Union met and finally came up with a list of criteria for defining what makes a planet. The decision to do so came after the discovery of Eris and Makemake, which confused astronomers. They didn't know how to classify these two celestial bodies. It was at this famed IAU meeting that Pluto was downgraded from a planet to a new category of dwarf planets because of its small size. This was an unpopular decision at the time as Pluto had been the ninth planet for more than seventy years."

"Wow!" Tracey said, understanding.

"Pluto was found in 1930," Arty continued. "It is super

cold because it is farther from the sun than any of the planets. In 2017, we finally got the first close-up pictures of Pluto, so we know now that it is a rocky planet with ice and red snow. Although it is smaller than the Earth's moon, it has several moons itself, the largest of which is named Charon. A day on Pluto lasts 153 hours, and it takes Pluto about 248 Earth years to travel around the sun."

The Sassafrases remembered the strange time frames in regard to some of the planets and the speed of their revolutions and orbits around the sun.

"Eris is a bit larger than Pluto and is believed to be made of solid rock," the local expert continued. "It was discovered in 2003, and its appearance led to that same IAU meeting where Pluto was demoted. Eris has a day that lasts just under twenty-six hours and an elliptical orbit around the sun that takes a whopping 557 earth years to complete just one lap around the sun."

"Wow!" The twins exclaimed. "That's a whole lot of years for just one orbit."

Arty nodded at the twin's statement, chuckled at the twin's statement, and then continued. "Haumea, the next dwarf planet, is a bit of an astronomical oddball as it is oval-shaped more like a football than a round sphere. It orbits the sun just beyond Pluto, a day only takes four hours, but it does take 285 Earth years to make one lap around the sun. Next is Makemake, and it also orbits the sun just beyond where Pluto can be found. Like Eris, it was first spotted in 2003, a day lasts just under twenty-three hours, and it takes about 305 Earth years to complete a lap around the sun."

"Do you think it has red snow too?" Blaine asked. "Like Pluto?"

"It's quite possible," Arty Stone answered.

"So," Blaine said with a smile. "If Santa Claus were delivering toys on Pluto or Makemake, he would be camouflaged!"

Tracey sighed and shook her head. Even after twelve years

of knowing him, she was still surprised sometimes at what came out of her brother's mouth. The Sassafras boy's comment made the space walker chuckle once more before he continued.

"And, last but not least, we have Ceres. It is the only dwarf planet not found in the region known as the Kuiper Belt. Instead it is found between Mars and Jupiter. It was first spotted way back in 1861 and was thought to be an asteroid. However, at the 2006 IAU meeting, it was determined that Ceres met the criteria to be classified as a dwarf planet. It has a solid core that is covered with ice. A day on Ceres lasts about nine hours, and it takes just over four and half years to complete a lap around the sun."

The twins nodded, understanding both a little more about the planets as well as the game.

Blaine laughed at himself. "I barely made it past Mercury on the 2001 version of Planet Prowess. I can't even begin to imagine how Robbie Thistler made it through all the planet checkpoints, and then beyond, to set his record."

"It's pretty impressive," Tracey agreed.

"In the VR version I only made it a smidge past Pluto," Blaine added. "It's gonna be fun to watch later today how the pro gamers do it."

"It sure is," Arty Stone said with a smile. "And it's all going to begin in a little bit. Why don't the two of you come backstage right now and help me run through the final checklist with some of the other space walkers."

"Sure thing, Arty," the twins agreed, happy to help out.

A couple hours later Blaine and Tracey found themselves with some of the best seats in the house. This was the most exciting production they had been a part of since the TOBA talent competition in Sydney Australia. Even now, they were peeking out from their prime spots as space walkers, stationed behind the stage's big, colorful backdrop. Arty had put them here because later, they were going to help with the virtual reality equipment.

The twelve-year-olds smiled excitedly as the stage exploded with lights and music. The two retro arcade machines were blinking and ready for the gamers. The Professional Gaming Championship was about to start!

They had opened the gates to the venue only about half an hour ago, and already the valley was completely filled with excited gaming fans. It was a massive crowd abuzz with kinetic energy. All at once a person brushed right past the Sassafrases and out onto the stage. It was none other than the bald and grumpy production manager, Mr. Sebastian. Only, right now, he was neither bald nor grumpy because he was wearing a PGC-branded stocking cap and was using tons of positive emotion as he spoke to the gathered thousands.

"Gaming fans big and small, welcome to this year's Professional Gaming Championship in beautiful New Zealand!"

The crowd let out the collective, booming cheer they had been waiting to release.

"Our marquee game for this year's championship is none other than the legendary rocket-racing game: Planet Prowess!"

Now the crowd started a Planet Prowess chant. "Planet Prowess!" Clap, clap, clap-clap-clap. "Planet Prowess!" Clap, clap, clap-clap-clap.

Mr. Sebastian smiled and joined in the chant for a couple rounds before he spoke into the echoing microphone again. "This year, every single one of the world's top five ranked gamers has come to participate in the PGC!"

More vivacious cheering came from the throngs.

"I will introduce them shortly, but first I would like to announce the local gamer who has been selected to stack up his Planet Prowess skills against the world's best."

Now the crowd hushed a bit in deep anticipation of who the lucky local gamer might be.

"Hailing from Christchurch, New Zealand, is a young and fairly new gamer on the world's stage but who already has wins in both the Oceana and European circuits," Mr. Sebastian said with joy that was still surprising the twins. "Fans of the Professional Gaming Championships, let me introduce to you 14-year-old New Zealand gamer, Kiwi Jones!"

The crowd cheered as a somewhat shy but strong-looking teenager walked onto the stage and stood next to Mr. Sebastian. The kid smiled sheepishly and looked out over the multitudes that were now chanting his name.

"Kiwi! Kiwi! Kiwi!"

Blaine and Tracey looked at each other with possible realization. Could it be that Kiwi Jones was the mysterious figure they had seen last night? Was this the individual who had topped the insurmountable Thistler record on the 1981 machine?

Mr. Sebastian let the cheering for the local favorite go on a little longer before he spoke into the mic again. "And now, gaming fans, it is with great pleasure that I introduce to you the top five gamers in the world!"

Again, the lively crowd filled the beautiful valley with sound.

"Ranked number five is the masked gamer from Mexico: *El Cohete Loco!*"

The big luchador-looking gamer with the carefree smile walked from behind the backdrop, opposite of where the twins were, out onto the stage to the cheers of his fans. Many of his fans were wearing luchador masks themselves. He waved his big arms around at the crowd and then took his place next to Sebastian and Kiwi.

"Next, from Canada, we have the current fourth-ranked gamer in the world: Agnes the Librarian!"

The production manager announced Agnes with energy, but the reaction of the crowd was as if they didn't know who Agnes was. As the middle-aged woman walked onto the stage and took her place, one small cohort of fans, who looked to be middle-aged themselves, gave the eldest gamer some love by shouting for her. Slowly but surely the younger fans joined in, giving the librarian a decent welcome.

"Number three in the world, from the country of England, and with taller hair than any other competitor, is Mohawk Wellington!"

Only now, as the British player's fans cheered did the Sassafrases' see how many Mohawks there were out in the crowd. They were also beginning to notice how much pink hair there was out there as the emcee continued his introductions.

"And with the most colorful hair of any competitor, from the country of Russia, is the number two ranked gamer in the world: Pink Rocker!"

Both the Brit and the Russian now took their places at center stage to the cheers of the crowd.

"And now fans of games, gamers, and gaming, let me introduce you to the number one ranked gamer in the world. From the USA and holding this number one spot for over a year is a gamer by the name of Wayne Hammer!"

The second his name was announced, Wayne bolted out from behind the backdrop straight toward Mr. Sebastian, grabbed the microphone out of the skinny man's hand, and then made his way to the front and center of the stage.

"It's time to bring the hammer down!" He shouted to the applause of most in the crowd. Then with his second little motto he yelled, "Who's gonna Wayne; I'm gonna Wayne!"

Again, he shouted, "Who's gonna Wayne?"

This time he left the question hanging as he took the

microphone from underneath his mouth and held it out toward the crowd. The number one gamer was probably expecting the crowd to respond enthusiastically, but it ended up being more of a confused murmur, because no one knew if they were supposed to shout "I'm gonna Wayne!" like he said the first time or change it to "You're gonna Wayne!"

The pompous gamer was about to shout out something else, but before he could, Mr. Sebastian took back the microphone. "Okay PGC fans, let's get straight to it. Right now, these six gamers will compete against each other on the original 1981 Planet Prowess arcade machine!"

Now the energy of the crowd started to rile up again.

"As they compete live, right here on the stage, you will be able to view their every move as their play is projected onto the screens around you. Only the gamers with the top four scores will get to move on to compete on the 2001 machine."

Upon this statement, Wayne Hammer cast a victorious glance toward his fellow competitors, most of whom ignored him, except for Kiwi Jones, who looked pretty intimidated.

Mr. Sebastian continued. "The two gamers who score the highest on the 2001 machine will then move on to the championship round. This will place them in a head-to-head, simultaneous virtual reality battle!"

There was more cheering as the gaming fans expressed their sentiments. They were excited and could hardly wait to see all that was about to happen.

The lights on the stage suddenly shifted, and the intensity of the music shot up as Mr. Sebastian held the mic close to his mouth and said, "PGC fans, the wait is over. Let the games begin!"

The crowd cheered. Blaine and Tracey cheered. All the backstage space walkers cheered. It was time to see some prowess!

Way back at the back of the crowd, three friends cheered

with the throng. One had a Mohawk, one had dreadlocks, and one had ears covered in all kinds of earrings.

"Dude, this summer keeps getting better and better!" The one with the Mohawk exclaimed.

"Yeah, man, this championship is awesome, man!" The one with dreads added.

"And New Zealand is sick!" The only female among the three said. "Totally sick!"

"We have gotten to travel to some gnarly cool places, man, and this is now one of my favorites, man!"

"Right on, dude! From Peru, to that great wall in China, to scary So-Cal, to Switzerland, to surfing in Sri Lanka, and now here. It's been a wild ride, dude!"

"And now we're at these sick gaming championships! It's gonna be totally sick to see who wins!"

"Dude, I like the Mohawk dude of course."

"I think I'm pulling for the local kid, man."

"And me, I'm all in with the Russian chick. She has some sick pink hair!"

"Dude!"

"Man!"

"Sick!"

"This is gonna be awesome, man. I wish those gnarly cool Sassafras twins were here to see it, man."

Black Hole Humor

Blaine and Tracey found themselves watching with great excitement from their backstage spots as the first player took his stance in front of the 1981 Planet Prowess arcade machine. Right off the bat, the number one gamer in the world was getting the chance to prove why he was the best.

The game started, and the Hammer raced his rocket up the screen with tenacious skill. He made dodging the asteroids look easy. He made avoiding fire from alien spacecraft look simple. He made maneuvering away from black holes seem like a walk in the park. He hit the "fire" button at just the right times. He pulled and tilted the joystick like a bi-vocational astronaut and surgeon. His rocket raced up the screen, and the Sassafrases were sure that his point total was racing up the all-time scoreboard. The twins, along with the rest of the crowd, could see Wayne's every skillful move on the screens.

As the asteroids, black holes, and enemy fire grew in number, Wayne Hammer's video game prowess continued to shine as he kept racing onward and upward with evident ease. After what seemed farther than humanly possible, the hammer-clad gamer's rocket was eventually sucked into a black hole as he jerked the joystick a tad too much to dodge a shot from an angry alien. Wayne threw up his hands and turned to the crowd, pointing toward the screens that were about to reveal his point total. He looked confident and assured of a great score.

The 1981 leaderboard for Planet Prowess blinked up on the screens, but instead of the crowd cheering for Wayne Hammer, the mass of people gasped. They were now seeing the new K-I-W-I record for the first time. The top-ranked gamer's score was impressive, but his four letters, H-A-M-M, appeared in the third slot, only a few hundred points shy of the Thistler record.

Wayne Hammer was also seeing the record for the first time. He was shocked but not speechless. "What is this?" He yelped into the microphone on his gaming headset. "Is this some kind of joke? Who put the K-I-W-I up there on top? That can't be real!"

Mr. Sebastian made his way back out onto the stage, and this time he was accompanied by Arty Stone.

"Well, Mr. Hammer, this new K-I-W-I record is a surprise to

us all here at the PGC, but we have checked with our top expert, Arty Stone, and he said the new point total set by player K-I-W-I is in fact a new authentic and bona fide record."

Mr. Sebastian gestured toward Arty as he said "top expert," and when he did, the space walker gave a thumbs-up to affirm it was indeed true and authentic. The sounds from the crowd now began to morph from gasping to cheering, but Wayne Hammer was having none of it.

"No, no, no!" He shouted into his mic. "There is no way this new record is bona fide. If anything, the game I played is the new record!"

"I'm sorry, Hammer, but this year you'll just have to settle for number three," Mr. Sebastian said to Wayne. The production manager then turned to the crowd as Arty Stone and several other space walkers escorted the complaining gamer off the stage.

"Okay PGC fans, now it's time for the next gamer to take on the 1981 Planet Prowess machine! Let your cheers be heard for *El Cohete Loco*!"

The crowd obeyed joyfully and met the mask-wearing Mexican gamer with loud applause as he walked out onto the stage to face the arcade original. The fifth-ranked gamer tilted his head back and let out an exhilarating, trill-laced shout. He then took the joystick authoritatively in his right hand and started the game.

From the beginning, Blaine and Tracey were awed by *El Cohete Loco*'s rocket racing skills. They couldn't tell any difference between this fifth-ranked gamer they were watching now and the number one ranked gamer they had watched before him. The barrage of enemy fire and asteroids seemed to be only minor annoyances as he zipped by them with ease. The black holes seemed virtually powerless as *Loco* raced his rocket effortlessly away from their pull. As the obstacles became more numerous and the game seemed to get faster, the masked gamer remained calm and steadfast. He continued maneuvering the rocket masterfully with the joystick, like a snake slithering over a rock, a bird soaring through the air, an artist painting on a canvas, or a luchador fighting in the ring. The Sassafrases smiled with excitement as they watched The Crazy Rocket play.

All at once, as it had happened with Wayne Hammer, *El Cohete Loco*'s rocket was gobbled up by a black hole. Tracey grunted. Blaine slapped his hand against his leg. The two twelve-year-olds had wanted *El Cohete* to keep going.

The twins turned their attention toward the screens to see what his final score was going to be. As the numbers blinked up, Blaine and Tracey gasped with the rest of the crowd. *El Cohete Loco*'s score was . . . only ten points behind the score Wayne Hammer had set.

Unlike Wayne, *El Cohete* was completely stoked about his game. He pumped his fist in victory and smiled widely from behind his mask as he exited the stage to make way for the next gamer, who Mr. Sebastian announced to be Pink Rocker. It was time for the Russian gamer to make her attempt at surpassing her number one nemesis: Wayne Hammer.

As the pink-haired female gamer got her game underway, Arty Stone made his way to where the Sassafrases were watching.

"This is pretty fun huh?" He commented with a smile. "Those first two games were definitely impressive, and I'll bet the Pink Rocker won't disappoint either," Arty said. "But man, oh man, the black holes have been brutal today."

"They sure have," the twins agreed.

"You know, real black holes out in space seem to be pretty brutal too," Stone informed as he continued speaking of science. "Albert Einstein initially predicted the existence of black holes with his theory of relativity, but it was Stephen Hawking who eventually used math to prove their existence. Still yet, black holes are a bit of a mystery. We know there are regions of space where the gravity

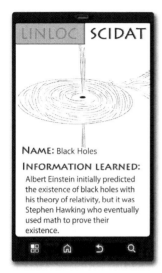

LINLOC SCIDAT

NAME: Black Holes

INFORMATION LEARNED:
Albert Einstein initially predicted the existence of black holes with his theory of relativity, but it was Stephen Hawking who eventually used math to prove their existence.

is so strong that it sucks everything, including light, into it. We also know that black holes act more like space whirlpools than space vacuums."

"Space whirlpools?" Blaine asked.

"Yes," The local expert confirmed. "Black holes are invisible, but we can spot them based on what goes on around them, and like a whirlpool, everything around a black hole swirls around and gets sucked in. This creates a circle or disk of particles that collect around them. Black holes also have a quasar, which is a jet of super-hot gas that shoots out above and below each black hole."

"Do the Planet Prowess black holes have quasars?" Blaine questioned as he took a glance at Pink Rocker, who was currently dodging black holes like a pro.

"No, I don't think so," Arty chuckled. "Planet Prowess's black holes are a lot simpler, especially on the '81 version. Real black holes can be complex. In fact, scientists believe there are three different types of black holes."

"Three different types?" Tracey questioned.

Stone nodded and then listed the three types. "Stellar, super massive, and miniature."

The twins watched the Pink Rocker's game play but also listened to their local expert closely as he expounded.

"Stellar black holes are believed to form when a massive star dies. Super massive black holes are extremely large black holes that can be found at the center of a galaxy, including the Milky Way. Miniature black holes are a type of black hole that has never actually been seen. However, scientists do believe these kinds of smaller black holes can exist."

Right as Arty Stone finished giving SCIDAT about black holes, the Pink Rocker let out a loud shout of disgust as her rocket was swallowed by a black hole in the video game.

"Another one bites the dust," Stone said to the twins with neither disappointment nor pleasure.

The scores blinked up on the screens, and the Russian's score hadn't even made it into the top 50, much less the new top spot. The pink-haired gamer walked off the stage muttering "vhatever" as Mr. Sebastian introduced the next gamer, who was Mohawk Wellington. The Brit with the prep school clothing and the street school haircut gave the 1981 machine his best, but his score ended up being even lower than the Pink Rocker's.

Agnus the Librarian was next, and although she walked out onto the stage with slow steps and folded hands, she wowed the crowd once she started the game. The middle-aged woman had the fastest fire button fingers of all the gamers, and she didn't disappoint on the joystick either as she maneuvered it with lightning-quick movements in all the right directions. The librarian posted a score in the top twenty, knocking Mohawk Wellington out of the competition and ensuring herself a spot in the next round.

The Pink Rocker was now on the bubble as the local favorite walked out onto the stage for his chance to compete against the professionals. Kiwi Jones shyly kept his head down as he approached the '81 arcade machine. He let out a long, nervous sigh and then placed his hands on the joystick and fire button. The game started, and as soon as it did, the real show started. Kiwi Jones may have been shy and timid in person, but he was not shy and timid in the game. He flew his rocket up the screen as though he was one with the game, as though he knew where the asteroids were going to be before they were there. He played like he knew when the alien spacecraft were going to shoot before they fired.

And he maneuvered as if he could calculate the pull and spin of the black holes before they appeared.

The Sassafrases were awed along with the crowd. They wished the scores were visible while the gamers played so they could see how Jones was doing right now, but they would have to wait until his game was over to see his score—if, in fact, his game ever came to an end, which by the way he was currently playing, looked like it might never happen.

The video screen became so full of black holes, asteroids, and alien spacecraft that there didn't look to be any open spaces big enough for Jones's rocket, but still he flew on. Eventually proving he was human after all, Kiwi Jones's game came to an end as his rocket was clipped by an asteroid and crashed.

The crowd fell silent as they waited to see the local teenager's score. However, when the score blinked up on the screens for all to see, the large crowd stayed silent no longer but erupted in uproarious applause. Kiwi Jones had just set a new all-time record. The top two scores were now both K-I-W-I and K-I-W-I.

The Sassafras twins looked at each other with joyful realization. It had been Kiwi Jones they had seen last night on the stage. And now, he hadn't just beaten the Thistler record once; he'd beaten it twice. And maybe even better than that, he'd beaten the score of the arrogant Wayne Hammer.

Arty Stone, who was still standing next to the twins, started up his good-natured chuckling again. "All hail the new king of Planet Prowess," he said as he looked at the New Zealand teenager admiringly. After several minutes of lively cheering and chants of "Kiwi! Kiwi! Kiwi!" Mr. Sebastian was finally able to get the attention of the crowd and move the competition on from the 1981 version of Planet Prowess to the 2001 version, which would serve as the next round for this gaming competition.

The four gamers moving on were Agnus the Librarian, *El Cohete Loco*, Wayne Hammer, and the new fan favorite: Kiwi

Jones. The first player to sit down at the sleeker version of the classic game was *El Cohete Loco*. He was a large, muscular man, so he adjusted the seat all the way back, chose the "cockpit view" with the mode button, and placed his big hands on the steering wheel. His right foot hovered over the rocket thruster pedal and he was ready to go. The second the game started, and the big gamer stomped down hard on the pedal, and shot off, racing his rocket through space.

Now instead of a simple pixelated rocket moving up a screen, the video screen made it look like the player was actually navigating the rocket forward. With skill and savvy, El Cohete raced around asteroids, dodged enemy fire, and steered like a crazy rocket away from black holes. He was passing the planet checkpoints with flare like the crazy rocket he was until he was shot down by an alien blaster somewhere on the backside of Jupiter. The death shot had seemingly come out of nowhere, and it caused the entire crowd of gaming fans to gasp and then to commiserate the popular gamer's end.

The Sassafras twins looked at each other with raised eyebrows. This 2001 version looked much more difficult than the 1981 version. They wondered how the other three gamers would fare.

El Cohete Loco stood from the machine, flashed his patented, lighthearted smile to the crowd, took a small bow, and then exited the stage. His score blinked up on the screens as he left, and more than likely it wouldn't be enough to move on.

Agnes the Librarian was next, and like the first time around, she took her place slowly but then dazzled the fans with her frenetic pace of play. She fared a little better than her Mexican counterpart, but the Sassafrases wondered, too, if the librarian's score would be high enough to move her into the finals.

Shouts of "Kiwi! Kiwi! Kiwi!" rose again from the crowd as the young New Zealander took his place in the seat of the 2001 machine. Even after his amazing, record-setting win earlier, Kiwi still looked extremely nervous. His hands were visibly shaking as he placed them on the steering wheel. Once again, he let out a long exhale before he started the game, and when the game got underway, he put on a show. It was as if the New Zealand native could telegraph what was going to be thrown his way and then could almost predetermine what moves needed to be made to dodge them and move forward.

He zipped past Jupiter and Mars and all the other planet checkpoints, including Pluto, which in 2001 was still considered to be the ninth planet. Out beyond Pluto, where the Thistler record was waiting somewhere, he raced his rocket past all the Planet Prowess obstacles.

His game eventually came to an end farther out than any gaming fan had thought humanly possible. As the young man's score blinked up on the screens, there was a slight moan from the mass of fandom that quickly turned to congratulatory applause. Kiwi Jones had not broken the Thistler record, but he had set the number two highest score. The crowd was squarely behind the local now, and they had wanted him to break the old record.

Before Kiwi was able to get all the way off the stage, Wayne Hammer barreled out from behind the backdrop and began his brash antics. He ran right up to the edge of the stage and tried to pump the gaming fans up with shouting and wild, swinging arms.

"It's time to bring the Hammer down," he yelled. "Who's gonna Wayne? I'm gonna Wayne!"

The crowd was making a lot of noise, but Blaine and Tracey couldn't tell if it was cheering or jeering.

"Who's gonna Wayne?" Hammer shouted. Again, he held a hand out toward the crowd, looking for a responsive shout from them. But like the first time he'd attempted it, the fans didn't know how to respond. Were they supposed to shout with him or what?

One guy with dreadlocks in the back of the crowd actually

responded with, "Kiwi's gonna win, man!"

This sent a wave of laughter rippling throughout the sea of people that surged forward and hit Wayne Hammer with an ocean of realization. This crowd was behind Kiwi Jones, not the Hammer. The number one gamer sat down angrily in the seat of Planet Prowess 2001, aggressively grabbing the steering wheel.

The Sassafras twins wondered if the fans had given Wayne Hammer the motivation he needed to obliterate both Kiwi's score and the age-old Thistler record. The highest-ranked gamer in the world immediately showcased his talent. He was every bit as good as Kiwi Jones. He also had the unnatural ability to seemingly telegraph obstacles and then make the best moves possible. Hammer made quick work of the eight planet checkpoints and then soared out beyond Pluto.

Again, the twins wished they could watch the scores as they accumulated in real time, but that was not the way the PGC was set up. They would have to wait.

After what seemed like forever, the number one gamer's run came to a crashing end, to which he responded with shouts of disgust and slammed fists. The leaderboard scores blinked up on the screens and they read: Number one was T-H-I-S; number two was K-I-W-I, and number three was H-A-M-M. Kiwi Jones had edged out Wayne Hammer by only five small points during this second round.

The mass of gaming fans cheered as Mr. Sebastian walked out and announced the two finalists for the Professional Gamer Championships. "Kiwi Jones and Wayne Hammer!"

The top-ranked gamer looked disgusted as he stumbled out of the seat of the 2001 machine. Kiwi, on the other hand, looked surprised and grateful as he emerged out onto the stage from behind the backdrop.

"Who do you think you are?" Hammer shouted and then

suddenly charged toward Jones. "You're a zero! A zilch! A nobody! And you think you can come in here and lay down some lucky scores like you're something?"

Wayne looked like he was mad enough to actually attack Kiwi, but before that was able to happen, a swarm of space walkers rushed out onto the stage and stopped him. The PGC roadies formed a protective circle around the local gamer. Blaine and Tracey were part of the swarm, mainly because they had been pushed forward by the space walkers behind them. Now they found themselves face-to-face with Wayne Hammer as he continued to spew insults in Kiwi Jones's direction.

"You think you can beat me, kid? Huh? Do you? You're nothing! I'm going to destroy you in the final round! Virtual reality is my forte! You'll wish you never set foot on this stage!"

"Whoa, whoa, whoa there, little buddy, that's enough. Settle down." Arty Stone commanded.

"Shut your trap, old man!" Wayne yelled, now turning his attention toward Arty. "You're a nobody, too. You think you can hold me back? You think you can talk to me like that? I'm the number one gamer in the world. You're just some nonessential backstage grunt. Get out of my way!"

Instead of getting out of his way, Stone reached out and picked up Wayne Hammer over his shoulder like a sack of potatoes. He then single-handedly carried the golden-hammer-clad gamer off the stage kicking and screaming. The rest of the space walkers gently ushered Kiwi Jones off the stage in the opposite direction. The crowd, who had been shocked by the ordeal they had witnessed, seemed like they didn't know what to do.

Sebastian stepped up as if he'd expected things to play out as they had. "Well, gaming fans, the stage couldn't be set any better for the finals! It's what you all came here to see: an epic showdown between two of the worlds' best gamers! It's guaranteed to be a legendary finish. Kiwi Jones, the newcomer from New Zealand will battle against American Wayne Hammer in Virtual Reality Planet Prowess! Who will win this year's Professional Gamer Championship? Everyone stick around to see how it all plays out!"

Now the sea of fans knew how to react, and they showed it with thunderous applause. Blaine and Tracey cheered along with the crowd. They too thought this was going to be an unforgettable finish to the PGC.

CHAPTER 16: THE SET OF *STAR CHECK*

Constellation Display

With colorful, flashing lights and resounding music pumping from a multitude of speakers, the final round of the Professional Gamer Championships got underway. The huge crowd was squarely behind the local unranked gamer, Kiwi Jones. They had been showing their support with well-wishing cheers and chants of his name throughout the final.

Wayne Hammer was still visibly frustrated about this fact, but he had calmed himself enough to play his game. He was showing why he was ranked number one in the world, and much to the dismay of the crowd, he appeared to be beating Kiwi handily.

During this final virtual reality round, the two finalists were playing Planet Prowess at the same time. The entire crowd could see every move both players were making via large screens as they raced their virtual rockets through space. Hammer's moves were fluid and agile. His rocket was already well beyond all the dwarf planet checkpoints and deep into the great beyond. Jones's moves, on the other hand, looked jerky and abrupt. He had made it past the last dwarf planet, and that was a surprise with how uncomfortable he looked. The Sassafrases wondered if the reason for this was because he had to play side by side with Wayne Hammer. Or maybe he wasn't as good at virtual reality as he was with the more classic-style video games. Whatever the reason, he looked extremely shaky and every bit the underdog he was.

The two gamers continued peering into the headsets and using the handheld accessories to shoot at asteroids and alien spacecraft and to glide past monstrous, spinning black holes. Then, suddenly, what no one wanted or expected to happen happened. Kiwi Jones's rocket was blown up by a single shot from a stealthy alien. The cheering crowd immediately deflated. Kiwi's shoulders slumped, and he slowly reached up and pulled off his virtual reality headset.

Wayne Hammer, however, puffed up even more and continued racing his rocket farther and farther. He started laughing an arrogant laugh because he knew he had won the championship, but he wasn't about to stop. He didn't just want to beat Jones. He also wanted to beat the all-time VR record.

After a showcase of otherworldly skill, the Hammer was finally downed by an asteroid. He immediately ripped off the headset and raised his hands in victory. The VR leaderboard scores blinked up on the screens, and there it was for all to see. Number one by far was H-A-M-M. Kiwi Jones's score hadn't even made the top twenty.

"Look at that loser!" Wayne shouted, sticking a finger in Kiwi's face. "Your name's not up there, is it? That's because you stink! You don't belong here! So go back to whatever hole you crawled out of, and never come back!"

Jones's shoulders slumped even lower as he was being heckled. Hammer drew up closer to him and continued shouting insults. The throng of space walkers was ready to rush the stage again to pull the two apart, but before they could, a single individual walked out onto the stage.

The person's presence stopped the roadies in their tracks and even silenced Wayne Hammer. The Sassafrases were confused. Why was it a big deal that he had walked out onto the stage? It was only Arty Stone. He looked a little different now, but it was just Arty. Their local expert had removed his hat, he had put on glasses, and he had shaved off his salt-and-pepper beard. The twins thought all this was a little strange, but it was just Arty, right?

Rumblings from the crowd could now be heard up on stage. They were saying the name, "Robbie Thistler."

"Robbie Thistler?" The twins thought. "Where was Robbie Thistler?"

Mr. Sebastian now emerged onto the stage and looked speechless, although he wasn't actually speechless because he started mumbling into the microphone. "Arty, I had no idea . . . I thought you were just a space walker . . . a really good space walker, but I didn't know you were . . . him."

Arty smiled. His face was displayed on all the screens.

Wayne, unwilling to be silent, started a brand-new rant. "Hey! Mr. Producer Man. Who cares who this old guy is? I just won the PGC! Why don't you announce my name as the winner?"

Mr. Sebastian looked at Hammer like he was crazy. "Because Robbie Thistler showed up; that's why."

"Sure, he looks a little bit like him," Wayne rebutted. "But I think this guy is just a space walker—Arty Stone or something like that. Who cares? Let's talk about me and my big win!"

"It's R. T. Not Arty," Stone corrected.

"What? R. T.?" Hammer questioned.

"That's right. R. T.—short for Robbie Thistler."

"What about Stone?" Hammer questioned, still shouting.

"Stone is my middle name. I was born Robert Stone Thistler."

The rumblings from the crowd now turned into shouts and cheers of joy. Robbie Thistler, the legend, had returned, and they were here to witness it. Blaine and Tracey looked at each other with shocked smiles. Their local expert just so happened to be the best Planet Prowess gamer who had ever lived!

"Okay, okay, but who cares?" Wayne said, facing Stone, and trying to raise his voice louder than the cheering crowd. "I'm the champion here! I'm the number one gamer in the world, and I brought the hammer down! Who are you? Some old washed-up yesterday's champion? Sure, you were good in 1981 and 2001, but what about now? What about virtual reality? VR is a whole new ball game, old man! You are way too geriatric to handle all that

VR can throw at you. It's much more complex than a joystick or a steering wheel. You'd have no chance in today's game. You old geezer!"

Instead of responding with words, R. T. Stone responded by picking up a virtual reality headset and putting it on. The crowd cheered so loudly that the twins were sure it measured on the Richter scale.

What happened in the glorious moments that followed was nothing short of miraculous—R. T. Stone, or rather Robbie Thistler, blew Wayne Hammer's virtual reality record out of the water. Wayne was left speechless. Although he was the champion of the PGC and was still the world's number one ranked gamer, he held no Planet Prowess records. T-H-I-S held the records on both the 2001 and the virtual reality versions, and K-I-W-I held the new record on the 1981 original.

As the PGC came to a close and the sun began to set in beautiful New Zealand, the cheering fans slowly and joyfully filed out of the venue. Mr. Sebastian breathed a sigh of relief that it was all over then switched back to his normal grumpy but lovable self. R. T. Stone couldn't congratulate Kiwi Jones enough on breaking his 1981 record. It was apparent the two would become fast friends.

The Sassafras twins found the same spot where they had landed, and then they entered their SCIDAT data and pictures. They put on their harnesses, calibrated their three-ringed carabiners, and prepared to disappear again from their science-learning location. As they got ready to zip, they wondered if Robbie Thistler was going to disappear again to leave the gaming world in suspense. They didn't know, but they sure did like Arty Stone, and they were appreciative of all he had taught them.

The twelve-year-old space walkers zipped off into swirls of free-flowing light toward their next location, which LINLOC had shown as Mumbai, India. There they would be studying

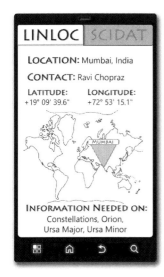

LINLOC SCIDAT

LOCATION: Mumbai, India

CONTACT: Ravi Chopraz

LATITUDE: LONGITUDE:
+19° 09' 39.6"   +72° 53' 15.1"

INFORMATION NEEDED ON:
Constellations, Orion,
Ursa Major, Ursa Minor

constellations in general and then, more specifically, Orion, Ursa Major, and Ursa Minor. Their local expert's name was Ravi Chopraz. At least that's what LINLOC said—maybe he had a couple different names like Arty.

The Sassafrases landed with a jerk, and when their strength and sight returned, they saw they had landed in comfortable chairs, comfortable movie-director-style chairs that were each situated in front of mirrors. Under each mirror was a shelf covered with a wide assortment of what looked like makeup products.

The twins took off their helmets and backpacks. "Wow," Tracey thought. "We've landed in a makeup and powder room!"

For this reason, Tracey was about to turn toward Blaine and

smile, and for the same reason, Blaine was about to turn toward Tracey and fake dry heave. But before they could, two stylists rushed into the room and approached them.

"Oh, good, you're here!" The first one said and took her place next to Tracey.

"Now, it's time to spruce you up and give you some pop and pizzazz!" The second one said, sidling up to Blaine.

Both women were Indian, energetic, and excited about whatever it was they were about to do. Tracey's stylist started playing with the girl's hair and talking through style options. Blaine's stylist started pushing on the boy's cheek bones and mentioned how they could use a little color. A smile now found its way to Tracey's face as Blaine's dry heave resurfaced, only this time it was for real.

As though they had done it a thousand times, the two women grabbed this and that from the makeup shelf and went to work on the twelve-year-olds' appearances. To Tracey, the makeover felt like a dream come true. She'd always dreamed of being primped and pampered by a professional stylist. To Blaine, it felt like a nightmare—the nightmare of being stuck in a tornado of blush, eyeliner, and hairspray. Tracey kept her eyes open and gazed into the mirror in front of her. Blaine kept his eyes shut and made wish after wish that it would soon be over.

When it was over, both twins looked into their mirrors with their stylists standing proudly behind them. The brother and sister could see they now looked like . . . movie stars! Tracey was still smiling and excited to be wearing makeup and boldly styled hair. Blaine's original look of horror was now slowly turning into a smile to match his sister's. Sure, he had a little makeup on, but with fluffed, wavy hair—Wow!—he looked good! The twins didn't know who these stylists thought the two of them were or why they had received the treatment they had, but they had never been so gussied up in their whole lives!

Blaine was about to turn toward his sister and attempt to say something debonair, but before he could, a new rich, loud, and confident voice filled the room.

"We're going to be fine, Varun. With my acting skills combined with Preathi's editing skills, how could they even think about cancelling us? C'mon let's be serious."

The voice was coming from a tall, handsome Indian man with a jawline set like a king's and a wave of perfectly styled hair that look surfable. He looked at the twins and their stylists and smiled, his eyes twinkling and his teeth perfectly white. He was wearing some kind of form-fitting, futuristic-looking jumpsuit and had a holster and belt around his waist.

Another man had entered with him, and he looked shorter, rounder, and less sparkly. "Ravi, I am being serious. They can cancel us, and I think they might," the shorter man said, full of worry.

The handsome one named Ravi, whom the Sassafrases immediately presumed was their local expert, Ravi Chopraz, walked to a mirror and gazed at his own reflection admiringly. "Varun, this face is not a cancelable face."

The man named Varun sighed.

"And as I was saying," Ravi continued, "have you seen the latest stuff Preathi has been up to? Have you seen her latest green screen work?"

"Yes, I have, and it's great, but . . ."

"But what, Varun? It's incredible! Did you know she can superimpose all eighty-eight of the internationally recognized constellations into the background of our set with a green screen?"

"Yes, but will it look real?" Varun asked. "If the constellations don't look real, the executives will probably cancel us. In the past, the best our editors could do was make the stars look like marshmallows floating in the background."

"But you know Preathi can do better than that!" Ravi reassured with another sparkle of his teeth.

"Like the rest of the cast and crew, and me of course, Preathi is a star! She's such a star that they should name a star after her. You know, Varun, constellations are collections of stars that have been named and are visible from Earth. All constellations have Latin names. Some have a local nickname, but all have a story behind them. Many were named after characters in Greek mythology."

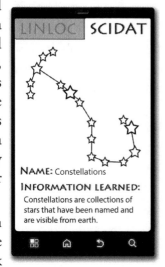

NAME: Constellations

INFORMATION LEARNED:
Constellations are collections of stars that have been named and are visible from earth.

"Greek mythology, huh?" Varun said with a shake of the head. "We're trying to do a sci-fi here, not Greek mythology."

"That is correct," Ravi said. "But why not mix a little science fact in with our science fiction? For example, did you know that stars within a constellation can be fifty to six hundred light-years away from each other even though they look a lot closer to us here on Earth?"

Varun shook his head "no" and also shook it like he didn't care to know what Ravi was talking about.

The actor continued nonetheless. "Astronomers once believed the constellations of stars resided in a globe around the Earth, which they called the Celestial Sphere. Although we now know this is not true, it is still used as a helpful way of pinpointing the stars. The celestial sphere is cut into two halves: the northern and the southern celestial spheres. The constellations you see and when you see them depends on where you live on Earth. For instance, here in India, we live in the northern hemisphere, so we can see the constellations in the northern celestial sphere."

Ravi paused for a moment, turned toward his companion, grabbed him by the shoulders, gazed deep into his eyes, and then asked him, "Have you ever gazed at the stars, Varun? Have you ever laid on your back in an open field and set your attention to the great beyond? Have you stared at that hazy river of stars, known as the Milky Way, that we can see in our night sky? Have you ever noticed that the stars don't stay still all night long, but that they appear to move through the sky as the Earth rotates? Have you, Varun? Have you?"

The shorter, rounder man broke from the gaze, took Ravi's hands off his shoulders, and then seemingly got more frustrated than he had been thus far. "Ravi! Enough about constellations! You're a television star, not a scientist, and I am a director, not a student. I need you to focus and come up with your best performance today. You're the star of *Star Check*. My direction is important, but everything rises and falls on you. We don't want to lose our jobs. We can't let *Star Check* get cancelled. Do you understand?"

Ravi smiled at Varun with his million-dollar smile and replied with a wink. "Reading you loud and clear, boss."

The television show director walked off, shaking his head and mumbling something under his breath. Ravi turned his attention toward the two stylists and the two children.

"Sana! Puja! Good morning. How are the two best stylists on the planet doing this morning?"

"We are wonderful, Mr. Chopraz," the stylist standing behind Tracey responded with a smile.

"Sana, I've told you that Mr. Chopraz is my father. Please call me Ravi."

The actor then gestured toward the Sassafrases. "Are these our twins?" He asked with a smile.

"Yes, they are," Puja, Blaine's stylist, answered.

The twins sat up straight, alarmed. How did these people already know them?

"Ah, the two Orion siblings who we are going to rescue from Riggamorak and the clutches of the Borbothians. These two siblings look perfect for the part!"

Blaine and Tracey laughed nervously. Riggamorak? Borbothians? Orion siblings? What in the world was this guy talking about?

Ravi Chopraz approached them and put his hands on their shoulders.

"Welcome to Bollywood!" He said with a wide smile.

Presenting Orion

"Bollywood?" Blaine asked.

"Yes, Bollywood!" Ravi confirmed. "Centralized in Mumbai India and the world's number one producer of movies and also some amazing TV shows! One of the best, of course is ours, *Star Check*!"

"*Star Check*?" Tracey asked.

"Why, yes! *Star Check*, the show you two are guest starring on today! *Star Check* with me, Ravi Chopraz, starring as the brave and dashingly handsome Captain Cutta. *Star Check*, with the catchy theme music and the tagline you've heard hundreds of times, 'A crew of bold adventurers, flying among the outreaches of space, checking out stars strange and mysterious.'"

Both Sassafras faces were blank. This caused Chopraz to lean down and look deep into their eyes.

"There is no need to be nervous. You two can do this," he said reassuringly. "Just feel the part. Be the part. Be the Orion siblings."

"The Orion siblings?" Blaine asked.

"Yes, the Orion siblings. That's the part you're here to play. The characters you're here to be."

"Oh, well, I think maybe there has been some sort of mistake," Tracey said, and then was about to say more, but was cut off by the Bollywood star.

"There has been no mistake! I can tell by looking at you two that you were born to play these parts! You were born to be the Orion siblings!"

"Well, actually, we are the Sassafras siblings," Blaine explained. "Blaine and Tracey Sassafras. And we're spending this summer traveling around the world studying science face-to-face. And we—"

"And today you are here to be the Orion siblings," Ravi announced as if Blaine and Tracey were destined to play these parts. "You are from a star somewhere beyond Orion's belt. Your lives were going great until you were kidnapped by an evil alien race called the Borbothians. They took you against your will to a space asteroid called Riggamorak where you have been forced to mine for spices, which the Borbothians plan to use for intergalactic trade. Luckily you were rescued by me, Captain Cutta and the courageous crew of the starship Ishani."

Both Sassafras faces were blank again. Ravi Chopraz took his hands off their shoulders, turned from them ,and started to pace.

"In the real world, Orion is a well-known constellation that is visible to both the northern hemisphere during winter, and the southern hemisphere during summer," he said, switching to factual astronomy for the moment. "The Orion constellation is the shape of a man formed from about twenty stars, two of which, Rigel and Betelgeuse, are part of the top ten brightest stars in the sky. The three stars in the middle of the constellation form Orion's belt, which is the area your characters are from, and are often visible at night from Earth even from the city."

Now the twins' faces changed from blank to thoughtful as they memorized the SCIDAT their local expert was covering for them.

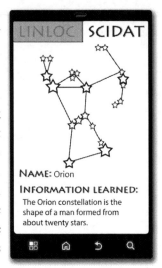

NAME: Orion

INFORMATION LEARNED:
The Orion constellation is the shape of a man formed from about twenty stars.

"The story behind the Orion constellation is rooted in Greek mythology," Chopraz continued. "It says Orion was a great hunter who roamed the forest with his dog, Sirius. One day, Orion ran across seven beautiful sisters. Hoping to marry one of them, he ran after the girls. The seven girls were scared and fled to Zeus for help. Zeus turned them all to birds, and they flew off, leaving Orion all alone. So the constellation is named after Orion, the lonely hunter, because it appears to move westward during the winter months, along with Sirius, the faithful Dog Star, close behind."

The TV captain turned his attention back toward the Sassafrases. "From this you must find your motivation. From somewhere within your soul, you must well up and become the Orion siblings."

"Are we ready to become Bollywood television stars? Do we have the proper theatrical motivation?" Blaine and Tracey noiselessly twin-telegraphed to each other, deciding they didn't know, but it sure looked like they were about to get the chance to find out.

Chopraz looked toward the two stylists, who were beaming in his presence. "Sana, Puja, are these two finished with their makeup and hair?"

"Yes, Ravi, they are," Puja answered for the both of them.

"Okay, you know what to do with them next. Take them to costumes, and then I'll see all four of you over on the set."

Ravi then winked with his eyes twinkling, smiled with his teeth sparkling, and left the room with movie star swagger.

The two Indian stylists doted over the twins for a couple more minutes like proud mothers. Then they stood them up out of their chairs and whisked them out of the room.

As they exited the room and entered a series of wide corridors, both indoors and outdoors, the Sassafrases saw they were right in the middle of a series of large, bustling television and movie studios.

"Look at all the colors!" Tracey exclaimed as they moved along. It was quite possible neither of the twins had ever seen such an assortment of bright and vibrant colors as it pertained to clothing and decorations. Most of the costumes the actors were wearing were stylishly ornamented and were an exciting array of blues, greens, reds, pinks, and yellows. The different movie sets they were passing were also crazy colorful and looked to be a variety of comedies, romances, musicals, and dramas. It was an electrifying place with overflowing creativity.

Eventually, Sana and Puja ushered the twelve-year-olds into a room titled "Costumes," where there were dozens of rows of assorted clothing hanging on hangers.

Tracey looked at her brother with excitement. "I wonder what kind of bright and beautiful clothes they'll give us to wear!"

Blaine smiled, but he wasn't nearly as excited as his sister about playing dress up. The two followed Sana and Puja down a long aisle and then rounded a corner where the stylists stopped. Sana grabbed a plastic-wrapped costume and handed it to Tracey. Puja grabbed another and handed it to Blaine.

Tracey excitedly pulled up the plastic to see what kind of dazzling outfit she would get to wear. Her smile widened in anticipation, but then it dropped when she realized that the costume she was looking at was not bright or beautiful. It looked like a tunic that was dull, brown, and may have even been dirty.

Blaine felt badly for his sister, but he couldn't help but chuckle as he saw his costume was the same. "Evidently, the 'Orion siblings' aren't flashy," he laughed.

"If you remember from the story line Ravi shared, the Orion siblings have been rescued from a spice mine," Puja reminded the two.

"So, I guess these outfits are the latest in Riggamorak mining fashion," Blaine laughed again, but Tracey did not.

"What about the hair and the makeup?" the girl asked. "Why do all of that if we have to wear these tunics?"

"Because this is Bollywood, sweetie," Sana said with a smile. "No matter what you're wearing, your face and hair are gonna look good!"

A few minutes later, the Sassafras twins found themselves standing on the set of *Star Check*. It was designed to look like the bridge of a spaceship, and it actually reminded the twins a little of the navigational bridge in the International Space Station. However, the I.S.S. was filled with seasoned astronauts. This place was filled with actors in spandex.

Even though they felt a little silly standing here in their mining tunics, they were ready for some more information about astronomy, even if it meant they had to guest star in a Bollywood sci-fi TV show to get it.

"Blaine! Tracey!" Ravi gestured toward the twins with his patented smile. "Come meet the crew!"

The Sassafrases stepped over to where the star actor was standing, and they were plunged into a wave of introductions. "This is the lovely Jaya Amin. She plays First Lieutenant Ursa, my wiser and better-looking counterpart."

The beautiful Indian actress smiled at the twins.

"This is Rom Basu. He plays the factual and stoic Second

Lieutenant Denab." Maybe he was already in character, but Basu hardly acknowledged the twins as he was introduced.

"Next we have one of the most versatile actors I know, Chiku Kapadia, who plays Third Lieutenant ☒❶≋❷≋." The Sassafrases gasped—what had their local expert said? Had he spoken in another language? Their surprise continued as they took in the creature before them. It was either a real alien or an actor with a good makeup job.

"Chiku and I share the same hometown of McCleod Ganj, but on *Star Check* he plays a Worbflyster from the planet Worbflyse, who only speaks Worbflystian. I, Captain Cutta, also happen to be fluent in Worbflystian. Isn't that right, Third Lieutenant ☒❶≋❷≋?"

"☞⑥⑨⑨≋🐍❶!" The actor confirmed; at least the twins thought he had. Evidently, they were speaking in Worbflystian.

Captain Cutta then turned from his three lieutenants to the rest of the cast, who were moving about on the set. "And all of these men and women . . . who I'm sure have names and important parts . . . here they are." Although Ravi stumbled through this last introduction, the smile never left his face.

Suddenly, a grotesque-looking character burst up through a panel in the floor and pointed a dramatic looking gun right in the captain's direction. With a quick flick of the wrist and a handsome squint of the eyes, Ravi grabbed the gun that hung in his holster and blasted the creature, who upon impact did a few backward somersaults and then landed flat. The twins were shocked, but as they looked around, nobody else seemed to be. Then they saw why as the grotesque creature popped up to his feet, took off his mask, and said, "All's well that falls well."

"Oh, Blaine and Tracey, you should meet Dhruv Dalal," Ravi introduced as he gestured toward the man under the mask. "He is our resident stuntman and is usually playing the part of a Borbothian alien who is out to get me."

Dhruv laughed at that statement along with the rest of the crew.

All at once another character burst onto the scene, but this time the Sassafras twins knew exactly who it was. It was Varun, the worried and frantic-seeming director whom they had briefly met in the makeup room.

"Okay. Places, everyone, take your places!" He snapped, and everyone, except Blaine and Tracey, immediately obeyed. Blaine and Tracey didn't know where their places were.

"Okay, people, as some of you know, two top studio executives are coming to the set today to do a review on our show." This announcement from Varun received grumbles from many in the cast.

"I know, I know. It's not our favorite, but it has to happen. Sadly, I think they are leaning toward canceling *Star Check*."

Now there were more grumbles and even some gasps.

"So we've got one shot today, people, one shot to show those executives that not only is *Star Check* worth renewing, but it's one of the best shows in all of India!"

Now the cast and crew cheered. This response brought a smile to Varun's face, which is the first one the Sassafrases had ever seen there. The short, round man walked over and sat down in a chair that said, "Varun Gowda: Director," on the back of it. He took a deep breath and then continued addressing his cast.

"The scene we're going to start with today is number seven, which just so happens to be the last scene of this episode, but I think it's a good one for our executive friends to peek in on. It is the scene in which the Borbothians have pulled Starship Ishani in with a tractor beam and are attempting to board the ship to forcefully take back the Orion siblings."

Varun looked toward the Sassafrases. "It's Blaine and Tracey, right?"

The twelve-year-olds nodded.

"I want the two of you to be standing by the big oval-shaped window over there with the green screen behind it, okay?"

The twins nodded again and began making their way toward the window. As they did, the director continued to give instructions.

"I need you two to be huddled together in apparent shock and fear. Remain that way until it's time for your lines."

Gowda turned to a crew member standing near him who was wearing a headset and holding a tablet. "What are their lines?" He asked her, snapping his fingers like he wanted the lines yesterday.

The crew member flipped furiously through her tablet and then responded. "Right after Dhruv jumps out with his gun, the girl says, 'Oh no, they're here to take us back.' And the boy says . . . let's see here . . . oh yes, right here. The boy says, 'Eeek!'"

"Okay, thank you," Varun said to the crew member and then turned back toward the twins, who were now in their spots. "So, Tracey, immediately after the Borbothian alien jumps out, you respond with 'Oh no, they're here to take us back!' And Blaine, you follow that with, 'Eeek!'"

Tracey smiled. Even in her tunic, she felt glamorous because she had a real line in a real TV show. Blaine did not smile. He had gotten makeup plastered all over his face to say one word—eeek. He wasn't actually sure it was even a word. It was just a sound.

Varun Gowda sat up straight in his chair and looked at the rest of the cast. "Everyone else knows their lines, right?"

Everyone nodded.

"Okay, then, people. I think we probably have time to run through the scene once before the executives get here, so let's get right to it!"

The director turned to the lady who had provided the lines

and ordered, "Grab me a clapboard."

She jumped into action and had one of the black and white things directors snap shut to start scenes in his hands in seconds. Varun lifted it up, took one more glance over every facet of the production, then announced, "Scene seven, take one. Lights, camera . . ."

CHAPTER 17: THE ORION SIBLINGS IN BOLLYWOOD

Ursa Major Fanfare

Before Varun Gowda could say "Action," the two dreaded visitors arrived on the set. The first studio executive was a tall, striking Indian woman in a gray skirt-suit wearing heels, glasses, and her hair up on top of her head in a tight bun. The second executive was a man who was a little shorter than the woman but also had striking characteristics. His gray suit was sleek, as was his hair. The woman held in her hands a briefcase, whereas the man held a notebook and an expensive-looking fountain pen. Both their faces looked patronizing.

Varun stood up from his chair, awkwardly shook both of their hands, and then introduced them to the cast and crew. "Everyone, this is Aja and Ru Katri. They are siblings and are two of the top executives who run these studios for us. As all of you know, they are here to watch us film today, so let's welcome them by giving our best performances and show them what *Star Check* is all about."

"*Star Check* is about a crew of bold adventurers," Ravi Chopraz explained, flashing his pearly whites and approaching the two executives as he spoke. "They're flying among the outreaches of space, checking out stars strange and mysterious."

He reached Aja Katri, stood in his most attractive stance possible, winked a couple of times, then said, "Hello, I'm Ravi Chopraz, star of *Star Check*. I'm enchanted to make your acquaintance."

Not seeming impressed at all, Aja simply said, "I know who you are."

Varun laughed nervously and then addressed his lead actor. "Okay, Ravi, that was so nice. Now go back and take your place. Let's get to scene seven please."

Undaunted in any way, Ravi took his place again, which was in the captain's chair in the middle of the set.

"Okay, people," the director shouted, addressing his cast. "Here we go. Attempt two at scene seven, take one. Lights, camera . . ."

Again, before Gowda could say "Action," he was interrupted. This time it was by an artistic-looking, young Indian woman wearing a beanie and juggling an armful of technical equipment with which she promptly bumped into Ru Katri.

"Oh, man! I'm so sorry! I didn't mean to run into you! It's that I'm running a little late, and I didn't . . ."

"Preathi, Preathi!" Varun cut in, getting the woman's attention through a fake smile. "Let's leave Mr. Katri alone. Come over here and tell me what in the world you're up to right now."

"That's just it, Mr. Gowda!" Preathi said excitedly. "It's out of this world! Did Ravi tell you what I can do with the stars and the green screen and stuff?"

Varun was about to answer, but Preathi was too excited to let him.

"Just watch! You see the oval window over there, the one those two baby cavemen are standing near?"

"Preathi, they're not baby cavemen, they are the Orion siblings and . . ."

"That window is equipped with a green screen as its backdrop," Preathi continued, not even aware the director had attempted to correct her. "Which, of course, I can put any images on, but my new tech allows me to put live, authentic-looking images on that green screen while you are filming! So that means instead of the actors staring at a green screen that won't have any images on it until later, they can gaze at real-looking constellations while they are acting. You know, this'll give them extra motivation and stuff!"

"Preathi, that's all fine and good, but right now we are trying to—"

"Just look, Mr. Gowda, you gotta see this!" Preathi exclaimed, still talking and not focusing on what the director was saying but instead focusing on one of the pieces of equipment she was holding. "Watch, Mr. G! If I push this right here, look what happens on the green screen!"

Preathi pushed whatever it was she was talking about, and immediately the oval window directly behind the Sassafrases lit up with a bright array of stars. Blaine and Tracey couldn't help but gasp in delight because the image didn't look like anything superimposed. It looked real. The twins felt like they were actually looking out a real window into real space! Again, they were reminded of what it had been like to be on the International Space Station.

Everyone else in the cast and crew seemed to be enamored with the new tech as well—everyone, that is, except for the director,

Varun Gowda. He looked more flustered than enamored.

"Okay, people, your oohing and aahing can be over now. Settle down and take your places. And Preathi, if you will please make your way off the set. Thank you for your new tech, but we are trying to film a scene."

Actually hearing the director this time, the tech specialist took her armful of equipment and exited the set. One more time the disheveled director raised the clapboard, looked around at everything on the set and said, "Attempt three at scene seven, take one. Lights, camera . . ."

"Oh, I see! It's Ursa Major!" Ravi Chopraz suddenly shouted out, looking at the formation of stars shining in the oval-shaped window like he'd totally forgotten they were trying to film a TV show.

All Varun could do was drop his head and shake it back and forth.

"Ursa Major is also known as the Great Bear, the Plough, or most commonly the Big Dipper because it's made of seven stars with four in its bowl and three in its handle," the actor said, still sitting in his captain's chair. "This constellation is helpful for locating other constellations. In the northern hemisphere it is visible year-round, so it is often used for navigating and orienting the night sky."

SCIDAT

NAME: Ursa Major
INFORMATION LEARNED:
Ursa Major is also known as the Great Bear, the Plough, or, the Big Dipper. The constellation is made of seven stars with four in its bowl and three in its handle.

As the television star spoke, the television executives evaluated. Aja seemed to be doing most of her evaluating in her mind, whereas her brother Ru was scribbling down notes with his expensive fountain pen.

"As it is with pretty much all constellations, the story behind Ursa Major is rooted in Greek mythology," Chopraz continued. "The story says Hera, the queen of the gods, was jealous of a beautiful, young woman named Callisto. Hera made a plan to hurt Callisto, but Zeus, the king of the gods, found out about their plan. To keep Callisto safe, he changed her into a bear and eventually set her in the sky."

Ravi finished his piece about Ursa Major, then leaned back in his chair, and smiled his sparkly white smile.

"Are you finished?" Varun asked his lead actor, not impressed with his scientific knowledge. "Is it okay with you and with everyone else if we start filming a TV show now?" Gowda wasn't really asking.

The entire cast nodded, sensing their director's disapproval and growing frustration—everyone, that is, except Ravi whose smile remained.

Varun jerked the clapboard back into the air. He took a deep breath; then he said once again, "Attempt four at scene seven, take one. Lights, camera . . ."

The director paused for quite a long time, expecting some kind of interruption, but this time none came. Gowda finally got to say, "Action!"

Rom Basu, who played second Lieutenant Denab, started the scene off. He was standing near a wall covered with monitors and controls. He turned toward Cutta's chair and declared, "Captain, they have us securely locked in their tractor beam."

"Well, that is not good, now; is it?" Ravi Chopraz said, completely in character. He swiveled in his chair away from the second lieutenant to face the alien-like cast member. "Third Lieutenant ☒𝟎⤳❷⤳, is there anything we can do to break free?"

Messing around with some different controls he was standing near, the actor Chiku Kapadia answered in Worbflystian. "◌⤳

ℭℭ⑤   ④ℭ②☙   ①⑥②☙⑩▤   ☙☙❶   ❶☙☙④   ❶⑥
③ℭ❶☙☙   ℭ⑤ℭ   ⑨☙③☙ℭ⑩☙   ❶⑩!"

To which Captain Cutta responded, "I totally agree, but that would only work if we had a dozen bananas and a bag of marbles."

Blaine and Tracey attempted not to laugh at that line as they stood by the oval window and tried to look scared and shocked. They didn't know when their lines were coming, but it could be soon.

"Captain, we must do everything we can to protect the Orion siblings." The actress, Jaya Amin, delivered her first line. "Look at them. Look how scared they are."

"First Lieutenant Ursa, your beautiful soul shines through yet again," Chopraz said with a twinkle in his eye. "And yes, we must protect these siblings, whatever the cost."

Suddenly, a panel in the wall swung open, and the Borbothian bad guy, played by Dhruv Dalal, jumped out with his blaster. Tracey tried to say her line, but Blaine was so nervous and wound up, he blurted out, "Eeeeeekkk!" with a long, high pitch before she had a chance.

Tracey looked sideways at him and then again attempted to say her line anyway. "Oh, no! They're here to take to . . . to . . . take us . . ."

Ravi jumped out of his chair with his blaster pointed at the alien antagonist and cut off the fumbling Sassafras girl with his line. "Not on my watch, Borbothian scum!" He then shot Dhruv, who flew back against the wall and bounced off and landed on the floor.

"Cut, cut, cut!" Director Gowda shouted, interrupting the scene while the two studio executives shook their heads in apparent dissatisfaction.

"I'm so sorry. That was my fault," Tracey volunteered.

"No, no, no, it wasn't," Blaine interjected. "I accidentally said, 'ee—,'"

"Blaine and Tracey," Varun said, stopping Blaine. "There is no need to fess up to anything. Just stay quiet and when I say 'cut.' Let me do the directing, okay?"

The twins nodded and obeyed, embarrassed not only for their line debacle but now also for breaking set protocol.

Gowda turned his attention away from the twins and toward the rest of the cast. "The Orion siblings' lines were the least of the problems in that scene, people! C'mon, show me a little more urgency, okay? Let's do it again."

"Urgency?" Ravi asked.

"Yes, urgency, Chopraz, urgency."

The lead star nodded and took his place back in the captain's chair as the director lifted the clapboard once more. "Scene seven, take two. Lights, camera . . . action!"

"Captain, they have us securely locked in their tractor beam," the second lieutenant actor, Rom Basu, asserted a little more urgently than he had the first time.

Ravi, however, had a different take on urgency. Evidently, he had translated the directive to deal with speed. He shouted out his first line so fast that the twins hardly heard it. "That's not good; is it? Third Lieutenant ⊠❶↝❷↝, can we break free?"

"⊘↝ 🐍❻⑤ ④❻②↝ ①⑥②↝⑩🖹 ↝↝❶ ❶↝↝④ ❶⑥ ③❻❶↝↝ ❻⑤❷ ⑨↝③↝❻⑩↝ ❶⑩!" Chiku Kapadia answered as quickly as Ravi.

"That would only work with bananas and marbles!" Ravi screeched quickly in reply.

"Captain, we must protect the Orion siblings!" Jaya Amin shouted out her line. She wasn't saying her line quite as quickly as Ravi and Chiku, but she had sped up her delivery a little.

"Look at them! Look at how scared they are!" Ravi responded with his next line as quickly as a lightning strike. "First Lieutenant Ursa, your beautiful soul shines through yet again, and yes, we must protect these siblings, whatever the cost," he finished, as Dhruv Dalal jumped super rapidly out of the floor panel.

This time around Tracey got her line out before Blaine could cut her off, and she got it out fast. "Oh, no, they're taking us back!"

"Eeek!" Blaine shouted so quickly it sounded like a mouse that had drank too much coffee.

"Not on my watch, Borbothian scum!" Ravi raged as he shot the stuntman once again, sending him careening across the set.

"Cut, cut, cut!" Varun Gowda shouted out, speaking faster than normal, too.

"C'mon, people, what was that?" He said, flabbergasted. "I asked for urgency, not speed. Everyone except for Rom said your lines so quickly I could hardly make out what you were saying. Let's do it again, and let's slow it way down this time. And add some thought and pause to your words."

"Pause?" Ravi asked.

"Yes, pause, Chopraz, pause! Now, let's do it! Scene seven, take three. Lights, camera . . . action!"

"Captain, they have us securely locked in their tractor beam," Basu conveyed thoughtfully.

Ravi leaned slowly forward in his chair in a pose that almost looked like the famous French statue "The Thinker."

"Well," he mused, not saying anything more. He sat there in complete silence for a long moment until he finally said, "That's not good, now; is it?"

He then began to swivel in his chair away from Rom toward Chiku, but it was so slow it was more like a granny in a rocker than a captain in his chair. When he finally got to the point where he was facing Chiku, he delivered his words at a sloth's pace.

"Third Lieutenant . . . ⊠❶⪰❷⪰ . . . is there . . . anything . . . we can do . . . to break free?"

Chiku gave his Worbflystian response in the same slow fashion as Ravi had asked in English, "⊘⪰ ⛰⌘⑤ . . . ④⌘②⪰ ①⑥②⪰⑩▤ . . . ⪯⪰❶ ❶⪰⪰④ ❶⑥ ③⌘❶⪯⪯ . . . ⌘⑤⌘ ⑨⪰③⪰⌘⑩⪰ . . . ❶⑩ . . ."

"I totally agree," Ravi responded. "But that would . . . only work . . . if . . . we had a dozen bananas and . . ."

"Cut, cut, cut!" Varun shouted and then hung his head in dismay with a long pause of his own. Aja and Ru Khatri also hung their heads in dismay. Blaine and Tracey gulped. The two studio executives seemed far from impressed. It wasn't looking good for *Star Check,* which made the twins sad because they'd already grown to adore the cast and the show.

"Just as I didn't mean speed when I said urgency, I didn't mean slow when I said pause," Varun addressed his cast. "It's not as much about the pace of your lines as it is about the feeling coming from your heart. I need more emotion from you, you know, more . . . fervor and passion. Play your roles with some joy."

The twins saw Ravi silently repeat the last few words Gowda had said as he sat all the way back in his captain's chair and prepared for the next take. The director took another long, deep breath as he looked from his cast toward the two executives and then back at his cast. Then, with the clapboard raised in front of him he said, "Scene seven, take four. Lights, camera . . . action!"

With the consistency of a clock, Rom Basu kicked the scene off again with his line, "Captain, they have us securely locked in their tractor beam."

"Well, that's not good now; is it?" Chopraz said with an explosion of happiness. "Third Lieutenant ⊠❶⪰❷⪰, is there anything we can do to break free?" He asked the alien crew member with a smile.

"⊘☙ ㋛◖◖⑤ ④◖◖②☙ ①⑥②☙⑩🗎 ☙☙⓿ ⓿☙☙④ ⓿⑥ ③◖◖⓿☙☙ ◖◖⑤◖◖ ⑨☙③☙◖◖⑩☙ ⓿⑩!" Chiku answered, and even though it was in Worbflystian, it somehow sounded happy to the Sassafrases.

"Ha, ha, ha, I totally agree," Captain Cutta answered, actually laughing. "But of course, as you know old friend, that would only work if we had a dozen bananas and a bag of marbles."

"Captain, we must do everything we can to protect the Orion siblings," Jaya chimed in, in an almost sing-songy way. "Look at them. Look at how scared they are."

"First Lieutenant Ursa, your beautiful soul shines through yet again!" Ravi exclaimed through a big, white-toothed smile. "And, yes, we must protect these siblings whatever the cost, ha, ha, ha!"

Dhruv popped out of the floor in his alien costume, and as he did, Tracey delivered her line in the spirit of the current feel. "Oh, no, they're here to take us back," the Sassafras girl said happily.

"Eeek!" Blaine sang with a smile on his face.

Captain Cutta then jumped out of his chair and actually did a couple of skipping steps before he blasted the stuntman. "Not on my watch, Borbothian buddy!"

"Cut, cut, cut!" Varun stopped the scene without a smile on his face. "What was that? Why in the world would you be so happy about a Borbothian coming to take the children back?"

"Well, because you said you wanted fervor, passion, and joy, of course," Ravi responded, teeth sparkling.

"Fervor and passion, yes," Gowda said fervently and passionately. "But not joy. What I meant by saying 'joy' was that I want you all to take joy in your work as actors, but for this scene, there should be no happiness. A Borbothian is coming to take back the children, for goodness sake. You should be doleful about that fact, not joyful."

"Doleful?" Ravi asked.

"Yes, doleful, Chopraz, doleful!"

Viewing Ursa Minor

The actors all got set once more, Varun took the clapboard, and raised it back in the air to cue the next take. The Sassafrases were pretty sure they knew what doleful meant, and as they watched Ravi repeat that word to himself, they were pretty sure they knew what was going to happen in the next take.

"Scene seven, take five. Lights, camera . . . action!" Gowda directed.

"Captain, they have us securely locked in their tractor beam."

"No! No! This is not good! Why? How?" Ravi cried out as though overcome by sorrow. "Third Lieutenant ⊠❶≳❷≳, is there anything, anything at all we can do to break free? Please, Lieutenant! Please tell me there is!"

"◯≳ ⒮⒞⑤ ④⒞②≳ ①⑥②≳⑩▤ ≪≳❶ ❶⌇≳④ ❶⑥ ③⒞❶≪⌇ ⒞⑤⒭ ⑨≳③≳⒞⑩≳ ❶⑩!" Chiku responded as dolefully as an actor under thick layers of makeup could.

"Bah, hah, hah!" Chopraz cried now with what looked like actual tears. "I agree with you. I do. But . . ." He sniffed. "That would only work if we had a dozen bananas and a bag of marbles. Bah hah hah!"

The cryfest continued as Jaya Amin delivered her line. "Captain, we must do everything we can to protect the Orion siblings. Look at them! Just look at them!" She cried convincingly. "Look at how scared they are."

Ravi stood up from his chair, walked over to Jaya, and took her tear-filled face in both his hands. "Oh, sweet First Lieutenant Ursa, your beautiful soul shines through yet again," he cried. "You're absolutely right. We must protect these siblings whatever the cost."

Dhruv popped up with his blaster, and now Tracey knew it was her turn. She wanted to deliver her line in a way that would please the director, but as she opened her mouth and tried to be passionate, she found herself and her emotions going along with her fellow overacting actors.

"Oh, no!" The girl literally cried with real tears. "They're here to take us back!

Blaine then followed his sister with an ugly, and possibly even a little snotty, cry of his own. "Eeek!"

"Not on my watch, Borbothian scum!" Ravi screamed through tears and then shot at the stuntman.

Dhruv fell back into a temporary heap on the floor.

"Cut, cut, cut!" Varun Gowda said as he held back some doleful, angry tears of his own. Aja and Ru Khatri actually looked doleful, too, a change from the patronizing looks they'd worn when they had first arrived. Maybe they were feeling sorry for Varun and his actors. Watching these over dramatic takes that were supposed to be the performances that were going to save the show was probably somewhat like watching a sinking ship go down. Ravi and the rest of the actors recovered quickly from all their tears and looked as though they hadn't cried at all as they retook their places on the set with their director scowling at them.

Varun Gowda was nearly at a loss for words. He did manage to get some out, but he was so frustrated they came out rather haltingly.

"C'mon people . . . You guys should . . . I know you can, but . . . Can you just give me . . . Today it's been . . . You have to do it for . . . You know, c'mon"

The Sassafras twins had no idea what the director had tried to say, but Ravi Chopraz did. The Captain Cutta actor looked as though he understood every word.

"Our intrepid director is absolutely right!" He confirmed, standing up from his chair to address his fellow actors. "To the world, we are the crew of *Star Check*! It is our responsibility to be that crew! And what exactly is that crew? It's a crew of bold adventurers flying among the outreaches of space, checking out stars strange and mysterious. We do things on TV that those at home sitting on couches wish they could do in real life. So, we should be doing those things with a boldness that will inspire! We should be acting in a way that will cause those couch potatoes to get up off their couches and go attempt bold things themselves! C'mon crew! Let's give a take that relays this sentiment, and that relays what's truly in our hearts! The world needs *Star Check*!"

Most of the cast affirmed the lead actor's sentiment with positive-sounding grunts.

"However, the only one of us who has delivered lines perfectly in character every time has been Rom," Ravi affirmed. "He has been the brightest star in our sky today."

Rom dipped his head toward Ravi in appreciation of the compliment.

"He has been true to his character's name," Chopraz continued. "Did you all know that Denab is the brightest star in the sky? In the northern hemisphere during the summer, three of the brightest stars: Vega, Altair and Denab, form a triangle that can be used to spot the constellations called Cygnus, Lyra, and Aquila. It's called the Summer Triangle. Rom Basu, our own Second Lieutenant Denab, has been a bright star and a guiding star for us, just like the real Denab."

"In the southern hemisphere, the Southern Cross is the most

important constellation. It is in the shape of a cross or kite made up of four stars. It's a small constellation, but the bar in the cross has been used for years in navigation and orienting the night sky down in the southern hemisphere."

Ravi paused and looked around at all the cast members with the intense eyes of a real captain. "So, who's going to step up for our next take? Who's going to be our Southern Cross? Who's going to be our Summer Triangle? Who's going to be our Vega, our Altair, our Denab?"

Blaine, completely won over by Captain Cutta's passionate, science-filled speech, raised his hand. "I will," he offered boldly.

Tracey smiled at her brother. Then she raised her hand too. "I will," she repeated.

From there, slowly and surely, the entire cast and even many in the crew raised their hands and said, "I will."

This wave of passion and determination brought a smile to Director Gowda's face. The two studio executives, however, did not raise their hands and did not seem impressed. Aja continued to stand and hold her briefcase with an expression on her face that was next to impossible to read. Her brother, Ru, also basically expressionless, again took notes with his fancy pen.

Varun Gowda's face, however, was readable, and he was looking more confident than he had all day. He lifted the clapboard into the air and said, "Scene seven, take six. Lights, camera . . . action!"

Rom Basu again started the scene solidly with his stone-cold line. "Captain, they have us securely locked in their tractor beam."

"Well, that's not good, now; is it?" Ravi replied with the perfect amount of concern mixed with brash confidence.

Turning in his chair toward Chiku Kapadia, he then asked, "Third Lieutenant ⊠❶↷❷↷, is there anything we can do to break free?"

"⊘⌀ ᎒CᏚ⑤ ④CᏚ②⌀ ①⑥②⌀⑩▤ ⤳⌀❶
❶⤳⌀④ ❶⑥ ③CᏚ❶⤳⤳ CᏚ⑤CᏞ ⑨⌀③⌀CᏚ⑩⌀
❶⑩!" Chiku answered in perfect Worbflystian.

"I totally agree, but that would only work if we had a dozen bananas and a bag of marbles." Ravi answered in perfect form.

"Captain, we must do everything we can to protect the Orion siblings. Look at them. Look how scared they are." Jaya delivered her line with strength and compassion.

"First Lieutenant Ursa, your beautiful soul shines through yet again. And yes, you're absolutely right. We must protect these siblings whatever the cost!"

Out came Dhruv from the floor panel dressed like a Borbothian and aiming his blaster.

Everything up to this point had gone perfectly during this take, and Tracey being next didn't want to mess it up. She wanted to be a bright Bollywood star, not a scene wrecker.

She summoned all the dramatic moxie inside of her and screamed out, "Oh, no! They're here to take us back!"

Now it was her brother's turn. Welling up with emotion, some dramatic and some real, Blaine opened up his mouth, "Eeek!" It was the best eek he had ever eeked in his entire life.

Now was the scene's climactic end. Captain Cutta jumped up out of his seat, aimed his blaster at the stuntman, and said with certainty, "Not on my watch, Borbothian scum!"

He then fired at Dhruv, who proceeded to flip, flail, and fall backward, perfectly defeated.

"This is it," thought the twins. "We've finally filmed the perfect scene." But then they saw the look on Director Gowda's face, and evidently it was not so.

"Cut, cut, cut, kittens!" He yelled.

"Kittens?" Everyone in the cast questioned, confused.

THE SASSAFRAS SCIENCE ADVENTURES

The director pointed toward the oval-shaped window in disgust. Everyone looked and saw that instead of stars, the window held an image of three adorable kittens.

Instinctively, everyone in the cast and crew turned their heads from the oval window toward Preathi, the technical expert, who was standing behind a couple boom mic operators. When she saw everyone looking at her, she smiled happily at them, not yet knowing what was happening. Then she saw the window herself.

"Uh oh. Oops." She laughed. "I must've bumped my laptop or something because that's my screensaver. Aren't those three little things cute?"

"No," Varun answered immediately. "They are not cute. They are gross and deplorable scene destroyers."

"Oh, don't lose your marbles," Preathi chortled, not taken aback by the seething director. "I can fix it."

She tapped a couple keys on her laptop, and immediately the image on the oval-shaped window turned back into real-looking stars. "See? Look, good as new," the beanie-wearing techie said with a smile.

"But it's not as good as . . . We finally had the perfect . . ." Varun tried to say.

Ravi Chopraz walked over to his friend and put his hand on his shoulder. "Don't worry, boss. We can do it again," he reassured, brashly confident, as though he were still channeling Captain Cutta. "We can give you another perfect take. We can save this show. We can be the stars that you believe us to be!"

"Stars? Stars?" Gowda asked. "Do we have any stars here? Or do we only have a bunch of kittens?"

Chopraz looked like he was about to reply to his director's comment quickly, but then he paused and instead responded scientifically.

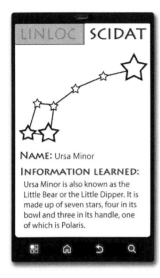

"The oval-shaped window no longer has kittens on it," the actor informed, pointing over toward the Sassafrases' spot on the set. "It also no longer has Ursa Major on it. It is now displaying Ursa Minor. Varun, there are so many stars in the sky. Even more stars than you have right here in this studio. Did you know that Ursa Minor is also known as the Little Bear or the Little Dipper? Just like the Big Dipper, it is made up of seven stars, four in its bowl and three in its handle. One of the stars in the handle is Polaris."

"Polaris, also known as the Pole Star, or the North Star, is not the brightest star in the sky, but it is the brightest star in the Little Dipper constellation. It can be found at the tip of the Little Dipper's handle, and if you follow it to the left, you will find the edge of the bowl of the Big Dipper.'

Blaine and Tracey looked at the window as Ravi spoke, and they were again amazed at how real the images looked. They looked so real, in fact, that it prompted both to pull out their phones and each take a picture of the Little Dipper.

"The Greek mythological story behind Ursa Minor goes like this," Chopraz continued. "One day Callisto's son, Arcas, was out hunting when he came across a bear. It was actually his mother, whom Zeus had recently turned into a bear to protect her from Orion. Zeus saw the encounter, and before Arcas could shoot, he turned the boy into a small bear and then eventually placed him in the sky alongside his mother. Because a little bear is always found with its mother, Ursa Minor is said to always be near Ursa Major."

Ravi paused again and looked deep into the eyes of his

director. "Again, I say there are so many stars in the sky, and there are so many stories I could tell you about them. But you also have many stars right here on this set, and we have a story to tell— an important story about protecting a pair of siblings from the Borbothians. So, let's not give up. We can do this. We can give you another perfect take, and we can do it right now. After this take, those executives over there will be begging us to stay on the air for twenty more seasons."

Varun smiled. "Take your places, people," he said with confidence. Then, with clapboard raised and his entire cast and crew ready, the director said resolutely, "Scene seven, take seven. Lights, camera . . . action!"

What followed was a thing of cosmic beauty. All the actors nailed their lines. All the blasts and stunts went off without a hitch. All the tech was on point. It was the best *Star Check* had to offer on all fronts. Now every eye of every cast member and crew member was on Aja and Ru Khatri. Would the two studio executives have anything to say? Would they make their decision now on whether or not to cancel the show?

Ru finished a flurry of scribbling in his notebook and then looked at his sister. She looked at him, almost like they had made an unspoken agreement. Aja then faced all the eyes that were looking her way.

"Ru and I do not need to deliberate. We've already made a decision regarding your show." She said, addressing the anxious group. "We were not impressed with what we saw."

Upon this statement, an almost audible deflation could be heard from the set, and Varun Gowda looked like he almost fell out of his director's chair.

"However," Aja continued. "Everything changed when we started seeing your passion for the show and your determination to go until you got it right."

Varun sat back up in his chair. Ravi flashed a perfect, sparkling white smile. And the rest of the cast and crew re-inflated.

"We were also eventually impressed with Preathi's new technology," Aja said, glancing at the tech expert. "And then there's all this." The studio executive said grabbing her brother's notebook. She flipped through its pages, in a way that everyone could see, and it was now apparent Ru had not been writing down criticisms. Rather, he had been taking notes about all the scientific data Ravi had covered.

"I'm a big fan." Ru gushed toward the Captain Cutta actor.

"So, are we going to cancel *Star Check*?" Aja asked. "Not on my watch!" She answered happily and then added with enthusiasm. "Bring on the dance party!"

"Dance party?" The twins thought, looking at each other with confused smiles.

CHAPTER 18: BACK TO UNCLE CECIL'S

Bonus Data

"Soc and Ari," the wild-haired Cecil Sassafras said to his two mannequins. "I don't mean to be paranoid, but I think I'm gonna run down to the Left-Handed Turtle to get some aluminum foil because we're all out here at the house."

Neither mannequin replied nor moved a muscle, but Cecil continued as he glanced at the tracker screen. "It looks like Train and Blaisey are close to being finished, so if they show up here while I'm gone, you tell them where I went, okie dokie?"

Still no reply from Socrates or Aristotle, and still Cecil continued his conversation with them, probably because they were currently the only "friends" he had around.

"When the twins land, they will automatically receive their bonus data about UFO's which—wowie willikers, wow—that is so ironic right now; is it not?" He said with raised eyebrows.

"Coolio McDoolio! You guys are real pals." Cecil patted both mannequins on their backs and then raced up the basement stairs and into the house where he hurriedly grabbed his money-filled left shoe. He crashed out onto the sidewalk, which he followed to the Left-Handed Turtle neighborhood supermarket.

Cecil sped toward his destination with urgency and curiosity. A few moments ago, while he had been lounging in his backyard sipping some lemonade, taking a rare break, he had seen something curious. Or at least he thought he had seen something curious. A halfway invisible aircraft of some sort had raced up from the blue horizon and then slowed to a hover over the neighborhood. Cecil had not been able to identify it because it hovered for only a second and then disappeared. He immediately second-guessed himself and started to wonder if he had seen anything at all.

He stood up from his lemon-flavored lounging with half a mind to dismiss what he had seen, but he couldn't shake it. He skipped down to the basement where he told Socrates and Aristotle about the sighting. They didn't seem to believe him, but Cecil was becoming more convinced he had indeed seen something. Being a man of science, he was sure that all unidentifiable flying objects could be explained with science. However, before this sighting was explained, to be safe, Cecil needed some aluminum foil. He would use the foil to make a hat to wear that would stop any aliens from scanning his brain.

The bunny house slippers flipped and flopped on his feet as the redheaded scientist booked it down the sidewalk. Cecil glanced back across the street as he ran, and to his shock and amazement, he thought he could see another half-invisible craft slowly landing next to Old Man Grusher's house.

"Amazi-riff-tastic!" He exclaimed to himself, a little bit scared and a lot bit excited.

As he passed Mrs. Pascapali's house, Cecil saw another craft landing in between her house and the house at 1108. The kindly old woman waved to Cecil as he passed.

"Mrs. Pascapali, I think invisible alien aircraft are landing in our neighborhood!" The scientist shouted as he ran.

"Well, isn't that nice," the woman replied.

"Do you want me to pick you up some aluminum foil at the supermarket?"

"No, sweetie, I have plenty of foil, but could you bring me a dozen eggs and a gallon of milk?"

"Sure thing, Mrs. Pascapali!"

"What a nice young man," Mrs. Pascapali said to herself as Cecil ran by.

The Sassafras twins were finding out that in Bollywood, dance parties were commonplace, especially at the end of a good movie, or in this case, at the end of a perfect take of a TV show episode. The bright colors and exuberant joy that were overflowing on the set of *Star Check* as the cast and crew danced was exhilarating.

Blaine and Tracey didn't know exactly what they were doing, but they felt like a welcomed part of the community as they danced in a line with Ravi Chopraz, Jaya Amin, Rom Basu, Chiku Kapadia, Dhruv Dalal, and other cast members. Some of the crew were dancing as well, including the director Varun Gowda, stylists Sana and Puja, and the tech expert Preathi. The most surprising dancers were the Khatris. Ru had dropped his notebook and fountain pen and had started dancing. Then, maybe even more surprisingly, Aja had taken off her glasses, let her hair down from the tight bun, thrown a colorful sari on, and was dancing the Indian-style dance with gusto.

The twins were relieved they had remembered their lines. They were overjoyed *Star Check* wasn't going to be cancelled, and they were grateful to share in this celebratory dance party.

"Of course, Cecil won't mind!" Summer said into the headset with a smile as she carefully landed her heliquickter in his backyard.

Ulysses S. Grant, President Lincoln, and REESE the Robot were all on board, and they were all almost as excited as Summer to see the Sassafras scientist. They were chomping at the bit to share with him all about their adventures in space.

After successfully getting their asteroid rock displayed at the National Air and Space museum, thanks to curator Paul Sims, they had briefly returned to Alaska for a debriefing and cleaning of the underground science lab. Then they had boarded Summer's heliquickter, which was just like a normal helicopter only much quicker. Now they were on North Pecan Street to reunite with Cecil.

Summer guided the flying vehicle to a nice, soft landing. She then shut off the engine and the propellers, took off her headset, and hopped out. She was excited to see Cecil again, but there was a little angst in her heart as she wondered if she was about to run into Cecil's rude new assistant, with whom she had talked on the phone while in D.C.

The one human, the one robot, and the two animals filed into the kitchen through the back door, which was unlocked. They walked through another door and then straight down into the basement. Their excited faces froze when they saw that Cecil was not there.

"I wooka, wooka, wooka, wonder where he went?" REESE asked in his robotic hip-hop voice.

Ulysses shrugged. Summer shrugged, hoping Cecil had not gone somewhere with that new assistant. But President Lincoln did not shrug. Instead, he scurried over to inspect Socrates and Aristotle, Cecil's two mannequins. When he did, he found something attached to their backs. Summer now saw it too, and she came over to join Lincoln.

Both mannequins had sticky notes on their backs. Socrates's note said, "Went to buy aluminum foil . . ." And Aristotle's note said, "at the Left-Handed Turtle."

"Okey madokey, friends," Summer said with a smile. "Now we know where that Stud-a-fras is. Let's go find him!"

It had been years since Captain Marolf had been out in the field, but this Adrianna Archer incident was the biggest breach of security Triple S had ever faced. So here he was now, leading a cohort of his best secret agents to capture her. Evan DeBlose and Q-Tip, both of whom were with him now, had fixed the satellite she had damaged by remotely taking down its shield. Therefore, they had been able to use said satellite to pinpoint Archer's location in this particular neighborhood.

Additionally, the satellite had shown that Yuroslav Bogdanovich, the terrorist Adrianna had conspired with, was also in this neighborhood. Marolf wanted them both. He stroked his flat-top haircut and then his thick mustache in turn as the pilot of the craft he was in set the vehicle safely on the ground.

The Swiss Secret Service was using their small, stealthy

fleet of chameleon heliquickters for this mission because they could discreetly land anywhere with almost no sound, and their adaptable camouflaging capability made them almost invisible. They knew how dangerous Archer and Bogdanovich could be, so they were setting down heliquickters all over the neighborhood. Upon landing, the secret agents would fan out and cover every block, street, house, and business of this place until they found the two fugitives.

The aircraft Marolf was in had landed in between a couple houses, and as he, Evan, and Q-Tip began to alight, they saw a curious sight. Running down the sidewalk in front of them was a woman, a robot, and two rodents.

"What is this place?" The captain muttered to himself.

In all the years he had lived here, he had never seen anything this crazy happen in his old neighborhood. That was saying something, considering the fact that he had lived two doors down from Cecil Sassafras. Right now, he watched as silent and mostly invisible aircraft of some kind landed all over the place. As they landed, side doors were opening up, and men and women in black suits were pouring out of them and spreading out covertly in all directions.

Were they here for him? He didn't know, but he had done a lot of bad things over the past few weeks, including stealing this Dark Cape suit he was standing in right now. It allowed him to be completely invisible, and for that he was especially thankful because he knew all of these agents, or whoever they were, couldn't see him.

Cautiously, he resumed the direction he'd been going in before he'd seen this swarm of agents, and that was in the direction of the Left-Handed Turtle neighborhood supermarket. He was going there because whatever Adrianna was planning was happening there. This blonde-headed woman he once loved was now bent on partnering with Cecil, his nemesis, and it didn't look like she was going to stop until that happened.

Over the past couple of days, he had watched her make plans in the basement of his old residence at 1108 North Pecan Street. Then today, she had scurried off to the Left-Handed Turtle with a red wig on and a big box of clothing, cologne, and hair care products. He had no idea how that could possibly snag the allegiance of the redheaded scientist, but he did know that Adrianna was smart, sly, and convincing.

A few minutes ago, he had seen Cecil running down the sidewalk toward the supermarket. Then interestingly, he'd seen Summer Beach and a few of her companions head that way as well. He squinted his invisible, eyebrow-less forehead as he moved stealthily forward.

A lot was happening in the neighborhood today.

Blaine and Tracey happily filled their SCIDAT applications with all the pictures and data from this Mumbai India location. When it was successfully sent, they opened their LINLOC apps to see where they would be zipping next.

"Uncle Cecil's basement!" Tracey exclaimed in joy.

"Eeek! We did it! We successfully finished Astronomy!" Blaine squealed in elation.

Tracey looked at her brother. "Did you just say 'eeek?'"

"Well, yeah . . . you know . . . because . . . it was my line in the . . . I'm just happy, okay?"

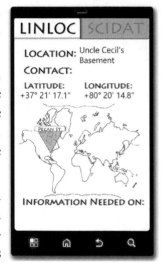

Tracey laughed. "I'm happy, too, bro. I'm happy we've had all these cool opportunities. I'm happy we've completed another subject of science. And I'm happy we now get to go see Uncle Cecil!"

The twelve-year-old twins put on their harnesses and helmets, and then they excitedly calibrated their three-ringed carabiners to the coordinates that would send them to their favorite basement.

When the carabiners snapped shut, they automatically found the correct invisible zip lines, pushing the twins up into the air where they dangled for approximately seven seconds. Then, in an instant, they disappeared into a swirling tunnel of light.

It was all over almost as soon as it had begun as the invisible lines brought them to their destination. The carabiners automatically became unclipped, and the two Sassafrases sprawled onto the floor of Cecil's basement with their bodies slightly tingling, devoid of sight and strength.

As Blaine and Tracey waited for their faculties to return to normal, they were expecting a congratulatory shout from their uncle and maybe even a happy, jumping dance-hug from Summer Beach, who had been hanging around their uncle's house a lot more lately, but no shouts or hugging came. The brother and sister stood to their feet with normalized bodies and looked around the messy basement. Nobody was here. All at once, they felt their smartphones vibrate in their backpacks.

"Bonus data!" Tracey exclaimed and then immediately slid

the backpack off her shoulders to retrieve her phone.

Blaine did the same and was the one to read the bonus data aloud when he brought it up on his screen.

Blaine raised his eyebrows. This was some pretty interesting bonus data.

Tracey finished reading the information they were seeing on their screens.

BONUS DATA

The most famous UFO sighting in American history happened in 1947 in Roswell, New Mexico. Residents found debris they claimed came from a flying saucer, but the Air Force said it was just pieces of a top-secret weather balloon. This explanation appeased some, but many doubted it was the truth. Today, Roswell is home to the International UFO Museum and Research Center.

Tracey raised her eyebrows to match her brother's. Studying science was interesting, and sometimes the difference between scientific fact and science fiction seemed pretty small.

Their eyebrows dropped as they both let out long, satisfied sighs. Studying astronomy had been wonderful, and now they were finished. But where in the world was Uncle Cecil?

Invasion of the Pecan Neighborhood

"He turned on aisle three, but if he needs aluminum foil like he said he did, he needs to be on aisle four." Preston muttered to himself before rushing around the corner to help his all-time favorite customer.

"Mr. Sassafras, sir!" The teenager shouted out in a squeaky puberty-stricken voice. "Our aluminum foil is actually one aisle over."

"Preston! Thankity thank you oh so very muchity much! You're always so helpful and manny oh nanny do I ever need some aluminum foil today!"

Preston nodded, happy to assist the scientist.

"I don't mean to alarm you, and I think that it will eventually be explainable with factual science," Cecil continued somewhat frantically. "But alien spacecraft may or may not be landing in our neighborhood today, and I am making myself an aluminum hat so they can't scan my brain. I will probably make one for both Socrates and Aristotle as well—and really, anyone who wants one. Preston, do you want me to make one for you too?"

The teenager was a little confused, but the smile remained on his face as he responded, "Sure, Mr. Sassafras. That would be nice of you."

Preston proceeded to guide Cecil around the corner of aisle four where the duo quickly found all the varieties of aluminum foil the Left-Handed Turtle had to offer. Cecil grabbed a few boxes off the shelf, and without yet paying for them, he opened the boxes and immediately began making a slew of cone-shaped hats. Preston didn't mind because he knew Cecil would eventually pay like he always did.

"Okay, Mr. Sassafras, sir. I'm going to go back up to the front register." The teenager squeaked as he walked away.

"Okay, Preston! Thanks a zillion!"

When the young clerk arrived at the front of the store, he saw a curious sight, not that curious sights in this place were a phenomenon, but he had never seen anything like this before. In the short time he had been gone from the front helping Mr. Sassafras, a woman he had never seen had come in and set up some kind of a booth at the end of the row of registers.

"Ummm, hello, ma'am," Preston said curiously, kindly, and squeakily. "May I ask what you're doing?"

"Preston! Good morning," the redheaded woman said like she knew the teenager, even though he was sure he didn't know her. "I set up a makeover station that your customers can stop by after they've bought their groceries and receive a free makeover or styling."

"A makeover station?" Preston asked.

The woman nodded.

"Do you have permission from management to do this?"

"Well, of course I do, Preston!" The woman laughed. "You don't think I would walk in here off the street with nefarious plans of world domination; do you?"

"Ummm, no, I guess not, ma'am."

"That's right, Preston. You keep doing what you do so well, and I will be over here giving free transformations."

Preston smiled kindly, but he was still curious. The teenager was about to ask a few more questions when all of a sudden, four new patrons plunged through the sliding front doors of the grocery store.

"Welcome to the Left-Handed Turtle," Preston greeted happily, as his mouth opened out of muscle memory.

A barrage of more warm Left-Handed greetings hit the four entering as Rona, Tank, Itsy, Rama, Kingman, Itja, and Yuroslav— the newest Left-Handed employees—did their duty and welcomed every single patron who walked through the store's front doors too.

"Hello, Preston! Where is your aluminum foil located?"

"Oh, hello, Miss Beach. It's over on aisle four."

"Thanks, friend!" Summer acknowledged as she raced past the teenager toward the aluminum foil. Ulysses, Lincoln, and REESE followed closely behind her.

Preston turned his attention back toward the lady who had set up the booth and was about to question her again when the front door of the supermarket opened once more.

"Welcome to the Left-Handed Tur—" Preston started to say, but there was no one there. "That's strange," the teenager thought. "Our doors have never malfunctioned or opened on their own before. It's almost like an invisible person walked in. What a silly thought. Oh, well, I guess things like this happen."

Evan DeBlose winked confidently at Q-Tip and Captain Marolf, who were both by his side, hunching down behind a recycling bin in the parking lot of the Left-Handed Turtle neighborhood supermarket.

"We're going to get her," the handsome, sandy-haired Triple S agent assured like there was no doubt in him at all. Q-Tip winked back, growing more and more confident as an agent.

Captain Marolf answered with a short gruff, "We'd better."

The Swiss Secret Service had successfully landed their fleet of heliquickters and then had fanned out throughout the neighborhood, covertly covering every square inch of ground. All that had led them here to this supermarket where they had spotted Adrianna Archer and Yuroslav Bogdanovich inside. Adrianna was wearing a red wig and setting up some sort of booth. Yuroslav was holding a mop and wearing an apron, almost as if he was an employee at the store.

"I wonder what those two are up to," Evan mused out loud.

"Whatever it is, we're about to stop them," Marolf said with a determined frown on his face. "When all our agents are in place, we're going in!"

"Well, hello, Soc and Ari," Blaine said to his favorite mannequins. "What's that there on your backs? Is that something for us?"

The Sassafras twins had been a little confused when they had landed in their uncle's basement to find no one there to meet them. Blaine had seen the sticky notes on the backs of Socrates and Aristotle.

THE SASSAFRAS SCIENCE ADVENTURES

"Went to buy aluminum foil," Blaine read the first note.

"At the Left-Handed Turtle." Tracey read the second and then clapped her hands once and said, "All right, it's off to the Left-Handed Turtle we go!"

Summer, Ulysses, Lincoln, and REESE made it to aisle four and found the aluminum foil, but they did not find Cecil.

"Huh, I can tell he's been here, but he's not here anymore. I wonder where he went?" Summer questioned.

She looked toward her three companions through a half-smile. "I guess let's start checking this place aisle by aisle."

Cecil tilted up his left shoe and dropped the correct amount of money onto the counter to pay for all the aluminum foil he'd used as well as the milk and eggs he'd grabbed for Mrs. Pascapali.

"Thanks, Mr. Cecil, sir," Preston said, taking the money and putting it in the cash register. "Did you happen to see your friend Summer? She came in a few minutes after you."

"Well, golly, golly, goodness, Preston. I sure did not. What did she say she was looking for?"

"I think she was looking for you, sir. I sent her to aisle fo—"

"Excuse me! Excuse me, sir!" The two were interrupted by the mystery makeover lady.

Cecil silently pointed to himself as if asking, "Me?"

"Yes, you," the woman smiled. "You with the crazy red hair, the messy lab coat, and the bunny house slippers. Today I want to make you an offer you can't refuse: a transformation!"

"A transformation?" Cecil asked.

"Yes, sir, a free transformation! Haven't you ever wanted to trade that messy lab coat in for a power suit? Haven't you ever wanted your wild red hair combed down and styled for success? Haven't you ever wanted to spray on cologne and walk away smelling of confidence?"

"Ummm . . . no . . . not really," Cecil answered, still not sure who this lady was but at the same time thinking there was something awfully familiar about her.

"Yes, you sir can be transformed!" The woman continued. "Come right over here to my booth, and I can do all these things for you for free! You will then feel confident, successful, and powerful! And then together we can take over the world!"

"Huh?" Cecil questioned as the woman walked over, grabbed him by the arm, led him over to her 'transformation' booth, and physically forced him to sit down. She quickly grabbed a bottle of hair gel and a comb and started working on taming the scientist's wild hair.

"Ma'am, I don't want—"

"Oh, just quiet down, you brilliant man. If I can get you transformed just a bit, then maybe you'll finally let me join you, and then the world will be ours for the taking."

"Please, lady, if you'll let me get up, I'd like to lea—"

"Stay still and quit squirming!" Adrianna forced Cecil back down into the seat as he tried to escape.

Preston didn't like this one bit. He didn't know who this redheaded lady was, and he didn't think she actually had managerial permission for this booth of hers. He didn't like the way she was treating his favorite customer. He looked at all his fellow Left-Handed Turtle store clerks.

"C'mon, everybody," he squeaked. "I think we're going to have to force this woman to leave."

Rona, Tank, Itsy, Rama, Kingman, Itja, and Yuroslav all nodded and, as a group, started moving slowly toward the transformation booth.

"Oh! There he is!" A jubilant voice suddenly shouted out.

Summer Beach and her posse had rounded the corner, and they'd finally found Cecil. The female scientist and her three companions skipped through the registers, brushed past the group of clerks, and plunged toward Cecil with the intention of a happy, jumping dance-hug. However, before they could reach their friend, the makeover lady with the red hair jumped forward to stand between them with an outstretched arm signaling for them to stop.

"Hold it right there, missy," she addressed Summer in a perturbed tone. "We're in the middle of a transformation here, and you're about to mess everything up!"

Summer skidded to a stop and looked at the woman, taken aback. She then peeked around the woman toward the man she considered her best friend in the whole world.

"Cecil?" She asked. "Do you think you need a transformation?"

The male scientist smiled sheepishly and gave a finger-wiggling wave.

"Of course, he needs a transformation!" The redheaded woman said with an air of authority, picking up a cologne bottle. "Look at him. He looks ridiculous, and he's wasting all his power."

"Wasting? Ridiculous?" Summer asked as she stood fully upright to face the woman eye to eye. "Cecil Sassafras is not wasting anything, and he doesn't need any kind of transformation.

He's perfect just the way he is."

"Listen here, missy. I—"

"My name is not Missy. It's Summer, Summer T. Beach, and I'm not going to let you . . . Hey wait a second . . . I recognize your voice. You're not even a makeover artist; are you? You're Cecil's new assistant!"

Summer's statement caused a fake curious look to form on the redheaded woman's face, while everyone else, especially Cecil, now had authentic curious looks on their faces.

"Yeah, I talked with you on the phone a few days ago. I'm sure of it," Summer said. "Why do you have this booth set up? Why are you acting like a makeover artist?"

"Because I . . . well I . . ." the woman stammered.

"And what about this red hair of yours? It doesn't even look real. Are you wearing a wig?"

On a whim, Summer reached up, grabbed the woman's red hair, and yanked. And to the surprise of everyone, the wig came right off.

"Who are you?" Summer asked, staring at the woman.

"Adrianna!" A new voice suddenly shouted out. "Adrianna Archer. Hello, darling."

Everyone turned to see a handsome man in a black suit standing in the open front doors of the supermarket.

"I'm not your darling," Adrianna spat back to the man, dropping her guise.

"No, I guess you're not," Even DeBlose agreed with a sad smile. "You could've been, but instead you decided to become a traitor."

Instead of denying anything, Adrianna looked at Evan with a sly smile of her own. "How'd you find me?"

"We fixed the satellite," Evan responded.

Adrianna nodded her head like she knew that had been inevitable. "Impressive," she said flatly.

DeBlose gazed at the beautiful turncoat agent for one more long second and then spoke into the earpiece he was wearing. "C'mon in, boys; we got her."

At that, a swarm of black-suit-wearing agents rushed in through the front doors of the Left-Handed Turtle and surrounded Adrianna Archer. Their former Triple S agent didn't put up a fight. She knew it was over for her. She was quickly handcuffed and led out of the store without another word.

"We're taking this one, too," Evan declared. He winked confidently, then he turned, and walked out the door. The group of Triple S agents grabbed Yuroslav, cuffed him, and led him out.

Preston, Ulysses, Lincoln, REESE, Rona, Tank, Itsy, Rama, Kingman, and Itja all stood where they were, speechless and dumbfounded.

Summer was as shocked as everyone else at what she had witnessed, but she was also relieved. She was so happy that Adrianna had turned out to be a backward agent instead of Cecil's new assistant.

Cecil, who sat in the transformation chair with awkward-looking, slicked-down hair, also didn't know what to say. But at least he did know now, they didn't need all the aluminum hats he had made.

Suddenly, the doors of the store opened back up. In walked Blaine and Tracey Sassafras. "Well, hello, everybody!" Blaine exclaimed. "What did we miss?"

THE SASSAFRAS SCIENCE ADVENTURES

As the twins walked into the store, he slid out invisible and undetected. He was reeling from what he had witnessed. Adrianna was now gone for good. She would never again be by his side. Nor would she be by Cecil's side or anybody's side for that matter. She was in the custody of the Swiss Secret Service, and they had inadvertently but effectively exacted revenge on her for what she had done to him.

He was satisfied yet sorrowful at the same time. He would now make his way back to his underground lab in Siberia where his army of servile scientists was currently working on a couple projects. With Adrianna now a nonfactor, he could again refocus all his vengeful thoughts and plans against those Sassafrases.

"I wonder how the new extra-large Forget-O-Nator and the swarm of Dark Cape suits are coming along?" He thought to himself as he calibrated his carabiner.

"Your bond has been paid," the guard announced to the three prisoners as he used a key to unlock their cell and then swung the squeaky, metal door open wide for them. "You are free to go."

The three prisoners looked at each other curiously for a second but then sprung up and went out the door, not daring to question this good fortune even if it had come unexpectedly. The two brothers and one sister made their way swiftly through the corridors of the jail and then outside into blue skies of freedom.

All three were tempted to twirl, shout, and dance over the elation of this surprising release, but before they could, a black limousine with dark tinted windows pulled up and stopped right where they were. A hefty driver who looked like he could double as a bodyguard got out of the car, walked around, and opened the back door.

"Get in," he ordered gruffly. Choosing not to argue, the three siblings slowly obeyed the driver's command.

Once inside the car, things started to make a little more sense. They knew the man sitting across from them. With a slightly annoyed look on his face, he reached inside a box sitting next to him and pulled out an object they had been trying to get their hands on for a long time: the guidance component to an SS-20 Soviet missile.

"Thanks, Paul," Graham acknowledged, reaching out to grab the component.

"Not so fast," Paul Sims said, pulling the component back out of the eager Rotary Club members' reach. "First let's talk about payment. I bailed the three of you out of jail on my own dime. That means the price has gone up."

Graham leaned back, but his brother Alexander leaned forward.

"We are willing to pay whatever you want," Alexander offered boldly.

Paul Sims smiled.

That's what he had wanted to hear. The museum curator held the component back out to the three siblings. Graham successfully grabbed it.

Paul watched as Alexander, Graham, and Belle Slote, the three members of the Rotary Club, ogled their prize. Sure, they were going to take this component, complete their rocket, and destroy all the world's cell phones. But that didn't matter to him right now because it was going to make him rich—richer than he already was.

Stay in touch with the Sassafras twins!

The adventure doesn't have to end just because you've finished the book! Connect with the twins and the other characters of the series through the Sassafras Science blog. You'll find articles in where:

* ✯ The Prez shares his wrap-up videos;
* ✯ Summer shares about the solar system;
* ✯ The twins share about constellations;
* ✯ And Paul Simms shares about the moon.

Plus, Blaine and Tracey regularly pop in to say hi and share their thoughts. The Sassafras twins would also love to keep in touch with you through their Facebook page. They share updates about future books, fun science-related activities, and cool nature news!

Visit ElementalScience.com/Sassafras to discover more!

Made in the USA
Las Vegas, NV
19 May 2021